SOME
REMARKS

Neal Stephenson

WILLIAM MORROW
An Imprint of HarperCollins*Publishers*

Some Remarks

Essays and Other Writing

CONTENTS

SOME
REMARKS

INTRODUCTION

Certain persons who know what they are talking about where publishing is concerned have assured me that I have reached the stage in my life and career where it is not only possible, but advisable, to release a compilation of what are drolly referred to as my "shorter" works. You are reading its introduction, which I'll try to make *especially* short.

Two general approaches could be taken to editing such a volume. One would be to make of it a pitilessly accurate historical record and trust the reader to make allowances for the widely varying levels of maturity, self-regard, and financial desperation that might have figured into the author's motives while the component pieces were being produced. That might have been an interesting strategy twenty years ago, but now we have the Internet for that.

The second approach, of course, is to conduct a shameless whitewashing of that historical record, picking only the good stuff, and editing even that to make it look better. This, within reason, is what I have done here. Which is not to say that these pieces don't contain material that might strike the sophisticated reader as dated or jejune; a bit of that has been left in because it makes me feel young. I have, however, removed some material that must have been topical when I wrote it but now seems merely inexplicable. As an example, the Slashdot interview, the second piece in the book, contains some answers that develop into essays that seem about as worth reading today as they ever were, while others were of interest only to that website's clientele (lovely people, but they know how to find the original if they really want to reread it) eight years ago. The latter have been removed. I have made similar edits to some of the other stories.

As has been pointed out by some critics, writing short fiction is not my strong point, but I have published a small number of short stories in my day. Two of these, "Spew" and "The Great Simoleon Caper," made the cut. A third, "Jipi and the Paranoid Chip," seemed extraordinarily ponderous and labored upon rereading and so has been left out.

During the mid-1990s I produced two very long pieces of what might generously be defined as journalism for *WIRED* magazine. The second of these, "Mother Earth, Mother Board," has not aged too badly and has been included intact. The first, "In the Kingdom of Mao Bell," was not as good to begin with and has gotten worse since, as many of the remarks that, at the time, I thought of as insights have now either become bromides or simply been proven wrong. For all that, it does have a few decent anecdotal bits, and so what you will find in this volume is a heavily cut-down series of excerpts.

Finally, the book contains two original, previously unpublished pieces: an essay about sitting entitled "Arsebestos," and a one-sentence work of fiction, unfinished, and, for very sound artistic and legal reasons, never to *be* finished, which I will allow the reader to discover in due course.

It only remains for me to thank the people who helped these

pieces come into being: as always, my supernaturally patient and understanding wife, and my agent, Liz Darhansoff, who has been a fount of infallible advice for thirty years; Kevin Kelly at *WIRED*, who talked me past my initial skepticism that an article about cables could ever be any good and turned a blind eye to some rather odd expense reports; the readers/members of Slashdot; the Royal Society and Gresham College for inviting me to take part in forums where I would never have expected to find myself in any capacity above the level of bootblack; and the editorial page staff of the *New York Times* for randomly entering my life every few years and asking me to write short pieces on odd topics.

ARSEBESTOS
(2012)

As a boy, watching screen adaptations of Dickens's *A Christmas Carol*, knowing nothing of Victorian England, I had only the vaguest understanding of what Bob Cratchit did for a living. Yet I sensed just how unpleasant his life was from the fact that he had to spend the whole day sitting on his bum. Scrooge, on the other hand, was generally depicted up on his feet, prowling through the countinghouse. Somehow, that was enough to tell a little boy in the 1960s everything about the class divide separating these two characters.

At about the same time, a few of my schoolmates began to show up occasionally in leather shoes, as opposed to sneakers. I sensed the beginning of a trend that would lead, in a few years' time, to all of us wearing cramped, hard shoes, impossible to walk in, and imprisoned at desk jobs to the end of our days, supervised and sniped at by ambulatory Scrooges. I began to take inventory of careers in which it was allowable to stand up and walk around.

I have enough media savvy now to understand that the real-life Scrooges of the Victorian age probably spent at least as many hours on their arses as their Cratchits, and that the people who adapted the story for the screen were employing a visual shorthand: people who can move around have more freedom, hence higher status, than the deskbound. The metaphor is carried through faithfully to Tiny Tim, Cratchit's son, who is the only person in Victorian London even less mobile than his dad. More mawkish screen adaptations of the story sometimes end with Tim, suddenly cured by Scrooge-subsidized medical care, spiking his crutch and doing a fandango around the Christmas tree.

The same shorthand is, of course, universal in film and television, where heroes stride and pace and run and dive. The deskbound are dweebs, losers, nebbishes. The class divide even extends to seating on airplanes. When the jet taxis to its gate and comes to a stop and the little *ding* sounds, the aisle-seat dwellers jump to their feet, claim space, and haul down their bags, while those stuck in the window seats can only crane their necks and meekly await permission to move.

All this was of merely abstract interest to me for a good number of years, until I found myself attending conferences and meetings with people who, unlike me, had not gone to irrational lengths to establish themselves in ambulatory careers. They racked up an amount of chair time that I simply could not believe was real. My ability to be of any use whatsoever in such contexts was limited strictly by how long I was able to remain on my arse: not very long, as it turned out.

Later, informed by health-care pros that years or even decades would be guillotined from my life expectancy if I didn't spend a certain amount of time every week in aerobic exercise, I got into the habit of playing video games while pumping an elliptical trainer. This worked surprisingly well, but only kept my legs moving for forty-five minute stretches, a few times a week. During the rest of the time, my workday underwent a gradual and almost insensible transition that will sound familiar to anyone over the age of forty.

It used to be that reading the mail required walking to the mailbox, slicing open envelopes, and other small but real physical exertions. Now we do it by twitching our fingers. Similar remarks could be made about talking on the phone (now replaced by Skype), filing or throwing away documents (now a matter of dragging icons around or, if that's too strenuous, using command-key combinations), watching television (YouTube), and meeting with coworkers (videoconferencing). The portion of the day allocated to staring at pixels kept growing, and my physical movements were increasingly restricted to minute, repetitive movements of the finger and the hand. Wrist, shoulder, and back problems ensued. I spent a lot of money on fancy ergonomic chairs and keyboards. Each of them helped for a few months and then led to a new constellation of injuries. I've lost track of the number of times I've switched between mouse and trackball, left hand and right, trying to stay one step ahead of the pain. After a couple of decades of this, I finally got it through my skull that the problem wasn't that I didn't have just the right chair, keyboard, or pointing device; it was that I stayed in the same position all day long.

So more recently I obtained a treadmill specifically designed for use while working. For several hours a day I amble along at one to one point five miles per hour, clicking and typing and talking on the phone.

This is easy, by the way. I was worried that it would be difficult to type while walking. It isn't, as long as your keyboard has a wrist rest.

I have not had any neck, shoulder, or arm trouble since I began doing this. I am convinced, though I can't prove, that this is because I'm continually in motion and so whenever I click that mouse button or hit the "e" key on the keyboard, I'm doing it from a slightly different angle. According to the digital readout on the treadmill, I'm covering as much as four or five virtual miles per day and burning hundreds of calories.

Now my knee hurts a little, though. But more about that in a minute.

I switched to a treadmill desk because I hate sitting down and because I suspected it would help with my neck and shoulder troubles. Beyond that there was no particular rationale. But scientific research, released during the last couple of years, now reveals that sitting all day isn't just a little bit unhealthy; it's seriously and actively bad for you to an extent that goes beyond merely vindicating my childhood intuitions and is actually just a bit shocking. Or at least I'd be shocked if I were the legal department of a large corporation employing many people obliged to spend most of each day sitting on their bottoms. Ergonomic swivel chairs, it turns out, are the next asbestos.

Let us be clear about the import of this research. It's not just that a bit of exercise is a good thing. It's not the usual suggestion that desk-bound office workers might want to spend a few minutes out of every hour on leisurely stretching exercises. What we have here is hard scientific data telling us that if you sit for any significant amount of time per day, it will kill you. Maybe with a heart attack, maybe with a stroke, maybe with cancer, maybe with diabetes. The reaper comes first for those who sit. In a society with a lot of coal miners, consumptives, and smokers, this might be drowned out in the statistical noise. Today it stands out like a siren on an empty road.

The bosses of the mid-twentieth century can't be blamed. Sitting in a chair all day behind a desk: What could be safer, compared to the grueling factory, mining, and agricultural toil that took so many lives during the age of industrialization? They must have believed they were only doing the best for their employees. Actually they were setting in motion a slow-moving and mostly inadvertent Cratchitization of the workforce.

It sneaked up on us. The Cratchits of the 1950s could only spend so much time sitting before their typewriters. They still had to pivot in their chairs to reach a filing cabinet, take a telephone call, or communicate with a coworker. But because computers can now do everything, the only reason a worker now has to stand up is to use the bathroom; and if it were possible to get an app for that, we'd all download it. It's a case of unfortunate timing, and unintended consequences: first, we all bought in to the idea that a normal job involved sitting in a chair, and then we found ourselves imprisoned by our own furniture and by the culture, expectations, employee manuals, and insurance policies built around them.

TWO KINDS OF COSTS ARE BEING INFLICTED BY THE NEARLY UNIVERSAL MISconception that sitting in chairs all day is reasonable.

The first, already mentioned, is simply the long-term health effects of sitting.

The second, less obvious one is the opportunity cost caused by the fact that millions of otherwise smart and energetic people simply cannot bring themselves to spend much time in chairs, and therefore end up taking forms of employment that don't really challenge their intellectual capacities, merely so that they can have the freedom, and, yes, the dignity to move.

Such people are frequently predisposed to think that they may have nothing to offer the modern economy because they may have done poorly in school. That people with dyslexia and ADHD are statistically overrepresented among physical trainers, building trades workers, and so on, may be noticeable to those who interact frequently with them. But even among those who don't have those diagnosable conditions, I think that a good number are just fidgety boys who found themselves in a place called school where even during recess running was outlawed and knew, literally in their bones, that this was no place for them. We all know highly intelligent persons who failed to reach their potential because they simply could not find a place in the world of work. I put it to you that a considerable number of these just don't like chairs. They walk into a modern office, with its grid of cubicles, and it morphs, in their mind's eyes, into a classroom with its grid of desks, and they get itchy and want to turn around and run out into the fresh air.

I emphasize boys because the problem is so obvious and acute in their case, and statistics show that they are falling behind girls in educational achievement, college enrollment, and participation in the postgraduate workforce. Females, however, who face brutal strictures regarding how heavy they are allowed to be and what sorts of shoes they are expected to wear, obviously face their own set of issues around Cratchitization and may be more vulnerable to its effects simply because they don't have as many options outside of the office-bound economy. A simple thought experiment: try to imagine Hope Solo spending forty years in a desk job. Or run the numbers and calculate the odds that a woman with a normal metabolism can spend forty hours a week sitting down (and, most likely, another ten hours a week commuting on her keister) and not gain weight.

DR. JAMES LEVINE OF THE MAYO CLINIC HAS EARNED A SORT OF MOSES-LIKE status among the growing community of "walk while you work" partisans. Sprinkled across the developed world, we trudge behind him at a stately pace of one to one and a half miles per hour as he leads us forth out of Aeronic bondage. His most recent opus, "Health-Chair Reform: Your Chair: Comfortable but Deadly," is a small masterpiece of dry humor and hard data that would improve this essay considerably if I were allowed to quote it whole. A few nuggets:

"The articles in this issue of *Diabetes* . . . suggest that chair-living is lethal. Of concern is that for most people in the developed world, chair-living is the norm."

"Modernity has imposed a Chair Sentence: work, home, and play are the shackles."

"Sitting is not bad for you in moderation, but in excess it is addictive and harmful."

" . . . repeated frequent bouts of low-intensity meandering-style activity may be more health-beneficial than occasional bouts at the gym . . . a primary risk of ill health is sitting time per se."

"There are solutions to chair-associated ill health that range from population-wide gym attendance, pharmacological administration, or genetic manipulation. Alternatively, people could get up."

In the last of these quotes, Levine is referring, probably not with a straight face, to serious research suggesting that administration of pharmaceuticals could help boost people's metabolic rates. Put the stuff in the water supply and everyone would get skinny. But it's clear that his heart is in the final sentence: "people could get up." Levine has pioneered development of treadmills, desks, and other office furniture intended to support mobile office workers. His work has drawn the attention of a growing network of "office walkers" who use Internet forums to exchange tips, advice, product reviews, and, all too often, disheartening tales of how they tried to get a treadmill desk at work but got shot down by nervous higher-ups or rigidly conform- ist coworkers.

The most commonly cited reason for refusing to allow an office worker to swap chair for treadmill seems to be the perception that, if it caught on, it might increase the number of workman's comp claims. Another justification heard with surprising frequency is that it just plain looks funny and somehow poses a distraction to co- workers. Some fear that the equipment will be noisy. Others wrongly assume that office walking is like what is seen in health clubs, where exercisers work up a sweat by pounding along at four or five miles an hour. People who just plain dislike the idea, and who are willing to grasp at any rhetorical straw to shoot it down, will complain about in- creased electricity usage or the weight of the device. All these objec- tions are based on some combination of bad information, faulty logic, or outright disingenuousness. The kinds of treadmills designed for office use are no noisier than other office equipment; using mine in a quiet room I can participate in speakerphone conversations with- out anyone being the wiser. Their weight per square foot is no more than that of a normal human in an office chair (treadmill plus human has more weight than the human alone, of course, but it is spread out over a larger area). Walking at one to one and a half miles per hour is a completely different proposition from speed-walking in a health club; you amble along at about the rate of a coach-class traveler moving through an airport security queue, and breaking a sweat is unlikely.

While on the topic of sweat, it might be helpful here to distinguish among three different general levels of physical exertion, from most to least intense.

Aerobic exercise is something that everyone is supposed to perform for at least thirty minutes a day, five days a week. The heart is beating at 60 to 80 percent of its maximum rate (where maximum rate is a figure calculated mostly on the basis of age; a fifty-year-old man's maximum is something like 170, so, doing the math, aerobic exercise should put his pulse rate in the band of about 100 to 136 beats per minute).

The heart beats faster in response to a demand for more oxygen. What uses oxygen is muscles. Bigger muscles use more. You can easily consume enough oxygen to bring your heart rate up into the 60-to-80-percent band if you work the larger muscles of your legs and lower abdomen, but it's more difficult to do so if you are only using your arms. If you are not sweating, then you are probably not in aerobic exercise mode. The advantages of regular aerobic exercise have been well publicized and so I won't rehearse them here. At some level everyone understands that this kind of exercise is good for you, and knows roughly why.

Aerobic exercise is usually contrasted against its evil complement, the sedentary state, and so everyone who can dutifully recite the benefits of aerobics can probably list the corresponding bad qualities of being sedentary: aerobics burns calories, sitting down doesn't, and so on.

Dr. Levine and other researchers have made us aware of an intermediate state between sedentary and aerobic, which for purposes of this piece, I'm going to call "ambulatory." We have already seen Dr.

Levine refer to it as "low-intensity meandering-style activity." Another term in the literature is NEAT, or "Non-Exercise Activity Thermogenesis." Until recently we were told that mere strolling about, subaerobically, without breaking a sweat, wasn't doing us that much good. Or to put it another way, it wasn't delivering us from the negative effects of the sedentary state. But recent research has revealed some new dangers associated with being sedentary (the bad news, if you will) and shown that those dangers may be eliminated by going into the ambulatory, but subaerobic, level of physical activity—which is good news, and which is a new result.

The research shows that when you become sedentary, the big muscle groups all drop into a sort of coma (my word choice) that causes immediate, and bad, changes in blood chemistry. Those changes persist and continue to wreak damage on health until the muscle groups are brought back to life by going into movement. To quote from a 2010 paper by Alpa Patel et al. in the *American Journal of Epidemiology*:

> . . . *prolonged time spent sitting, independent of physical activity, has important metabolic consequences that may influence specific biomarkers (such as triglycerides, high density lipoprotein cholesterol, fasting plasma glucose, resting blood pressure, and leptin) of obesity and cardiovascular and other chronic diseases. Animal studies have also shown that sedentary time substantially suppresses enzymes centrally involved in lipid metabolism within skeletal muscle, and low levels of daily life activity are sufficient to improve enzyme activity.*

The key here is that the movement needn't be strenuous; hence the careful word choice in the NEAT acronym. "Thermogenesis" just means that the body is burning fuel. "Non-Exercise Activity" means that the big muscles are turned on, but at a low level. The muscles just need to be doing *something*. Even jiggling your feet while seated is worth something. Standing up is good, but better is ambulating at a modest pace. This is the condition that office treadmills are designed to produce in their users.

This distinction between what I'm calling ambulatory and aerobic styles of movement is the basis for the entire office walking trend. Since the research is new, it's understandable that many who have been brought up to believe that subaerobic exercise is worthless are jumping to the assumption that what office walkers are asking for, when they propose installing treadmills in their cubicles, is the right to engage in full-on aerobic workouts all day long. In some cases this may be genuine confusion, in others a straw man used to defeat a proposal that makes managers skittish.

To this point it probably looks like I am setting this up as a slam-dunk case for ambulating while working, and getting ready to lambaste treadmill-resistant managers as insensitive and tragically shortsighted knuckle draggers. Well, they are. But in all fairness my knee did begin to hurt after I had been using my treadmill for a little while, and it hurt in a way that I had not experienced after other sorts of athletic exertions. The details aren't important. I ended up seeing a physical therapist who took a close look at my gait and then prescribed a regimen of stretching exercises and some changes to how I walk. For one thing, I had to think a lot harder about shoes. Which is obvious enough in retrospect. Any sensible person about to set out on a five-mile hike will have the presence of mind to don reasonable footwear. If you are going to cover a comparable distance on a treadmill, you need to take the same precautions.

The knee has been getting better ever since I came to my senses concerning the shoes. With luck it will all blow over and I'll be able to continue using my treadmill desk indefinitely without further difficulties.

But that's not the point. The point is that I had to see a physical therapist to solve the problem, and doing so cost money. Not a lot of money, but some.

If I hadn't used the treadmill, I wouldn't have seen a physical therapist about my knee. Oh, I very likely would have seen one about my upper back and shoulders. And down the road I might have seen any number of medical specialists about heart disease, diabetes, and other disorders resultant from a sedentary lifestyle. But large organizations tend to prefer the devil they know to the devil they don't. They're accustomed to their workers suffering carpal tunnel syndrome, back pain, and the like. But an epidemic of knee or foot problems would show up on their books as a new cost, directly chargeable to the use of treadmills at work. A reduction in sitting-related medical claims probably wouldn't be credited to the same program, though, since there's no way to prove that a reduction in someone's triglycerides or an easing of their shoulder pain is down to their use of a treadmill.

PRESUMABLY, PLAIN OLD WALKING AROUND IS EVEN BETTER FOR THE BODY than the somewhat unnatural gait that one adopts on a slow-moving treadmill. Treadmills are necessary for those who can't work without continuous access to an immobile piece of equipment: almost always a computer.

Actually, since computers are now small enough to carry around in the pocket, the crucial, nonmoving piece of equipment to which office workers are now anchored is not the computer but its monitor. The advent of cheap high-resolution flat-panel monitors seems only to have made this worse, since they can display so much information at such high quality, offering at least the illusion of greater productivity and connectedness. Miniaturization and the move to wireless connectivity have increased the (at least theoretical) ability of workers to get up and move around in every respect save this one.

The question then poses itself whether wearable displays have yet advanced to the point where they are adequate substitutes for monitors. If so, and if some sort of walking-friendly input devices could

be scrounged up or invented, then there would be no reason in principle why many workers couldn't wander around freely for a substantial part of their workday. Cubicle farms could be replaced by large
open spaces, devoid of furniture or other obstructions, where workers could move around in any way they liked. In good weather they
could go outside and stroll around in the fresh air. Imagine taking a
large call center and replacing it with a park dotted with wandering
pedestrians, each equipped with a phone headset and an augmented-
reality display giving them access to whatever data they needed to
handle customer-service inquiries. Employee retention, which tends
to be a serious headache in such operations, might be improved, and
employee health ought to improve markedly. There need be no loss of
supervisory control; whatever apparatus is now used for monitoring
and recording calls would work just as well in this kind of setup as it
does on a cubicle farm. Perhaps better, since an ambulatory worker
can just stroll over to talk to a supervisor when needed, or vice versa.
It sounds a bit odd, and it would definitely constitute a revolution in
office culture, but we already heading in that direction; it's getting
difficult to walk safely in places like airports and Manhattan streets
because of all the busy people striding blindly ahead with their eyes
fixed on the screens of their iPhones. Putting them in a place devoid
of brick walls and speeding taxicabs would make the world healthier
for them, and safer for all of us.

SLASHDOT INTERVIEW (2004)

[questions contributed by Slashdot readers]

THE LACK OF RESPECT... —BY MOSESJONES

Science Fiction is normally relegated to the specialist publications rather than having reviews in the mainstream press. Seen as "fringe" and a bit sad it's seldom reviewed with anything more than condescension by the "quality" press.

Does it bother you that people like Jeffery Archer or Jackie Collins seem to get more respect for their writing than you?

NEAL

OUCH! *(removes mirrorshades, wipes tears, blows nose, composes self)*

Let me just come at this one from sort of a big picture point of view.

(the sound of a million Slashdot readers hitting the "back" button . . .)

First of all, I don't think that the condescending "quality" press look too kindly on Jackie Collins and Jeffrey Archer. So I disagree with the premise of the last sentence of this question and I'm not going to address it. Instead I'm going to answer what I think MosesJones is really getting at, which is why SF and other genre and popular writers don't seem to get a lot of respect from the literary world.

To set it up, a brief anecdote: a while back, I went to a writers' conference. I was making chitchat with another writer, a critically acclaimed literary novelist who taught at a university. She had never heard of me. After we'd exchanged a bit of of small talk, she asked me "And where do you teach?"

I was taken aback. "I don't teach anywhere," I said.

Her turn to be taken aback. "Then what do you do?"

"I'm . . . a writer," I said. Which admittedly was a stupid thing to say, since she already knew that.

"Yes, but what do you do?"

I couldn't think of how to answer the question—I'd already answered it!

"You can't make a living out of being a writer, so how do you make money?" she tried.

"From . . . being a writer," I stammered.

At this point she finally got it, and her whole affect changed. She wasn't snobbish about it. But it was obvious that, in her mind, the sort of writer who actually made a living from it was an entirely different creature from the sort she generally associated with.

And once I got over the excruciating awkwardness of this conversation, I began to think she was right in thinking so. One way to classify artists is by to whom they are accountable.

The great artists of the Italian Renaissance were accountable to wealthy entities who became their patrons or gave them commissions. In many cases there was no other way to arrange it. There is only one Sistine Chapel. Not just anyone could walk in and start daubing paint on the ceiling. Someone had to be the gatekeeper—to hire an artist and give him a set of more or less restrictive limits within which he was allowed to be creative. So the artist was, in the end, accountable to the Church. The Church's goal was to build a magnificent structure that would stand there forever and provide inspiration to the Christians who walked into it, and they had to make sure that Michelangelo would carry out his work accordingly.

Similar arrangements were made by writers. After Dante was banished from Florence he found a patron in the Prince of Verona, for example. And if you look at many old books of the Baroque period you find the opening pages filled with florid expressions of gratitude from the authors to their patrons. It's the same as in a modern book when it says "this work was supported by a grant from the XYZ Foundation."

Nowadays we have different ways of supporting artists. Some painters, for example, make a living selling their work to wealthy collectors. In other cases, musicians or artists will find appointments at universities or other cultural institutions. But in both such cases there is a kind of accountability at work.

A wealthy art collector who pays a lot of money for a painting does not like to see his money evaporate. He wants to feel some confidence that if he or an heir decides to sell the painting later, they'll be able to get an amount of money that is at least in the same ballpark. But that price is going to be set by the market—it depends on the perceived value of the painting in the art world. And that in turn is a function of how the artist is esteemed by critics and by other collectors. So art criticism does two things at once: it's culture, but it's also economics.

There is also a kind of accountability in the case of, say, a composer who has a faculty job at a university. The trustees of the university have got a fiduciary responsibility not to throw away money. It's not the same as hiring a laborer in factory, whose output can be easily reduced to dollars and cents. Rather, the trustees have to justify the composer's salary by pointing to intangibles. And one of those intangibles is the degree of respect accorded that composer by critics, musicians, and other experts in the field: how often his works are performed by symphony orchestras, for example.

Accountability in the writing profession has been bifurcated for many centuries. I already mentioned that Dante and other writers were supported by patrons at least as far back as the Renaissance. But I doubt that *Beowulf* was written on commission. Probably there was a collection of legends and tales that had been passed along in an oral tradition—which is just a fancy way of saying that lots of people liked those stories and wanted to hear them told. And at some point perhaps there was an especially well-liked storyteller who pulled a few such tales together and fashioned them into what we now know as *Beowulf*. Maybe there was a king or other wealthy patron who then caused the tale to be written down by a scribe. But I doubt it was created at the behest of a king. It was created at the behest of lots and lots of intoxicated Frisians sitting around the fire wanting to hear a yarn. And there was no grand purpose behind its creation, as there was with the painting of the Sistine Chapel.

The novel is a very new form of art. It was unthinkable until the invention of printing and impractical until a significant fraction of the population became literate. But when the conditions were right, it suddenly became huge. The great serialized novelists of the 19th Century were like rock stars or movie stars. The printing press and the apparatus of publishing had given these creators a means to bypass traditional arbiters and gatekeepers of culture and connect directly to a mass audience. And the economics worked out such that they didn't need to land a commission or find a patron in order to put bread on the table. The creators of those novels were therefore able to have a connection with a mass audience and a livelihood fundamentally different from other types of artists.

Nowadays, rock stars and movie stars are making all the money. But the publishing industry still works for some lucky novelists who find a way to establish a connection with a readership sufficiently large to put bread on their tables. It's conventional to refer to these as "commercial" novelists, but I hate that term, so I'm going to call them Beowulf writers.

But this is not true for a great many other writers who are every bit as talented and worthy of finding readers. And so, in addition, we have got an alternate system that makes it possible for those writers to pursue their careers and make their voices heard. Just as Renaissance princes supported writers like Dante because they felt it was the right thing to do, there are many affluent persons in modern society who, by making donations to cultural institutions like universities, support all sorts of artists, including writers. Usually they are called "literary" as opposed to "commercial" but I hate that term too, so I'm going to call them Dante writers. And this is what I mean when I speak of a bifurcated system.

Like all tricks for dividing people into two groups, this is simplistic, and needs to be taken with a grain of salt. But there is a cultural difference between these two types of writers, rooted in to whom they are accountable, and it explains what MosesJones is complaining about. Beowulf writers and Dante writers appear to have the same job, but in fact there is a quite radical difference between them— hence the odd conversation that I had with my fellow author at the writer's conference. Because she'd never heard of me, she made the quite reasonable assumption that I was a Dante writer—one so new or obscure that she'd never seen me mentioned in a journal of literary criticism, and never bumped into me at a conference. Therefore, I couldn't be making any money at it. Therefore, I was most likely teaching somewhere. All perfectly logical. In order to set her straight, I had to let her know that the reason she'd never heard of me was because I was famous.

All of this places someone like me in critical limbo. As everyone knows, there are literary critics, and journals that publish their work, and I imagine they have the same dual role as art critics. That is, they are engaging in intellectual discourse for its own sake. But they are also performing an economic function by making judgments. These judgments, taken collectively, eventually determine who's deemed worthy of receiving fellowships, teaching appointments, etc.

The relationship between that critical apparatus and Beowulf writers is famously awkward and leads to all sorts of peculiar misunderstandings. Occasionally I'll take a hit from a critic for being somehow arrogant or egomaniacal, which is difficult to understand from my point of view sitting here and just trying to write about whatever I find interesting. To begin with, it's not clear why they think I'm any more arrogant than anyone else who writes a book and actually expects that someone's going to read it. Secondly, I don't understand why they think that this is relevant enough to rate mention in a review. After all, if I'm going to eat at a restaurant, I don't care about the chef's personality flaws—I just want to eat good food. I was slagged for entitling my latest book *The System of the World* by one critic who found that title arrogant. That criticism is simply wrong; the critic has completely misunderstood why I chose that title. Why on earth would anyone think it was arrogant? Well, on the Dante side of the bifurcation it's implicit that authority comes from the top down, and you need to get in the habit of deferring to people who are older and grander than you. In that world, apparently one must never select a grand-sounding title for one's book until one has reached Nobel Prize status. But on my side, if I'm trying to write a book about a bunch of historical figures who were consciously trying to understand and invent the System of the World, then this is an obvious choice for the title of the book. The same argument, I believe, explains why the accusation of having a big ego is considered relevant for inclusion in a book review. Considering the economic function of these reviews (explained above) it is worth pointing out which writers are and are not suited for participating in the somewhat hierarchical and political community of Dante writers. Egomaniacs would only create trouble.

Mind you, much of the authority and seniority in that world is benevolent, or at least well-intentioned. If you are trying to become a writer by taking expensive classes in that subject, you want your teacher to know more about it than you and to behave like a teacher. And so you might hear advice along the lines of "I don't think you're ready to tackle Y yet, you need to spend a few more years honing your skills with X" and the like. All perfectly reasonable. But people on the Beowulf side may never have taken a writing class in their life. They just tend to lunge at whatever looks interesting to them, write whatever they please, and let the chips fall where they may. So we may seem not merely arrogant, but completely unhinged. It reminds me somewhat of the split between Christians and Faeries depicted in Susannah Clarke's wonderful book *Jonathan Strange and Mr. Norrell.* The faeries do whatever they want and strike the Christians (humans) as ludicrously irresponsible and "barely sane." They don't seem to deserve or appreciate their freedom.

Later at the writers' conference, I introduced myself to someone who was responsible for organizing it, and she looked at me keenly and said, "Ah, yes, you're the one who's going to bring in our males 18–32." And sure enough, when we got to the venue, there were the males 18–32, looking quite out of place compared to the baseline lit-festival crowd. They stood at long lines at the microphones and asked me one question after another while ignoring the Dante writers sitting at the table with me. Some of the males 18–32 were so out of place that they seemed to have warped in from the Land of Faerie, and had the organizers wondering whether they should summon the police. But in the end they were more or less reasonable people who just wanted to talk about books and were as mystified by the literary people as the literary people were by them.

In the same vein, I just got back from the National Book Festival on the Capitol Mall in D.C., where I crossed paths for a few minutes with Neil Gaiman. This was another event in which Beowulf writers and Dante writers were all mixed together. The organizers had queues set up in front of signing tables. Neil had mentioned on his blog that he was going to be there, and so hundreds, maybe thousands of his readers had showed up there as early as 5:30 A.M. to get stuff signed. The organizers simply had not anticipated this and so—very much to their credit—they had to make all sorts of last-minute rearrangements to accommodate the crowd. Neil spent many hours signing. As he said on his blog, the *Washington Post* later said he did this because he was a "savvy businessman." Of course Neil was actually doing it to be polite; but even simple politeness to one's fans can seem grasping and cynical when viewed from the other side.

Because of such reactions, I know that certain people are going to read this screed as further evidence that I have a big head. But let me make at least a token effort to deflect this by stipulating that the system I am describing here IS NOT FAIR and that IT MAKES NO SENSE and that I don't deserve to have the freedom that is accorded a Beowulf writer when many talented and excellent writers—some of them good friends of mine—end up selling small numbers of books and having to cultivate grants, fellowships, faculty appointments, etc.

Anyway, most Beowulf writing is ignored by the critical apparatus or lightly made fun of when it's noticed at all. Literary critics know perfectly well that nothing they say is likely to have much effect on sales. Let's face it, when Neil Gaiman publishes a new book, all of his readers are going to know about it through his site and most of them are going to buy it and none of them is likely to see a review in the *New York Review of Books*, or care what that review says.

So what of MosesJones's original question, which was

entitled "The lack of respect"? My answer is that I don't
pay that much notice to these things because I am aware
at some level that I am on one side of the bifurcation and
most literary critics are on the other, and we simply are not
that relevant to each other's lives and careers.

What is most interesting to me is when people make
efforts to "route around" the apparatus of literary criticism and publish their thoughts about books in place
where you wouldn't normally look for book reviews. For
example, a year ago there was a piece by Edward Rothstein
in the *New York Times* about *Quicksilver* that appears to have
been a sort of wildcat review. He just got interested in the
book and decided to write about it, independent of the *New
York Times*'s normal book-reviewing apparatus. It is not the
first time such a thing has happened with one of my books.

It has happened many times in history that new systems will come along and, instead of obliterating the old,
will surround and encapsulate them and work in symbio-
sis with them but otherwise pretty much leave them alone
(think mitochondria) and sometimes I get the feeling that
something similar is happening with these two literary
worlds. The fact that we are having a discussion like this
one on a forum such as Slashdot is Exhibit A.

SINGULARITY—BY RANDALX

*What are your thoughts on Vernor Vinge's Singularity predic-
tion. Is it inevitable? Will humans become a part of it or be left
behind by this new "species"?*

NEAL:

I can never get past the structural similarities between
the Singularity prediction and the apocalypse of St. John
the Divine. This is not the place to parse it out, but the
key thing they have in common is the idea of a rapture, in

which some chosen humans will be taken up and made one with the infinite while others will be left behind.

I know Vernor. To know him is to respect him. He kicked my ass (as well as J. K. Rowling's and Greg Bear's and a few other people's) at the 2000 Hugo Awards, and on top of that he knows more physics than I ever will. So I don't for a moment think that he is peddling any such ideas with his prediction of a singularity. I am only telling you why I have a personal mental block as far as the Singularity prediction is concerned.

My thoughts are more in line with those of Jaron Lanier, who points out that while hardware might be getting faster all the time, software is shit (I am paraphrasing his argument). And without software to do something useful with all that hardware, the hardware's nothing more than a really complicated space heater.

RIGHT TO KEEP AND BEAR CODE—BY ARASHIAKARI

Do you think that hacking tools should be protected (in the United States) under the Second Amendment?

NEAL:

Such is the intensity of issues like this that I can't tell whether this is a troll. I'm going to assume it's not, and answer the question seriously.

I'm no constitutional scholar but I'm pretty sure that the Founding Fathers were thinking of flintlocks, not perl scripts, when they wrote the Second Amendment. Now you can dispute that and say "No, anything that enables citizens to defend themselves against an oppressive government is covered by the Second Amendment." There might be something to such an argument. But pragmatically, the question is whether you can get nine (or at least five) non-hacker Supreme Court Justices to see it that way. I suspect the answer is no. It's just too easy for them to say "it is not a weapon." To me it seems a lot easier simply to invoke the First Amendment.

Also, remember that there might be unwanted side effects to classifying code as weapons. In the U.S., where the right to bear certain weapons is written into the Constitution, it might seem like a clever way to secure access to such code. But authorities in other countries might say "look, even the U.S. Government defines this string of bits as a weapon—so we are going to outlaw it."

It's difficult to form an intelligent opinion on issues like this without doing a lot of work. One has to learn a lot about the issues and then think about them pretty hard. I haven't really done so, and so I'm inclined to trust people who have, like Matt Blaze. At crypto.com he has posted some interesting material that is germane to this topic.

See http://www.crypto.com/masterkey.html and especially

http://www.crypto.com/hobbs.html.

To make a long argument short, what I have learned from Matt's writings on the topic is that (1) it's not a new issue, (2) it's a First Amendment issue, and (3) it's best in the long run, for all concerned, if vulnerabilities are exposed in public.

WHO WOULD WIN? (SCORE:5, FUNNY)—BY CALL ME BLACK CLOUD

In a fight between you and William Gibson, who would win?

NEAL:

You don't have to settle for mere idle speculation. Let me tell you how it came out on the three occasions when we did fight.

The first time was a year or two after *Snow Crash* came

out. I was doing a reading/signing at White Dwarf Books in Vancouver. Gibson stopped by to say hello and extended his hand as if to shake. But I remembered something Bruce Sterling had told me. For, at the time, Sterling and I had formed a pact to fight Gibson. Gibson had been regrown in a vat from scraps of DNA after Sterling had crashed an LNG tanker into Gibson's Stealth pleasure barge in the Straits of Juan de Fuca. During the regeneration process, telescoping Carbonite stilettos had been incorporated into Gibson's arms. Remembering this in the nick of time, I grabbed the signing table and flipped it up between us. Of course the Carbonite stilettos pierced it as if it were cork board, but this spoiled his aim long enough for me to whip my wakizashi out from between my shoulder blades and swing at his head. He deflected the blow with a force blast that sprained my wrist. The falling table knocked over a space heater and set fire to the store. Everyone else fled. Gibson and I dueled among blazing stacks of books for a while. Slowly I gained the upper hand, for, on defense, his Praying Mantis style was no match for my Flying Cloud technique. But I lost him behind a cloud of smoke. Then I had to get out of the place. The streets were crowded with his black-suited minions so I turned into a swarm of locusts and flew back to Seattle.

The second time was a few years later when Gibson came through Seattle on his *Idoru* tour. Between doing some drive-by signings at local bookstores, he came and devastated my quarter of the city. I had been in a trance for seven days and seven nights and was unaware of these goings-on, but he came to me in a vision and taunted me, and left a message on my cellphone. That evening he was doing a reading at Kane Hall on the University of Washington campus. Swathed in black, I climbed to the top of the hall, mesmerized his snipers, sliced a hole in the roof using a plasma cutter, let myself into the catwalks above the stage, and then leapt down upon him from forty feet above. But I had forgotten that he had once studied in the same monastery as I, and knew all of my techniques. He rolled away at the last moment. I struck only the lectern, smashing it to kindling. Snatching up one jagged shard of oak I adopted the Mountain Tiger position just as you would expect. He pulled off his wireless mike and began to whirl it around his head. From there, the fight proceeded along predictable lines. As a stalemate developed we began to resort more and more to the use of pure energy, modulated by Red Lotus incantations of the third Sung group, which eventually led to the collapse of the building's roof and the loss of eight hundred lives. But as they were only peasants, we did not care.

Our third fight occurred at the Peace Arch on the U.S./ Canadian border between Seattle and Vancouver. Gibson wished to retire from that sort of lifestyle that required ceaseless training in the martial arts and sleeping outdoors under the rain. He only wished to sit in his garden brushing out novels on rice paper. But honor dictated that he must fight me for a third time first. Of course the Peace Arch did not remain standing for long. Before long my sword arm hung useless at my side. One of my psi blasts kicked up a large divot of earth and rubble, uncovering a silver metallic object, hitherto buried, that seemed to have been crafted by an industrial designer. It was a nitro-veridian device that had been buried there by Sterling. We were able to fly clear before it detonated. The blast caused a seismic rupture that split off a sizable part of Canada and created what we now know as Vancouver Island. This was the last fight between me and Gibson. For both of us, by studying certain ancient prophecies, had independently arrived at the same conclusion, namely that Sterling's professed interest in industrial design was a mere cover for work in superweapons. Gibson and I formed a pact to fight Sterling. So far we have made little headway in seeking out his lair of brushed steel and white LEDs, because I had a dentist appointment and Gibson had to attend a writers' conference, but keep an eye on Slashdot for any further developments.

STORYGRAMMING—BY DOC RUBY

You programmed computers before you wrote novels. Greg Egan shares that hyphenated career, and continues to illustrate his stories with Java applets [netspace.net.au]. Do you still program, possibly targeting the same subjects with your word processor as your compiler?

As Snow Crash *was originally designed as an interactive game, and such landmarks as* Myst *have regenerated as (usually bad) novels, do you see the arrival of a truly multimedia story, delivered simultaneously in multiple media, anytime soon? By whom, specifically or generally?*

NEAL:

It has already happened in the form of the I Love Bees alternate reality game, which, as many of you must know, is a promotional campaign for Halo 2. I know the people who did it, but I have lost track of what I promised not to reveal publicly, and so will shut up for now.

I still program, but I tend to do it as a diversion from writing, and so there is little crossover between it and fiction writing. Modern programming is hairy and difficult for me to get a grip on. This is because (1) there is so much user interface code, which kind of makes my eyes glaze over, and (2) GNU type code is crammed with macros, compiler directives and switches that make it very difficult for me to read the source files. Lately my platform of choice has been Mathematica, which is expensive (compared to gcc) but makes it easy to do anything with a few lines of code. Mathematica makes it easy to do proper documentation, in that you can mix narrative material freely with executable statements.

For *Cryptonomicon* I needed to generate some illustrations of a cutaway view of the mountain where Goto Dengo was building his tunnels. It needed to have a rough, natural-looking profile that maintained its roughness, but still had the same overall shape, when I zoomed in on it for more detailed illustrations. I did this with a Mathematica notebook that used the classic fractal technique of midpoint displacement.

For the Baroque Cycle books I needed to convert my manuscripts, which were all TeX files, into a Quark format used by the publisher. So I wrote an emacs lisp program that churned through the TeX files looking for TeX escape codes and converting them to their equivalents in Quark. This was nasty and tedious but, in the end, reasonably satisfying.

MONEY—BY QUERENCIA

One of the major themes in Cryptonomicon *that carried over (in a big way) to the Baroque Cycle is money. You introduced some "futuristic" views of currency and of where money might be going in* Cryptonomicon, *and you skillfully managed to do the same thing, while explaining some of the history of modern monetary systems, in the most recent books.*

You've obviously spent a lot of time thinking about money lately. Is there anything going on in the modern world with monetary systems (barter networks, for example) that you find particularly interesting?

What do you see on the horizon with respect to money?

NEAL:

Actually, what's interesting about money is that it doesn't seem to change that much at all. It became fantastically sophisticated hundreds of years ago. Back before people knew about germs, evolution, the Table of Elements, and other stuff that we now take for granted, people were engaging in financial manipulations that seem quite modern in their sophistication. So if I had to take a wild guess—and believe me, it is a wild guess—I'd say that money and the way it works is going to be a constant, not a variable.

TRAVEL TIPS FOR MODERN PRIMITIVES?—BY TIMOTHY

Mr. Stephenson:

I greatly enjoy your travel stories, both non-fiction (Mother Earth, Mother Board) and in particular your descriptions of the Philippines in Cryptonomicon.

Can you share some of the ideas you've developed for savvy trav'lin? For instance, how do you deal with carrying sufficient technology (whatever level you deem this to be) while minimizing the risk of theft, breakage, or loss by other means? Do you dress native or carry your entire wardrobe? [And broader, do you travel with something close to nothing, picking up necessary items as the need arises? What do you not leave home without?]

Do you carry any sort of self-defense means in some places, and if so What and Where?

NEAL:

I haven't done that much in the way of adventuresome travel lately. Even when I was doing so, I was never the sort

of hardened third-world travel geek that you are imagining. The thing is that when you go to such countries you
can typically get a room in a five-star hotel for less than a
hundred bucks a night. At that rate, it's easy to be a sellout
and wallow in luxury. Staying in a dive is more romantic,
but makes it harder to write. My excuse (if I need one) is
that typically I'm not writing about backpackers and rural
people in those countries; I'm writing about well-heeled
expats whose natural habitat is airport bars and Shangri-
La hotels. So that's where I tend to end up.

Re "self-defense means": I am reminded of a history book I read recently entitled *Skeletons on the Zahara*
by Dean King. It is about some American sailors who
get shipwrecked on the Atlantic Coast of Africa and go
through hell. Eventually most of them make it back to
freedom with the help of some Arab traders based in Mo-
rocco. These traders range across the Sahara on incredibly arduous journeys. They are just about the toughest
and meanest hombres you can possibly imagine. They've
been through all kinds of fights and ambushes, plagues
of locusts, sandstorms, etc. and come out on top. Because
of their success they have acquired camels, horses, and
weapons: not only swords and daggers but rifles and shot-
guns too. After having rescued the Americans, these guys
go out on another journey in the desert, and find themselves surrounded by a few dozen people who are wretched
even by the standards of the Sahara: no animals, little in
the way of clothing, and no weapons except for bags containing stones. A fight breaks out. The traders discharge
their weapons and kill everyone they shoot at: maybe half
a dozen. Then before they can reload they are all killed by
flying stones.

The best "self-defense means" when you are surrounded by a hundred million people of some other culture is to avoid dangerous places and figure out some way to get along with the folks around you.

CONFIDENTIAL PROPOSAL, OFF SHORE DATA HAVEN (SCORE:5, FUNNY)—BY SLASHDREAD

Greetings to you in the name of the most high God, from my beloved country Nigeria.

I am sorry and I solicit your permission into your privacy. I am Barrister Leonardo Akume, lawyer to the late Dr. Koffi Abachus, a brilliant Nigerian mathematician.

My former client, late Dr. Koffi Abachus, died in a mysterious plane crash in the year 1994 on the way to a scientific conference to make an announcement of the utmost importance to mankind.

He was planning to present a paper regarding his extensive work on data storage. It is said the data storage device he had developed would be roughly ten times more secure compared to the latest quantum excyption techniques. The device was about the size of a steamer trunk and stored on a privately owned island close to the coast of Nigeria. Dr Koffi Abachus is also the King of the local tribe by heritage . . .

Oh well . . . Should there BE a data haven? If so, where?

NEAL:

Your proposition sounds quite reasonable. In order for me to provide you with the support that you need, I will need for you to wire $100,000 into my Swiss bank account . . .

NEAL:

At this point, that is probably a technical question that I might not be competent to answer. I can carry a gig of encrypted data on a thumb drive now, and it doesn't cost much. Soon it'll be smaller and cheaper. Millions of people in different countries carrying gigs of data on thumb drives, iPods, cellphones, etc. make for a pretty robust distributed data storage system. It is difficult to imagine how one could build a centralized, hardened facility that would be more robust than that. But perhaps there's some technical or regulatory angle that I'm failing to appreciate here. I have not kept up to speed on this since *Cryptonomicon*.

BLUE ORIGIN—BY CONCERNED ONLOOKER

The Wikipedia lists you as a part-time advisor for Blue Origin [blueorigin.com], a company that is working to "develop a crewed, suborbital launch system." What is it that you do for them and has the recent winning of the X-Prize by the SpaceshipOne team had any effect on Blue Origin's plans? What are your visions of future private space flight?

NEAL:

Like Spock on the deck of the *Enterprise*, I sit in the corner and await opportunities to jump out and yammer about Science. Unlike Spock, I don't have anyone reporting to me and I never get to sit in the captain's chair and aim the phasers. This is probably good.

Though the X-Prize is cool and good, Blue Origin never intended to compete for it. Consequently, it has had no effect, other than destroying productivity whenever a SpaceShipOne flight is being broadcast.

As for my visions of future private space flight: here I have to remind you of something, which is that, up to this point in the interview, I have been wearing my novelist hat, meaning that I talk freely about whatever I please. But private space flight is an area where I wear a different hat (or helmet). I do not freely disseminate my thoughts on this one topic because I have agreed to sell those thoughts to Blue Origin. Admittedly, this feels a little strange to a novelist who is accustomed to running his mouth whenever he feels like it. But it is a small price to pay for the once-in-a-lifetime opportunity to become a minor character in a Robert Heinlein novel.

DO NEW PUBLISHING MODELS MAKE SENSE?—BY INFONAUT

Have you contemplated using any sort of alternative to traditional copyright for your works of fiction, such as a flavor of Creative Commons [creativecommons.org] license? Do you feel that making money as a writer and more open copyright are compatible in the long term, or do you think that writers like Lessig who distribute electronically via CC are merely indulging in a short-lived fad?

NEAL:

Publishing is a very ancient and crafty industry that existed and flourished before the idea of copyright even existed. When copyright came into existence, the publishing industry dealt with it and moved on. My suspicion is that everything that's been going on lately will amount to a sort of fire drill that will force publishing to scurry around and make some new arrangements so that they can get back to making money for themselves and for authors.

You can use the brick-and-mortar bookstore as a way to think about this. There was a time maybe five years ago when many people were questioning whether brick-and-mortar bookstores were going to survive the onslaught of online retailers. Now, if you take the narrow view that a bookstore is nothing more than a machine that swaps money for books, then it follows that there's no need for a physical store. But here we are five years later. Some bookstores have gone out of business, it's true. But there are big, beautiful bookstores all over the place, with sofas and coffee bars and author appearances and so on. Why? Because it turns out that a bookstore is a lot more than a machine that swaps money for books.

Likewise, if you think of a publisher as a machine that makes copies of bits and sells them, then you're going to predict the elimination of publishers. But that's only the smallest part of what publishers actually do. This is not to say that electronic distribution via CC is just a fad, any more than online bookstores are a fad. They will keep on going in parallel, and all of this will get sorted out in time.

METAPHYSICS IN THE ROYAL SOCIETY 1715–2010 (2012)

> This philosophy is a gift of God to this old world, to serve as the only plank, as it were, which pious and prudent people may use to escape the shipwreck of atheism which now threatens us.
>
> —LEIBNIZ, IN A 1669 LETTER TO THOMASIUS

Isaac Newton was slow to join to the Royal Society—in the Charter Book that lives in the Society's vault, his signature does not appear until the ninth page—but by the second decade of the Eighteenth Century he had become its President. His unquestioned status as the greatest mind of his generation, combined with his political connections as Master of the Mint and his ruthlessness toward those he perceived as rivals, had given him an unusual degree of power. This he brought to bear against the only living person who could even hope to challenge his intellectual supremacy: Gottfried Wilhelm Leibniz, who despite being a foreigner (he was Hanoverian) had been made a Fellow of the Royal Society in 1673, largely in recognition for his invention of the Stepped Reckoner, a mechanical computer.

The contrasts between Newton and Leibniz were lavish. Newton seems to have had an entirely accurate sense of just how he compared to his contemporaries, and acted accordingly without concern for dusty precedents or the personal feelings of those who clung to them. When confronted with anything less than uncritical acceptance of his work, he lashed out and then secluded himself. He published rarely but ex cathedra, handing down nearly flawless treatises over which he had toiled for years or decades, perfectly organized into definitions, axioms, lemmas, and laws, framing a mathematical physics that could be used to explain past observations and to make verifiable predictions.

Leibniz was an accomplished courtier who maintained long friendships with the Electress of Hanover, the first Queen of Prussia, the sister-in-law of Louis XIV, and the future Queen Consort of England, while moonlighting, late in his career, for Peter the Great. He corresponded so heavily that scholars are still sorting through his unpublished papers today. In his philosophy he practiced an ecumenicism that in a lesser mind would strike us as suspicious or even craven. Leibniz seems never to have met a philosopher or a theologian he didn't like, and his metaphysics developed out of an effort to harmonize the ancient thinking of (both) Plato and Aristotle with tenets of Christian and Jewish theology and with the "mechanical philosophy" the Royal Society had been created to champion. It is impossible to know precisely what he was thinking without perusing his vast legacy of papers. In effect, Leibniz's philosophy ceased to exist at the moment he died. Since then, anyone who has wanted to know it has first had to reconstruct it, which is only possible for forensically inclined scholars, fluent in Latin, French, and German,

and well versed in the history of Western philosophy, Christian theology, and Enlightenment science.

Given Leibniz's stature as one of the great thinkers of Western
history, one might expect that, as of the 350th anniversary of the
founding of the Royal Society, all of his writings would long since
have have been published, and that everything would be known
about his philosophy. But the question of "what did Leibniz believe,
and when did he believe it?" is unsettled and is the topic of current
research and debate.

A squalid row over the origins of the calculus, which these two
men had independently co-invented decades earlier, became the
public face of the conflict, which is regrettable since it is not very
interesting and since it reflects dreadfully on the combatants. Much
more significant in the long run was a debate on topics that reach so
deeply into the foundations of science that they are still discussed
in our times. This broke the surface in the last year of Leibniz's life,
in an exchange of letters that has come to be known as the Leibniz-
Clarke Correspondence.

The year was 1715, and because of two royal deaths (in England,
Queen Anne; in Hanover, Electress Sophie), Princess Caroline of
Brandenburg-Ansbach had just become the Princess of Wales. To
the modern reader, Caroline seems less like a real historical person-
age than a plucky, clever, independent-minded heroine from some
post-feminist historical novel. A noble but poor orphan, raised as a
ward of the Prussian court, she was conversant with scientific topics
of the day, largely because she had been tutored in them by Leibniz. She had married into the Hanoverian dynasty and had moved
with it to London, where her father-in-law had been crowned King
George I. The 69-year-old Leibniz, who had become unfashionable
and, because of the dispute over the calculus, something of a political
problem, had been left behind in Germany. He wrote a short letter to
Caroline, warning her that religion was declining in England; that
John Locke did not believe in the immortality of the soul; and that

Sir Isaac Newton held to some strange views about the relationship between God and the physical universe.

Anyone who has blithely forwarded a private email to a corporate mailing list, with incalculable consequences, will recognize what happened next: Caroline made Leibniz's letter known, and one Samuel Clarke stepped forward to rebut Leibniz's charges. The result was a series of letters (five each by Leibniz and Clarke) over the course of a year, at which point Leibniz died. Clarke, though he had serious credentials in his own right both as theologian and scientist, was acting as a spokesman for Newton, and so the Correspondence can fairly be read as a debate between Leibniz and Newton.

In the opening round, the combatants practically trip over each other in their eagerness to remind the Princess that atheism is bad and that true natural philosophy in no way conflicts with religion. There is no reason to think that either of them is being disingenuous. The scientific revolution had created doubts about the existence of God, or at least the veracity of religious dogma, in the minds of many; but not Newton or Leibniz.

These concerns are dispensed with in a few paragraphs. The bulk of the Correspondence, which runs to about eighty pages, resembles an email exchange that devolves, as it goes on, into several distinct threads, each concerning a specific sub-topic. The correspondents begin to number their paragraphs (Leibniz's fifth letter contains 130 of them), the better to keep track of all the rebuttals and counter-rebuttals. The over-arching theme is the relationship of God to the universe, and more specifically the universe as perceived, measured, and understood by scientists. Leibniz, in the universal manner of authors promoting their latest work, finds frequent occasion to mention his books *Theodicy* and *Monadology*. Even when he isn't mentioning them by name, he is presenting arguments, and using terminology, derived from them.

My theme is the legacy of Leibniz's metaphysics from the time of his death down to the present day, and so a direct summary of that system, based on the scholarship of latter-day researchers, will do better service than any attempt to untangle the points and counterpoints in the Correspondence. The account presented below is patterned after the work of Christia Mercer of Columbia University. Her book *Leibniz's Metaphysics: Its Origins and Development*, published in 2001 by Cambridge University Press, is a formidable work of forensic scholarship that can in no way be improved by my attempts to summarize it.

In 1661, at the age of 14, Leibniz had formed a resolution to embrace the new mechanical philosophy. For most natural philosophers of the era, this meant rejecting the Aristotelian worldview of the medieval schoolmen. As mentioned, though, Leibniz was an ecumenicist and a conciliator, and so for him it meant, rather, the beginning of a lifelong quest to reconcile certain select, precisely defined tenets of Aristotelian and Platonic thought with modern science.

In his metaphysical reasoning, Leibniz is at least as meticulous as is Newton in his mathematical physics. Bertrand Russell called Leibniz's system "profound, coherent, largely Spinozistic, and amazingly logical." Newton, however, can verify his results by comparing them to observations while Leibniz is beholden to no one except Leibniz. By pure thinking, Leibniz fabricated a metaphysical system that could hardly be more at odds with that of Newton, or indeed any other person who attempts to think in a commonsensical way about how the world might work.

Where Newton's work is grounded in Euclidean geometry, Leibniz begins with certain precepts that he takes to be axiomatic, such as the Principle of Sufficient Reason (nothing exists without a reason; there is no effect without a cause) and the Identity of Indiscernibles (two individual things cannot differ in number alone; it must be possible to explain why they are distinct based on some intrinsic difference). Newton developed calculus because it enabled him to solve problems in his theory of gravitation; Leibniz developed it as an outgrowth of his fascination with the problem of the Continuum, which asks how a line can be made up out of points, a span of time from instants, or a thought from the minute perceptions and endeavours of a mind. Just as Newton would not bother developing a physics that could not explain the fact that planets move in elliptical orbits, Leibniz had no time for any metaphysics that was incompatible with the transubstantiation of the Eucharist (both the Protestant and the Catholic versions!) and the incarnation of God in Christ. Much of the pick-and-shovel work of his Monadology came from a 1671 tract about the Incarnation of God.*

The modern reader, following the development of Leibniz's ideas over the years between 1661 and his death in 1716, veers between finding it all quite reasonable and feeling as though it must have come from an alien planet. Just when one is about to judge Leibniz as having the strangest mind of anyone who ever lived, one remembers Newton and his lifelong obsession with alchemy and his strenuous efforts to predict the exact date of the End Times by ransacking the Book of Revelation for encrypted clues.

It takes an entire book such as Mercer's to explain Leibniz's full chain of reasoning, so there is not room here to attempt any such thing. The end point—Leibniz's mature system, as described in *Monadology*—may be summarized as follows:

Matter, assumed by most to be the primary stuff of the universe, extended in space and time, is, in fact, unreal. Atomism in its conventional form—the idea that physical objects can be divided and subdivided up to a certain point, but (for some, usually unspecified, reason) no further, and that the result is a collection of tiny indivisible matter-bits moving around in empty space and banging into one another—is all wrong. The true atoms—the fundamental, indivisible units that make up the universe—are not spatiotemporal and so are not bound by spatial and temporal constraints; rather, space and

---

* This perennial theological chestnut seems to have occasioned some soul-searching for Newton as well, since he risked serious trouble by semi-openly espousing the Arian heresy, which denies the Trinity.

time are epiphenomena of their activities, which are mental (today we might say computational) rather than physical. Leibniz calls these mind-atoms by the name of monads.

Use of "mind" and "mental" is apt to give modern readers the wrong idea. Many translators of Leibniz (including Russell) choose the word "soul" instead of "mind," which is even more confusing. A word about those words is, therefore, in order. Extension (occupying physical space) and duration (persisting through time) are obvious properties of matter that had long been of interest to natural philosophers. Beginning around 1671, Leibniz began to add a third element, namely *cognitio*, which can be translated as "thought" or "knowledge." In his metaphysics, *cognitio* is a property that things can possess and that makes them different from inert matter. Early in his career, it is as fundamental as extension. Later, it becomes more so. Previously, he had admitted God and the human mind as the only two incorporeal principles in his system; the key move he now made was to admit the possibility of cogitating entities ("minds" or "souls") that were neither divine nor human, and to make them and "endeavour"—the smallest possible unit of cogitation, which is to *cognitio* as a point is to a line or an instant is to time—as fundamental as space and time. Later, he goes on to deny the primary reality of space and time altogether and to assert that the created world consists entirely of these unextended monads and that the universe is created from moment to moment as a result of their cognition. In this he breaks from the metaphysics assumed by Newton (and almost anyone else who has thought in a commensensical way about space, time and atoms) in which space and time have an absolute reality, and form a sort of lattice on which the laws of physics are enacted, and, indeed, without which they cannot even be written down.

Because the monads do not exist in space and time, they are free to take on certain powers and properties that would otherwise be implausible: (1) each monad perceives the state of every other monad in the universe, and (2) each exists in a certain state, and is capable of changing that state. This process of continual internal state-change is the cogitation that is the raison d'etre of the monad and the fundamental process of the universe.

Internal and intrinsic to each monad is a rule (dubbed by Mercer the Production Rule) that governs how it changes its state in response to its current state and the perceived state of all of the other monads. And just as the constraints of space and time are inapplicable to monads, so cause and effect work differently, for each monad is causally independent of all other monads. It makes its own decisions by its own lights, obeying its intrinsic rule.

This raises the obvious objection that if the states of the other monads serve as inputs to the production rule, then there would seem to be a cause-and-effect relationship at work, but Leibniz doggedly maintains that no such relationship exists and that coordination among monads comes about, not through causal linkages, but as the result of a divinely ordained pre-established harmony that brings all of the monads into a kind of synchronization without encroaching on their independence. For minds and cogitation are, to Leibniz, the ultimate reality, and unless the minds have free will, they are not minds at all, but physical mechanisms numbly obeying deterministic rules.

This is the one feature of the monadology that might (I speculate) have aroused some competitive anxiety in Newton's mind. The Leibniz-Clarke correspondence probably would not have drawn the attention of so many important people were it not that traditional (spatiotemporal) atomism, combined with the then-new science of mathematical physics, seems to lead ineluctably to what was later called Laplacian determinism. If the behavior of all objects can be explained in terms of spatiotemporal atoms, and if the atoms' behavior, in turn, is subject to Newton's deterministic mathematical laws, then there is no room for free will. Humans are robots and religion is a fraud.

Newton was aware of this problem. He had no intention of promulgating a philosophy that stripped humans of free will. He seems to have gotten around it by positing supernatural intervention, i.e., by recourse to entities and powers that lay outside of the system described by his science. Leibniz's approach, bizarre as it might be in many respects, was, in a sense, more scientific; free will was no longer a problem that needed to be explained away, but an intrinsic feature of every monad.

Monadology spent the next two centuries on the ash-heap of intellectual history. After Leibniz's death, a faulty version was published by one of his disciples, and its errors laid at Leibniz's feet. Then it swam into the gunsights of Immanuel Kant. In his *Critique of Pure Reason*, Kant begins by saying a few complimentary things about Leibniz. Three hundred pages later, having carefully set his pieces out on the board, he annihilates Leibniz's metaphysics in a few sentences. According to Kant's philosophy, Leibniz is correct in thinking that space and time, cause and effect, are not ultimate realities, but rather constructs of mental activity. But by the same token, Kant says, the human mind is powerless to think in any useful or productive way about anything that is outside of space and time, cause and effect, and so Leibniz's entire Monadology—or any thinking that attempts to transcend spatiotemporality—is rubbish.

In the day of Newton and Leibniz, metaphysics had been as respectable as mathematics, but the hard-headed empiricists of the scientific world began to kick dirt on it during the Nineteenth Century and, in the first half of the Twentieth, the logical positivists buried it. And indeed, Leibniz's work seems unsound at best, ludicrous at worst, by the scientific standards of the era before relativity, quantum mechanics, and Gödel's Proof.

Today, metaphysics in general has regained much of its former respectability among philosophers. For almost everyone else, though, it retains the connotations of wooliness that it picked up during that century or so of rough treatment at the hands of empiricists and positivists. Many hard scientists still use "metaphysics" as a byword for undisciplined, conjectural thinking. Nevertheless, metaphysics is still being practiced today: by philosophers openly, by physicists under other names.

A straightforward way of defining metaphysics is as the set of assumptions and practices present in the scientist's mind before he or she begins to do science. There is nothing wrong with making such assumptions, as it is not possible to do science without them. The lepidopterist who records in her notebook that a butterfly is blue may not stop to consider that this is true only because the giant ball of nuclear fuel 93 million miles away happens to maintain a surface temperature just right for shedding certain wavelengths of electromagnetic radiation on the earth; that the eyes of humans have evolved to be sensitive to those wavelengths; that the eye can discriminate slightly different wavelengths as colors; that one of those colors has, by cultural consensus, been defined as "blue," and so on. Nevertheless, science benefits from the lepidopterist's note that the butterfly is blue.

Even the hardest of hard sciences is replete with assumptions that may fairly be classified as metaphysical. Almost all mathematicians, for example, presume that they are discovering, rather than creating, mathematical truths. Ask a room full of mathematicians whether three was a prime number a billion years ago (i.e. before there were humans to define it as such) and every hand will go up. And yet to say so is to espouse the metaphysical position that primeness and all the other subject matter of mathematics have a reality independent of the human mind. This assumption goes under various names, one of which is Mathematical Platonism. Likewise physicists can hardly go about their work without assuming that the physical world answers to laws that may be expressed and proved mathematically—an assumption for which there is plenty of empirical evidence, dating back (at least) to Galileo, but no proof as such.

The revival of Leibniz's fortunes may be dated to approximately 1900, when Bertrand Russell began to publish his studies of Leibniz's unpublished work. While unsparing in his criticisms of Leibniz's character and of his more popular writings, Russell had a high opinion of Leibniz's work on mathematical logic and was fascinated by some of the ramifications of the Monadology. In his *History of Western Philosophy* (1945) he ends his chapter on Leibniz as follows: "What I . . . think best in his theory of monads is his two kinds of space, one subjective, in the perceptions of each monad, and one objective, consisting of the assemblage of points of view of the various monads. This, I believe, is still useful in relating perception to physics."

Leibniz then came to the attention of a wide range of thinkers. To tell the story in chronological order, including all of the requisite details about those who have knowingly or unknowingly echoed Leibniz's views, would require a substantial book in and of itself, of which the following might serve as a brief sketch or outline.

1. The debate on free will vs. determinism is no more settled today than it was at the time of the Leibniz-Clarke Correspondence, and so in that sense (at least) Monadology is still interesting as a gambit, which different observers might see as heroic, ingenious, or desperate, to cut that Gordian knot by making free minds or souls into the fundamental components of the universe.

2. Leibniz's interpreters made use of the vocabulary at their disposal to translate his terminology into words such as "mind," "soul," "cognition," "endeavour," etc. This, however, was before the era of information theory, Turing machines, and digital computers, which have supplied us with a new set of concepts, a lexicon, and a rigorous science pertaining to things that, like monads, perform a sort of cogitation but are neither divine nor human. A translator of Leibniz's work, beginning in A.D. 2010 from a blank sheet of paper, would, I submit, be more likely to use words like "computer" and "computation" than "soul" and "cognition." During Leibniz's era, the only

person who had thought seriously about such machines was Leibniz himself; building on earlier work by Blaise Pascal, he designed, and caused to be built, a mechanical computer, and envisioned coupling it to a formal logical system called the *Characteristica Universalis*. He invented binary arithmetic, and, according to no less an authority than Norbert Wiener, pioneered the idea of feedback.

3. In particular, the monads' production rule scheme clearly presages the modern concept of cellular automata. Quoting from Mercer's work: "The Production Rule of F is a rule for the continuous production of the discrete states of F so that it instructs F about exactly what to think at every moment of F's existence. Following Leibniz's suggestion, if F exists from t1 to tn and has a different thought at each moment of its existence, then at every moment, there will be an instruction about what to think next. The present thought occurring at t1, together with the Production Rule, will determine what F will think at t2." Combined with the monadic property of being able to perceive the states of all other monads, this comes close to being a mathematically formal definition of cellular automata, a branch of mathematics generally agreed to have been invented by Stanislaw Ulam and John von Neumann during the 1940s as an outgrowth of work at Los Alamos. The impressive capabilities of such systems have, in subsequent decades, drawn the attention of many luminaries from the worlds of mathematics and physics, some of whom have proposed that the physical universe might, in fact, consist of cellular automata carrying out a calculation—a hypothesis known as Digital Physics, or It from Bit.

4. Leibniz insisted that each monad perceived the states of all of the others, a premise that runs counter to intuition, given that this would seem to require that an infinite amount of information be transmitted to and stored in each monad. Of all

the claims of monadology, this must have seemed the easiest to refute a hundred years ago. Since then, however, it has been given a new lease on life by quantum mechanics. Consider, for example, the Pauli Exclusion Principle, which states (for example) that, in a helium atom with two electrons in the same orbital, the two must have opposite spins. It is not possible for both of them to possess exactly the same state. Each of the two electrons somehow "knows" the direction of the other's spin and "obeys" the rule that its spin must be different. The Pauli Exclusion Principle is Leibniz's Identity of Indiscernibles principle translated directly into physics. Moreover, the ability of an electron to "know" the state of another electron, without any physical explanation as to how this information is transmitted and stored, is strongly reminiscent of Monadology. Elementary descriptions of quantum mechanics tend to limit themselves to extremely simple systems, such as individual particles or atoms, since beyond there the mathematics become intractable. But the same principles apply, albeit in vastly more complex form, in larger systems: the quantum state of each particle is dependent upon the states of all the other particles in the system.

5. Leibniz's notion that the ultimate entities in the universe were non-spatiotemporal received a kind of weak boost from General Relativity, which called into question the idea of absolute space and time as a fixed lattice on which the laws of physics were enacted. More recently, absolute space and time have come under more concerted attack as some physicists have sought to develop so-called background-independent theories. The idea of background independence is explained in more detail in Lee Smolin's *The Trouble with Physics*, and the history of the concept of absolute space and time, from the Babylonians forwards, is told by Barbour in his magisterial *The Discovery of Dynamics*. That space and time have an

absolute reality, and that the laws of physics must be hung on a fixed spatiotemporal lattice, are metaphysical assumptions. Very reasonable, empirically grounded assumptions to be sure, but assumptions nonetheless. Resulting theories are called background-dependent. Various efforts have been made to derive background-independent theories that make no assumptions as to the fundamental reality of space and time. Barbour in particular has done seminal work along these lines, showing that General Relativity is a realization of a relational, i.e. Leibnizian view of space and time. More recently, other researchers, notably Smolin, have sought to unify Barbour's formulation of general relativity with quantum mechanics, the aim being to develop a background-independent theory of quantum gravity according to which space and time are emergent properties resulting from interactions of more fundamental entities joined together in a graph of connections. This theory, which is called Loop Quantum Gravity, is proposed as an alternative to string theory, which is background-dependent.

6. The Leibnizian concept of pre-established harmony was viciously mocked by Voltaire in *Candide*, and has become no easier for sophisticated people to accept since then. Stripped of its theological overtones and saccharine connotations, though, the concept has a reasonably clear analog in modern physics.

   a. Newtonian mechanics exactly describes the behavior of individual bodies (provided, as Einstein later discovered, that they are reasonably large and slow-moving). Its laws are expressed in terms of individual particles: a particle moves in a straight line unless acted upon by a force. The force acting on a particle

is equal to the product of its mass and acceleration (F = ma). As any first-year physics student
learns the hard way, naively using the F = ma
approach to describe systems comprising many
independent parts soon becomes mathematically intractable.

b.   Leibniz is credited with having written down
the law now known as conservation of energy
(which he denoted *vis viva*). In any system of particles, the product of the mass and the square
of the velocity of each particle, summed over
all of the particles in the system, remains constant. When this, and the law of Conservation
of Momentum, are imposed as constraints on a
system, the mathematics frequently gets easier,
to the point where it becomes possible to produce results not obtainable otherwise. Conservation of energy does not contradict Newton's
laws, and, in fact, is derivable from them, and
so from a strictly mathematical point of view
it adds nothing to Newtonian physics. It does,
however, introduce a different way of thinking
about physical systems. The naive reductionist
strategy of the first-year physics student gives
way to a global approach in which the system
as a whole must obey certain rules, to which
the detailed movements and interactions of its
components are seen as subordinate.

c.   The physicists of the late 18th and early 19th
Century developed new tools based on the
notion of state or configuration spaces framed,
not of spatial dimensions, but of all the generalized coordinates and momenta needed to

specify the state of the system. Any possible state can be represented as a point in that space, and its evolution over time as a trajectory. The behavior of such trajectories is governed by an "action principle" that encodes all of the applicable physical laws, such as conservation of momentum and of energy. Action principles in classical state space are a mathematical reformulation of Newton's laws, not an alternative to them. The change in point of view from physical trajectories in Cartesian space to action in state space is nonetheless significant. It is a further step away from the reductionist and toward the global approach. It seems to inject a teleological aspect that is not present in the older formulation, and so has occasioned some introspection among philosophically inclined scientists. In his *Lectures on Physics*, Richard Feynman interpolated a single, anomalous chapter on the topic, simply because of his abiding fascination with it. It allows the physicist to predict the behavior of a complex system without having to work out the detailed interactions among its physical atoms. It leads to important results from thermodynamics and it is directly applicable to quantum mechanics. It is a way of thinking, in a systematic and rigorous way, about compossibility, a concept important to Leibniz. Many possible states of affairs might exist or, to put it another way, there are an infinite number of possible worlds. But not all states of affairs are *compossible*; some are mutually contradictory, and while it is possible to imagine a universe in

which contradictory states of affairs coexist, it
is not possible for such a universe to come into
practical being. The configuration space that
describes the universe contains an infinity of
points, each of which represents a different state
of affairs, but most of these are incoherent. Only
certain points—certain universes—make sense
internally, and those points lie on trajectories
that describe the logical evolution, according to
physical law, of those universes over time. If one
adopts this frame of reference for considering
Leibniz's concept of the pre-established harmony, and excludes (or at least adopts an agnos-
tic stance toward) the notion that it was all set up
at the beginning by God, it is easier to come to
grips with Leibniz's idea that the monads act in
a coherent way somehow transcending detailed
cause-and-effect interactions.

d. That much is true of classical (i.e. pre-quantum)
state space theory, even though it adds nothing
beyond Newton's original laws. The quantum
version of the theory, on the other hand, requires
that actions over all possible worlds be brought
together in a calculation yielding the probability
that any one state of affairs will eventuate. As
Feynman puts it, "It isn't that a particle takes the
path of least action but that it smells all the paths
in the neighborhood and chooses the one that has
the least action. . . ." The picture is reminiscent
of Leibniz's "best of all possible worlds."

7. Possible-world theory has come in for serious study in recent
decades both by philosophers and physicists. For impres-

sively technical reasons that are likely to leave lay readers nonplussed, David Lewis (*Plurality of Worlds*) posited that all possible worlds really exist and are no less real than the one we live in. Such notions are the subject of current philosophical research, under the rubrics of modal realism and actualist realism. Among physicists, Hugh Everett launched the many-worlds interpretation of quantum mechanics in the late 1950s, since which time it has slowly but steadily garnered support. A particularly eloquent latter-day treatment can be found in David Deutsch's *The Fabric of Reality*.

8. Kurt Gödel (1906–1978), who early in his life became known as "the greatest logician since Aristotle" because of his astonishingly original work on the foundations of mathematics, devoted much of the second half of his life to the development of a rigorous metaphysical system that was to be based upon the work of Leibniz, with whom he had a fascination that became notorious. Gödel was a strong mathematical Platonist who thought in a serious way about the notion that the entities that are the subject matter of mathematics really exist, though not in our physical universe, and that when we do mathematics we in some sense perceive those entities. An almost painfully meticulous scholar, he was well aware of Kant's objections to Leibniz's metaphysics, and understood that those objections would have to be dealt with in order for him to make any progress. According to his friend and biographer Hao Wang, Gödel discovered the works of Edmund Husserl (1859–1938) in the late 1950s and devoted much of the remainder of his life to studying them. He felt that Husserl had solved many, if not all, of the metaphysical problems that Gödel had set for himself, including doing away with Kant's objections to Leibniz's work. Husserl is prolix, prolific, and infamously difficult to read (even Gödel complained of this) and so a reader of sub-Gödel I.Q., eyeing a heap of Husserl translations on a table,

might despair of ever putting his finger on the passages that
Gödel is thinking of. Fortunately, Hao Wang did us the favor
of listing the specific Husserl books that Gödel most admired.
One of them is *Cartesian Meditations*, based on a series of lectures that Husserl delivered late in his career. In the fifth and
last of these, Husserl gets around to mentioning, in an ap-
proving way, Leibniz and monads. Husserl has come round to
Leibniz's way of thinking, but he has got there by taking a different route, pioneered by Husserl, through phenomenology,
the premises and development of which I'll spare the reader.
Since Gödel's death, Mathematical Platonism has come in for
serious study both by philosophers such as Edward N. Zalta, a
metaphysician at Stanford University, and scientists such as
Max Tegmark, an MIT cosmologist. Zalta and Tegmark (like
Deutsch) have been influenced by David Lewis's work on
modal realism. Beginning from different premises, they have
arrived at markedly similar approaches.

NONE OF THESE LATTER-DAY ECHOES OF LEIBNIZIAN THINKING HAS GENER-
ated traceable, exact results in the same way that, for example, Newtonian mechanics was able to predict the orbit of the moon. If such
a thing happens in the future—if, for example, the practitioners of
Loop Quantum Gravity use their theory to make predictions that are
verified by experiment—then credit will have to go to them and not to
Leibniz, who could never have imagined such a science. It's not the
point of this chapter, in other words, to argue that Leibniz was right,
much less that Newton was wrong. Leibniz was not even doing science as we now define the term. My conclusions are two. First of all,
that the infamous duel between Newton and Leibniz—which was only
superficially about who had invented the calculus—came back from
the dead a hundred years ago to exert remarkable influence over the
course of modern science. Secondly, that Leibniz's most fundamen-

tal assumption, namely that the universe makes sense and that the human has the power to make sense of it and that, consequently, pure metaphysics is no waste of time, remains perhaps the central question of all science. In 1960, Eugene Wigner wrote a paper, *The Unreasonable Effectiveness of Mathematics in the Physical Sciences*, in which he addressed the nearly miraculous way in which pure mathematics— seemingly a product of human cognition, and nothing else—predicts the behavior of the physical world. The examples cited by Wigner would have made sense to Leibniz. Leibniz, however, would have been baffled by Wigner's use of the adjective "unreasonable" in the title of his paper. Wigner was a modern: a product of a skeptical age. He was uneasy (or felt obliged to pretend to be uneasy) with the philosophical implications of the way in which the physical world answered to mathematics. This unease could not have been more alien to Leibniz, who, during his long philosophical career, questioned many things that would have been easier to leave alone, but believed, with a kind of medieval serenity, in the reasonableness of Creation.

IT'S ALL GEEK TO ME
(2007)

A week ago Friday, moments before an opening-day showing of the movie "300" at Seattle's Cinerama, a 20-something moviegoer rushed to the front of the theater, dropped his shoulders, curled his arms into a mock-Schwarzenegger pose and bellowed out a timeless remark of King Leonidas of Sparta that has in the last week become the catchphrase of the year: "Spartans! Tonight we dine in hell!"

Groans, roars, macho hooting noises and sardonic applause rained down on him. The audience had been standing in line for an hour. Only a few of them were dressed as Greek hoplites. They were much better balanced between men and women than I'd expected and, racially, looked like a fair cross section of Seattle's populace. Over the next couple of hours, they enjoyed "300" with roughly the same level of energy and audience participation as one would expect in an N.C.A.A. Final Four game.

The film contains a lot of over-the-top material, reflecting its origin in a graphic novel. As often as not, when I found myself rolling my eyes at something particularly mortifying (the tactical corpse-pile avalanche, the Persian executioner with serrated fins for arms), the crowd reacted much as I did, some even hurling catcalls from the balcony or blurting their own lines of dialogue. It was all pretty festive for a movie about ancient history in which almost all of the characters end up dead.

This, apparently, was no anomaly. Though it opened on a relatively small number of screens, "300" made money far beyond the most optimistic projections of its producers, racking up the third-best opening weekend ever for an R-rated movie.

The critics, however, were mostly hostile, and frequently venomous. Many reviews made the same points:

- "300" is not sufficiently ironic. It takes its themes (duty, loyalty, sacrifice, the preservation of Western civilization against enormous odds) too seriously to, well, be taken seriously.
- "300" is campy—meaning that many things about it can be read as sexual double entendres—yet the filmmakers don't show sufficient awareness of this.
- All of the good guys are white people and many of the bad guys are brown. (How this could have been avoided in a film about Spartans versus Persians is never explained; the distinctly non-Greek viewers at my showing seemed to have no trouble placing themselves in the sandals of ancient Spartans.)

But such criticisms aren't really worth arguing with, because they are not serious in the first place—and that is their whole point. Many critics dislike "300" so intensely that they refused to do it the honor of criticizing it as if it were a real movie. Critics at a festival in Berlin walked out, and accused its director of being on the Bush payroll.

Thermopylae is a wedge issue!

Lefties can't abide lionizing a bunch of militaristic slave-owners (even if they did happen to be long-haired supporters of women's rights). So you might think that righties would love the film. But they're nervous that Emperor Xerxes of Persia, not the freedom-loving Leonidas, might be George Bush.

Our so-called conservatives, who have cut all ties to their own intellectual moorings, now espouse policies and personalities that would get them laughed out of Periclean Athens. The few conservatives still able to hold up one end of a Socratic dialogue are those in the ostracized libertarian wing—interestingly enough, a group with a disproportionately high representation among fans of speculative fiction.

The less politicized majority, who perhaps would like to draw inspiration from this story without glossing over the crazy and defective aspects of Spartan society, have turned, in droves, to a film from the alternative cultural universe of fantasy and science fiction. Styled and informed by pulp novels, comic books, video games and Asian martial arts flicks, science fiction eats this kind of material up, and expresses it in ways that look impossibly weird to people who aren't used to it.

Lack of critical respect means nothing to sci-fi's creators and fans. They made peace with their own dorkiness long ago. Oh, there was momentary discomfort around the time of William Shatner's 1987 "Saturday Night Live" sketch, in which he exhorted Trekkies to "get a life." But this had been fully resolved by 2000, when sci-fi fans voted to give the Hugo Award for best movie to "Galaxy Quest," a film that revolves around making fun of sci-fi fans.

The growing popularity of science fiction, the rise of graphic novels, anime and video games, and the fact that geeks can make lots of money now, have given creators and fans of this kind of art a confidence, even a swagger, that—hard as it is for some of us to believe—is kind of cool.

Video games have turned everyone under the age of 20 into experts on military history and tactics; 12-year-olds on school buses argue about the right way to deploy onagers and cataphracts while outflanking a Roman triplex acies formation. The near exhaustion of Asian martial arts themes has led a small but growing number to begin reconstructing, or imagining, the forgotten martial arts of the West. And science fiction, by its nature, has had to equip itself with a full toolkit for dealing with alien cultures, mindsets and landscapes.

Which is exactly how the creators of "300" approach the Spartans and the Persians. The only people in the film who don't seem as if they came from another planet are the Arcadians (non-Spartan Greeks), who turn tail once the battle becomes hopeless.

Classics-based sci-fi is nothing new. To name the most recent of many examples, the novelist Dan Simmons published "Ilium" and "Olympos," science-fictional takes on Homer. When science fiction tackles classical themes, the results may look a bit odd to some, but the audience—which is increasingly the mainstream audience—is sufficiently hungry for this kind of material (and, perhaps, suspicious of anything that's overly polished) that it is willing to overlook the occasional mistake, or make up for it by shouting hilarious things from the balcony. These people don't need irony or campiness self-consciously pointed out to them, any more than they need a laugh track to enjoy "The Simpsons."

The Spartan phalanx presents itself to foes as a wall of shields, bristling with spears, its members squatting behind their defenses, anonymous and unknowable, until they break formation and stand out alone, practically naked, soft, exposed and recognizable as individuals.

The audience members watching them play the same game: media-weary, hunkered down behind thick irony, flinging verbal jabs at the screen—until they see something that moves them. Then they'll come out and feel. But at the first hint of politics, they'll jump back behind their shield-wall, just like the Spartans when millions of Persian arrows blot out the sun, and wait until the noise stops.

TURN ON, TUNE IN,
VEG OUT
(2006)

In the spring of 1977, some friends and I made a 40-mile pil-grimage to the biggest and fanciest movie theater in Iowa so we could watch a new science fiction movie called "Star Wars." Expecting long lines, we got there early, and found the place deserted.

As we sat on the sidewalk waiting for the box office to open, others like us drifted in from the towns, farms and colleges of central Iowa and queued up behind. When the curtain in front of the big Cinerama screen finally parted, the fanfare sounded and the famous opening crawl appeared against a backdrop of stars, there were still some empty seats. "Star Wars" wasn't famous yet. The only people who had heard about it were what are now called geeks.

Twenty-eight years later, the vast corpus of "Star Wars" movies,

novels, games and merchandise still has much to say about geeks—
and also about a society that loves them, hates them and depends
upon them.

In the opening sequence of the new Star Wars movie, "Episode
III: Revenge of the Sith," two Jedi knights fight their way through an
enemy starship to rescue a hostage. Ever since I saw the movie, I have
been annoying friends with a trivia question: "Who is the enemy?
What organization owns this vessel?"

We ought to know. In 1977, we all knew who owned the Death Star
(the Empire) and who owned the Millennium Falcon (Han Solo). But
when I ask my question about the new film, everyone reacts in the
same way: with a sudden intake of breath and a sideways dart of the
eyes, followed by lengthy cogitation. Some confess that they have no
idea. Others think out loud for a while, developing and rejecting various theories. Only a few have come up with the right answer.

One hyperverbal friend was able to spit it out because he had read
and memorized the opening crawl. Another, a hard-core science
fiction fan, had been boning up on supplemental materials: "Clone
Wars," an animated TV series consisting of "epic adventures that
bridge the story arc between 'Episode II: Attack of the Clones' and
'Episode III: Revenge of the Sith.' "

If you have watched these cartoons—or if you've enjoyed some
of the half-dozen "Clone Wars" novels, flipped through the graphic
novels, read the short stories or played the video game—you will know
that the battle cruiser in question is owned by the New Droid Army
of the Confederacy of Independent Systems, which is backed by the
Trade Federation, a commercial guild that is peeved about taxation
of trade routes.

And that is not the only aspect of Episode III that you will see in a
different light. If you watch the movie without doing the prep work,
General Grievous—who is supposed to be one of the most formidable bad guys in the entire Star Wars cycle—will seem like something that just fell out of a Happy Meal. But if you've been boning up,
you'll have seen Grievous slay many a Jedi. Hayden Christensen, who

plays Anakin Skywalker/Darth Vader, has taken flak for his performance. Anakin is supposed to be a tragic figure endowed with cosmic powers, wrestling with an impossible moral dilemma. In the movie, he seems more like a homecoming king who has just found a scratch on his Camaro. If you've seen the Clone Wars cartoons and read the books, you'll understand that the kid is a seriously damaged veteran, a poster child for post-traumatic stress disorder. But since none of that background is supplied by the Episode III script, Mr. Christensen has been given an impossible acting task. He's trying to swim in air.

In sum, very little of the new film makes sense, taken as a free-standing narrative. What's interesting about this is how little it matters. Millions of people are happily spending their money to watch a movie they don't understand. What gives?

Modern English has given us two terms we need to explain this phenomenon: "geeking out" and "vegging out." To geek out on something means to immerse yourself in its details to an extent that is distinctly abnormal—and to have a good time doing it. To veg out, by contrast, means to enter a passive state and allow sounds and images to wash over you without troubling yourself too much about what it all means.

In corporate-speak, there is a related term used when someone has committed the faux pas of geeking out during a meeting. "Let's take this offline," someone will suggest, when the PowerPoint slides grow dark with words. Literally, it means, "I look forward to geeking out on this topic—later." But really it's a polite synonym for "shut up already!"

The first "Star Wars" movie 28 years ago was distinguished by healthy interplay between veg and geek scenes. In the climactic sequence, where rebel fighters attacked the Death Star, we repeatedly cut away from the dogfights and strafing runs—the purest kind of vegging-out material—to hushed command bunkers where people stood around pondering computer displays, geeking out on the strategic progress of the battle.

All such content—as well as the long, beautiful, uncluttered shots of desert, sky, jungle and mountain that filled the early episodes—was banished in the first of the prequels ("Episode I: The Phantom Menace," 1999). In the 16 years that separated it from the initial trilogy, a new universe of ancillary media had come into existence. These had made it possible to take the geek material offline so that the movies could consist of pure, uncut veg-out content, steeped in day-care-center ambience. These newer films don't even pretend to tell the whole story; they are akin to PowerPoint presentations that summarize the main bullet points from a much more comprehensive body of work developed by and for a geek subculture.

"Concentrate on the moment. Feel, don't think. Trust your instincts," says a Jedi to the young Anakin in Episode I, immediately before a pod race in which Anakin is likely to get killed. It is distinctly odd counsel coming from a member of the Jedi order, the geekiest people in the universe: they have beards and ponytails, they dress in army blankets, they are expert fighter pilots, they build their own laser swords from scratch.

And (as is made clear in the "Clone Wars" novels) the masses and the elites both claim to admire them, but actually fear and loathe them because they hate being dependent upon their powers.

Anakin wins that race by repairing his crippled racer in an ecstasy of switch-flipping that looks about as intuitive as starting up a nuclear submarine. Clearly the boy is destined to be adopted into the Jedi order, where he will develop his geek talents—not by studying calculus but by meditating a lot and learning to trust his feelings. I lap this stuff up along with millions, maybe billions, of others. Why? Because every single one of us is as dependent on science and technology—and, by extension, on the geeks who make it work—as a patient in intensive care. Yet we much prefer to think otherwise.

Scientists and technologists have the same uneasy status in our society as the Jedi in the Galactic Republic. They are scorned by the cultural left and the cultural right, and young people avoid science and math classes in hordes. The tedious particulars of keeping ourselves alive, comfortable and free are being taken offline to countries where people are happy to sweat the details, as long as we have some foreign exchange left to send their way. Nothing is more seductive than to think that we, like the Jedi, could be masters of the most advanced technologies while living simple lives: to have a geek standard of living and spend our copious leisure time vegging out.

If the "Star Wars" movies are remembered a century from now, it'll be because they are such exact parables for this state of affairs. Young people in other countries will watch them in classrooms as an answer to the question: Whatever became of that big rich country that used to buy the stuff we make? The answer: It went the way of the old Republic.

GRESHAM COLLEGE
LECTURE
(2008)

When Professors Mainelli and Connell did me the honor of inviting me here, I cautioned them that I would have to attend as a sort of Idiot Savant. An Idiot because I am not a scholar, or even a particularly accomplished reader, of SF. A Savant because I get paid to write it.

And so if this were a lecture, the purpose of which is to impart erudition, I would have to decline. Instead, though, it is a seminar, which feels more like a sort of conversation, and so all I need to do, I suppose, is to get people talking, which is almost easier for an idiot than for a savant.

I'm going to come back to this idiot savant theme in Part 3 of this talk, when I speak about the distinction between vegging out and geeking out— two quintessentially modern ways of spending one's time—but first to

PART 1: THE STANDARD MODEL

If you don't run with this crowd, you might assume that SF is an ab-
breviation of Science Fiction. But here it means Speculative Fiction.
This coinage is a way to cope with the problem that Science Fiction
is mysteriously, inextricably conjoined with the seemingly unrelated
literature of Fantasy. Many who are fond of one are fond of the other,
to the point where they perceive them as The Same Thing in spite of
the fact that they seem quite different to non-fans.

I also use SF to denote a third thing which I'll call the new wave
of historical fiction that is heavily influenced by SF and clearly aimed
at SF fans. To get a quick fix on what this means, consider the recent
movie 300, and compare it to its predecessor, a 1962 film called The
300 Spartans, starring Richard Egan. Both take as their subject the
Battle of Thermopylae. But 300 is quite obviously informed by graphic
novels, video games, and Asian martial arts films, and therefore, in
my opinion, belongs to the SF world even though it's technically a
historical drama.

I need another term to denote things that aren't SF, such as The
300 Spartans. Conventionally, one would call this a mainstream, as
opposed to a genre, film. But the entire thrust of my talk is going to
be that it no longer makes sense to speak of a mainstream and some
number of genres. So I'm going to borrow another term that is used in
the SF world to denote all that is Not SF, and call it Mundane.

I first happened upon this when I saw a mass mailing that was sent
out to a number of SF fans who were attending a convention being
held in a high-rise hotel in a major city. The document contained a
polite request that attendees not brandish swords, battle axes, or
other medieval weaponry in elevators and other common spaces of
the hotel, as some of the other guests were, after all, mundanes, who
might not understand.

What I'm going to call the Standard Model of our culture states
that there is a mainstream and, peripheral to it, inferior in intel-

lectual content, moral stature, production values, and economic importance, some number of genres. And here we could get lost in the weeds trying to enumerate, and differentiate between, different genres and subgenres, so to keep things moving along I'm going to restrict my comments to four: SF, Romance, Westerns, and Crime-slash-Mystery.

Now, I think that the Standard Model was reasonably accurate, say, 50 years ago. But I put it to you that if an alien culture sent a xeno-ethnologist to Earth today with the mission "observe their culture and submit a report," the xeno-ethnologist would not perceive or describe anything like the Standard Model.

First of all, the genre known as the Western no longer exists. Before people send me email, I'll happily stipulate that Western movies are still made. I saw the recent remake of *3:10 to Yuma* and enjoyed it. And Western books can still be found in bookstores. But it has been a long time since one could walk into an average, or even an extraordinarily large, bookstore and find a separate shelf labeled "Westerns," and that is a change from how things were when I was a child. Similarly, when I was a child, many prime-time television series were Westerns. Now, none are. Fifty years ago, unless you lived in a very small town indeed, you could probably go to the cinema and see a Western on any given weekend. Now, when Western films are made, they are always remarkable or exceptional in some way, and not the routine produce of a genre.

Romance and Mystery most certainly do have their own sections in bookstores, and probably will for a long time. So our xeno-ethnologist might perceive them as genres, provided that all that he or she looked at was bookstores. But outside of bookstores, something interesting has happened, and I'm going to sum it up by saying that Romance fused with the film industry, and Crime fused with the television industry.

Not all movies are romances, of course, and so if you count the number of films produced, my assertion is very debatable. But if you weight the count by the number of tickets sold, or the amount of money that financiers are willing to invest in the production, marketing, and distribution of films, I think you'll see that almost any prospective film project that does not contain a romance as a major, if not *the* major, line of its plot, is unlikely to find support. Again, before the emails roll in, I'll stipulate that there are exceptions. I've already mentioned one: the recent remake of *3:10 to Yuma* starring Russell Crowe and Christian Bale. There are a couple of women in it, but romantic relationships certainly are not a major element of the plot, unless you count the strange kind of seduction that goes on between the two main male characters. What the movie does offer, though, is hunks, riding around and looking good. Compare the movie stars of fifty years ago with those of today. On average, the ones we have today are simply better looking. Of course, there are exceptions. But the bar has been set much higher than it used to be, and I think that it is all a reflection of the way romance, and the romantic sensibility, has stopped being confined to a particular genre and has become an intrinsic part of the modern, industrial movie-making business. If you'd like to know, I think it all started with *Gone with the Wind*, which proved that a story that came out of the romance genre could become enormously successful with sufficiently attractive and charismatic actors. Put simply, romance and violence are two things that easily cross borders and jump language barriers. You can make a lot of money on films that consist entirely of action, but there are only so many young males in the world; romance appeals to more people. Romance is versatile. All by itself, it's enough to make a successful movie. Added to a screenplay, it works like monosodium glutamate in food, which is to say, it doesn't matter whether the underlying material is poor or excellent to begin with; adding some of this wonder ingredient always makes it better.

What Romance became to the film industry, Mystery-slash-Crime became to the television industry. They are made for each other. A television series needs to tell a fresh story each episode.

Romance is not a good fit; you can't have your lead character fall in love with a different person each week. Westerns worked okay for a while, but eventually, the writers ran out of things that could possibly happen on ranches, and began to jump the shark with ideas like *The Wild, Wild West*. By comparison, TV shows about detectives have it easy. I won't try your patience by reciting particulars. There's never been a time during my life when there weren't several different very popular crime and mystery series on prime-time television.

Thus Westerns have become too few and far between to constitute a genre, while Romance and Crime have become too ubiquitous to be considered as genres.

PART 2: IN LIGHT OF ALL THE ABOVE, WHAT ARE WE TO THINK ABOUT SF?

Unlike Westerns, SF has grown rather than withered.

Unlike Romance and Mystery, it has maintained its separateness rather than becoming part of the mainstream.

Why not then speak of SF as the genre that survived? Because "genre" connotes features that simply would not be perceived by our xeno-ethnologist, who would, presumably, gather data and go about the work scientifically. In movies, SF dominates utterly: by my count, 57 of the top 100 movies of all time, and nine of the top ten. The only top ten film that isn't SF is *Titanic*, made by a director who cut his teeth making SF films.

In television, SF is not nearly as important, though obviously there have been any number of quite successful and more or less famous SF television series.

In books things are much more diffuse and complicated and the statistics difficult to process because of the maddening way in which publishers chop books up into genres. Harry Potter is obviously SF. If you want to know how the latest Harry Potter book is making out in my country, go to the *New York Times* website, find the page where all of the bestseller lists are listed, and follow the link to "Children's." There you'll find separate lists for picture books, chapter books, paperbacks, and series books. Harry Potter is on the latter, and I think he was moved there just because people got sick of seeing his name on the main bestseller list month after month and year after year. Many other books are arguably SF, but not published as such. Whatever you may think of *The Da Vinci Code*, you have to admit that its premises are somewhat fantastic and hence SF-like. My colleague Bruce Sterling has defined a thriller as a science fiction novel that includes the President of the United States. If you agree with Bruce's definition, the size of the SF market suddenly becomes very much larger.

Finally, in graphic novels and video games, SF is, of course, dominant.

So rather than trying to salvage anything from the Standard Model, I believe that it makes more sense to speak of a bifurcated culture. Of course the bifurcation isn't absolute or perfectly clean but it's clear that there are two distinct audience groups and that they have different characteristics. One carries swords in elevators and the other doesn't.

That probably sounds merely flippant, but consider the following anecdote. I was in New York City a few weeks ago. I had dinner with friends. Thanks to their hospitality, we dined in a highly civilized, but by no means flashy or famous, Italian restaurant just off of midtown, where the office buildings begin to give way to townhouses. One of the pleasures of dining in such places is that you get real professional waiters: not just kids trying to make a few bucks, or out-of-work actors, but middle-aged people who've done it before, who take it seriously as their life's work, and who do it with dignity and grace. Our waiter was one of those. Probably in his late forties, impeccably dressed, knew how to show up when we needed something and to disappear otherwise. I was telling my companions about a trip I had recently made to Vegas. Not normally my idea of a place to go, but the

Sci Fi channel had flown me down there to take part in a panel discussion. One of the other panelists was Lucy Lawless.

Now, if you're not an SF kind of person, then I will probably have
to tell you that she is an actor best known for her title role on the television series *Xena: Warrior Princess* and more recently appearing on
Battlestar Galactica. If you are an SF person, you already know this,
and much more, about her. Well, it turned out that our waiter that
evening, contrary to appearances, was very much an SF person. And
as soon as he heard me mention the name of Lucy Lawless, he spun
around to face us and came over to join the conversation. Now remember, this man hears the names of the rich and famous dropped
all the time. He probably *serves* the rich and famous all the time. It's
his job to pretend he doesn't notice, and he does his job very well—in
the Mundane world. But as soon as he heard me mention Lucy Lawless, the Mundane shell dropped away and he turned into a fan.

Not quite the same as carrying a sword in an elevator but very
closely related. Both this waiter, and the elevator sword people,
are displaying a trait that is epitomized, for better or worse, by the
cruel Mundane stereotype of SF fans wearing rubber Vulcan ears.
In a sense, all of us—all SF fans—are forever carrying those rubber
ears around, concealed in the pockets of our business suits, military
uniforms, waiter's jackets, or doctor's smocks. No one knows they're
there. But when we find ourselves around like-minded persons, even
if they happen to be total strangers, we absent-mindedly reach into
our pockets, pull out the ears, and slap them on. We identify ourselves as geeks. We geek out.

Lucy Lawless is one example of an actor with a bifurcated career:
a topic I would like to explore for a few minutes. It might sound to
you like a trivia game, but I think that it works as a kind of natural
experiment that gives us information about the bifurcated culture.

I first noticed this when I was watching the first Lord of the Rings
movie and the character of Elrond made his first appearance. He
looked strangely familiar to me. Later I looked him up on IMDB and
figured out that he was, of course, the same guy who portrays Agent

Smith in the *Matrix* movies. His name is Hugo Weaving. In the Mundane world, he has a perfectly respectable career going. It is difficult to make a living as an actor! One has to be very good, and to work very hard, to make a go of it. Hugo Weaving has done this, and has appeared in various Mundane plays and films; if he'd never done any SF work at all, he'd have a career that other actors would envy. It's likely, however, that none of us would have seen him or heard of him, because in the Mundane world he's not a huge star. In the SF world, he is one of the biggest stars of all time. Why the difference? What is it about him that accounts for this imbalance?

Once I noticed this phenomenon, other examples came to mind. I've already mentioned Lucy Lawless. And it is by no means a historical curiosity, because there are *incipient* bifurcated stars. *The Sarah Connor Chronicles*, a new TV series based on the *Terminator* movies, features two: Lena Headey, who looked familiar to me because I'd previously seen her in *300*, as the unfortunately named Gorgo, Queen of Sparta, and Summer Glau, who played one of the characters on the SF series *Firefly*.

Sigourney Weaver has had a bifurcated career. Again, this isn't to say that she didn't do perfectly well for herself in Mundane films and theatrical productions, in *Alien* and *Aliens*, though, she attained a level of fame that far exceeded her Mundane work. And I don't think she would mind my saying so, because she took a role in the film *Galaxy Quest* that made light of exactly this kind of situation.

Is there any common thread linking the actresses I've mentioned? Lucy Lawless, Lena Headey, and Sigourney Weaver are all athletic, statuesque, good at doing action stuff. The cynical interpretation, then, is that male SF fans like to ogle Amazons. A more generous take on it is that SF is more forgiving toward strong women. I suspect that both of these are true, but they're not enough to explain the bifurcated career phenomenon.

Galaxy Quest, of course, was transparently based on *Star Trek*, which brings to mind the archetypal bifurcated actor: Leonard Nimoy, who attained such perfection in his portrayal of Spock that it led to two unintended consequences. The one everyone knows about is that he afterwards found it difficult to get non-Vulcan work. The less obvious one is that never again, in the ongoing history of the franchise, were the producers of any of those films or television episodes able to find an actor who could convincingly portray a Vulcan.

Just as an exercise, I spent a while trying to think whether there was any actor, living or dead, who could possibly portray a Vulcan as convincingly as Leonard Nimoy. I assumed that this experiment would end in failure, but, surprisingly, the answer came to me immediately: Hugo Weaving. Hugo Weaving would make a totally convincing Vulcan. And it's not just because we've already seen him with pointy ears. It's something else.

I think that it is the ability to portray intelligence. When I first saw Weaving as Elrond, I didn't think I was going to like him, because he looked very different from how I had imagined this character when I read The Lord of the Rings. But I ended up liking his performance very much. He was able to convince me that he really was a three-thousand-year-old Elf lord. Part of this is simply that he's a professional actor who is good at what he does, but it also, I'm convinced, has something to do with this ability to project intelligence.

Consider some of the other characters in the *Star Trek* franchise. Out of the entire cast of *Star Trek: The Next Generation*, I would say that the two most beloved, successful characters, at least to fans in the SF world, are Commander Data, portrayed by Brent Spiner, and Jean-Luc Picard, played by Patrick Stewart. These are very different characters, but what they have in common is that they are intelligent people, portrayed convincingly by actors who are either very intelligent or else good at seeming that way. Some other characters in this series did not ring true, for SF fans, in the same way.

Going back to the female actors I was talking about earlier, I believe that the same is true. Oh, it helps that they are statuesque, beautiful, and athletic, but there is more to it than that. It is conspicuous in the first two *Alien* films that Sigourney Weaver's character is the smartest person in the room at any given time. The only possible exception is Bishop, the android in the second film, played by Lance Henriksen, in another fine example of an intelligence-projecting performance. One believes in this character in the same way that one believes in Nimoy's Spock or that I, at least, believe in Weaving's Elrond. All of these actors can somehow convey that there is complexity behind the eyes.

The intelligence of these characters isn't just a slapped-on trait— these are not token nerds, thrown into an ensemble piece to solve technical problems. Their intelligence is an intrinsic reason why you are supposed to find them interesting, to identify with them. It is what makes them human—even—especially—when they are not actually humans. If the actor can't portray that intelligence, the character fails altogether. This is why I have devoted a bit of time to what might strike some as a fairly lowbrow pop culture analysis: because I think that the bifurcated-career phenomenon can tell us something about what differentiates SF from Mundane culture.

PART 3: VEGGING OUT AND GEEKING OUT

The cheap, and, since I'm an SF person, self-congratulatory answer is that SF is for intelligent people. But, saying that—even supposing it were true—doesn't actually get us very far, since there are so many different kinds, and different definitions, of intelligence. And so here is where this talk has to pick its away along the spine of a narrow ridge, if you will, with fatal drop-offs to either side. If I stray one direction, I end up talking endlessly about intelligence, or intelligences, and what they mean, and end up defining it out of existence. If I go the other way, I run afoul of invidious class distinctions, since intelligence is still linked, in many people's minds, with expensive educations and high-status jobs. Neither explains SF very well. If the first were true, everyone would be an SF fan. Clearly that's not the case. If the second were true, the only people who liked SF would be those with Ph.D.s. And that is slightly closer to the truth—but still not very close. No doubt there is a sort of vague correlation between having higher education and being an SF fan, but there are so many exceptions—so many Ph.D.s who can't abide SF, and so many waiters and welders who live for it—that it doesn't serve well as a model.

The correct way to think about intelligence, in this case, is as a human quality shared by just about everyone, at least until it gets beaten out of us. Not a special gift that is bestowed on only a few. And secondly that it is a functional trait that most people find some way of using in their careers, or whatever it is that they spend their days doing. Sometimes, this trait is put to use doing theoretical physics, but much more often, it's used in raising children or building houses or operating farm machinery.

Counter-examples are legion. We have all suffered through movies that were ruined by characters doing stupid things. The classic example is in suspense movies, when someone, usually a pretty girl, is running away from a monster or a serial killer, when she happens to trip and fall down. Whereupon, instead of simply getting back to her feet and running some more, she sits on the ground whimpering until the threat catches up with her. And we've all seen bad horror movies in which the protagonists blunder into situations that no one who has ever actually watched a bad horror movie would ever get into. The satisfaction, and the solace, offered by good SF, is that its characters don't behave that way. Consider how Ripley, the character played by Sigourney Weaver, responds to the threat posed by the aliens. In the second film, once she and the Marines she's with have made first contact with the aliens, and had a chance to catch their breath, they very quickly agree that they should simply go back to the orbiting ship and nuke the place. It's a brilliant move on the part of the filmmakers, precisely because it is the obvious and intelligent thing to do—it's exactly what we in the audience are all thinking to ourselves—

but because it's a kind of horror movie, and we've been conditioned to expect stupid behavior from characters in horror movies, it's the last thing we're expecting. When the idea is raised and agreed on, we wake up, sit a little straighter in our chairs and say "Oh! This is a movie about REAL people—which is to say, people who behave intelligently." And for the rest of the film, that promise is largely borne out, as Ripley goes on to do a number of more or less intelligent things, such as using a cigarette lighter to set off a fire alarm when she needs to draw the others' attention, and so on.

So, in SF, intelligence is just how people behave, and it is what you expect in a well-wrought piece. But by this definition, intelligence is something that has undergone some changes during the last fifty years or so. The Heinleinian hero who knows everything, who can do everything, is gone. The world is complicated. No one can be good at everything. I bought a new car a couple of weeks ago, and I still haven't read more than a few pages of the inch-and-a-half-thick pile of instruction books that came with it. It, like everything else in our lives, has too many features, too many details for our minds to hold. The best we can do is to be good at something, or a few things. We come home tired, and we feel the need to veg out—a recent coinage, meaning to drop voluntarily into a kind of vegetative coma, typically in front of the TV. I should know; in my family, I am infamous for my lowbrow tastes in entertainment, my sluggishness to attend art films and theatrical productions. It's a miracle, actually, that Gresham College was able to get me over here right in the middle of the NBA Playoffs.

But many people, after they have vegged out long enough to recharge their batteries, derive fun and profound satisfaction from *geeking* out on whatever topic is of particular interest to them. Choose any person in the world at random, no matter how non-geeky they might seem, and talk to them long enough, and in most cases you will eventually hit on some topic about which they are exorbitantly knowledgeable and, if you express interest, on which they are willing to talk, enthusiastically, for hours. You have found their inner geek. Sometimes the inner geek may be hidden very deeply indeed. The grizzled, taciturn machinist, who normally speaks in sentences of one or two words, will light up and deliver an extemporaneous dissertation about his favorite alloys of steel. The forklift operator at Wal-Mart will turn out to be a Civil War reenactor who can recite the full history of the Battle of Shiloh down to the level of individual squads and soldiers. This is how knowledge works today, and how it's going to work in the future. No more Heinleinian polymaths. Instead, a web of geeks, each of whom knows a lot about something.

Twenty years ago, we called them nerds, and we despised them; we didn't like the power that they seemed to have over the rest of us, and we identified them as something different from normal society. Now, we call them geeks, and we like them just fine, because they are us. Nerds were limited to math and science and computers. Geeks also do those kinds of things—which isn't saying much, because everyone works with computers all the time now—but geeks can also be experts on welding or Civil War battles or fine cabinetmaking. Everyone gets, now, that this is how society is going to work, and as long as geeks bathe frequently enough and don't commit the faux pas of geeking out at the wrong time, in the wrong company, it's okay. It's better than okay. It's desirable. We're all geeks now.

But we're all geeks in different subject areas, and so the only thing that links us all together is what we watch on the tube when our geek energies have been spent and we feel the need to veg out—the lowest common denominator stuff. Almost everyone knows and agrees that this material is idiotic. It doesn't reflect the way the world actually works, because it doesn't contain as many geeks as the real world that we all inhabit. In that sense, it's more unrealistic, more fantastical, than the material that actually gets tagged as fantasy. It is when we turn on a movie or a television show and observe people behaving intelligently that we sit up a little straighter in our seats and get interested, begin to take the story and its characters a little more seriously.

It would be a little too simplistic and, again, self-congratulatory to say, flat-out, that the first category of entertainment, the veg-out stuff, is Mundane and the latter type, the geek-out stuff, is SF. It would be like saying that people from the United States drink coffee and people from the U.K. drink tea. But there is a more than faint trend that bears thinking about and that, I believe, helps to explain the bifurcated career phenomenon that I mentioned in Part 2 of this talk.

PART 4: GENRE REDUX

In this, the last and shortest part of this talk, I'm going to revisit the genre question. Despite the fact that this seminar is supposed to be about literature, I've devoted most of my time so far to speaking about movies and television. That's because I believe that certain movies and TV programs that almost everyone has seen can provide insights into SF culture that translate directly to the literary side.

In Part 1 I mentioned that, in the Standard Model, some of the traditional markers of genrehood were its low intellectual content and depraved moral stature. In the literary world as it existed back in the days when the Standard Model was still operative, this would presumably mean that real literature was written by respected authors with credentials while pulp genre novels were churned out by semi-anonymous hacks in cheap hotel rooms. All of which of course, is just a set of stereotypes, and I don't mean to suggest that we should take them too seriously. Let's instead look at how things are today.

As I mentioned, the bestseller lists have been exquisitely tweaked so as to ensure that the books that show up on the main list are—what, exactly? It's easier to say what they're *not*. Most so-called genre fiction is in paperback, so it doesn't taint the hardcover list. Young adult books get shunted to a different list, so we don't have to know how many copies Harry Potter is selling. Other special categories, such as business books or series books or media-related books, further winnow the field. I gather that the people who make these lists have got an idea in their heads as to what constitutes a proper book: a hard-cover work of fiction, written recently, not too genre-esque, and so on. Literary fiction is the closest thing this has to a name.

Now. People who aspire to write literature often study it first. It's logical. If you want to build bridges, you study engineering. If you want to write literary fiction, you study . . . literature!

The lecture halls, the editorships, the endowed chairs that might have been occupied 50 years ago by academics and intellectuals of a more traditional stripe are now occupied—and have been for decades—by insurgents who gained sway beginning in the 1960s and who, ever since then, have been teaching a kind of literary theory variously called post-modernist or post-structuralist or deconstructionist.

What literary theorists—post-structuralists, anyway—are teaching, might be fascinating and encouraging to people who aspire to be critics, but must be just a bit unsettling to people who would like to become authors. One of the founding documents of post-structuralism is "The Death of the Author" by Roland Barthes!

And I am not here to try to explain post-structuralism, or to argue with it, but I will say that if I were a would-be author studying literature, one hundred years ago, from professors who were willing to grant that authors actually created, understood, and controlled the meaning of their own work, I'd feel more encouraged than I would studying it from post-structuralists.

Or perhaps it's more accurate to say that I'd feel more sanguine writing certain types of fiction than others.

I haven't been in this situation myself, but based on what I read of post-structuralism, I'd imagine there'd be a weeding-out effect. It's fun to imagine a comedy sketch with Robert Heinlein in a writer's workshop having the first draft of *Starship Troopers* evaluated by a circle of earnest young post-structuralists.

I don't imagine that there is anything like out-and-out censorship, but I do suspect that people who write about relationships, who write autobiographical, introspective fiction, from a subjective point of view, are going to have an easier time of it, in this environment, than those who write SF. On the science fiction side of SF, such writers are working with abstract ideas from science. And scientists, who believe, and who can prove, that they are right, are notoriously at odds with post-structuralists, who are always looking for ways to bring science into the realm of criticizibility. On the fantasy side, writers are creating entire worlds inside of their brains and populating them with species and civilizations and histories: an undertaking that seems fantastically arrogant from a post-structuralist standpoint.

The characteristics I spoke of earlier, that lead SF fans to want to see intelligence at work in the faces of movie characters, when rolled over into literature, mean that they want ideas. They want to learn something or to join with the author in speculating about a future or about a fantastical other world. Naturally they will see the aliens as dangerous predatory creatures that have to be killed, while literary theorists would say that perhaps the real reason we're afraid of the Alien Other is because it represents the eruption into our discourse of heretofore subjugated knowledges.

Post-structuralist critics, assuming they have the courage of their convictions, would say to the young Heinlein: I see that you are intelligent, that you know a lot, that you've worked hard and put a lot of ingenuity into this book, but the whole thing is pre-theoretical and therefore naive and as such, simply of lesser intellectual stature than something that was written taking into account the intellectual trends of the last half-century.

And this is the same attitude—for completely different reasons— that the occupants of those lecture halls and editorships and endowed chairs fifty or a hundred years ago would have taken toward the pulp genre fiction of their day: namely, that it was intellectually inferior to literary fiction. The author of a fantasy or a science fiction novel may be an Oxford linguist like J.R.R. Tolkien or a Ph.D. astrophysicist like Gregory Benford, but by taking their own ideas seriously enough to write fantasy or science fiction about them, they reduce themselves, in the eyes of critics, to pre-theoretical knuckle-draggers. A curious inversion has taken place in which the very intellectual credentials that, back in the heyday of the Standard Model, might have given such authors the credibility needed to escape from the stigma of genrehood, today consign them irrevocably to the same.

Another feature of genrehood in the Standard Model is moral depravity. This was easy to talk about back in the day when universities were strongly linked to churches, and professors, among other responsibilities, were the guardians of a religiously-based moral code. It might seem more difficult to talk about now, because we no longer have a shared idea of what it is to be moral. And yet post-modern academics are nothing if not censorious.

Mind you, I don't mean to say that all SF writers are oblivious to the last fifty years' developments in critical theory, or that there is no SF literature that is alive to those changes. But there are entire swathes of SF—for example, a whole, vast subgenre called military science fiction—that I'm pretty sure would be considered not only intellectually naive, but morally bankrupt as well, by many members of the Modern Language Association. The incredulous hostility with which the movie 300 was greeted by a good many film critics serves as an especially vivid and entertaining example.

So, having gone to some lengths in Part 1 to dismantle the idea that there are genres and that SF is one of them, I conclude Part 4, and this talk, with the observation that, in the current critical-theoretical environment, SF does possess at least two of the classic markers of genrehood, namely intellectual disreputability and moral salaciousness. SF thrives because it is idea porn.

SPEW
(1994)

Yeah, I know it's boring of me to send you plain old Text like this, and I hope you don't just blow this message off without reading it.

But what can I say, I was an English major. On video, I come off like a stunned bystander. I'm just a Text kind of guy. I'm gambling that you'll think it's quaint or something. So let me just tell you the whole sorry tale, starting from the point where I think I went wrong.

I'd be blowing brown smoke if I said I wasn't nervous when they shoved in the needles, taped on the trodes, thrust my head into the Big Cold Magnet, and opened a channel direct from the Spew to my immortal soul. Of course they didn't call it the Spew, and neither did I—I wanted the job, after all. But how could I not call it that, with its Feeds multifarious as the glistening strands cascading sunnily from the supple scalps of the models in the dandruff shampoo ads.

I mention that image because it was the first thing I saw when they turned the Spew on, and I wasn't even ready. Not that anyone could ever *get ready* for the dreaded Polysurf Exam. The proctors came for me when *they* were ready, must have got my address off that job app yellowing in their infinite files, yanked me straight out of a fuzzy gray hangover dream with a really wandering story arc, the kind of dream concussion victims must have in the back of the ambulance. I'd been doing shots of vodka in the living room the night before, decided not to take a chance on the stairs, turned slowly into a mummy while I lay comatose on our living-room couch—the First Couch Ever Built, a Couch upholstered in avocado Orlon that had absorbed so much tar, nicotine, and body cheese over the centuries that now the centers of the cushions had developed the black sheen of virgin Naugahyde. When they buzzed me awake, my joints would not move nor my eyes open: I had to bolt four consecutive 32-ounce glasses of tap water to reconstitute my freeze-dried plasma.

Half an hour later I'm in Television City. A million stories below, floes of gray-yellow ice, like broken teeth, grind away at each other just below the surface of the Hudson. I've signed all the releases and they're lowering the Squid helmet over me, and without any warning BAM the Spew comes on and the first thing I see is this model chick shaking her head in ultra-slow-mo, her lovely hairs gleaming because they've got so many spotlights cross-firing on her head that she's about to burst into flame, and in voice-over she's talking about how her dandruff problem is just a nasty, embarrassing memory of adolescence now along with pimples and (if I may just fill in the blanks) screwing skanky guys who'll never have a salaried job. And I think she's cute and everything but it occurs to me that this is really kind of sick—I mean, this chick has *admitted* to a history of shedding *blizzards* every time she moved her head, and here she is *getting down* under eight megawatts of color-corrected halogen light, and I just *know* I'm supposed to be thinking about *how much head chaff* would be sifting down in her personal space right now if she hadn't ditched her old hair care product lineup in favor of—

Click. Course, it never really clicks anymore, no one has used mechanical switches since like the '50s, but some Spew terminals emit a synthesized click—they wired up a 1955 Sylvania in a digital sound lab somewhere and had some old gomer in a tank-top stagger up to it and change back and forth between Channel 4 and Channel 5 a few times, paid him off and fired him, then compressed the sound and inseminated it into the terminals' fundamental ROMs so that we'd get that reassuring *click* when we jumped from one Feed to another. Which is what happens now; except I haven't touched a remote, don't even *have* a remote, that being the whole point of the Polysurf. Now it's some fucker picking a banjo, *ouch* it is an actual *Hee Haw* rerun, digitally remastered, frozen in pure binary until the collapse of the Universe.

Click. And I resist the impulse to say, "Wait a minute. *Hee Haw* is my favorite show."

Well, I have lots of favorite shows. But me and my housemates, we're always watching *Hee Haw.* But all I get is two or three twangs of the banjo and a glimpse of the eerily friendly grin of the banjo picker and then *click* it's a '77 Buick LeSabre smashing through a guardrail in SoCal and bursting into a fireball *before it has even touched the ground,* which is one of my favorite things about TV. Watch that for a while and just as I am settling into a nice Spew daze, it's a rap video, white trailer park boys in Clackamas who've actually got their moho on hydraulics so it can tilt and bounce in the air while the homeboys are partying down inside. Even the rooftop sentinels are boogieing, they have to boogie, using their AK-47s like jugglers' poles to keep their balance. Under the TV lights, the chrome-plated bayonets spark like throwaway cameras at the Orange Bowl Halftime Show.

And so it goes. Twenty clicks into the test I've left my fear behind, I'm Polysurfing like some incarnate sofa god, my attention plays like a space laser across the Spew's numberless Feeds, each Feed a torrent, all of them plexed together across the panascopic bandwidth of the optical fiber as if the contents of every Edge City in Greater America have been rammed into the maw of a giant pasta machine and extruded as endless, countless strands of polychrome angel hair. Within an hour or so I've settled into a pattern without even knowing it. I'm surfing among 20 or so different Feeds. My subconscious mind is like a retarded homunculus sacked out on the couch of my reptilian brain, his thumb wandering crazily around the keypad of the world's largest remote control. It looks like chaos, even to me, but to the proctors, watching all my polygraph traces superimposed on the video feed, tracking my blood pressure and pupil dilation, there is a strange attractor somewhere down there, and if it's the right one. . . .

"Congratulations," the proctor says, and I realize the chilly mind-sucking apparatus has been retracted into the ceiling. I'm still fixated on the Spew. Bringing me back to reality: the nurse chick ripping off the handy disposable self-stick electrodes, bristling with my body hair.

So, a week later I'm still wondering how I got this job: patrolman on the information highway. We don't call it that, of course, the job title is Profile Auditor 1. But if the Spew is a highway, imagine a hard-jawed, close-shaven buck lurking in the shade of an overpass, your license plate reflected in the quicksilver pools of his shades as you whoosh past. Key difference: we never bust anyone, we just like to watch.

We sit in Television City cubicles, VR rigs strapped to our skulls, grokking people's Profiles in n-dimensional DemoTainment Space, where demographics, entertainment, consumption habits, and credit history all intersect to define a weird imaginary universe that is every bit as twisted and convoluted as those balloon animals that so eerily squelch and shudder from the hands of feckless loitering clowns in the touristy districts of our great cities. Takes killer spatial relations not to get lost. We turn our heads, and the Demosphere moves around us; we point at something of interest—the distinct galactic cluster formed by some schmo's Profile—and we fly toward it, warp speed. Hell, we fly right through the middle of it, we do barrel rolls through said schmo's annual mortgage interest statements and gambol in his urinalysis records. Course, the VR illusion doesn't track just right, so most of us get sick for the first few weeks until we learn to move our heads slowly, like tank turrets. You can always tell a rookie by the scope patch glued beneath his ear, strong mouthwash odor, gray lips.

Through the Demosphere we fly, we men of the Database Maintenance Division, and although the Demosphere belongs to General Communications Inc., it is the schmos of the world who make it—every time a schmo surfs to a different channel, the Demosphere notes that he is bored with program A and more interested, at the moment, in program B. When a schmo's paycheck is delivered over the I-way, the number on the bottom line is plotted in his Profile, and if that schmo got it by telecommuting we know about that too—the length of his coffee breaks and the size of his bladder are an open book to us. When a schmo buys something on the I-way it goes into his Profile, and if it happens to be something that he recently saw advertised there, we call that interesting, and when he uses the I-way to phone his friends and family, we Profile Auditors can navigate his social web out to a gazillion fractal iterations, the friends of his friends of his friends of his friends, what they buy and what they watch and if there's a correlation.

So now it's a year later. I have logged many a megaparsec across the Demosphere, I can pick out an anomalous Profile at a glance and notify my superiors. I am dimly aware of two things: (1) that my yearly Polysurf test looms, and (2) I've a decent chance of being promoted to Profile Auditor 2 and getting a cubicle some 25 percent larger and with my choice from among three different color schemes and four pre-approved decor configurations. If I show some stick-to-it-iveness, put out some Second Effort, spread my legs on cue, I may one day be issued a *chair with arms*.

But let's not get ahead of ourselves. Have to get through that Polysurf test first. And I am oddly nervous. I am nervous because of *Hee Haw*.

Why did my subconscious brain surf away from *Hee Haw*? That wasn't like me at all. And yet perhaps it was this that had gotten me the job.

Disturbing thought: the hangover. I was in a foul mood, short-tempered, reactionary, literal-minded—in short, the temporary brain insult had turned me into an ideal candidate for this job.

But this time they will come and tap me for the test at a random time, while I am at work. I cannot possibly arrange to be hung over, unless I *stay* hung over for two weeks straight—tricky to arrange. I am a fraud. Soon they will know; ignominy, poverty will follow.

I am going to lose my job—my salaried job with medical and dental and even a *pension plan*. Didn't even know what a pension was until the employee benefits counselor clued me in, and it nearly blew the top of my skull off. For a couple of weeks I was like that lucky con-quistador from the poem—stout what's-his-name silent upon a peak in Darien—as I dealt this wild surmise: 20 years of rough country ahead of me leading down to an ocean of Slack that stretched all the way to the sunlit rim of the world, or to the end of my natural life expectancy, whichever came first.

So now I am scared shitless about the next Polysurf test. And then, hope.

My division commander zooms toward me in the Demosphere, an alienated human head wearing a bowler hat as badge of rank. "Follow me, Stark," he says, launching the command like a bronchial loogie, and before I can even "yes sir" I'm trying to keep up with him, dodging through DemoTainment Space.

And 10 minutes later we are cruising in a standard orbit around your Profile.

And from the middle distance it looks pretty normal. I can see at a glance you are a 24-year-old single white female New Derisive with post-Disillusionist leanings, income careening in a death spiral around the poverty line, you spend more on mascara than is really appropriate compared to your other cosmetics outlays, which are Low

Modest—I'd wager you're hooked on some exotic brand—no appendix, O positive, HIV-negative, don't call your mother often enough, spend an hour a day talking to your girlfriends, you prefer voice phone to video, like Irish music as well as the usual intelligent yet primal, sludgy yet danceable rock that someone like you would of course listen to. Your use of the Spew follows a bulimic course—you'll watch for two days at a time and then not switch on for a week.

But I know it can't be that simple, the commander wouldn't have brought me here because he was worried about your mascara imbalance, there's got to be something else.

I decide to take a flyer. "Geez, boss, something's not right here," I say, "this profile looks normal—too normal."

He buys it. He buys it like a set of snow tires. His disembodied head spins around and he looks at me intently, an oval of two-dimensional video in DemoTainment Space. "You saw that!?" he says.

Now I'm in deep. "Just a hunch, boss."

"Get to the bottom of it, and you'll be picking out color schemes by the end of the week," he says, then streaks off like a bottle rocket.

So that's it then; if I nab myself a promotion before the next Polysurf, they'll be a lot more forgiving if, say, the little couch potato in my brain stem chooses to watch *Hee Haw* for half an hour, or whatever.

Thenceforward I am in full Stalker Mode, I stake out your Profile, camp out in the middle of your income-tax returns, dance like an arachnid through your Social Telephony Web, dog you through the Virtual Mall trying to predict what clothes you're going to buy. It takes me about 10 minutes to figure out you've been buying mascara for one of your girlfriends who got fired from her job last year, so that solves that little riddle. Then I get nervous because whatever weirdness it was about you that drew the Commander's attention doesn't seem to be there anymore. Almost like you know someone's watching.

OK, let's just get this out of the way: it's creepy. Being a creep is a role someone has to take for society to remain free and hence prosperous (or is it the other way around?).

I am pursuing a larger goal that isn't creepy at all. I am thinking of Adderson. Every one of us, sitting in our cubicles, is always
thinking of Adderson, who started out as a Profile Auditor 1 just like
us and is now Vice President for Dynamic Programming at Dynastic
Communications Inc. and making eight to nine digits a year depending on whether he gets around to exercising his stock options. One
day young Adderson was checking out a Profile that didn't fit in with
established norms, and by tracing the subject's social telephony web,
noticed a trend: Post-Graduate Existentialists who *started going to
church*. You heard me: Adderson single-handedly discovered the New
Complacency.

It was an unexploited market niche of cavernous proportions: up-
wards of one-hundredth of one percent of the population. Within six
hours, Adderson had descended upon the subject's moho with a Rapid
Deployment Team of entertainment lawyers and development assis-
tants and launched the fastest-growing new channel ever to wend its
way into the thick braid of the Spew.

I'm figuring that there's something about you, girl, that's going to
make me into the next Adderson and you into the next Spew Icon—
the voice of a generation, the figurehead of a Spew channel, a straight
polished shaft leading direct to the heart of a *hitherto unknown and
unexploited market*. I know how awful this sounds, by the way.

So I stay late in my cubicle and dig a little deeper, rewinding your
Profile back into the mists of time. Your credit record is fashion-
ably cratered—but that's cool, even the God of the New Testament is
not as forgiving as the consumer credit system. You've blown many
scarce dollars at your local BodyMod franchise getting yourself
pierced ("topologically enhanced"), and, on one occasion, tattooed: a
medium #P879, left breast. Perusal of BodyMod's graphical database
(available, of course, over the Spew) turns up "(c) 1991 by Ray Troll
of Ketchikan, Alaska." BodyMod's own market research on this little
gem indicates that it first become widely popular within the Seattle
music scene.

So the plot thickens. I check out of my cubicle. I decide to go undercover.

Wouldn't think a Profile Auditor 1 could pull that off, wouldja? But I'm just like you, or I was a year ago. All I have to do is dig a yard deeper into the sediments of my dirty laundry pile, which have become metamorphic under prolonged heat and pressure.

As I put the clothes on it occurs to me that I could stand a little prolonged heat and pressure myself.

But I can't be thinking about *that*, I'm a professional, got a job to do, and frankly I could do without this unwanted insight. That's just what I need, for the most important assignment of my career to turn into a nookie hunt. I try to drive it from my mind, try to lose myself in the high-definition Spew terminals in the subway car, up there where the roach motel placards used to be. They click from one Feed to another following some irrational pattern and I wonder who has the job of surfing the channels in the subway; maybe it's what I'll be doing for a living, a week from now.

Just before the train pulls into your stop, the terminal in my face surfs into episode #2489 of *Hee Haw*. It's a skit. The banjo picker is playing a bit part, sitting on a bale of hay in the back of a pickup truck—chewing on a stalk of grass, surprisingly enough. His job is to laugh along with the cheesy jokes but he's just a banjo picker, not an actor, he doesn't know the drill, he can't keep himself from looking at the camera—looking at me. I notice for the first time that his irises are different colors. I turn up the collar on my jacket as I detrain, feeling those creepy eyes on my neck.

I have already discovered much about the infrastructure of your life that is probably hidden even from you, including your position in the food chain, which is as follows: the SRVX group is the largest *zaibatsu* in the services industry. They own five different hotel networks, of which Hospicor is the second-largest but only the fourth most profitable. Hospicor hotels are arranged in tiers: at the bottom we have Catchawink, which is human coin lockers in airports, everything covered in a plastic sheet that comes off a huge roll, like sleeping inside a giant, loose-fitting condom. Then we have Mom's Sleep Inn, a chain of motels catering to truckers and homeless migrants; The Family Room, currently getting its ass kicked by Holiday Inn; Kensington Place, going for that all-important biz traveler; and Imperion Preferred Resorts.

I see that you work for the Kensington Place Columbus Circle Hotel, which is too far from the park and too viewless to be an Imperion Preferred, even though it's in a very nice old building. So you are, to be specific, a desk clerk and you work the evening shift there.

I approach the entrance to the hotel at 8:05 p.m., long-jumping across vast reservoirs of gray-brown slush and blowing off the young men who want to change my money into Hong Kong dollars. The doorman is too busy tapping a fresh Camel on his wrist bone to open the door for me so I do it myself.

The lobby looks a little weird because I've only seen it on TV, through that security camera up there in the corner, with its distorting wide-angle lens, which feeds directly into the Spew, of course. I'm all turned around for a moment, doing sort of a drunken pirouette in the middle of the lobby, and finally I get my bearings and establish missile lock on You, standing behind the reception desk with Evan, your goatee-sporting colleague, both of you looking dorky (as I'm sure you'd be the first to assert) in your navy blue Kensington Place uniforms, which would border on dignified if not for the maroon piping and pseudo-brass name tags.

For long minutes I stand more or less like an idiot right there under the big chandelier, watching you giving the business to some poor sap of a guest. I am too stunned to move because something big and heavy is going upside my head. Not sure exactly what.

But it feels like the Big L. And I don't just mean Lust, though it is present.

The guest is approaching tears because the fridge in her room is broken and she has some kind of medicine that has to be kept cold or else she won't wake up tomorrow morning.

No it's worse than that, there's no fridge in her room *at all*.

Evan suggests that the woman leave the medicine outside on her windowsill overnight. It is a priceless moment, I feel like holding up a big card with 9.8 written on it. Some of my all-time fave Television Moments have been on surveillance TV, moments like this one, but it takes patience. You have to wait for it. Usually, at a Kensington Place you don't have to wait for long.

As I have been watching Evan and you on the Stalker Channel the past couple of days, I have been trying to figure out if the two of you have a thing going. It's hard because the camera doesn't give me audio, I have to work it out from body language. And after careful analysis of instant replays, I suspect you of being one of those dangerous types who innocently give good body language to everyone. The type of girl who should have someone walking 10 paces in front of her with a red flashing light and a clanging bell. Just my type.

The woman storms out in tears, wailing something about lawyers. I resist the urge to applaud and stand there for a minute or so, waiting to be greeted. You and Evan ignore me. I approach the desk. I clear my throat. I come right up to the desk and put my bag down on the counter right there and sigh very loudly. Evan is poking randomly at the computer and you are misfiling thousands of tiny little oaktag cards, the color of old bananas, in a small wooden drawer.

I inhale and open my mouth to say *excuse me*, but Evan cuts me off: "Customerrrrzz . . . gotta love 'em."

You grin wickedly and give him a nice flirty conspiratorial look. No one has looked at me yet. That's OK. I recognize your technique from the surveillance camera: good clerk, bad clerk.

"Reservation for Stark," I say.

"Stark," Evan says, and rolls it around in his head for a minute or so, unwilling to proceed until he has deconstructed my name. "That's German for 'strong,' right?"

"It's German for 'naked,' " I say.

Evan drops his gaze to the computer screen, defeated and temporarily humble. You laugh and glance up at me for the first time. What do you see? You see a guy who looks pretty much like the guys you hang out with.

I shove the sleeves of my ratty sweater up to the elbows and rest one forearm across the counter. The tattoo stands out vividly against my spudlike flesh, and in my peripheral I can see your eyes glance up for a moment, taking in the black rectangle, the skull, the crossed fish. Then I pretend to get self-conscious. I step back and pull my sleeve down again—don't want you to see that the tattoo is only about a day old.

"No reservation for Stark," Evan says, right on cue. I'm cool, I'm expecting this; they lose all of the reservations.

"Dash these computers," I say. "You have any empty rooms?"

"Just a suite. And a couple of economy rooms," he says, issuing a double challenge: do I have the bucks for the former or the moxie for the latter?

"I'll take one of the economy rooms," I say.

"You sure?"

"HIV-positive."

Evan shrugs, the hotel clerk's equivalent of issuing a 20-page legal disclaimer, and prods the computer, which is good enough to spit out a keycard, freshly imprinted with a random code. It's also spewing bits upstairs to the computer lock on my door, telling it that I'm cool, I'm to be let in.

"Would you like someone to show you up?" Evan says, glancing in mock surprise around the lobby, which is of course devoid of bell-hops. I respond in the only way possible: chuckle darkly—*good one, Ev!*—and hump my own bag.

My room's lone window looks out on a narrow well somewhere between an air shaft and a garbage chute in size and function. Patches of the shag carpet have fused into mysterious crust formations, and in the corners of the bathroom, pubic hairs have formed into gnarled drifts. There is a Robobar in the corner but the door can only be opened halfway because it runs into the radiator, a 12-ton cast-iron model that, randomly, once or twice an hour, makes a noise like a rock hitting the windshield. The Robobar is mostly empty but I wriggle one arm into it and yank out a canned Mai Tai, knowing that the selection will show up instantaneously on the computer screens below, where you and Evan will derive fleeting amusement from my offbeat tastes.

Yes, now we are surveiling each other. I open my suitcase and take my own Spew terminal out of its case, unplug the room's set and jack my own into the socket. Then I start opening windows: first, in the upper left, you and Evan in wide-angle black-and-white. Then an episode of *Starsky and Hutch* that I happened to notice. Starsky's hair is very big in this one. And then I open a data window too and patch it into the feed coming out of your terminal down there at the desk.

Profile Auditors can do this because data security on the Spew is a joke. It was deliberately made a joke by the Government so that they, and we, and anyone else with a Radio Shack charge card and a trade school diploma, can snoop on anyone.

I sit back on the bed and sip my execrable Mai Tai from its heavy, rusty can and watch *Starsky and Hutch*. Every so often there's some activity at the desk and I watch you and Evan for a minute. When Evan uses his terminal, lines of ASCII text scroll up my data window. I cannot help noticing that when Evan isn't actively slacking he can type at a burst speed in excess of 200 words per minute.

From *Starsky and Hutch* I surf to an *L.A. Law* rerun and then to *Larry King Live*. There's local news, then Dave comes on, and about the time he's doing his Top Ten list, I see activity at the desk.

It is a young gentleman with hair way down past the epaulets of his tremendously oversized black wool overcoat. Naked hairy legs protrude below the coat and are socketed into large, ratty old basketball shoes. He is carrying, not a garment bag, but a guitar.

For the first time all night, you and Evan show actual hospitality. Evan does some punching on his computer, and monitoring the codes I can see that the guitarist is being checked into a room.

Into my room. Not the one I'm in, but the one I'm supposed to be in. Number 707. I pull out the fax that Marie at Kensington Place Worldwide Reservation Command sent to me yesterday, just to double-check.

Sure enough, the guitarist is being checked into my room. Not only that—Evan's checking him in *under my name*.

I go out into the streets of the city. You and Evan pretend to ignore me, but I can see you following me with your eyes as I circumvent the doorman, who is planted like a dead *ficus benjamina* before the exit, and throw my shoulder against the sullen bulk of the revolving door. It has commenced snowing for the 11th time today. I walk cross-town to Television City and have a drink in a bar there, a real Profile Auditor hangout, the kind of joint where I'm proud to be seen. When I get back to the hotel, the shift has changed, you and Evan have apparently stalked off into the rapidly developing blizzard, and the only person there is the night clerk.

I stand there for 10 minutes or so while she winds down a rather involved, multithreaded conversation with a friend in Ireland. "Stark," I say, as she's hanging up, "Room 707. Left my keycard in the room."

She doesn't even ask to see ID, just makes up another keycard for me. Bad service has its charms. But I cruise past the seventh floor and go on up to my own cell because I want to do this right.

I jack into the Spew. I check out what's going on in Room 707.

First thing I look at is the Robobar transcript. Whoever's in there has already gone through four beers and two non-sparkling mineral waters. And one bad Mai Tai.

Guess I'm a trendsetter here. A hunch thuds into my cortex. I pop a beer from my own Robobar and rewind the lobby security tape to midnight.

You and Evan hand over the helm to the Irish girl. Then, like Picard and Riker on their way to Ten Forward after a long day of sensitive negotiations, you head straight for Elevator Three, the only one that seems to be hooked up. So I check out the elevator activity transcript too—not to be monotonous or anything, but it's all on the Spew—and sho nuff, it seems that you and Evan went straight to the seventh floor. You're in there, I realize, with your guitar-player bud who wears shorts in the middle of the winter, and you're drinking bad beer and Mai Tais from my Robobar.

I monitor the Spew traffic to Room 707. You did some random surfing like anyone else, sort of as foreplay, but since then you've just been hoovering up gigabyte after gigabyte of encrypted data.

It's gotta be media; only media takes that many bytes. It's coming from an unknown source, definitely not the big centralized Spew nodes—but it's been forwarded six ways from Sunday, it's been bounced off Indian military satellites, divided into tiny chunks, disguised as credit card authorizations, rerouted through manual telephone exchanges in Nigeria, reassembled in pirated insurance-company databases in the Netherlands. Upshot: I'll never trace it back to its source, or sources.

What is 10 times as weird: *you're putting data out*. You're talking *back* to the Spew. You have turned your room—*my* room—into a broadcast station. For all I know, you've got a *live studio audience* packed in there with you.

All of your outgoing stuff is encrypted too.

Now. My rig has some badass code-breaking stuff built into it, Profile Auditor warez, but all of it just bounces off. You guys are cypherpunks, or at least you know some. You're using codes so tough they're illegal. Conclusion: you're talking to other people—other people like you—probably squatting in other Kensington Place hotel rooms all over the world at this moment.

Everything's falling into place. No wonder Kensington Place has such legendarily shitty service. No wonder it's so unprofitable. The whole chain has been infiltrated.

And what's really brilliant is that all the weird shit you're pulling off the Spew, all the hooch you're pulling out of my Robobar, is going to end up tacked onto my Profile, while you end up looking infuriatingly normal.

I kind of like it. So I invest another half-hour of my life waiting for an elevator, take it down to the lobby, go out to a 24-hour mart around the corner and buy two six-packs—one of the fashionable down-market swill that you are drinking and one of your brand of mineral water. I can tell you're cool because your water costs more than your beer.

Ten minutes later I'm standing in front of 707, sweating like a high school kid in a cheesy tuxedo on prom night. After a few minutes the sheer patheticity of this little scene starts to embarrass me and so I tuck a six under my arm and swipe my card through the slot. The little green light winks at me knowingly. I shoulder through the door saying, "Honey, I'm home!"

No response. I have to negotiate a narrow corridor past the bath and closets before I can see into the room proper. I step out with what I hope is a non-creepy smile. Something wet and warm sprays into my face. It trickles into my mouth. It's on the savory side.

The room's got like 10 feet of open floor space that you have increased to 15 by stacking the furniture in the bathroom. In the midst of this is the guitar dude, stripped to his colorful knee-length shorts. He is playing his ax, but it's not plugged into anything. I can hear some melodious plinks, but the squelch of his fingers on the strings, the thud of calluses on the fingerboard almost drown out the notes.

He sweats hard, even though the windows are open and cold air is blowing into the room, the blinds running with condensation and whacking crazily against the leaky aluminum window frame. As he works through his solo, sighing and grunting with effort, his fingers drumming their way higher and higher up the fingerboard, he swings his head back and forth and his hair whips around, broadcasting sweat. He's wearing dark shades.

Evan is perched like an arboreal primate on top of the room's Spew terminal, which is fixed to the wall at about head level. His legs are spread wide apart to expose the screen, against which crash waves of black-and-white static. The motherly warmth of the cathode-ray tube is, I guess, permeating his buttocks.

On his lap is just about the bitchingest media processor I have ever seen, and judging from the heavy cables exploding out of the back it looks like he's got it crammed with deadly expansion cards. He's wearing dark shades too, just like the guitarist's; but now I see they aren't shades, they are VR rigs, pretty good ones actually. Evan is also wearing a pair of Datagloves. His hands and fingers are constantly moving. Sometimes he makes typing motions, sometimes he reaches out and grabs imaginary things and moves them around, sometimes he points his index finger and navigates through virtual space, sometimes he riffs in some kind of sign language.

You—you are mostly in the airspace above the bed, touching down frequently, using it as trampoline and safety net. Every 3-year-old bouncing illicitly on her bed probably aspires to your level of intensity. You've got the VR rig too, you've got the Datagloves, you've got Velcro bands around your wrists, elbows, waist, knees, and ankles, tracking the position of every part of your body in three-dimensional space. Other than that, you have stripped down to voluminous plaid boxer shorts and a generously sized tank-top undershirt.

You are rocking out. I have never seen anyone dance like this. You have churned the bedspread and pillows into sufferin' succotash. They get in your way so you kick them vindictively off the bed and get down again, boogieing so hard I can't believe you haven't flown off the bed yet. Your undershirt is drenched. You are breathing hard and steady and in sync with the rhythm, which I cannot hear but can infer.

I can't help looking. There's the SPAWN TILL YOU DIE tattoo. And there on the other breast is something else. I walk into the room for a better look, taking in a huge whiff of perfume and sweat and beer. The second tattoo consists of small but neat navy-blue script, like that of names embroidered on bowling shirts, reading, HACK THE SPEW.

It's not too hard to trace the connections. A wire coils out of the guitar, runs across the floor, and jumps up to jack into Evan's badass media processor. You have a wireless rig hanging on your waist and the receiver is likewise patched into Evan's machine. And Evan's output port, then, is jacked straight into the room's Spew socket.

I am ashamed to notice that the Profile Auditor 1 part of my brain is thinking that this weird little mime fest has UNEXPLOITED MARKET NICHE—ORDER NOW! superimposed all over it in flashing yellow block letters.

Evan gets so into his solo that he sinks unsteadily to his knees and nearly falls over. He's leaning way back, stomach muscles knotting up, his wet hair dangling back and picking up detritus from the carpet as he swings his head back and forth.

This whole setup is depressingly familiar: it is just like high school, when I had a crush on some girl, and even though I was in the same room with her, breathing the same air, sharing the same space, she didn't know I existed; she had her own network of friends, all grooving on some frequency I couldn't pick up, existing on another plane that I couldn't even see.

There's a note on the dresser, scrawled on hotel stationery with a dried-up hotel ball-point. WELCOME CHAZ, it says, JACK IN AND JOIN US! followed by 10 lines of stuff like:

A073 49D2 CD01 7813 000F B09B 323A E040

which are obviously an encryption key, written in the hexadecimal system beloved of hackers. It is the key to whatever plane you and your buds are on at the moment.

But I am not Chaz.

I open the desk drawer to reveal the room's fax machine, a special Kensington Place feature that Marie extolled to me most tediously. I put the note into it and punch the Copy key, shove the copy into my pocket when it's finished and leave the note where I found it. I leave the two six-packs on the dresser as a ritual sacrifice, and slink out of the room, not looking back. An elevator is coming up toward me, L M

2 3 4 5 6 and then DING and the doors open, and out steps a slacker who can only be Chaz, thousands of snowflakes caught in his hair, glinting in the light like he's just stepped out of the Land of Faerie. He's got kind of a peculiar expression on his face as he steps out of the elevator, and as we trade places, and I punch the button for the lobby, I recognize it: Chaz is happy. Happier than me.

IN THE KINGDOM OF MAO BELL OR, DESTROY THE USERS ON THE WAITING LIST (SELECTED EXCERPTS) (1994)

In the inevitable rotating lounge atop the Shangri-La Hotel in the Shenzhen Special Economic Zone, a burly local businessman, wearing a synthetic polo shirt stretched so thin as to be semitransparent, takes in the view, some drinks, and selections from the dinner buffet.

He is accompanied by a lissome consort in a nice flowered print dress. Like any face-conscious Chinese businessman he carries a large boxy cellular phone. It's not that he can't afford a "prawn," as the newer flip phones are called. His model is prized because it stands up on a restaurant table, antenna in the fully erect position, flaunting the owner's connectivity.

The lounge spins disconcertingly fast—you have to recalibrate your inner ear when you enter, and I half expect to see the head of my Guinness listing. Furthermore, it is prone to a subtly disturbing oscillation known to audio engineers as wow. Outside the smoked windows, Typhoon Abe is gathering his forces. Shenzhen spins around me, wowing sporadically.

Thirty-one floors below is the Shen Zhen (Deep River) itself, which separates China-proper's Special Economic Zone from Hong Kong and eventually flows into the vast estuary of the Pearl River. The boundary serves the combined functions of the Iron Curtain and the Rio Grande, yet in cyberspace terms it has already ceased to exist:

—The border is riddled with leased lines connecting clean, comfortable offices in Hong Kong with factories in Shenzhen, staffed with nimble and submissive girls from rural China. Shenzhen's population is 60 percent female.

—The value of many Hong Kong stocks is pegged to arcane details of PRC government policy, which are announced from time to time by ministries in Beijing. For a long time, the Hong Kong market has fluctuated in response to such announcements; more recently, the fluctuations have begun to happen hours or days before the policies are made public.

—Hong Kong television is no longer targeted at a Hong Kong audience; it is now geared for the 20 million people in the Pearl Delta—the 80-mile-long region defined by Guangzhou (Canton) in the interior, Hong Kong and the Shenzhen SEZ on the eastern bank, and Macao and the Zhuhai SEZ on the western bank. Thickets of television antennas, aimed toward Hong Kong, fringe the roof of every Pearl Delta apartment block. Since TV Guide and its ilk are not available, Star TV regularly flashes up a telephone number bearing the Hong Kong prefix. Dial this number and they will fax you a program guide. This is easy for Shenzhen residents, because . . .

—Every telephone in Shenzhen has international direct dial.

THE FIRST THING THAT HAPPENED DURING JARUZELSKI'S MILITARY COUP IN Poland was that the narcs invaded the telephone exchanges and severed the trunk lines with axes, ensuring that they would take months to repair. This and similar stories have gotten us into the habit of thinking that modern information technology is to totalitarianism what crosses are to vampires. Skeptics might say it's just a coincidence that glasnost and perestroika came just after the photocopier, the fax, and the personal computer invaded Russia, but I think there's a connection, and if you read *WIRED*, you probably do too. After all, how could any country whose power structure was based on controlling the flow of information survive in an era of direct-dial phones and ubiquitous fax machines?

Now (or so the argument goes), any nation that wants a modern economy has to have information technology—so economic modernization will inevitably lead to political reform, right?

I went to China expecting to see that process in action. I looked everywhere for hardy electronic frontierfolk, using their modems and fax machines to push the Communists back into their holes, and I asked dang near everyone I met about how communications technology was changing Chinese culture.

None of them knew what the hell I was talking about.

I was carrying an issue of *WIRED* so that I wouldn't have to explain it to everyone. It happened to be the issue with Bill Gibson on the cover. In one corner were three characters in Hanzi (the script of the Han Chinese). Before I'd left the States, I'd heard that they formed the Chinese word for "network."

Whenever I showed the magazine to a Chinese person they were baffled. "It means network, doesn't it?" I said, thinking all the warm and fuzzy thoughts that we think about networks.

"Yes," they said, "this is the term used by the Red Guards during the Cultural Revolution for the network of spies and informers that they spread across every village and neighborhood to snare enemies of the regime."

GOING TO CHINA AND ASKING PEOPLE ABOUT THE HACKER ETHIC IS LIKE going to Peoria and talking to the folks down at Ned's Feed & Grain about Taoism. The hacking part comes to them easily enough—China is, in a sense, a nation of analog hackers quickly entering the digital realm. But I didn't see any urge to draw profound, cosmic conclusions from the act of messing around with technology.

SHENZHEN HAS THE LOOK OF AN INFORMATION-AGE CITY, WHERE LOCATION IS basically irrelevant. Unlike, say, Shanghai (which is laid out the old-fashioned way, on an armature of heavy industry and transportation lines), Shenzhen seems to have grown up without any clear central plan, the office blocks and residential neighborhoods springing into being like crystals from a supersaturated solution. Think of the difference between Los Angeles and New York City, and you might get a general idea of what I mean. Streets tend to be straight, wide, and many-laned, with endless iron fences running down the middle so that pedestrians and bicyclists are forced, against all cultural norms, to cross only at major intersections. Shenzhen has more cars and fewer bicycles than most Chinese cities. This has shifted the balance of power somewhat; in, say, Shanghai, mobs of bicyclists play chicken with the cars and frequently win. But in Shenzhen they stand defeated on the curbs, waiting for the light to change. Occasionally some young scoundrel will dart out and try to claim a lane and be driven back by taxi drivers, scolding him with horns and shaking fingers.

Even on a humid day (which is to say, every day) the place is rather dusty, like a construction site where things haven't been tamped down yet. Houses are rare, though there is one district that looks something like an American suburban housing development, albeit more tightly packed. But this one looks like it's been abandoned and then recolonized by survivalists: Every house is surrounded by a high wall topped with something sharp, and if you peer between the iron bars of the gates, you can see that the windows and patio doors of the houses are additionally protected by iron bars and expanding metal security gates. Beyond that, everyone lives in high-rises.

On every block in central Shenzhen, clean new high-rises protrude from organic husks of bamboo scaffolding. Nissan flatbed trucks rumble away from the waterfront stacked with sheets of Indonesian mahogany plywood on its way to construction sites, where it will be used in concrete forms and then thrown away. The darkness is troubled by the report of nocturnal jackhammers, and all-night arc-welders hollow immense spheres of blue light out of the translucent, steamy atmosphere.

Only a quarter mile away from this scene of hysterical development, a green hillside rises, covered with an undisturbed mat of tropical vegetation and empty except for an ancient cemetery. It doesn't make sense until you realize that you're looking across the Shen Zhen into Hong Kong territory. Running parallel to the river is a border defense system meant to keep the mainland Chinese out. A chain of sodium-vapor lamps and a high fence topped with razor ribbon cuts across lakes and wetlands that have become wildlife refuges by default.

CORRUPTION IN CHINA IS NO SECRET, BUT THE WAY IT'S COVERED IN WESTERN media suggests that it's just an epiphenomenon attached to the government. In fact, corruption is the government. It's like jungle vines that have twined around a tree and strangled it—now the tree has rotted out and only the vines remain. Much of this stems from the way China is modernizing its economy.

If you thought zaibatsus were creepy, if Singapore's brand of state-backed capitalism gives you the willies, wait until you see the Sino-foreign joint venture. The Russians, in their efforts to turn capitalist, have at least tried to break up some of the big state monopolies and privatize their enterprises—but since China is still Communist, there's no reason for any of that nonsense. Instead, foreign companies form joint ventures with enterprises that are still part of the government—and, of course, everything is part of the government.

On every block you see an entrepreneur sitting at a sidewalk card table with one or two telephones, jury-rigged by wires strung down an alley, up the side of a building, and into a window. There is a phone book, a price chart, and a cigar box full of cash (in Shenzhen, always Hong Kong dollars). Some fastidious operators have a jar full of mysterious disinfectant with which they wipe down the mouthpiece and even the buttons after each customer is finished. Most of these enterprises also feature a queue of anywhere from one to half a dozen people. The proprietor will step in and cut long-winded customers off, especially if someone in the queue makes it worth his while.

All of the phone wiring is kludgey. It looks like everyone went down to Radio Shack and bought reels of phone wire and began stringing it around, across roofs, in windows, over alleyways. Hundreds of wires explode from junction boxes on the sides of apartments, exposed to the elements.

I was checking out some electronics shops along one of Shenzhen's wide avenues. Above the shops were dimly lit office spaces housing small software companies or (more likely) software departments of Sino-foreign joint ventures. If there was a Chinese Silicon Valley, this was it. I wandered into an alley—the Silicon Alley, perhaps—and discovered a particularly gnarly looking cobweb of phone wires. My traveling companion Paul Lau, a Hong Kong–based photographer, started taking pictures of it. Within moments, a couple of attentive young Chinese men had charged up on bicycles and confronted him.

"Are you a reporter?" they demanded.

"No, I'm an artist," Paul said, leaving them too stunned to make trouble. The lesson I learned from this is that a sophisticated Hong Kong Chinese knows how to use the sheer force of culture shock to keep his mainland cousins at bay. The Shenzhenese are pretty worldly by Chinese standards, but compared to the Hong Kong Chinese, who may be the most cosmopolitan people on earth, they are still yokels. This cultural disparity is about the only thing Hong Kong has going for it as 1997 approaches; but more about that later.

MOTOROLA RUNS ONE OF THE TWO CELLPHONE NETWORKS IN SHANGHAI. THE local chief is a young American named Bill Newton, who came here a few years ago with two other people and worked around the clock at first—like new immigrants, he says, who've just come to America and have nothing to do but work. Now he's managing 55 employees; he's the only American. He thinks everyone should want his job: "To be in one of the fastest growing companies in one of the fastest growing sectors of the fastest growing economy in the world—how many times in your life is that going to happen?" In the context of Shanghai, "fast growing" means, for example, that cellular phone service is growing at 140 percent a year and pager use at 170 percent a year.

Motorola's offices are in the international center west of downtown Shanghai—the modern, high-rise equivalent of the Western enclaves where capitalists used to do business in the old days. It's got a Shangri-La luxury hotel, it's got modern offices identical to those you'd see in any big American city, it's got living quarters with purified water. Newton and I got in a taxi and took a long drive to the headquarters of the Shanghai Post and Telecommunications Administration (PTA)—Mao Bell, if you will.

Driving in Shanghai is like shouldering your way through the crowd at an overbooked trade convention. There's never any space in front of your vehicle that is large enough to let you in, so you just ooze along with the traffic, occasionally claiming a few extra square yards of pavement when the chance presents itself. I'm hardly the first Westerner to point this out, but the density of bicycle and foot traffic is amazing. I'm tempted to write that the streets are choked with bicycles, but, of course, the opposite is true: All those bicycles are moving, and they're all carrying stuff. If the same stuff was being moved on trucks, the way it is in, say, Manhattan, then the streets would be choked.

Everyone is carrying something of economic value. Eviscerated pigs slung belly-up over the rear tire; bouquets of scrawny, plucked chickens dangling from racks where they get bathed in splashed-up puddle water; car parts, mattresses, messages.

In network jargon, the Chinese are distributed. Instead of having One Big Enterprise, the way the Soviets did, or the way we do with our Wal-Marts, the Chinese have millions of little enterprises. Instead of moving stuff around in large hunks on trucks and trains, they move it around in tiny little hunks on bicycles. The former approach works great in say, the Midwestern U.S., where you've got thousands of miles of nearly empty interstate highways and railroad lines and huge chunks of rolling stock to carry stuff around. The latter approach works in a place like Shanghai.

The same problems of distribution arise in computer networks. As networks get bigger and as the machines that make them up become more equal, the whole approach to moving information around changes from centralized to distributed. The packet-switching system that makes things like the Internet work would be immediately familiar to the Chinese. Instead of requisitioning a hunk of optical fiber between Point A and Point B and slamming the data down it in one big shipment, the packet data network breaks the data down into tiny pieces and sends them out separately, just as a Chinese enterprise might break a large shipment down into small pieces and send each one out on a separate bicycle, knowing that each one might take a different route but that they'd all get there eventually.

Mao Bell is responsible, among other things, for setting up such data networks in China. The Shanghai headquarters is on the waterfront of the Huangpu River between the Shanghai stock exchange and a tall hotel used during the war by the Japanese as a high-rise concentration camp. A woman sits in the tiny lobby with her telephone and her jug of disinfectant, and allows you to call upstairs to announce yourself. A tiny, rickety elevator descends, hoists you up a few floors, and deposits you in a long corridor without artificial light. Some illumination enters through windows and glances down the shiny floor, but it's the gloomy steel-gray light of a northern industrial city. You'd never know that Mao Bell takes in over US$7 billion a year and that revenues are growing by something like 60 percent a year.

A bit of a spelunking expedition through these corridors takes you into a classic communist-style meeting room, the kind of place Coleridge might have been thinking of when he wrote of "caverns measureless to man." In this part of the world, the heavy hitters show up for meetings with large retinues of underlings, and all of them have to have a seat at the table, so the tables go on for miles. I established a foothold in a corner near the door and was met by Gao Kun, director of the import office of the Shanghai PTA, comfortable in a short-sleeved shirt. Gao, bless him, was the only government official who would talk to me the whole trip—the PRC was still pissed off at the Great Hegemon (as they now call the U.S.) about that incident in the Persian Gulf a few months back when our guys stopped and boarded a Chinese freighter allegedly full of chemical warfare ingredients. They found nothing.

Gao calmly rattled off a fairly staggering list of statistics on how rapidly the phone system there is growing—half to three-quarters of a million lines added per year for the foreseeable future. All of their local exchanges are webbed together with fiber, and they're running fiber down the coast toward Shenzhen. They're setting up packet-switching networks for their customers who want them—banks, import/export houses, and the like. The cellular and CT2 networks are also growing as rapidly as technology allows. He buys scads of high-bandwidth technology from the West and is actually trying to set up a sort of clearinghouse near Shanghai where Western manufacturers could gain access to the potentially stupendous Chinese market through a single point, instead of having to traffic separately with each regional PTA.

Gao is baffled by the fact that the U.S. makes all the most advanced technology, but our government won't allow him to buy it. He asked me to explain that fact. I didn't suppose that haranguing him about human rights would get me anywhere, so I mumbled some kind of rambling shit about politics.

He explained to me, through his interpreter, that the slogan of Shanghai PTA is "destroy the users on the waiting list." Indeed, it's the job of people like Gao to extend the net into every cranny of the society, making sure everyone gets wired. When nobody had phones, he says, nobody really missed them; the very few people who had them in their homes viewed them primarily as a symbol of status and power. Now, 61 percent of his customers are residential, everyone views it as a basic necessity of life, and Gao's company has to provide them with more services, like direct dial, pagers, and so on. Cellphones, he said, are so expensive that they're only used by businessmen and high-ranking officials. But the officials are uneasy with the whole concept because they have to answer the phone themselves, which is seen as a menial chore. I told him that in Hong Kong, businessmen walk down the streets followed at a respectful distance by walking receptionists who carry the phones for them. Gao thought that was pretty funny.

In one Chinese city, a woman spends all day running a sidewalk stand and keeping one eye on a construction project across the street. The construction project is backed by a couple of people who were running a software counterfeiting operation to the tune of some tens of millions of dollars until they got busted by Microsoft. They hid their money and have been sinking it into the real estate project. Microsoft is paying the woman a lot of money (by the standards of a Chinese sidewalk vendor) to watch the site and keep track of who comes and goes. She has a camera in her stand, and if the software pirates ever show up there and she takes a picture of them, she gets a whopping bonus, plus a free trip to the United States to testify.

Microsoft runs an office in Hong Kong that is devoted to the miserable task of trying to stop software piracy in Asia. In addition to
running their undercover operation in the sidewalk stand, they are
targeting a number of operations in other countries, which probably
provides a foretaste of what's going to happen in mainland China a
few years down the road.

Most East Asian countries have sort of a stolen intellectual property shopping mall where people sit all day in front of cheap computers swapping disks, copying the software while you wait—the vaunted
just-in-time delivery system. After a few of these got busted, many
switched to a networked approach. One guy in Taiwan is selling a set
of 7 CD-ROMs containing hundreds of pirated programs. He has no
known name or address, just a pager.

Taiwan, the most technologically advanced part of Greater China,
makes a lot of PCs, all of which need system software, so there the name
of the game is counterfeiting, not pirating. MS-DOS and Windows are,
naturally, the main targets. Microsoft tried to make the counterfeiters'
job harder by sealing their packages with holograms, but that didn't
stop the Taiwanese—they made a deal with the Reflective Materials Institute at, you guessed it, Shenzhen University, which cranked out hundreds of thousands of counterfeit holograms for them.

It often seems that, from the point of view of many entrepreneurial souls in East Asia, the West's tight-assed legal system and
penchant for ethical dithering have left many inviting niches to fill.
Perhaps this explains their compulsion to enter such perfectly sensible fields as driftnet fishing, making medicines from body parts of
nearly extinct species, creative toxic waste disposal, and, above all,
the wholesale, organized theft of intellectual property. It's not just
software, either—Indonesia has bootleg publishers who crank out
counterfeit bestsellers, and even Hong Kong's Saturday morning TV
clown wears a purloined Ronald McDonald outfit.

This has a lot to do with the collective Chinese approach to technology. The Chinese were born to hack. A billion of them jammed

together have created the world's most efficient system for honing
and assimilating new tech (they actually view Americans as being
somewhat backward and slow to accept new ideas—the Chinese are
considered, as Bill Newton put it, "not so much early adopters as
rapid adopters"). As soon as someone comes up with a new idea, all
the neighbors know about it, and through an exponential process
that you don't have to be a math major to understand, a billion people
know about it a week later. They start tinkering with it, applying it
to slightly different problems, trying to eke out hair-thin improvements, and the improvements propagate across the country until
everyone's doing things the same way—which also happens to be the
simplest and most efficient way. The infrastructure of day-to-day life
in China consists of a few simple, cheap, robust technologies that
don't belong to anyone: the wok, the bicycle, various structures made
from bamboo and lashed together with strips of rattan, and now the
286 box. A piece of Chinese technology, whether it's a cooking knife
or a roofing tile, has the awesomely simple functionality of a piece of
hand-coded machine language.

Introducing non-copy-protected software into this kind of an
environment may be the single most boneheaded thing that American business has ever done in its long history of stepping on rakes
in Asia. The Chinese don't draw any mystical distinctions between
analog and digital tech; whatever works, works, and so they're happy
to absorb things like pagers, cellphones, and computers if they find
that such things are useful. I don't think you find a lot of Chinese ex-
pressing hostility toward computers or cellphones in the same way
that technophobic Americans do. So they have not hesitated to en-
shrine the pager, the cellphone, and the 286 box in their pantheon of
simple, ubiquitous technology, along with the wok, the bicycle, and
the Kalashnikov assault rifle.

While avoiding technophobia, they've also avoided techno-
fetishism for the most part. They don't name their computers "Frodo,"
and they generally don't use them to play games, or for anything more

than keeping the accounts, running payroll, and processing a bit of text. In China, they treat computers like they treat dogs: handy for a few things, worth having around, but not worth getting overly attached to.

Shanghai's computer stores were all completely different. One place had a pathetic assortment of yellowed stuff from the Apple II Dynasty. Another specialized in circuit boards, catering to do-it-yourselfers. There were several of what we'd call box movers: stores crowded with stacks of brand-new 486 boxes and monitors. And I found one place hidden way off the street in a giant old Western-style house, which I thought was closed at first because all the lights were off and no one seemed to be there. But then people began to emerge from the shadows one by one and turn on lights, one fixture at a time, slowly powering up the building, shedding light on an amazing panoply of used computers and peripherals spanning the entire history of the industry. In more ways than one, the place was like a museum.

I GOT AROUND SHANGHAI IN A NONDESCRIPT WHITE FORD. BECAUSE OF ITS high fuel consumption, the driver called it the "Oil Tiger." Whenever it ran low, he was compelled by certain murkily described safety regulations to leave me a block away from the fuel pumps while he filled it up, which imparted an air of drama to the procedure.

One day, on the outskirts of Shanghai, I stumbled across a brand-new computer store with several large floral arrangements set up in front. A brass plaque identified it, imposingly enough, as the Shanghai Fanxin Computer System Application Technology Research Institute. Walking in, I saw the usual rack full of badly printed manuals for pirated software and a cardboard box brimming with long red skeins of firecrackers. The place was otherwise indistinguishable from any cut-rate consumer electronics outlet in the States, with the usual exception that it was smaller and more tightly packed together.

There were a couple of dozen people there, but they weren't acting like salespeople and customers; they were milling around talking.

It turned out that they had just opened their doors something like an hour before I arrived. I had accidentally crashed their opening-day party. Everyone stood around amazed by their good fortune: a writer for an American technology magazine showing up for their grand opening!

Dai Qing, the director, a young blade in an oversized suit, beckoned me into the back room, where we could sit around a conference table and watch the front through a large window. He bade a couple of females to scurry out for slices of cantaloupe and mugs of heavily sweetened coffee, and gave me the scoop on his company. There are 21 employees, 16 of whom are coders. It's a pure entrepreneurial venture—a bunch of people pooled their capital and started it rolling some three years ago. The engineers mostly worked in state enterprises or as teachers where they couldn't really use their skills; now they've developed, among other things, an implementation of the Li Xing accounting system, which is a standard developed in Shanghai and used throughout China.

The engineers make some 400 yuan per month, which works out to something like $600 a year at the black market exchange rate. This is a terrible salary—most people in Shanghai can rely on making four times that much. But here, the coders also get 5 percent of the profits from their software.

You can't pick out the coders by looking at them the way you can in the States. The gender ratio among coders is probably similar. Everyone is trim and nicely but uninterestingly dressed. No extremes of weight, facial hair, piercings, earrings, ponytails, wacky T-shirts, and certainly no flagrantly individualistic behavior. In other words, there's no evidence that being good at computers has caused these people to think of themselves as having a separate identity from other Chinese in the same wage bracket.

By the time I'd gotten out the door, the software engineers had already rolled a couple of dozen strings of firecrackers across the sidewalk. As soon as I jumped out of the way, they started lighting the fuses with their cigarettes (another habit not common among U.S. hackers), and everything went off in a massively parallel barrage, covering the sidewalk in dense smoke and kicking up a blizzard of shredded red paper. Several more coders came out carrying mortars and began launching bombs into the air, holding the things right in front of their faces as they disgorged fireballs with satisfying thuds. The strings of fireworks kept blowing themselves out, so as I backed slowly toward the Oil Tiger I was treated to the sight of excited Chinese software engineers lunging into the firestorm holding their cigarettes out like fencing foils, trying to reboot the strings without sacrificing eyes, fingers, or eardrums.

BACK IN SHENZHEN, WHEN I'D HAD ABOUT ALL I COULD TAKE OF THE SPECIAL Economic Zone, I walked over a bridge across the Shen Zhen and found myself back in the British Empire again, filling out forms in a clean well-lit room with the Union Jack flying overhead. A twenty-minute trip in one of Hong Kong's quiet, fast commuter trains took me through the New Territories, mostly open green land with the occasional grove of palm trees or burst of high-rise development, and into Kowloon, where I hopped into a taxi.

On the approach to the tunnel between Kowloon and Hong Kong, stuck in traffic beneath a huge electronic billboard showing animated stock market graphs in white, emerald, and ruby, I gazed into the next lane at a brand-new gray BMW 733i, smooth and polished as a drop of molten glass. Behind the wheel was a Chinese man, affluently fleshy. He'd taken off his suit jacket to expose a striped shirt, French cuffs, the cuff links flashing around the rim of the steering wheel. In the passenger seat to his left sat a beautiful young woman who had flipped her sunvisor down, centering her face in a pool of light from the vanity mirror; as she discussed the day's events with

the man, she deftly touched up her Shiseido—not that I would have
guessed she was wearing any, and not that she seemed especially vain
or preoccupied. The BMW kept pace with my taxi through the tunnel
and then the lanes diverged. I couldn't help wondering what the hell
was going to happen to this place when it becomes part of the People's
Republic in 1997. Needless to say, a lot of Hong Kong residents are
wondering the same thing.

People who think that America has a monopoly on gratuitous TV
violence have never watched what the Hong Kong stations radiate
across the Pearl Delta every night between 7 and 10. Their fake blood
technology is decades behind ours, but that doesn't seem to bother
this audience. The carnage is, of course, frequently interrupted by
ads, which also appeal to folks who are fairly new to the idiot box.
In my favorite TV ad, Beethoven's "Ode to Joy" was played as front-
end loaders fed boulders into a giant crusher and whole segments
of mountainside were blasted into rubble. And the Mitsubishi ads
looked like what you'd get if you hired Leni Riefenstahl to plug consumer electronics.

THE NETWORK IS SPREADING ACROSS CHINA, GETTING DENSER AND MORE SO-
phisticated with every kilometer of fiber that goes into the ground.
We'd like to think of it as the grass roots of democracy, but the Chinese are just as apt to think of it as a finely engineered snare for tying
the whole country together even more firmly than its predecessor,
the human Net of the Red Guards. Looking at all the little enterprises
that have sprung up in Shenzhen to write software and entertain visiting spacemen, it's easy to think that it's all the beginning of something permanent. But a longer historical perspective suggests that
it's only a matter of time before the northerners come pouring down
through the mountain passes to whip their troublesome southern
cousins back into line.

UNDER-CONSTABLE PROUDFOOT (2012)

[Author's note: This is the first sentence of a thriller that I will never complete about a serial killer on the loose in the Shire.]

From the angle of the stab wounds, Under-Constable Proud-foot could tell that, contrary to the opinions circulating in the tap-room at the Prancing Pony, the murder had not been committed by a Big Person.

MOTHER EARTH,
MOTHER BOARD
(1996)

IN WHICH THE HACKER TOURIST VENTURES
FORTH ACROSS THE WIDE AND WONDROUS
MEATSPACE OF THREE CONTINENTS, AC-
QUAINTING HIMSELF WITH THE CUSTOMS
AND DIALECTS OF THE EXOTIC MANHOLE VIL-
LAGERS OF THAILAND, THE U-TURN TUNNEL-
ERS OF THE NILE DELTA, THE CABLE NOMADS
OF LAN TAO ISLAND, THE SLACK CONTROL
WIZARDS OF CHELMSFORD, THE SUBTER-
RANEAN EX-TELEGRAPHERS OF CORNWALL,

AND OTHER PREVIOUSLY UNKNOWN AND UNCHRONICLED FOLK; ALSO, BIOGRAPHICAL SKETCHES OF THE TWO LONG-DEAD SUPREME NINJA HACKER MAGE LORDS OF GLOBAL TELECOMMUNICATIONS, AND OTHER MATERIAL PERTAINING TO THE BUSINESS AND TECHNOLOGY OF UNDERSEA FIBER-OPTIC CABLES, AS WELL AS AN ACCOUNT OF THE LAYING OF THE LONGEST WIRE ON EARTH, WHICH SHOULD NOT BE WITHOUT INTEREST TO THE READERS OF *WIRED*.

Information moves, or we move to it. Moving to it has rarely been popular and is growing unfashionable; nowadays we demand that the information come to us. This can be accomplished in three basic ways: moving physical media around, broadcasting radiation through space, and sending signals through wires. This article is about what will, for a short time anyway, be the biggest and best wire ever made.

Wires warp cyberspace in the same way wormholes warp physical space: the two points at opposite ends of a wire are, for informational purposes, the same point, even if they are on opposite sides of the planet. The cyberspace-warping power of wires, therefore, changes the geometry of the world of commerce and politics and ideas that we live in. The financial districts of New York, London, and Tokyo, linked by thousands of wires, are much closer to each other than, say, the Bronx is to Manhattan.

Today this is all quite familiar, but in the 19th century, when the first feeble bits struggled down the first undersea cable joining the Old World to the New, it must have made people's hair stand up on end in more than just the purely electrical sense—it must have seemed supernatural. Perhaps this sort of feeling explains why when Samuel Morse stretched a wire between Washington and Baltimore in 1844, the first message he sent with his code was "What hath God wrought!"—almost as if he needed to reassure himself and others that God, and not the Devil, was behind it.

During the decades after Morse's "What hath God wrought!" a plethora of different codes, signalling techniques, and sending and receiving machines were patented. A web of wires was spun across every modern city on the globe, and longer wires were strung between cities. Some of the early technologies were, in retrospect, flaky: one early inventor wanted to use 26-wire cables, one wire for each letter of the alphabet. But it quickly became evident that it was best to keep the number of individual wires as low as possible and find clever ways to fit more information onto them.

This requires more ingenuity than you might think. Wires have never been perfectly transparent carriers of data; they have always degraded the information put into them. In general, this gets worse as the wire gets longer, and so as the early telegraph networks spanned greater distances, the people building them had to edge away from the seat-of-the-pants engineering practices that, applied in another field, gave us so many boiler explosions, and toward the more scientific approach that is the standard of practice today.

Still, telegraphy, like many other forms of engineering, retained a certain barnyard, improvised quality until the Year of Our Lord 1858, when the terrifyingly high financial stakes and shockingly formidable technical challenges of the first transatlantic submarine cable brought certain long-simmering conflicts to a rolling boil, incarnated the old and new approaches in the persons of Dr. Wildman Whitehouse and Professor William Thomson, respectively, and brought the conflict between them into the highest possible relief in the form of an inquiry and a scandal that rocked the Victorian world. Thomson came out on top, with a new title and name—Lord Kelvin.

Everything that has occurred in Silicon Valley in the last couple of decades also occurred in the 1850s. Anyone who thinks that wild-ass high-tech venture capitalism is a late-20th-century California phenomenon needs to read about the maniacs who built the first transatlantic cable projects (I recommend Arthur C. Clarke's book *How the World Was One*). The only things that have changed since then are that the stakes have gotten smaller, the process more bureaucratized, and the personalities less interesting.

Those early cables were eventually made to work, albeit not without founding whole new fields of scientific inquiry and generating many lucrative patents. Undersea cables, and long-distance communications in general, became the highest of high tech, with many of the same connotations as rocket science or nuclear physics or brain surgery would acquire in later decades. Some countries and companies (the distinction between countries and companies is hazy in the telco world) became very good at it, and some didn't. AT&T acquired a dominance of the field that largely continues to this day and is only now being seriously challenged by a project called FLAG: the Fiberoptic Link Around the Globe.

IN WHICH THE HACKER TOURIST ENCOUNTERS: PENANG, A MICROCOSM OF THE INTERNET. RUBBER, PENANG'S CHIEF COMMODITY, AND ITS MANY USES: PROTECTING WIRES FROM THE ELEMENTS AND CONCUPISCENT WANDERERS FROM HARMFUL DNA. ADVANTAGES OF CHASTITY, BOTH FOR HACKER TOURISTS AND FOR CABLE LAYERS. BIZARRE SPECTACLES IN THE JUNGLES OF SOUTHERN THAILAND. FLAG, ITS ORIGINS AND ITS ENEMIES.

5° 241 24.932' N, 100° 241 19.748' E City of George Town, Island of Penang, Malaysia

FLAG, a fiber-optic cable now being built from England to Japan, is a skinny little cuss (about an inch in diameter), but it is 28,000 kilometers long, which is long even compared to really big things like the planet Earth. When it is finished in September 1997, it arguably will be the longest engineering project in history. Writing about it necessitates a lot of banging around through meatspace. Over the course of two months, photographer Alex Tehrani and I hit six countries and four continents trying to get a grip on this longest, fastest, mother of all wires. I took a GPS receiver with me so that I could have at least a general idea of where the hell we were. It gave me the above reading in front of a Chinese temple around the corner from the Shangri-La Hotel in Penang, Malaysia, which was only one of 100 peculiar spots around the globe where I suddenly pulled up short and asked myself, "What the hell am I doing here?"

You might well ask yourself the same question before diving into an article as long as this one. The answer is that we all depend heavily on wires, but we hardly ever think about them. Before learning about FLAG, I knew that data packets could get from America to Asia or the Middle East, but I had no idea how. I knew that it had something to do with wires across the bottom of the ocean, but I didn't know how many of those wires existed, how they got there, who controlled them, or how many bits they could carry.

According to legend, in 1876 the first sounds transmitted down a wire were Alexander Graham Bell saying "Mr. Watson, come here. I want you." Compared with Morse's "What hath God wrought!" this is disappointingly banal—as if Neil Armstrong, setting foot on the moon, had uttered the words: "Buzz, could you toss me that rock hammer?" It's as though during the 32 years following Morse's message, people had become inured to the amazing powers of wire.

Today, another 120 years later, we take wires completely for granted. This is most unwise. People who use the Internet (or for that matter, who make long-distance phone calls) but who don't know about wires are just like the millions of complacent motorists who pump gasoline into their cars without ever considering where it came from or how it found its way to the corner gas station. That works only until the political situation in the Middle East gets all screwed up, or an oil tanker runs aground on a wildlife refuge. In the same way, it behooves wired people to know a few things about wires—how they work, where they lie, who owns them, and what sorts of business deals and political machinations bring them into being.

In the hopes of learning more about the modern business of really, really long wires, we spent much of the summer of 1996 in pursuits such as: being arrested by toothless, shotgun-toting Egyptian cops; getting pushed around by a drunken smuggler queen on a Thai train; vaulting over rustic gates to take emergency shits in isolated fields; being kept awake by groovy Eurotrash backpackers singing songs; blowing Saharan dust out of cameras; scraping equatorial mold out of fountain pens; stuffing faded banknotes into the palms of Egyptian service-industry professionals; trying to persuade non-English-speaking taxi drivers that we really did want to visit the beach even though it was pouring rain; and laundering clothes by showering in them. We still missed more than half the countries FLAG touches.

Our method was not exactly journalism nor tourism in the normal sense but what might be thought of as a new field of human endeavor called hacker tourism: travel to exotic locations in search of sights and sensations that only would be of interest to a geek.

I will introduce sections with readings from my trusty GPS in case other hacker tourists would like to leap over the same rustic gates or get rained on at the same beaches.

5° 26.325' N, 100° 17.417' E Penang Botanical Gardens

Penang, one of the first sites visited by this hacker tourist partly because of its little-known historical importance to wires, lies just off the west coast of the Malay Peninsula. The British acquired it from the local sultan in the late 1700s, built a pathetic fort above the harbor, and named it, appropriately, after the hapless General Cornwallis. They set up a couple of churches and established the kernel of a judicial system. A vigorous market grew up around them. A few kilometers away, they built a botanical garden.

This seems like an odd set of priorities to us today. But gardens were not mere decorations to the British—they were strategic installations.

The headquarters was Kew Gardens outside of London. Penang was one of the forward outposts, and it became incomparably more important than the nearby fort. In 1876, 70,000 seeds of the rubber tree, painstakingly collected by botanists in the Amazon rain forest, were brought to Kew Gardens and planted in a greenhouse. About 2,800 of them germinated and were shipped to the botanical gardens in Sri Lanka and Penang, where they propagated explosively and were used to establish rubber plantations.

Most of these plantations were on the neighboring Malay Peninsula, a lumpy, bony tentacle of land that stretches for 1,000 miles from Bangkok in the north to Singapore in the south, where it grazes the equator. The landscape is a stalemate between, on one hand, the devastatingly powerful erosive forces of continual tropical rainstorms and dense plant life, and, on the other hand, some really, really hard rocks. Anything with the least propensity to be eroded did so a long time ago and turned into a paddy. What's left are ridges of stone that rise almost vertically from the landscape and are still mostly covered with rain forest, notwithstanding efforts by the locals to cut it all down. The flat stuff is all used for something—coconuts, date palms, banana trees, and above all, rubber.

Until artificial rubber was invented by the colony-impaired Germans, no modern economy could exist without the natural stuff. All of the important powers had tropical colonies where rubber was produced. For the Netherlands, it was Indonesia; for France, it was

Indochina; for the British, it was what they then called Malaya, as well as many other places.

Without rubber and another kind of tree resin called gutta-percha, it would not have been possible to wire the world. Early telegraph lines were just naked conductors strung from pole to pole, but this worked poorly, especially in wet conditions, so some kind of flexible but durable insulation was needed. After much trial and error, rubber became the standard for terrestrial and aerial wires while gutta-percha (a natural gum also derived from a tree grown in Malaya) was used for submarine cables. Gutta-percha is humble-looking stuff, a nondescript brown crud that surrounds the inner core of old submarine cables to a thickness of perhaps 1 centimeter, but it was a wonder material back in those days, and the longer it remained immersed in salt water, the better it got.

So far, it was all according to the general plan that the British had in mind: find some useful DNA in the Americas, stockpile it at Kew Gardens, propagate it to other botanical gardens around the world, make money off the proceeds, and grow the economy. Modern-day Penang, however, is a good example of the notion of unintended consequences.

As soon as the British had established the rule of law in Penang, various kinds of Chinese people began to move in and establish businesses. Most of them were Hokkien Chinese from north of Hong Kong, though Cantonese, Hakka, and other groups also settled there. Likewise, Tamils and Sikhs came from across the Bay of Bengal. As rubber trees began to take over the countryside, a common arrangement was for Chinese immigrants to establish rubber plantations and hire Indian immigrants (as well as Malays) as laborers.

The British involvement, then, was more catalytic than anything else. They didn't own the rubber plantations. They merely bought the rubber on an open market from Chinese brokers who in turn bought it from producers of various ethnicities. The market was just a few square blocks of George Town where British law was enforced, i.e.

where businessmen could rely on a few basics like property rights, contracts, and a currency.

During and after World War II, the British lost what presence they had here. Penang fell to the Japanese and became a base for German U-Boats patrolling the Indian Ocean. Later, there was a somewhat messy transition to independence involving a communist insurrection and a war with Indonesia. Today, Malaysia is one of Asia's economic supernovas and evidently has decided that it will be second to none when it comes to the Internet. They are furiously wiring up the place and have established JARING, which is the Malaysian Internet (this word is a somewhat tortured English acronym that happens to spell out the Malay word for the Net).

If you have a look at JARING's homepage *(www.jaring.my/jaring)*, you will be confronted by a link that will take you to a page reciting Malaysia's censorship laws, which, like most censorship laws, are ridiculously vague and hence sort of creepy and yet, in the context of the Internet, totally unworkable.

In a way, the architects of JARING are trying to run the Kew Gardens experiment all over again. By adopting the Internet protocol for their national information infrastructure, they have copied the same DNA that, planted in the deregulated telecom environment of the United States, has grown like some unstoppable exotic weed. Now they are trying to raise the same plant inside a hothouse (because they want it to flourish) but in a pot (because they don't want it to escape into the wild).

They seem to have misunderstood both their own history and that of the Internet, which run strangely parallel. Today the streets of George Town, Penang's main city, are so vivid, crowded, and intensely multicultural that by comparison they make New York City look like Colonial Williamsburg. Every block has a mosque or Hindu temple or Buddhist shrine or Christian church. You can get any kind of food, hear any language. The place is thronged, but it's affluent, and it works. It's a lot like the Internet.

Both Penang and the Internet were established basically for strategic military reasons. In both cases, what was built by the military was merely a kernel for a much vaster phenomenon that came along later. This kernel was really nothing more than a protocol, a set of rules. If you wanted to follow those rules, you could participate, otherwise you were free to go elsewhere. Because the protocol laid down a standard way for people to interact, which was clearly set out and could be understood by anyone, it attracted smart, adaptable, ambitious people from all over the place, and at a certain point it flew completely out of control and turned into something that no one had ever envisioned: something thriving, colorful, wildly diverse, essentially peaceful, and plagued only by the congestion of its own success.

JARING's link to the global Internet is over an undersea cable that connects it to the United States. This is typical of many Southeast Asian countries, which are far better connected to the US than they are to one another. But in late June of 1996, a barge called the *Elbe* appeared off the coast of Penang. Divers and boats came ashore, braving an infestation of sea snakes, and floated in a segment of armored cable that will become Malaysia's link to FLAG. The capacity of that cable is theoretically some 5.3 Gbps. Much of this will be used for telephone and other non-Internet purposes, but it can't help but serve as a major floodgate between JARING, the censored pseudo-Internet of Malaysia, and the rest of the Net. After that, it will be interesting to see how long JARING remains confined to its pot.

FLAG FACTS

The FLAG system, that mother of all wires, starts at Porthcurno, England, and proceeds to Estepona, Spain; through the Strait of Gibraltar to Palermo, Sicily; across the Mediterranean to Alexandria and Port Said, Egypt; overland from those two cities to Suez, Egypt; down the Gulf of Suez and the Red Sea, with a potential branching unit to Jedda, Saudia Arabia; around the Arabian Peninsula to Dubai, site of the FLAG Network Operations Center; across the Indian Ocean to Bombay; around the tip of India and across the Bay of Bengal and the Andaman Sea to Ban Pak Bara, Thailand, with a branch down to Penang, Malaysia; overland across Thailand to Songkhla; up through the South China Sea to Lan Tao Island in Hong Kong; up the coast of China to a branch in the East China Sea where one fork goes to Shanghai and the other to Koje-do Island in Korea, and finally to two separate landings in Japan—Ninomiya and Miura, which are owned by rival carriers.

Phone company people tend to think (and do business) in terms of circuits. Hacker tourists, by contrast, tend to think in terms of bits per second. Converting between these two units of measurements is simple: on any modern phone system, the conversations are transmitted digitally, and the standard bit rate that is used for this purpose is 64 kbps. A circuit, then, in telephony jargon, amounts to a datastream of 64 kbps.

Copper submarine cables of only a few decades ago could carry only a few dozen circuits—say, about 2,500 kbps total. The first generation of optical-fiber cables, by contrast, carries more than 1,000 times as much data—280 Mbps of data per fiber pair. (Fibers always come in pairs. This practice seems obvious to a telephony person, who is in the business of setting up symmetrical two-way circuits, but makes no particular sense to a hacker tourist who tends to think in terms of one-way packet transmission. The split between these two ways of thinking runs very deep and accounts for much tumult in the telecom world, as will be explained later.) The second generation of optical-fiber cables carries 560 Mbps per fiber pair. FLAG and other third-generation systems will carry 5.3 Gbps per pair. Or, in the system of units typically used by phone company people, they will carry 60,000 circuits on each fiber pair.

If you multiply 60,000 circuits times 64 kbps per circuit, you get a bit rate of only 3.84 Gbps, which leaves 1.46 Gbps unaccounted for. This bandwidth is devoted to various kinds of overhead, such as frame headers and error correction. The FLAG cable contains two sets of fiber pairs, and so its theoretical maximum capacity is 120,000 circuits, or (not counting the overhead) just under 8 Gbps of actual throughput.

These numbers really knock 'em dead in the phone industry. To the hacker tourist, or anyone who spends much time messing around with computer networks, they seem distinctly underwhelming. All this trouble and expense for a measly 8 Gbps? You've got to be kidding! Again, it comes down to a radical difference in perspective between telephony people and Internet people.

In defense of telephony people, it must be pointed out that they are the ones who really know the score when it comes to sending bits across oceans. Netheads have heard so much puffery about the robust nature of the Internet and its amazing ability to route around obstacles that they frequently have a grossly inflated conception of how many routes packets can take between continents and how much bandwidth those routes can carry. As of this writing, I have learned that nearly the entire state of Minnesota was recently cut off from the Internet for 13 hours because it had only one primary connection to the global Net, and that link went down. If Minnesota, of all places, is so vulnerable, one can imagine how tenuous many international links must be.

Douglas Barnes, an Oakland-based hacker and cypherpunk, looked into this issue a couple of years ago when, inspired by Bruce Sterling's *Islands in the Net*, he was doing background research on a project to set up a data haven in the Caribbean. "I found out that the idea of the Internet as a highly distributed, redundant global communications system is a myth," he discovered. "Virtually all communications between countries take place through a very small number of bottlenecks, and the available bandwidth simply isn't that great." And he cautions: "Even outfits like FLAG don't really grok the Internet. The undersized cables they are running reflect their myopic outlook."

So the bad news is that the capacity of modern undersea cables like FLAG isn't very impressive by Internet standards, but the slightly better news is that such cables are much better than what we have now. Here's how they work: Signals are transmitted down the fiber as modulated laser light with a wavelength of 1,558 nanometers (nm), which is in the infrared range. These signals begin to fade after they have traveled a certain distance, so it's necessary to build amplifiers into the cable every so often. In the case of FLAG, the spacing of these amplifiers ranges from 45 to 85 kilometers. They work on a strikingly simple and elegant principle. Each amplifier contains an approximately 10-meter-long piece of special fiber that has been doped with erbium ions, making it capable of functioning as a laser medium. A separate semiconductor laser built into the amplifier generates powerful light at 1,480 nm—close to the same frequency as the signal beam, but not close enough to interfere with it. This light, directed into the doped fiber, pumps the electrons orbiting around those erbium ions up to a higher energy level.

The signal coming down the FLAG cable passes through the doped fiber and causes it to lase, i.e., the excited electrons drop back down to a lower energy level, emitting light that is coherent with the incoming signal—which is to say that it is an exact copy of the incoming signal, except more powerful.

The amplifiers need power—up to 10,000 volts DC, at 0.9 amperes. Since public 10,000-volt outlets are few and far between on the bottom of the ocean, this power must be delivered down the same cable that carries the fibers. The cable, therefore, consists of an inner core of four optical fibers, coated with plastic jackets of different colors so that the people at opposite ends can tell which is which, plus a thin copper wire that is used for test purposes. The total thickness of these elements taken together is comparable to a pencil lead; they are contained within a transparent plastic tube. Surrounding this tube is a sheath consisting of three steel segments designed so that they interlock and form a circular jacket. Around that is a layer of about 20 steel "strength wires"—each perhaps 2 mm in diameter—

that wrap around the core in a steep helix. Around the strength wires goes a copper tube that serves as the conductor for the 10,000-volt power feed. Only one conductor is needed because the ocean serves as the ground wire. This tube also is watertight and so performs the additional function of protecting the cable's innards. It then is surrounded by polyethylene insulation to a total thickness of about an inch. To protect it from the rigors of shipment and laying, the entire cable is clothed in good old-fashioned tarred jute, although jute nowadays is made from plastic, not hemp.

This suffices for the deep-sea portions of the cable. In shallower waters, additional layers of protection are laid on, beginning with a steel antishark jacket. As the shore is approached, various other layers of steel armoring wires are added.

This more or less describes how all submarine cables are being made as of 1996. Only a few companies in the world know how to make cables like this: AT&T Submarine Systems International (AT&T-SSI) in the US, Alcatel in France, and KDD Submarine Cable Systems (KDD-SCS) in Japan, among others. AT&T-SSI and KDD-SCS frequently work together on large projects and are responsible for FLAG. Alcatel, in classic French fasion, likes to go it alone.

This basic technology will, by the end of the century, be carrying most of the information between continents. Copper-based coaxial cable systems are still in operation in many places around the world, but all of them will have reached the end of their practical lifetimes within a few years. Even if they still function, they are not worth the trouble it takes to operate them. TPC–1 (Trans Pacific Cable #1), which connected Japan to Guam and hence to the United States in 1964, is still in perfect working order, but so commercially worthless that it has been turned over to a team at Tokyo University, which is using it to carry out seismic research. The capacity of such cables is so tiny that modern fiber cables could absorb all of their traffic with barely a hiccup if the right switches and routers were in place. Likewise, satellites have failed to match some of the latest leaps in fiber capacity and can no longer compete with submarine cables, at least until such time as low-flying constellations such as Iridium and Teledesic begin operating.

Within the next few years, several huge third-generational optical fiber systems will be coming online: not only FLAG but a FLAG competitor called SEA-ME-WE 3 (Southeast Asia-Middle East-Western Europe #3); TPC–5 (Trans-Pacific Cable #5); APCN (Asia-Pacific Cable Network), which is a web of cables interconnecting Japan, Korea, Hong Kong, Taiwan, Malaysia, Thailand, Indonesia, Singapore, Australia, and the Philippines; and the latest TAT (Trans-atlantic) cable. So FLAG is part of a trend that will soon bring about a vast increase in intercontinental bandwidth.

What is unusual about FLAG is not its length (although it will be the longest cable ever constructed) or its technology (which is shared by other cables) but how it came into existence. But that's a business question which will be dealt with later. First, the hacker tourist is going to travel a short distance up the Malay Peninsula to southern Thailand, one of the two places where FLAG passes overland. On a world map this looks about as difficult as throwing an extension cord over a sandbar, but when you actually get there, it turns out to be a colossal project

$7°$ 3.467' N, 100° 22.489' E FLAG Manhole production site, southern Thailand

Large portions of this section were written in a hotel in Ban Hat Yai, Thailand, which is one of the information-transfer capitals of the planet regardless of whether you think of information transfer as bits propagating down an optical fiber, profound and complex religious faiths being transmitted down through countless generations, or genetic material being interchanged between consenting adults. Male travelers approaching Ban Hat Yai will have a difficult time convincing travel agents, railway conductors, and taxi drivers that they are coming only to look at a big fat wire, but the hacker tourist must get used to being misunderstood.

We stayed in a hotel with all the glossy accoutrements of an Asian business center plus a few perks such as partially used jumbo condom packages squirreled away on closet shelves, disconcertingly huge love marks on the sofas, and extraordinarily long, fine, black hairs all over the bathroom. While writing, I sat before a picture window looking out over a fine view of: a well-maintained but completely empty swimming pool, a green Carlsberg Beer billboard written in Thai script, an industrial-scale whorehouse catering to Japanese "businessmen," a rather fine Buddhist temple complex, and, behind that, a district of brand-new high-rise hotels built to cater to the bur-geoning information-transfer industry, almost none of which has anything to do with bits and bytes. Tropical storms rolled through, lightning flashed, I sucked down European beers from the minibar and tried to cope with a bad case of information overload. FLAG is a huge project, bigger and more complicated than many wars, and to visit even chunks of this cable operation is to be floored by it.

We first met Jim Daily and Alan Wall underneath that big Carls-berg sign, sitting out in a late-afternoon rainstorm under an um-brella, having a couple of beers—"the only *ferangs* here," as Wall told me on the phone, using the local term for foreign devil. Daily is American, 2 meters tall, blond, blue-eyed, khaki-and-polo-shirted, gregarious, absolutely plain-spoken, and almost always seems to be having a great time. Wall is English, shorter, dark-haired, impec-cably suited, cagey, reticent, and dry. Both are in their 50s. It is of some significance to this story that, at the end of the day, these two men unwind by sitting out in the rain and hoisting a beer, paying no attention whatsoever to the industrial-scale whorehouse next door. Both of them have seen many young Western men arrive here on business missions and completely lose control of their sphincters and become impediments to any kind of organized activity. Daily hired Wall because, like Daily, he is a stable family man who has his act together. They are the very definition of a complementary relationship, and they seem to be making excellent progress toward their goal, which is to run two really expensive wires across the Malay Peninsula.

Since these two, and many of the others we will meet on this journey, have much in common with one another, this is as good a place as any to write a general description. They tend to come from the US or the British Commonwealth countries but spend very little time living there. They are cheerful and outgoing, rudely humorous, and frequently have long-term marriages to adaptable wives. They tend to be absolutely straight shooters even when they are talking to a hacker tourist about whom they know nothing. Their openness would probably be career suicide in the atmosphere of Byzantine court-eunuch intrigue that is public life in the United States today. On the other hand, if I had an unlimited amount of money and woke up tomorrow morning with a burning desire to see a 2,000-hole golf course erected on the surface of Mars, I would probably call men like Daily and Wall, do a handshake deal with them, send them a blank check, and not worry about it.

Daily works out of Bangkok, the place where banks are headquartered, contracts are written, and 50-ton cranes are to be had. Alan "the ferang" Wall lives in Ban Hat Yai, the center of the FLAG operation in Thailand, cruising the cable routes a couple of times a week, materializing unpredictably in the heart of the tropical jungle in a perfectly tailored dark suit to inspect, among other things, FLAG's chain of manhole-making villages.

There were seven of these in existence during the summer of 1996, all lying along one of the two highways that run across the isthmus between the Andaman and the South China Seas. These highways, incidentally, are lined with utility poles carrying both power and communications wires. The tops of the poles are guarded by conical baskets about halfway up. The baskets prevent rats from scampering up the poles to chew away the tasty insulation on the wires and poisonous snakes from slithering up to sun themselves on the crossbars, a practice that has been known to cause morale problems among line workers.

The manhole-making village we are visiting on this fine, steamy summer day has a population of some 130 workers plus an unknown number of children. The village was founded in the shade of an old, mature rubber plantation. Along the highway are piles of construction materials deposited by trucks: bundles of half-inch rebar, piles of sand and gravel. At one end of the clearing is a double row of shelters made from shiny new corrugated metal nailed over wooden frames, where the men, women, and children of the village live. On the end of this is an open-air office under a lean-to roof, equipped with a whiteboard—just like any self-respecting high tech company. Chickens strut around flapping their wings uselessly, looking for stuff to peck out of the ground.

When the day begins, the children are bused off to school, and the men and women go to work. The women cut the rebar to length using an electric chop saw. The bars are laid out on planks with rows of nails sticking out of them to form simple templates. Then the pieces of rebar are wired together to create cages perhaps 2 meters high and 1.5 meters on a side. Then the carpenters go to work, lining the cage inside and out with wooden planks. Finally, 13 metric tons of cement are poured into the forms created by the planks. When the planks are taken away, the result is a hollow, concrete obelisk with a cylindrical collar projecting from the top, with an iron manhole cover set into it. Making a manhole takes three weeks.

Meanwhile, along the highway, trenches are being dug—quickly scooped out of the lowland soil with a backhoe, or, in the mountains, laboriously jackhammered into solid rock. A 50-ton crane comes to the village, picks up one manhole at a time using lifting loops that the villagers built into its top, and sets it on a flatbed truck that transports it to one of the wider excavations that are spaced along the trench at intervals of 300 to 700 meters. The manholes will allow workers to climb down to the level of the buried cable, which will stretch through a conduit running under the ground between the manholes.

The crane lowers the manhole into the excavation. A couple of hard-hatted workers get down there with it and push it this way and that, getting it lined up, while other workers up on the edge of the pit help out by shoving on it with a big stick. Finally it settles gingerly into place, atop its prepoured pad. The foreman clambers in, takes a transparent green disposable lighter from his pocket, and sets it down sideways on the top of the manhole. The liquid butane inside the lighter serves as a fluid level, verifying that the manhole is correctly positioned.

With a few more hours' work, the conduits have been mated with the tubes built into the walls of the manhole and the surrounding excavation filled in so that nothing is left except some disturbed earth and a manhole cover labeled CAT: Communications Authority of Thailand. The eventual result of all this work will be two separate chains of manholes (931 of them all told) running parallel to two different highways, each chain joined by twin lengths of conduit—one conduit for FLAG and one for CAT.

Farther west, another crew is at work, burdened with three enormous metal spools carrying flexible black plastic conduit having an inside diameter of an inch. The three spools are set up on stands near a manhole, the three ducts brought together and tied into a neat bundle by workers using colorful plastic twine. Meanwhile, others down in the manhole are wrestling with the world's most powerful peashooter: a massive metal pipe with a screw jack on its butt end. The muzzle of the device is inserted into one of the conduits on the manhole wall and the screw jack is tightened against the opposite wall to hold it horizontal. Next the peashooter is loaded: a big round sponge with a rope tied to it is inserted into an opening on its side. The rope comes off a long spool. Finally, a hefty air compressor is fired up above ground and its outlet tube thrown down into the manhole and patched into a valve on this pipe. When the valve is opened, compressed air floods the pipe behind the round sponge, which shoots forward like a bullet in a gun barrel, pulling the rope behind it and causing the reel to spin wildly like deep-sea fishing tackle that has hooked a big tuna.

"Next manhole! Next manhole!" cries the foreman excitedly, and pedestrians, bicyclists, motor scooters, and (if inspectors or hacker tourists are present) cars parade down the highway, veering around water buffaloes and goats and chickens to the next manhole, some half a kilometer away, where a torrent of water, driven before the sponge, is blasting out of a conduit and slamming into the opposite wall. One length of the conduit can hold some 5 cubic meters of water, and the sponge, ramming down the tube like a piston, forces all of it out. Finally the sponge pops out of the hole like a pea from a pea-shooter, bringing the rope with it. The rope is used to pull through a thicker rope, which is finally connected to the triple bundle of thin duct at one end and to a pulling motor at the other. This pulling motor is a slowly turning drum with several turns of rope around it.

Now the work gets harder: at the manhole with the reels, some workers bundle and tie the ducts as they unroll while others, down in the hole, bend them around a difficult curve and keep them feeding smoothly into the conduit. At the other end, a man works with the puller, keeping the tension constant and remaining alert for trouble. Back at the reels, the thin duct occasionally gets wedged between loose turns on the reel, and everything has to be stopped. Usually this is communicated to the puller via walkie-talkie, but when the afternoon rains hit, the walkie-talkies don't work as well, and a messenger has to buzz back and forth on a motor scooter. But eventually the triple inner duct is pulled through both of the conduits, and the whole process can begin again on the next segment.

Daily and Wall preside over this operation, which is Western at the top and pure Thai at the ground level, with a gradual shading of cultures in between. FLAG has dealings in many countries, and the arrangement is different in each one. Here, the top level is a 50–50 partnership between FLAG and Thailand's CAT. They bid the project out to two different large contractors, each of whom hired subcontractors with particular specialties who work through sub-sub-contractors who hire the workers, get them to the site, and make things happen. The incentives are shaped at each level so that the contractors will get the job done without having to be micromanaged, and the roads seem to be crawling with inspectors representing various levels of the project who make sure that the work is being done according to spec (at the height of this operation, 50 percent of the traffic on some of these roads was FLAG-related).

The top-level contracts are completely formalized with detailed specifications, bid bonds, and so on, and business at this level is done in English and in air-conditioned offices. But by the time you get to the bottom layer, work is being done by people who, although presumably just as intelligent as the big shots, are fluent only in Thai and not especially literate in any language, running around in rubber flip-flops, doing business on a handshake, pulling wads of bills out of their pockets when necessary to pay for some supplies or get drinks brought in. Consequently, the way in which the work is performed bears no resemblance whatsoever to the way it would be done in the United States or any other developed country. It is done the Thai way.

Not one but two entirely separate pairs of conduits are being created in this fashion. Both of them run from the idyllic sandy beach of Ban Pak Bara on the west to the paradisiacal sandy beach of Songkhla on the east—both of them are constructed in the same way, to the same specifications. Both of them run along highways. The southern route takes the obvious path, paralleling a road that runs in a relatively straight line between the two endpoints for 170 kilometers. But the other route jogs sharply northward just out of Ban Pak Bara, runs up the coast for some distance, turns east, and climbs up over the bony spine of the peninsula, then turns south again and finally reaches Songkhla after meandering for some 270 kilometers. Unlike the southern route, which passes almost exclusively over table-flat paddy land, easily excavated with a backhoe, the northern route goes for many kilometers over solid rock, which must be trenched with jackhammers and other heavy artillery, filled with galvanized steel conduit, and then backfilled with gravel and concrete.

This raises questions. The questions turn out to have interesting answers. I'll summarize them first and then go into detail.

Q: Why bother running two widely separated routes over the Malay Peninsula?

A: Because Thailand, like everywhere else in the world, is full of idiots with backhoes.

Q: Isn't that a pain in the ass?

A: You have no idea.

Q: Why not just go south around Singapore and keep the cable in the water, then?

A: Because Singapore is controlled by the enemy.

Q: Who is the enemy?

A: FLAG's enemies are legion.

The reason for the difficult northern route is FLAG's pursuit of diversity, which in this case is not a politically correct buzzword (though FLAG also has plenty of that kind of diversity) but refers to the principle that one should have multiple, redundant paths to make the system more robust. Diversity is not needed in the deep ocean, but land crossings are viewed as considerably more risky. So FLAG decided, early on, to lay two independent cables on two different routes, instead of one.

The indefatigable Jim Daily, along with his redoubtable inspector Ruzee, drove us along every kilometer of both of these routes over the course of a day and a half. "Let me ask you a naïve question," I said to him, once I got a load of the big rock ridge he was getting ready to cut a trench through. "Why not just put one cable on one side of that southern highway and another cable on the opposite side?" I found it hard to imagine a backhoe cutting through both sides of the highway at once.

"They just wanted to be sure that there was no conceivable disaster that could wipe out both routes at the same time," he shrugged.

FLAG has envisioned every possible paranoid disaster scenario that could lead to a failure of a cable segment and has laid action plans that will be implemented if this should happen. For example, it has made deals with its competitors so that it can buy capacity from them, if it has to, while it repairs a break (likewise, the competitors might reserve capacity from FLAG for the same reason). Despite all this, FLAG is saying in this case: "We are going to cut a trench across a 50-mile-wide piece of rock because we think it will make our cable infinitesimally more reliable." Essentially, they have to do it, because otherwise no one will entrust valuable bits to their cable system.

Why didn't they keep it in the water? Opinions vary on this: pro-FLAG people argue that the Straits, with all of their ship traffic, are a relatively hazardous place to put a submarine cable and that a terrestrial crossing of the Malay Peninsula is a tactical masterstroke. FLAG skeptics will tell you that the terrestrial crossing is a necessity imposed on them because Singapore Telecom made the decision that they didn't want to be connected to FLAG.

Instead, Singapore Telecom and France Telecom have been promoting SEA-ME-WE 3, that Southeast Asia-Middle East-Western Europe 3 cable, a system whose target date is 1999, two years later than FLAG. SEA-ME-WE 1 and 2 run from France to Singapore and 3 was originally planned to cover the same territory, but now its organizers have gotten other telecoms, such as British Telecom, involved. They hope that SEA-ME-WE 3 will continue north from Singapore as far as Japan, and north from France to Great Britain, covering generally the same route as FLAG. FLAG and SEA-ME-WE 3 are, therefore, direct competitors.

The competition is not just between two different wires. It is a competition between two entirely different systems of doing business, two entirely different visions of how the telecommunications industry should work. It is a competition, also, between AT&T (the juggernaut of the field, and the power behind most telecom-backed systems) and Nynex (the Baby Bell with an Oedipus complex and the power behind FLAG). Nynex and AT&T have their offices a short distance from each other in Manhattan, but the war between them is being fought in trenches in Thailand, glass office towers in Tokyo, and dusty government ministries in Egypt.

THE ORIGIN OF FLAG

Kessler Marketing Intelligence Corp. (KMI) is a Newport, Rhode Island, company that has developed a specialty in tracking the worldwide submarine cable system. This is not a trivial job, since there are at least 320 cable systems in operation around the world, with old ones being retired and new ones being laid all the time. KMI makes money from this by selling a document titled "Worldwide Summary of Fiberoptic Submarine Systems" that will set you back about US$4,500 but that is a must-read for anyone wanting to operate in that business. Compiling and maintaining this document gives a rare Olympian perspective on the world communications system.

In the late 1980s, as KMI looked at the cables then in existence and the systems that were slated for the next few years, they noticed an almost monstrous imbalance.

The United States would, by the late 1990s, be massively connected to Europe by some 200,000 circuits across the Atlantic, and just as massively connected to Asia by a roughly equal number of circuits across the Pacific. But between Europe and Asia there would be fewer than 20,000 circuits.

Cables have always been financed and built by telecoms, which until very recently have always been government-backed monopolies. In the business, these are variously referred to as PTTs (Post, Telephone, and Telegraphs) or PTAs (Post and Telecom Authorities) or simply as "the clubs." The dominant club has long been AT&T—

especially in the years since World War II, when most of the international telecommunications system was built.

Traditionally, the way a cable system gets built is that AT&T meets with other PTTs along the proposed route to negotiate terms (although in the opinion of some informed people who don't work for AT&T, "dictate" comes closer to the truth than "negotiate"). The capital needed to construct the cable system is ponied up by the various PTTs along its route, which, consequently, end up collectively owning the cable and all of its capacity. This is a tidy enough arrangement as those telecoms traditionally "own" all of the customers within their borders and can charge them whatever it takes to pay for all of those cables. Cables built this way are now called "club cables."

Given America's postwar dominance of the world economy and AT&T's dominance of the communications system, it becomes much easier to understand the huge bandwidth imbalance that the analysts at KMI noticed. Actually, it would be surprising if this imbalance didn't exist. If the cable industry worked on anything like a free-market basis, this howling chasm in bandwidth between Europe and Asia would be an obvious opportunity for entrepreneurs. Since the system was, in fact, controlled by government monopolies, and since the biggest of those monopolies had no particular interest in building a cable that entirely bypassed its territory, nothing was likely to happen.

But then something did happen. KMI, whose entire business is founded on knowing and understanding the market, was ideally positioned, not just to be aware of this situation, but also to crunch the numbers and figure out whether it constituted a workable business opportunity. In 1989, it published a study on worldwide undersea fiber-optic systems that included some such calculations. Based on reasonable assumptions about the cost of the system, its working lifetime, and the present cost of communications on similar systems, KMI reckoned that if a state-of-the-art cable were laid from the United Kingdom to the Middle East it would pay back its investors in two to five years. Setting aside for a moment the fact that it went against all the traditions of the industry, there was no reason in principle why a privately financed cable could not be constructed to fill this demand. Investors would pool the capital, just as they would for any other kind of business venture. They would buy the cable, pay to have it installed, sell the capacity to local customers, and make money for their shareholders.

The study was read by Gulf Associates, a group of New York–based moneyed Iranian expats who are always looking for good investments. Gulf Associates checked out KMI's prefeasibility study to get an idea of what the parameters of such a system would be. Based on that, other companies, such as Dallah Al-Baraka (a Saudi investment company), Marubeni Corp. (a Tokyo trading company), and Nynex got involved. The nascent consortium paid KMI to perform a full feasibility study. Neil Tagare, the former vice president for KMI, visited 25 countries to determine their level of need for such a cable. The feasibility study was completed in late 1990 and looked favorable. The consortium grew to include the Asian Infrastructure Fund of Hong Kong and Telecom Holding Co. Ltd. of Thailand. The scope of the project grew also, extending not just to the Middle East but all the way to Tokyo.

Nynex took on the role of managing sponsor for the FLAG project. A new company called Nynex Network Systems (Bermuda) Ltd. was formed to serve as the worldwide sales representative for FLAG, and FLAG's world headquarters was sited in Bermuda. This might seem a bit peculiar given that none of the money comes from Bermuda, the cable goes nowhere near Bermuda, and Nynex is centered in the northeastern United States. But since FLAG is ultimately owned and controlled by a Bermuda company and the capacity on the cable is sold out of Bermuda, the invoices all come out of Bermuda and the money all comes into Bermuda, which by an odd coincidence happens to be a major corporate tax haven.

Nynex also has responsibility for building the FLAG cable system. One might think that a Baby Bell such as Nynex would be a perfect choice for this kind of work, but, in fact, Nynex owned none of the factories needed to manufacture cable, none of the ships needed to lay it, and not enough of the expertise needed to install it. Nynex does know a thing or two about laying and operating terrestrial cable systems—during the mid-1990s, for example, it wired large parts of the United Kingdom with a "cable television" system that is actually a generalized digital communication network. But transoceanic submarine cables were outside of its traditional realm.

On the other hand, during the early '90s, Nynex found itself stymied from competing in the United States because of regulatory hassles and began looking overseas for markets in which to expand. By the time FLAG was conceived, therefore, Nynex had begun to gain experience in the countless pitfalls of doing business in the worldwide telecommunications business, making up a little bit of AT&T's daunting lead.

FLAG's business arrangements were entirely novel. The entire FLAG concept was unfeasible unless agreements could be made with so-called landing parties in each country along the route. The landing party is the company that owns the station where the cable comes ashore and operates the equipment that patches it into the local telecommunications system. The obvious choice for such a role would be a PTT. But many PTTs were reluctant to participate, partly because this novel arrangement struck them as dubious and partly because they weren't going to end up monopolizing the cable.

Overcoming such opposition was essentially a sales job. John Mercogliano, a high-intensity New Yorker who is now vice president—Europe, Nynex Network Systems (Bermuda) Ltd., developed a sales pitch that he delivers too rapidly for any hacker tourist to write down but goes something like this: "In the old days AT&T came in, told you how much to pay, and you raised the money, assumed all of the risk, and owned the cable. But now FLAG's coming in with investors who are going to put in $600 million of their own cash and borrow a billion more without any guaranteed sales, assuming all of the risk. You buy only as much capacity on FLAG as you want, and meanwhile you have retained your capital, which you can use to upgrade your outdated local infrastructure and provide better service to your customers—now what the hell is wrong with that?"

The question hangs in the air provocatively. What the hell is wrong with it? Put this way, it seems unbeatable. But a lot of local telecoms turned FLAG down anyway—at least at first. Why?

The short answer is that I'm not allowed to tell you. The long answer requires an explanation of how a hacker tourist operates; how his methods differ from those of an actual journalist; and just how weird the global telecom business is nowadays.

Let's take the last one first. The business is so tangled that no pure competition exists. There are no Coke-versus-Pepsi dichotomies. Most of the companies mentioned in this story are actually whole families of companies, and most of those have their fingers in pies in dozens of countries all around the globe. Any two companies that compete in one arena are, at the same time, probably in bed with each other on many other levels. As badly as they might want to slag each other in the press, they dare not.

So, like those "high-ranking officials" you're always reading about in news reports from Washington, they all talk on background. Anyone who wants to write about this business will come off as either a genius with an encyclopedic brain or a pathological liar with an axe to grind—depending on the reader's point of view—because all truly interesting information is dished out strictly on background.

Perhaps a real journalist would go into Woodward-and-Bernstein mode, find a Deep Throat, and lay it all bare. But I'm not a real journalist: I'm a hacker tourist, and trying to work up an exposé on monopolistic behavior by big bad telecoms would only get in the way of what are, to me, the more interesting aspects of this story.

So I'll just say that a whole lot of important and well-informed people in the telecom business, all over the planet, are laboring under the strange impression that AT&T used its power and influence to discourage smaller telecoms in other countries from signing deals with FLAG.

In the old days, this would have prevented FLAG from ever coming into existence. But these are the new days, telecom deregulation is creeping slowly across the planet, and many PTTs now have to worry about competition. So the results of the FLAG sales pitch varied from country to country. In some places, like Singapore, FLAG never made an agreement with anyone and had to bypass the country entirely. In other places, the PTT broke ranks with AT&T and agreed to land FLAG. In others, the PTT turned it down but an upstart competitor decided to land FLAG instead, and in still others, the PTT declined at first, and then got so worried about the upstart competitor that it changed its mind and decided to land FLAG after all.

It would be very easy for you, dear reader, to underestimate what a sea change this all represents for the clubs. They are not accustomed to having to worry about competition—it doesn't come naturally to them. The typical high-ranking telecom executive is more of a government bureaucrat than a businessperson, and the entire scenario laid out above is irregular, messy, and disturbing to someone like that. A telecrat's reflex is to assume, smugly, that new carriers simply don't matter, because no matter how much financing and business acumen they may have, no matter how great the demand for their services may be, and no matter how crappy the existing service is, the old PTT still controls the cable, which is the only way to get bits out of the country. But in the FLAG era, if the customers go to another carrier, that carrier will find a way to get the needed capacity somehow—at which point it is too late for the PTT.

The local carriers, therefore, need to stop thinking globally and start thinking locally. That is, they need to leave long-range cable laying to the entrepreneurs, to assume that the bandwidth will always somehow be there, and to concentrate on upgrading the quality of their customer service—in particular, the so-called last mile, the local loop that ties customers into the Net.

By the end of 1994, FLAG's Construction and Maintenance Agreement had been signed, and the project was for real. Well before this point, it had become obvious to everyone that FLAG was going to happen in some form, so companies that initially might have been hostile began looking for ways to get in on the action. The manufacture of the cable and the repeaters had been put out to bid in 1993 and had turned into a competition between two consortia, one consisting of AT&T Submarine Systems and KDD Submarine Cable Systems, and the other formed around Alcatel and Fujitsu. The former group ended up landing the contract. So AT&T, which evidently felt threatened by the whole premise of the FLAG project and according to some people had tried to quash it, ended up with part of the contract to manufacture the cable.

IN WHICH THE HACKER TOURIST RETURNS (TEMPORARILY) TO BRITISH SOIL IN THE FAR EAST. THE (TEMPORARY) CENTER OF THE CABLE-LAYING UNIVERSE. HOISTING FLAGONS WITH THE ÉLITE CABLE-LAYING FRATERNITY AT A WATERFRONT ESTABLISHMENT. CLASSIC REPRISE OF THE ANCIENT HACKER-VERSUS-SUIT DRAMA. HISTORICAL EXPLOITS OF THE FAMOUS WILLIAM THOMSON AND THE INFAMOUS WILDMAN WHITEHOUSE. THEIR RIVALRY, CULMINATING IN THE DESTRUCTION OF THE FIRST TRANSATLANTIC CABLE. WHITEHOUSE DISGRACED, THOMSON TRANSMOGRIFIED INTO LORD KELVIN . . .

$22°$ 15.745' N, $114°$ 0.557' E Silvermine Bay, Lan Tao Island,?b Hong Kong

"Today, Lan Tao Island is the center of the cable-laying universe," says David M. Handley, a 52-year-old Southerner who, like virtually all cable-laying people, is talkative, endlessly energetic, and gives every indication of knowing exactly what he's doing. "Tomorrow, it'll be someplace else." We are chug-a-lugging large bottles of water on a public beach at Tong Fuk on the southern coast of Lan Tao, which is a relatively large (25 kilometers long) island an hour's ferry ride west of Hong Kong Island. Arrayed before us on the bay is a collection of vessels that, to a layman, wouldn't look like the center of a decent salvage yard, to say nothing of the cable-laying universe. But remember that "layman" is just a polite word for "idiot."

Closest to shore, there are a couple of junks and sampans. Mind you, these are not picturesque James Clavell junks with red sails or Pearl Buck sampans with pole-wielding peasants in conical hats. The terms are now used to describe modern, motorized vessels built vaguely along the same lines to perform roughly the same functions: a junk is a large, square-assed vessel, and a sampan is a small utility craft with an enclosed cabin. Farther out, there are two barges: slabs with cranes and boxy things on them. Finally, there are several of what Handley calls LBRBs (Little Bitty Rubber Boats) going back and forth between these vessels and the beach. Boeing hydrofoils and turbo cats scream back and forth a few miles out, ferrying passengers among various destinations around the Pearl Delta region. It's a hot day, and kids are swimming on the public beach, prudently staying within the line of red buoys marking the antishark net. Handley remarks, offhandedly, that five people have been eaten so far this year. A bulletin board, in English and Chinese, offers advice: "If schooling fish start to congregate in unusually large numbers, leave the water."

This bay is the center of the cable-laying universe because cable layers have congregated here in unusually large numbers and because of those two barges, which are a damn sight more complicated and expensive than you would ever guess from looking at them. These men (they are all men) and equipment have come from all over the world, to land not only FLAG but also, at the same time, another of those third-generation fiber-optic cables, APCN (Asia-Pacific Cable Network).

In contrast to other places we visited, virtually no local labor is being used on Lan Tao. There is hardly a Chinese face to be seen around the work site, and when you do see an Asian it tends to be either an Indonesian member of a barge crew or a Singaporean of Chinese or Indian ancestry. Most of the people here are blue-eyed and sunburned. A good half of them have accents that originate from the British Isles. The remainder are from the States (frequently Dixie), Australia, or New Zealand, with a smattering from France and Germany.

Both FLAG and APCN are just passing through Hong Kong, not terminating here, and so each has to be landed twice (one segment coming in and one segment going back out). In FLAG's case, one segment goes south to Songkhla, Thailand, and the other goes north toward Shanghai and Korea. It wouldn't be safe to land both segments in the same place, so there are two separate landing sites, with FLAG and APCN cables running side by side at each one. One of the sites is at the public beach, which is nice and sandy. The other site is a few hundred meters away on a cobble beach—a hill of rounded stones, fist- to football-sized, rising up out of the surf and making musical clinking noises as the waves smash them up and down the grade. This is a terrible place to land a cable (Handley: "If it was easy, everybody would do it!") but, as in Thailand, diversity is the ultimate trump card. Planted above the hill of cobbles is a brand-new cable station bearing the Hong Kong Telecom logo, only one of the spoils soon to be reaped by the People's Republic of China when all this reverts to its control next year.

Lan Tao Island, like most other places where cables are landed, is a peculiar area, long home to smugglers and pirates. Some 30,000 people live here, mostly concentrated around Silvermine Bay on the island's eastern end, where the ferries come in every hour or so from Hong Kong's central district, carrying both islanders and tourists. The beaches are lovely, except for the sharks, and the interior of the island is mostly unspoiled parkland, popular among hikers. Hong

Kong's new airport is being built on reclaimed land attached to the north side of the island, and a monumental chain of bridges and tunnels is being constructed to connect it with the city. Other than tourist attractions, the island hosts a few oddities such as a prison, a Trappist monastery, a village on stilts, and the world's largest outdoor bronze Buddha.

Cable trash, as these characters affectionately call themselves, shuttle back and forth between Tong Fuk and Silvermine Bay. They all stay at the same hotel and tend to spend their off hours at Papa Doc's (no relation to the Haitian dictator), a beachfront bar run by expats (British) for expats (Australians, Americans, Brits, you name it). Papa Doc's isn't just for cable layers. It also meets the exacting specifications of exhausted hacker tourists. It's the kind of joint that Humphrey Bogart would be running if he had washed ashore on Lan Tao in the mid-1990s wearing a nose ring instead of landing in Casablanca in the 1940s wearing a fedora.

One evening, after Handley and I had been buying each other drinks at Papa Doc's for a while, he raised his glass and said, "To good times and great cable laying!" This toast, while no doubt uttered with a certain amount of irony, speaks volumes about cable professionals.

For most of them, good times and great cable laying are one and the same. They make their living doing the kind of work that automatically weeds out losers. Handley, for example, was a founding member of SEAL Team 2 who spent 59 months fighting in Vietnam, laid cables for the Navy for a few more years, and has done similar work in the civilian world ever since. In addition to being an expert diver, he has a master mariner's license good up to 1,500 tons, which is not an easy thing to get or maintain. He does all his work on a laptop (he claims that it replaced 14 employees) and is as computer-literate as anyone I've known who isn't a coder.

Handley is unusual in combining all of these qualities into one person (that's why he's the boss of the Lan Tao Island operation), but the qualities are as common as tattoos and Tevas around the tables of Papa Doc's. The crews of the cable barges tend to be jacks-of-all-trades: ship's masters who also know how to dive using various types of breathing rigs or who can slam out a report on their laptops, embed a few digital images in it, and email it to the other side of the world over a satellite phone, then pick up a welding torch and go to work on the barge. If these people didn't know what they were doing, there's a good chance they would be dead by now or would have screwed up a cable lay somewhere and washed out of the industry.

Most of the ones here work on what amounts to a freelance basis, either on their own or as part of small firms. Handley, for example, is Director of Technical Services for the ITR Corporation, which, among other functions, serves as a sort of talent agency for cable-layers, matching supply of expertise to demand and facilitating contracts. Most of the divers are freelancers, hired temporarily by companies that likewise move from one job to another. The business is as close to being a pure meritocracy as anything ever gets in the real world, and it's only because these guys know they are good that they have the confidence to call themselves cable trash.

It was not always thus. Until very recently, cable-laying talent was monopolized by the clubs. This worked just fine when every cable was a club cable, created by monopolies for monopolies. In the last couple of years, however, two changes have occurred at once: FLAG, the first major privately financed cable, came along; and at the same time, many experienced cable layers began to go into business for themselves, either because of voluntary retirement or downsizing. There clearly is a synergy between these two trends.

The roster of FLAG's Tong Fuk cable lay contains around 44 people, half of whom are crew members on either the cable barge *Elbe* or the accompanying tug *Ocean East*. The rest of them are here representing various contractors involved in the project. It would be safe to assume that at least that many are working on the APCN side for a grand total of around 100.

The size of the fraternity of cable layers is estimated by Handley to be less than 500, and the number is not increasing. A majority work full time for one of the clubs. Perhaps a couple hundred of them are freelancers, though this fraction gives every indication of rising as the club employees resign and go to work as contractors, frequently doing the same work for the same company. "No one can afford to hire these folks for long periods of time," Handley says. But their pay is not exceptionally high: benefits, per diem, and expenses plus a daily rate—but a day might be anything from 0 to 24 hours of work. For a diver the rate might be $200 per day; for the master of a barge, tug, or beach $300; and for the experts running the show and repping for contractors or customers it's in the range of $300 to $400.

The arrival of a shore-landing operation at a place like Lan Tao Island must look something like this to the locals: suddenly, it is difficult to obtain hotel rooms because a plethora of small, unheard-of offshore corporations have blocked out a couple of dozen rooms for a couple hundred nights. Sunburned Anglos begin to arrive, wearing T-shirts and carrying luggage emblazoned with the logos of Alcatel, AT&T, or Cable & Wireless. They fly in from all points of the compass, speaking in Southern drawls or Australian twangs or Scottish burrs and sometimes bringing their wives or girlfriends, not infrequently Thai or Filipina. The least important of them has a laptop and a cell phone, but most have more advanced stuff like portable printers, GPS units, and that ultimate personal communications device, the satellite telephone, which works anywhere on the planet, even in the middle of the ocean, by beaming the call straight up to a satellite.

Sample conversation at Papa Doc's:

Envious hacker tourist: "How much does one of those satellite phones cost, anyway?"

Leathery, veteran cable layer: "Who gives a shit?"

Within a day or two, the cable layers have established an official haunt: preferably a place equipped with a dartboard and a few other amenities very close to the waterfront so they can keep an eye on incoming traffic. There they can get a bite to eat or a drink and pay for it on the spot so that when their satellite phones ring or when a tugboat chugs into the bay, they can immediately dash off to work. These men work and play at completely erratic and unpredictable hours. They wear shorts and sandals and T-shirts and frequently sport tattoos and hence could easily be mistaken, at a glance, for vacationing sailors. But if you can get someone to turn down the volume on the jukebox, you can overhear them learnedly discoursing on flaw propagation in the crystalline structure of boron silicate glass or on seasonal variation of currents in the Pearl River estuary, or on what a pain in the ass it is to helm a large ship through the Suez Canal. Their conversation is filled with references to places like Tunisia, Diego Garcia, the North Sea, Porthcurno, and Penang.

One day a barge appears off the cove, and there is a lot of fussing around with floats, lots of divers in the water. A backhoe digs a trench in the cobble beach. A long skinny black thing is wrestled ashore. Working almost naked in the tropical heat, the men bolt segmented pipes around it and then bury it. It is never again to be seen by human eyes. Suddenly, all of these men pay their bills and vanish. Not long afterward, the phone service gets a hell of a lot better.

On land, the tools of cable laying are the tools of civil engineers: backhoes, shovels, cranes. The job is a matter of digging a ditch, laying duct, planting manholes. The complications are sometimes geographical but mostly political. In deep water, where the majority of FLAG is located, the work is done by cable ships and has more in common with space exploration than with any terrestrial activity. These two realms could hardly be more different, and yet the transition between them—the shore landing—is completely distinct from both.

Shallow water is the most perilous part of a cable's route. Extra precautions must be taken in the transition from deep water to the beach, and these precautions get more extreme as the water gets more shallow. Between 1,000 and 3,000 meters, the cable has a single layer of armor wires (steel rods about as thick as a pencil) around it. In less than 1,000 meters of water, it has a second layer of armor around the first. In the final approach to the shoreline, this double-armored cable is contained within a massive shell of articulated cast-iron pipe, which in turn is buried under up to a meter of sand.

The articulated pipe comes in sections half a meter long, which have to be manually fit around the cable and bolted together. Each section of pipe interlocks with the ones on either end of it. The coupling is designed to bend a certain amount so that the cable can be snaked around any obstructions to its destination: the beach manhole. It will bend only so much, however, so that the cable's minimum radius of curvature will not be violated.

At the sandy beach this manual work was done out in the surf by a team of English freelance divers based out of Hong Kong. At the cobble beach, it was done in a trench by a bikini-underwear-clad Frenchman with a New Zealand passport living in Singapore, working in Hong Kong, with a Singaporean wife of Chinese descent. Drenched with sweat and rain and seawater, he wrestles with the cast-iron pipe sections in a cobblestone ditch, bolting them patiently together. A Chinese man in a suit picks his way across the cobbles toward him, carrying an oversized umbrella emblazoned with the logo of a prominent stock brokerage, followed by a minion. Although this is all happening in China, this is the first Chinese person who has appeared on the beach in a couple of days. He is an executive from the phone company, coming to inspect the work. After a stiff exchange of pleasantries with the other cable layers on the beach, he goes to the brink of the trench and begins bossing around the man with the half-pipes, who, knowing what's good for him, just keeps his mouth shut while maintaining a certain bearing and dignity beside which the executive's suit and umbrella seem pathetic and vain.

To a hacker tourist, the scene is strikingly familiar: it is the ancient hacker-versus-suit drama, enacted for the millionth time but sticking to its traditional structure as strictly as a Noh play or, for that matter, a Dilbert cartoon. Cable layers, like hackers, scorn credentials, etiquette, and nice clothes. Anyone who can do the work is part of the club. Nothing else matters. Suits are a bizarre intrusion from an irrational world. They have undeniable authority, but heaven only knows how they acquired it. This year, the suits are from Hong Kong, which means they are probably smarter than the average suit. Pretty soon the suits will be from Beijing, but Beijing doesn't know how to lay cable either, so if they ever want to get bits in or out of their country, they will have to reach an understanding with these guys.

At Tong Fuk, FLAG is encased in pipe out to a distance of some 300 meters from the beach manhole. When the divers have got all of that pipe bolted on, which will take a week or so, they will make their way down the line with a water jet that works by fluidizing the seabed beneath it, turning it into quicksand. The pipe sinks into the quicksand, which eventually compacts, leaving no trace of the buried pipe.

Beyond 300 meters, the cable must still be buried to protect it from anchors, tickler chains, and otter boards (more about this later). This is the job of the two barges we saw off Tong Fuk. One, the *Elbe*, was burying FLAG. The other was burying APCN. *Elbe* did its job in one-third the time, with one-third the crew, perhaps exemplifying the difference between FLAG's freelance-based virtual-corporation business model versus the old club model. The *Elbe* crew is German, British, Filipino, Singaporean-of-Indian-ancestry, New Zealander, and also includes a South African diver.

In the center of the barge is a tank where the cable is spooled. The thick, heavy armored cable that the *Elbe* works with is covered with a jacket of tarred jute, which gives it an old-fashioned look that belies its high tech optical-fiber innards. The tar likes to melt and stick the cable together, so each layer of cable in the tank is separated from its neighbors by wooden slats, and buckets of talc are slathered over it. The cable emerges from the open top of the tank and passes through a series of rollers that curve around, looking very much like a miniature roller-coaster track—these are built in such a way as to bend the cable through a particular trajectory without violating its minimum radius of curvature. They feed it into the top of the injector unit.

The injector is a huge steel cleaver, 7 meters high and 2 or 3 meters broad, rigged to the side of the barge so it can slide up and down and thus be jammed directly into the seabed. But instead of a cutting blade on its leading edge, it has a row of hardened-steel injector nozzles that spurt highly pressurized water, piped in from a huge pump buried in the *Elbe*'s engine room. These nozzles fluidize the seabed and thus make it possible for the giant blade to penetrate it. Along the trailing edge of the blade runs a channel for the cable so that as the blade works its way forward, the cable is gently laid into the bottom of the slit. The barge carries a set of extensions that can be bolted onto the top of the injector so it can operate in water as deep as 40 meters, burying the cable as deep as 9 meters beneath the seabed. This sufficed to lay the cable out for a distance of 10 kilometers from Tong Fuk. Later, another barge, the *Chinann*, will come to continue work out to 100 meters deep and will bury both legs of the FLAG cable for another 60 kilometers out to get them through a dangerous anchorage zone.

The *Elbe* has its own tugboat, the *Ocean East*, staffed with an Indonesian crew. Relations between the two vessels have been a bit tense because the Indonesians butchered and ate all of the *Elbe*'s laying hens, terminating the egg supply. But it all seemed to have been patched up when we were there; no one was fretting about it except for the *Elbe*'s rooster. When the *Elbe* is more than half a kilometer from shore, *Ocean East* pulls her along by means of a cable. The tug's movements are controlled from the *Elbe*'s bridge over a radio link. Closer to shore, the *Elbe* drops an anchor and then pulls itself along by winching the line in. She can get more power by using the Harbormaster thruster units mounted on each of her ends. But the main purpose of these thrusters is to provide side propulsion so the barge's movements can be finely controlled.

The nerve center of the *Elbe* is a raised, air-conditioned bridge jammed with the electronic paraphernalia characteristic of modern ships, such as a satellite phone, a fax machine, a plotter, and a Navtex machine to receive meteorological updates. Probably the most important equipment is the differential GPS system that tells the barge's operators exactly where they are with respect to the all-important Route Position List: a series of points provided by the surveyors. Their job is to connect these dots with cable. *Elbe*'s bridge normally sports four different computers all concerned with navigation and station-keeping functions. In addition to this complement, during the Tong Fuk cable lay, Dave Handley was up here with his laptop, taking down data important to FLAG, while the representatives from AT&T and Cable & Wireless were also present with their laptops compiling their own data.

Hey, wait a minute, the hacker tourist says to himself, I thought AT&T was the enemy. What's an AT&T guy doing on the bridge of the *Elbe*, side-by-side with Dave Handley?

The answer is that the telecom business is an unfathomably complicated snarl of relationships. Not only did AT&T (along with KDD) end up with the contract to supply FLAG's cable, it also ended up landing a great deal of the installation work. Not that many companies have what it takes to manage an installation of FLAG's magnitude. AT&T is one of them and Nynex isn't. So it frequently happens at FLAG job sites that AT&T will be serving as the contractor, making the local contacts and organizing the work, while FLAG's presence will be limited to one or two reps whose allegiance is to the investors and whose job it is to make sure it's all done the FLAG way, as opposed to the AT&T way. As with any other construction project from a doghouse on upward, countless decisions must be made on the site, and here they need to be made the way a group of private investors would make them—not the way a club would.

If FLAG's investors spent any time at all looking into the history of the cable-laying business, this topic must have given them a few sleepless nights. The early years of the industry were filled with decision making that can most charitably be described as colorful. In those days, there were no experienced old hands. They just made everything up as they went along, and as often as not, they got it wrong.

THOMSON AND WHITEHOUSE

As of 1861, some 17,500 kilometers of submarine cable had been laid in various places around the world, of which only about 5,000 kilometers worked. The remaining 12,500 kilometers represented a loss to their investors, and most of these lost investments were long cables such as the ones between Britain and the United States and Britain and India (3,500 and 5,600 kilometers, respectively). Understanding why long cables failed was not a trivial problem; it defeated eminent scientists like Rankine and Siemens and was solved, in the end, only by William Thomson.

In prospect, it probably looked like it was going to be easy. Insulated telegraph wires strung from pole to pole worked just as one might expect, and so, assuming that watertight insulation could be found, similar wires laid under the ocean should work just as well. The insulation was soon found in the form of gutta-percha. Very long gutta-percha-insulated wires were built. They worked fine when laid out on the factory floor and tested. But when immersed in water they worked poorly, if at all.

The problem was that water, unlike air, is an electrical conductor, which is to say that charged particles are free to move around in it. When a pulse of electrons moves down an immersed cable, it repels electrons in the surrounding seawater, creating a positively charged pulse in the water outside. These two charged regions interact with each other in such a way as to smear out the original pulse moving down the wire. The operator at the receiving end sees only a slow upward trend in electrical charge, instead of a crisp jump. If the sending operator transmitted the different pulses—the dots and dashes—too close together, they'd blur as they moved down the wire.

Unfortunately, that's not the only thing happening in that wire. Long cables act as antennae, picking up all kinds of stray currents as the rotation of the Earth, and its revolution around the sun, sweep them across magnetic fields of terrestrial and celestial origin. At the

Museum of Submarine Telegraphy in Porthcurno, Cornwall (which we'll visit later), is a graph of the so-called Earth current measured in a cable that ran from there to Harbor Grace, Newfoundland, decades ago. Over a period of some 72 hours, the graph showed a variation in the range of 100 volts. Unfortunately, the amplitude of the telegraph signal was only 70 volts. So the weak, smeared-out pulses making their way down the cable would have been almost impossible to hear above the music of the spheres.

Finally, leakage in the cable's primitive insulation was inevitable. All of these influences, added together, meant that early telegraphers could send anything they wanted into the big wire, but the only thing that showed up at the other end was noise.

These problems were known, but poorly understood, in the mid-1850s when the first transatlantic cable was being planned. They had proved troublesome but manageable in the early cables that bridged short gaps, such as between England and Ireland. No one knew, yet, what would happen in a much longer cable system. The best anyone could do, short of building one, was to make predictions.

The Victorian era was an age of superlatives and larger-than-life characters, and as far as that goes, Dr. Wildman Whitehouse fit right in: what Victoria was to monarchs, Dickens to novelists, Burton to explorers, Robert E. Lee to generals, Dr. Wildman Whitehouse was to assholes. The only 19th-century figure who even comes close to him in this department is Custer. In any case, Dr. Edward Orange Wildman Whitehouse fancied himself something of an expert on electricity. His rival was William Thomson, 10 years younger, a professor of natural philosophy at Glasgow University who was infatuated with Fourier analysis, a new and extremely powerful tool that happened to be perfectly suited to the problem of how to send electrical pulses down long submarine cables.

Wildman Whitehouse predicted that sending bits down long undersea cables was going to be easy (the degradation of the signal would be proportional to the length of the cable) and William Thomson predicted that it was going to be hard (proportional to the length of the cable squared). Naturally, they both ended up working for the same company at the same time.

Whitehouse was a medical doctor, hence working in the wrong field, and probably trailed Thomson by a good 50 or 100 IQ points. But that didn't stop Whitehouse. In 1856, he published a paper stating that Thomson's theories concerning the proposed transatlantic cable were balderdash. The two men got into a public argument, which became extremely important in 1858 when the Atlantic Telegraph Company laid such a cable from Ireland to Newfoundland: a copper core sheathed in gutta-percha and wrapped in iron wires.

This cable was, to put it mildly, a bad idea, given the state of cable science and technology at the time. The notion of copper as a conductor for electricity, as opposed to a downspout material, was still extraordinary, and it was impossible to obtain the metal in anything like a pure form. The cable was slapped together so shoddily that in some places the core could be seen poking out through its gutta-percha insulation even before it was loaded onto the cable-laying ship. But venture capitalists back then were a more rugged—not to say crazy—breed, and there can be no better evidence than that they let Wildman Whitehouse stay on as the Atlantic Telegraph Company's chief electrician long after his deficiencies had become conspicuous.

The physical process of building and laying the cable makes for a wild tale in and of itself. But to do it justice, I would have to double the length of this already herniated article. Let's just say that after lots of excitement, they put a cable in place between Ireland and Newfoundland. But for all of the reasons mentioned earlier, it hardly worked at all. Queen Victoria managed to send President Buchanan a celebratory message, but it took a whole day to send it. On a good day, the cable could carry something like one word per minute. This fact was generally hushed up, but the important people knew about it—so the pressure was on Wildman Whitehouse, whose theories were blatantly contradicted by the facts.

Whitehouse convinced himself that the solution to their troubles was brute force—send the message at extremely high voltages. To that end, he invented and patented a set of 5-foot-long induction coils capable of ramming 2,000 volts into the cable. When he hooked them up to the Ireland end of the system, he soon managed to blast a hole through the gutta-percha somewhere between there and Newfoundland, turning the entire system into useless junk.

Long before this, William Thomson had figured out, by dint of Fourier analysis, that incoming bits could be detected much faster by a more sensitive instrument. The problem was that instruments in those days had to work by physically moving things around, for example, by closing an electromagnetic relay that would sound a buzzer. Moving things around requires power, and the bits on a working transatlantic cable embodied very little power. It was difficult to make a physical object small enough to be susceptible to such ghostly traces of current.

Thomson's solution (actually, the first of several solutions) was the mirror galvanometer, which incorporated a tiny fleck of reflective material that would twist back and forth in the magnetic field created by the current in the wire. A beam of light reflecting from the fleck would swing back and forth like a searchlight, making a dim spot on a strip of white paper. An observer with good eyesight sitting in a darkened room could tell which way the current was flowing by watching which way the spot moved. Current flowing in one direction signified a Morse code dot, in the other a dash. In fact, the information that had been transmitted down the cable in the brief few weeks before Wildman Whitehouse burned it to a crisp had been detected using Thomson's mirror galvanometer—though Whitehouse denied it.

After the literal burnout of the first transatlantic cable, Wildman Whitehouse and Professor Thomson were grilled by a committee of eminent Victorians who were seriously pissed off at Whitehouse and enthralled with Thomson, even before they heard any testimony—

and they heard a lot of testimony.

Whitehouse disappeared into ignominy. Thomson ended up being knighted and later elevated to a baron by Queen Victoria. He became Lord Kelvin and eventually got an important unit of measurement, an even more important law of physics, and a refrigerator named after him.

Eight years after Whitehouse fried the first, a second transatlantic cable was built to Lord Kelvin's specifications with his patented mirror galvanometers at either end of it. He bought a 126-ton schooner yacht with the stupendous amount of money he made from his numerous cable-related patents, turned the ship into a floating luxury palace and laboratory for the invention of even more fantastically lucrative patents. He then spent the rest of his life tooling around the British Isles, Bay of Biscay, and western Mediterranean, frequently hosting Dukes and continental savants who all commented on the nerd-lord's tendency to stop in the middle of polite conversation to scrawl out long skeins of equations on whatever piece of paper happened to be handy.

Kelvin went on to design and patent other devices for extracting bits from the ends of cables, and other engineers went to work on the problem, too. By the 1920s, the chore of translating electrical pulses into letters had been largely automated. Now, of course, humans are completely out of the loop.

The number of people working in cable landing stations is probably about the same as it was in Kelvin's day. But now they are merely caretakers for machines that process bits about as fast as a billion telegraphers working in parallel.

THE HACKER TOURIST TRAVELS TO THE LAND OF THE RISING SUN. TECHNOLOGICAL WONDERS OF MODERN CABLE STATIONS. WHY UGANDANS COULD NOT PLACE

TELEPHONE CALLS TO SEATTLE. TRAWL- ERS, TICKLER CHAINS, TEREDO WORMS, AND OTHER HAZARDS TO UNDERSEA CABLES. THE IMMENSE FINANCIAL STAKES INVOLVED—WHY CABLE OWNERS DO NOT CARE FOR THE COMPANY OF FISHERMEN, AND VICE VERSA.

$35°$ 17.690' N, $139°$ 46.328' E KDD Cable Landing Station, Ninomiya, Japan

Whether they are in Thailand, Egypt, or Japan, modern cable landing stations have much in common with each other. Shortly after touching down in Tokyo, we were standing in KDD's landing station in Ninomiya, Japan. I'll describe it to you.

A surprising amount of space in the station is devoted to electrical gear. The station must not lose power, so there are two separate, redundant emergency generators. There is also likely to be a transformer to supply power to the cable system. We think of optical fibers as delicate strands consuming negligible power, but all of those repeaters, spaced every few dozen kilometers across an ocean, end up consuming a lot of juice: for a big transoceanic cable, one or two amperes at 7,000 or so volts, for a total of something like 10,000 watts. The equipment handling that power makes a hum you can feel in your bones, kicking the power out not along wires but solid copper bars suspended from the ceiling, with occasional sections of massive braided metal ribbon so they won't snap in an earthquake.

The emergency generators are hooked into a battery farm that fills a room. The batteries are constantly trickle-charged and exist simply to provide power during an emergency—after the regular power goes out but before the generators kick in. Most of the equipment in the cable station is computer gear that demands a stable temperature, so there are two separate, redundant air-conditioning plants feeding into a big system of ventilation ducts. The equipment must not get dirty or get fried by sparks from the fingers of hacker tourists, so you leave your shoes by the door and slip into plastic antistatic flip-flops. The equipment must not get smashed up in earthquakes, so the building is built like a brick shithouse.

The station is no more than a few hundred meters from a beach. Sandy beaches in out-of-the-way areas are preferred. The cable comes in under the sand until it hits a beach manhole, where it continues through underground ducts until it comes up out of the floor of the cable station into a small, well-secured room. The cable is attached to something big and strong, such as a massive steel grid bolted into the wall. Early cable technicians were sometimes startled to see their cables suddenly jerk loose from their moorings inside the station—yanking the guts out of expensive pieces of equipment—and disappear in the direction of the ocean, where a passing ship had snagged them.

From holes in the floor, the cables pass up into boxes where all the armor and insulation are stripped away from them and where the tubular power lead surrounding the core is connected to the electrical service (7,500 volts in the case of FLAG) that powers the repeaters out in the middle of the ocean. Its innards then continue, typically in some kind of overhead wiring plenum (a miniature catwalk suspended from the ceiling) into the Big Room Full of Expensive Stuff.

The Big Room Full of Expensive Stuff is at least 25 meters on a side and commonly has a floor made of removable, perforated plates covering plenums through which wires can be routed, an overhead grid of open plenums from which wires descend like jungle vines, or both. Most of the room is occupied by equipment racks arranged in parallel rows (think of the stacks at a big library). The racks are tall, well over most people's heads, and their insides are concealed and protected by face plates bearing corporate logos: AT&T, Alcatel, Fujitsu. In the case of an optical cable like FLAG, they contain the Light Terminal: the gear that converts the 1,558-nanometer signal lasers coming down the fiber strands into digits within an electrical circuit, and vice versa. The Light Terminal is contained within a couple of racks that, taken together, are about the size of a refrigerator.

All the other racks of gear filling the room cope with the unfathomable hassles associated with trying to funnel that many bits into and out of the fiber. In the end, that gear is, of course, connected to the local telecommunications system in some way. Hence one commonly sees microwave relay towers on top of these buildings and lots of manholes in the streets around them. One does not, however, see a lot of employees, because for the most part this equipment runs itself. Every single circuit board in every slot of every level of every rack in the whole place has a pair of copper wires coming out of it to send an alarm signal in the event that the board fails. Like tiny rivulets joining together into a mighty river, these come together into bundles as thick as your leg that snake beneath the floor plates to an alarm center where they are patched into beautiful rounded clear plastic cases enclosing grids of interconnect pins. From here they are tied into communications lines that run all the way to Tokyo so that everything on the premises can be monitored remotely during nights and weekends. Ninomiya is staffed with nine employees and Miura, FLAG's other Japanese landing point, only one.

With one notable exception, the hacker tourist sees no particular evidence that any of this has the slightest thing to do with communications. It might as well be the computer room at a big university or insurance company. The one exception is a telephone handset hanging on a hook on one of the equipment racks. The handset is there, but there's no keypad. Above it is a sign bearing the name of a city far, far away. "Ha, ha!" I said, the first time I saw one of these, "that's for talking to the guy in California, right?" To my embarrassment, my tour guides nodded yes. Each cable system has something called the *order wire*, which enables the technicians at opposite ends of the cable to talk to each other. At a major landing station you will see several order wires labeled with the names of exotic-sounding cities on the opposite side of the nearest large body of water.

That is the bare minimum that you will see at any cable station. At Ninomiya you see a bit more, and therein lies something of a tale.

Ninomiya is by far the oldest of KDD's seven cable landing stations, having been built in 1964 to land TPC–1, which connected Japan to Guam and hence to the United States. Unlike many of FLAG's other landing sites, which are still torn up by backhoe tracks, it is surrounded by perfectly maintained gardens marred only by towering gray steel poles with big red lights on them aimed out toward the sea in an attempt to dissuade mariners from dropping anchor anywhere nearby. Ninomiya served as a training ground for Japanese cable talent. Some of the people who learned the trade there are among the top executives in KDD's hierarchy today.

During the 1980s, when Americans started to get freaked out about Japan again, we heard a great deal about Japanese corporations' patient, long-term approach to R&D and how vastly superior it was to American companies' stupid, short-term approach. Since American news media are at least as stupid and short-term as the big corporations they like to bitch about, we have heard very little follow-up to such stories in recent years, which is kind of disappointing because I was sort of wondering how it was all going to turn out. But now the formerly long-term is about to come due.

By the beginning of the 1980s, the generation of cable-savvy KDD men who had cut their teeth at Ninomiya had reached the level where they could begin diverting corporate resources into R&D programs. Tohru Ohta, who today is the executive vice president of KDD, managed to pry some money loose and get it into the hands of a protégé, Dr. Yasuhiko Niiro, who launched one of those vaunted far-sighted Japanese R&D programs at Ninomiya. The terminal building for TPC–1, which had been the center of the Japanese international telecommunications network in 1964, was relegated to a laboratory for

Niiro. The goal was to make KDD a player in the optical-fiber submarine cable manufacturing business.

Such a move was not without controversy in the senior ranks of KDD, who had devoted themselves to a very different corporate mission. In 1949, when Japan was still being run by Douglas MacArthur and the country was trying to dig out from the rubble of the war, Nippon Telephone & Telegraph (NT&T) split off its international department into a new company called Kokusai Denshin Denwa Co., Ltd. (KDD), which means International Telegraph & Telephone. KDD was much smaller and more focused than NT&T, and this was for a reason: Japan's international communications system was a shambles, and nothing was more important to the country's economic recovery than that it be rehabilitated as quickly as possible. The hope was that KDD would be more nimble and agile than its lumbering parent and get the job done faster.

This strategy seems to have more or less worked. Obviously, Japan has succeeded in the world of international business. It is connected to the United States by numerous transpacific cables; lines to the outside world are plentiful. Of course, since KDD enjoyed monopoly status for a long time, the fact that these lines are plentiful has never led to their being cheap. Still, the system worked. Like much else that worked in Japan's postwar economy, it succeeded, in those early years, precisely insofar as it worked hand-in-glove with American companies and institutions. AT&T, in other words.

Unlike the United States or France or Great Britain, Japan was never much of a player in the submarine cable business back in the prewar days, and so Ohta's and Niiro's notion of going into head-to-head competition against AT&T, its postwar sugar daddy, might have seemed audacious. KDD had customarily been so close to AT&T that many Japanese mocked it cruelly. AT&T is the sumo champion, they said, and KDD is its *koshi-ginchaku*, its belt-holding assistant. The word literally means *waist purse* but seems to have rude connotations along the lines of *jockstrap carrier*.

Against all of that, the only thing that Ohta and Niiro had to go on was the fact that their idea was a really, really good one. Building cables is just the kind of thing that Japanese industry is good at: a highly advanced form of manufacturing that requires the very best quality control. Cables and repeaters have to work for at least 25 years under some really unpleasant conditions.

KDD Submarine Cable Systems (KDD-SCS) built its first optical fiber submarine cable system, TPC–3, in 1989 and will soon have more than 100,000 kilometers of cable in service worldwide. It designs and holds the patents on the terminal equipment that we saw at Ninomiya, though the equipment itself is manufactured by electronics giants like Toshiba and NEC. KDD-SCS is building some of the cable and repeaters that make up FLAG, and AT&T-SSI is building the rest. A problem has already surfaced in the AT&T repeaters—they switched to a different soldering technique which turns out to be not such a good idea. Eleven of the repeaters that AT&T made for FLAG have this problem, and all of them are lying on the bottom of oceans with bits running through them—for now. FLAG and AT&T are still studying this problem and trying to decide how to resolve it. Still, everyone in the cable business knows what happened—it has to be considered a major win for KDD-SCS.

So when KDD threw some of its resources into one of those famous far-sighted long-range Japanese R&D programs, it paid off beautifully. In the field of submarine cable systems, the lowly assistant has taught the sumo champion a lesson and sent him reeling back—not quite out of the ring, but certainly enough to get his attention. How, you might ask, is the rest of KDD doing?

The answer is that, like most other PTTs, it's showing its age. Even the tactful Japanese are willing to admit that they have performed poorly in the world of international telecommunications compared to other countries. Non-Japanese will tell you the same thing more enthusiastically.

The telco deregulation wars have begun in Japan as they have almost everywhere else, and KDD now has competitors in the form of International Digital Communications Inc. (IDC), which owns the Miura station, the other FLAG landing spot. In order to succeed in this competition, KDD needs to invest a lot of money, but the very smallness that made it such a good idea in 1949 puts it at a disadvantage when large amounts of capital are needed.

Just as Ninomiya is a generic cable landing, so KDD is something of a generic PTT, facing many of the same troubles that others do. For example: the Japanese telecommunications ministry continues to set rates at an artificially high level. At first blush, this would seem to help KDD by making it much more difficult for upstarts like IDC to compete with them. But in fact it has opened the door to an unexpected form of competition: callback.

Callback and *Kallback* are registered trademarks of Seattle-based International Telcom Ltd. (ITL), but, like *band-aid* and *kleenex*, tend to be used in a generic way by people overseas. The callback concept is based on the fact that it's much cheaper to call Japan from the U.S. than it is to call the U.S. from Japan. Subscribers to a callback service are given a phone number in the U.S. When they want to make a call, they dial that number, wait for it to ring once, and then hang up so they won't be charged for the call. In the jargon of the callback world, this is the *trigger call*. A system in the U.S. then calls them back, giving them a cheap international line, and once that is accomplished, it's an easy matter to shunt the call elsewhere: to a number in the States or in any other country in the world.

Any phone call made between two countries is subject to a so-called settlement charge, which is assessed on a per-minute basis. The amount of the settlement charged is fixed by an agreement between the two countries' PTTs and generally provides a barometer of their relative size and power. So, for example, when working out the deal with Denmark, Pakistan might say, "Hey, Danes are rich, and we don't really care whether they call us or not, and they have no particular leverage over us—so POW!" and insist on a high settlement charge—say $4 per minute. But when negotiating against AT&T, Pakistan might agree to a lower settlement charge—say $1 per minute.

Settlement charges have long been a major source of foreign exchange for developing countries' PTTs and hence for their governments and any crooked officials who may be dipping into the money stream. In some underdeveloped nations, they have been the major—verging on the only—source of such income. But not for long.

Nowadays, a Dane who makes lot of international calls will subscribe to a service such as ITL's Kallback. He makes a trigger call to Kallback's computer in Seattle, which, since it is an incomplete call, costs him nothing. The computer phones him back within a few seconds. He then punches in the number he wants to call in Pakistan, and the computer in Seattle places the call for him and makes the connection. Since Pakistan's PTT has no way to know that the call originates in Denmark, it assesses the lower AT&T settlement charge. The total settlement charge ends up being much less than what the Dane would have paid if he'd dialed Pakistan directly. In other words, two calls from the U.S., one to point A and one to point B, are cheaper than one direct call from point A to point B.

KDD, like many other PTTs around the world, has tried to crack down on callback services by compiling lists of the callback numbers and blocking calls to those numbers. When I talked to Eric Doescher, ITL's director of marketing, I expected him to be outraged about such attacks. But it soon became evident that if he ever felt that way, he long ago got over it and now views all such efforts with jaded amusement. "In Uganda," he said, "the PTT blocked all calls to the 206 area code. So we issued numbers from different area codes. In Saudi Arabia, they disabled touch-tones upon connection so our users were unable to place calls when the callback arrived—so we instituted a sophisticated voice recognition system—customer service reps who listened to our customers speaking the number and keyed it into the system." In Canada, a bizarre situation developed in which calls from the Yukon and Northwest Territories to the big southeastern cities like

Ottawa and Toronto were actually cheaper—by a factor of three—when routed through Seattle than when dialed directly. In response to the flood of Kallback traffic, Canada's Northern Telecom had human operators monitor phone calls, listening for the distinctive pattern of a trigger call: one ring followed by a hang-up. They then blocked calls to those numbers. So ITL substituted a busy signal for the ringing sound. Northern Telecom, unwilling to block calls to every phone in the U.S. that was ever busy, was checkmated.

In most countries, callback services inhabit a gray area. Saudi Arabia and Kenya occasionally run ads reminding their people that callback is illegal, but they don't try to enforce the law. China has better luck with enforcement because of its system of informants, but it doesn't bother Western businesspeople, who are the primary users. Singapore has legalized them on the condition that they don't advertise. In Italy, the market is so open that ITL is about to market a debit card that enables people to use the service from any pay phone.

So settlement charges have backfired on the telcos of many countries. Originally created to coddle these local monopolies, they've now become a hazard to their existence.

KDD carries all the baggage of an old monopoly: it works in conjunction with a notoriously gray and moribund government agency, it still has the bad customer-service attitude that is typical of monopolies, and it has the whole range of monopoly PR troubles too. Any competitive actions that it takes tend to be construed as part of a sinister world domination plot. So KDD has managed to get the worst of both worlds: it is viewed both as a big sinister monopoly and as a cringing sidekick to the even bigger and more sinister AT&T.

Michio Kuroda is a KDD executive who negotiates deals relating to submarine cables. He tells of a friend of his, a KDD employee who went to the United States two decades ago to study at a university and went around proudly announcing to his new American acquaintances that he worked for a monopoly. Finally, some kind soul took him aside and gently broke the news to him that, in America, monopoly was an ugly word.

Now, 20 years later, Kuroda claims that KDD has come around; it agrees now that monopoly is an ugly word. KDD's detractors will say that this is self-serving, but it rings true to this reporter. It seems clear that a decision has been made at the highest levels of KDD that it's time to stop looking backward and start to compete. As KDD is demonstrating, fat payrolls can be trimmed. Capital can be raised. Customer service can be improved, prices cut, bad PR mended. The biggest challenge that KDD faces now may stem from a mistake that it made several years ago: it decided not to land FLAG.

$35°$ 11.535' N, $139°$ 36.995' E IDC Cable Landing Station, Miura, Japan

The Miura station of IDC, or International Digital Communications Inc., looks a good deal like KDD's Ninomiya station on the inside, except that its equipment is made by Fujitsu instead of KDD-SCS. At first approximation, you might think of IDC as being the MCI of Japan. Originally it specialized in data transmission, but now that deregulation has arrived it is also a long-distance carrier. This, by the way, is a common pattern in Asian countries where deregulation is looming: new companies will try to kick out a niche for themselves in data or cellular markets and hold on by their toenails until the vast long-distance market opens up to them. Anyone in Japan can dial an international call over IDC's network by dialing the prefix 0061 instead of 001 for KDD. The numerical prefixes of various competing long-distance companies are slapped up all over Tokyo on signs and across rear windows of taxicabs in a desperate attempt to get a tiny edge in mindshare.

Miura's outer surroundings are quite different from Ninomiya's. Ninomiya is on a bluff in the middle of a town, and the beach below it is a narrow strip of sand chockablock with giant concrete tetrapods, looking like vastly magnified skeletons of plankton and intended to keep waves from washing up onto the busy coastal highway that runs between the beach and the station. Miura, by contrast, is a resort area with a wide beach lined with seasonal restaurants. When we were there we even saw a few surfers, hunting for puny waves under a relentless rain, looking miserable in black wetsuits. The beach gives way to intensively cultivated farmland.

Miura is the Japan end of NPC, the Northern Pacific Cable, which links it directly to Pacific City, Oregon, with 8,380 kilometers of second-generation optical fiber (it carries three fiber pairs, each of which handles 420 Mbps). Miura also lands APC, the Asia-Pacific Cable, which links it to Hong Kong and Singapore, and by means of a short cable under Tokyo Bay it is connected to KDD's Chikura station, which is a major nexus for transpacific and East Asian cables.

When FLAG first approached KDD with its wild scheme to build a privately financed cable from England to Japan, there were plenty of reasons for KDD to turn it down. The U.S. Commerce Department was pressuring KDD to accept FLAG, but AT&T was against it. KDD was now caught between *two* sumo wrestlers trying to push it opposite ways. Also in the crowded ring was Japan's telecommunications ministry, which maintained that plenty of bandwidth already existed and that FLAG would somehow create a glut on the market. Again, this attitude is probably difficult for the hacker tourist or any other Net user to comprehend, but it seems to be ubiquitous among telecrats.

Finally, KDD saw advantages in the old business model in which cables are backed, and owned, by carriers—it likes the idea of owning a cable and reaping profits from it rather than allowing a bunch of outside investors to make all the money.

For whatever reasons, KDD declined FLAG's invitation, so FLAG made overtures to IDC, which readily agreed to land the cable at its Miura station, where it could be cross-connected with NPC.

A similar scenario played out in Korea, by the way, where Korea

Telecom, traditionally a loyal member of the AT&T family, turned FLAG down at first. FLAG approached a competitor named Dacom, and, faced with that threat, Korea Telecom changed its mind and decided to break with AT&T and land FLAG after all. But in Japan, KDD, perhaps displaying more loyalty than was good for it, held the line. Miura became FLAG's Japanese landing station by default—a huge coup for IDC, which could now route calls to virtually anywhere in the world directly from its station.

All of this happened prior to a major FLAG meeting in Singapore in 1992, which those familiar with the project regard as having been a turning point. At this meeting it became clear that FLAG was a serious endeavor, that it really was going to happen. Not long afterward, AT&T decided to adopt an "if you can't beat 'em, join 'em" strategy toward FLAG, which eventually led to it and KDD Submarine Cable Systems getting the contract to build FLAG's cable and repeaters. (AT&T-SSI is supplying 64 percent of the cable and 59 percent of the repeaters, and KDD-SCS is supplying the rest.) This was a big piece of good news for KDD-SCS, the competitive-minded manufacturer, but it put KDD the poky long-distance company in the awkward, perhaps even absurd situation of supplying the hardware for a project that it had originally opposed and that would end up being a cash cow for its toughest competitor.

So KDD changed its mind and began trying to get in on FLAG. Since FLAG was already coming ashore at a station owned by IDC, this meant creating a second landing in Japan, at Ninomiya. In no other country would FLAG have two landings controlled by two different companies. For arcane contractual reasons, this meant that all of the other 50-odd carriers involved in FLAG would have to give unanimous consent to the arrangement, which meant in practice that IDC had veto power. At a ceremony opening a new KDD-SCS factory on Kyūshū executives from KDD and IDC met to discuss the idea. IDC agreed to let KDD in, in exchange for what people on both sides agree were surprisingly reasonable conditions.

At first blush it might seem as though IDC was guilty of valuing harmony and cooperation over the preservation of shareholder value—a common charge leveled against Japanese corporations by grasping and peevish American investors. Perhaps there was some element of this, but the fact is that IDC did have good reasons for wanting FLAG connected to KDD's network. KDD's Ninomiya station is scheduled to be the landing site for TPC–5, a megaproject of the same order of magnitude as FLAG: 25,000 kilometers of third-generation optical fiber cable swinging in a vast loop around the Pacific, connecting Japan with the West Coast of the U.S. With both FLAG and TPC–5 literally coming into the same room at Ninomiya, it would be possible to build a cross-connect between the two, effectively extending FLAG's reach across the Pacific. This would add a great deal of value to FLAG and hence would be good for IDC.

In any case, the deal fell through because of a strong anti-FLAG faction within KDD that could not tolerate the notion of giving any concessions whatever to IDC. There it stalemated until FLAG managed to cut a deal with China Telecom to run a full-bore 10.6 Gbps spur straight into Shanghai. While China has other undersea cable connections, they are tiny compared with FLAG, which is now set to be the first big cable, as well as the first modern Internet connection, into China.

At this point it became obvious that KDD absolutely had to get in on the FLAG action no matter what the cost, and so it returned to the bargaining table—but this time, IDC, sensing that it had an overpoweringly strong hand, wanted much tougher conditions. Eventually, though, the deal was made, and now jumpsuited workers are preparing rooms at both Ninomiya and Miura to receive the new equipment racks, much like expectant parents wallpapering the nursery. At Ninomiya, an immense cross-connect will be built between FLAG and TPC–5, and Miura will house a cross-connect between FLAG and the smaller NPC cable.

The two companies will end up on an equal footing as far as FLAG is concerned, but the crucial strategic misstep has already been made by KDD: by letting IDC be the first to land FLAG, it has given its rival a chance to acquire a great deal of experience in the business. It is not unlike the situation that now exists between AT&T, which used to be the only company big and experienced enough to put together a major international cable, and Nynex, which has now managed to get its foot in that particular door and is rapidly gaining the experience and contacts needed to compete with AT&T in the future.

HAZARDS

Dr. Wildman Whitehouse and his 5-foot-long induction coils were the first hazard to destroy a submarine cable but hardly the last. It sometimes seems as though every force of nature, every flaw in the human character, and every biological organism on the planet is engaged in a competition to see which can sever the most cables. The Museum of Submarine Telegraphy in Porthcurno, England, has a display of wrecked cables bracketed to a slab of wood. Each is labeled with its cause of failure, some of which sound dramatic, some cryptic, some both: trawler maul, spewed core, intermittent disconnection, strained core, teredo worms, crab's nest, perished core, fish bite, even "spliced by Italians." The teredo worm is like a science fiction creature, a bivalve with a rasp-edged shell that it uses like a buzz saw to cut through wood—or through submarine cables. Cable companies learned the hard way, early on, that it likes to eat gutta-percha, and subsequent cables received a helical wrapping of copper tape to stop it.

A modern cable needn't be severed to stop working. More frequently, a fault in the insulation will allow seawater to leak in and reach the copper conductor that carries power to the repeaters. The optical fibers are fine, but the repeater stops working because its power is leaking into the ocean. The interaction of electricity, seawater, and other chemical elements present in the cable can produce hydrogen gas that forces its way down the cable and chemically attacks the fiber or delicate components in the repeaters.

Cable failure can be caused by any number of errors in installation or route selection. Currents, such as those found before the mouths of rivers, are avoided. If the bottom is hard, currents will chafe the cable against it—and currents and hard bottoms frequently go together because currents tend to scour sediments away from the rock. If the cable is laid with insufficient slack, it may become suspended between two ridges, and as the suspended part rocks back and forth, the ridges eventually wear through the insulation. Sand waves move across the bottom of the ocean like dunes across the desert; these can surface a cable, where it may be bruised by passing ships. Anchors are a perennial problem that gets much worse during typhoons, because an anchor that has dropped well away from a cable may be dragged across it as the ship is pushed around by the wind.

In 1870, a new cable was laid between England and France, and Napoleon III used it to send a congratulatory message to Queen Victoria. Hours later, a French fisherman hauled the cable up into his boat, identified it as either the tail of a sea monster or a new species of gold-bearing seaweed, and cut off a chunk to take home. Thus was inaugurated an almost incredibly hostile relationship between the cable industry and fishermen. Almost anyone in the cable business will be glad, even eager, to tell you that since 1870 the intelligence and civic responsibility of fishermen have only degraded. Fishermen, for their part, tend to see everyone in the cable business as hard-hearted blue-bloods out to screw the common man.

Most of the fishing-related damage is caused by trawlers, which tow big sacklike nets behind them. Trawlers seem designed for the purpose of damaging submarine cables. Various types of hardware are attached to the nets. In some cases, these are otter boards, which act something like rudders to push the net's mouth open. When bottom fish such as halibut are the target, a massive bar is placed across the front of the net with heavy tickler chains dangling from it; these flail against the bottom, stirring up the fish so they will rise up into the maw of the net.

Mere impact can be enough to wreck a cable, if it puts a leak in the insulation. Frequently, though, a net or anchor will snag a cable.

If the ship is small and the cable is big, the cable may survive the encounter. There is a type of cable, used up until the advent of optical fiber, called 21-quad, which consists of 21 four-bundle pairs of cable and a coaxial line. It is 15 centimeters in diameter, and a single meter of it weighs 46 kilograms. If a passing ship should happen to catch such a cable with its anchor, it will follow a very simple procedure: abandon it and go buy a new anchor.

But modern cables are much smaller and lighter—a mere 0.85 kg per meter for the unarmored, deep-sea portions of the FLAG cable— and the ships most apt to snag them, trawlers, are getting bigger and more powerful. Now that fishermen have massacred most of the fish in shallower water, they are moving out deeper. Formerly, cable was plowed into the bottom in water shallower than 1,000 meters, which kept it away from the trawlers. Because of recent changes in fishing practices, the figure has been boosted to 2,000 meters. But this means that the old cables are still vulnerable.

When a trawler snags a cable, it will pull it up off the seafloor. How far it gets pulled depends on the weight of the cable, the amount of slack, and the size and horsepower of the ship. Even if the cable is not pulled all the way to the surface, it may get kinked—its minimum bending radius may be violated. If the trawler does succeed in hauling the cable all the way up out of the water, the only way out of the situation, or at least the simplest, is to cut the cable. Dave Handley once did a study of a cable that had been suddenly and mysteriously severed. Hauling up the cut end, he discovered that someone had sliced through it with a cutting torch.

There is also the obvious threat of sabotage by a hostile government, but, surprisingly, this almost never happens. When cypherpunk Doug Barnes was researching his Caribbean project, he spent some time looking into this, because it was exactly the kind of threat he was worried about in the case of a data haven. Somewhat to his own surprise and relief, he concluded that it simply wasn't going to happen. "Cutting a submarine cable," Barnes says, "is like starting a nuclear war. It's easy to do, the results are devastating, and as soon as one country does it, all of the others will retaliate."

Bert Porter, a Cable & Wireless cable-laying veteran who is now a freelancer, was beachmaster for the Tong Fuk lay. He was on a ship that laid a cable from Hong Kong to Singapore during the late 1960s. Along the way they passed south of Lan Tao Island, and so the view from Tong Fuk Beach is a trip down memory lane for him. "The repeater spacing was about 18 miles," he says, "and so the first repeater went into the water right out there. Then, a few days later, the cable suddenly tested broken." In other words, the shore station in Hong Kong had lost contact with the equipment on board Porter's cable ship. In such cases it's easy to figure out roughly where the break occurred—by measuring the resistance in the cable's conductors—and they knew it had to be somewhere in the vicinity of the first repeater. "So we backtracked, pulling up cable, and when we got right out there," he waves his hand out over the bay, "we discovered that the repeater had simply been chopped out." He holds his hands up parallel, like twin blades. "Apparently the Chinese were curious about our repeaters, so they thought they'd come out and get one."

As the capacity of optical fibers climbs, so does the economic damage caused when the cable is severed. FLAG makes its money by selling capacity to long-distance carriers, who turn around and resell it to end users at rates that are increasingly determined by what the market will bear. If FLAG gets chopped, no calls get through. The carriers' phone calls get routed to FLAG's competitors (other cables or satellites), and FLAG loses the revenue represented by those calls until the cable is repaired. The amount of revenue it loses is a function of how many calls the cable is physically capable of carrying, how close to capacity the cable is running, and what prices the market will bear for calls on the broken cable segment. In other words, a break between Dubai and Bombay might cost FLAG more in revenue loss than a break between Korea and Japan if calls between Dubai and Bombay cost more.

The rule of thumb for calculating revenue loss works like this: for every penny per minute that the long distance market will bear on a particular route, the loss of revenue, should FLAG be severed on that route, is about $3,000 a minute. So if calls on that route are a dime a minute, the damage is $30,000 a minute, and if calls are a dollar a minute, the damage is almost a third of a million dollars for every minute the cable is down. Upcoming advances in fiber bandwidth may push this figure, for some cables, past the million-dollar-a-minute mark.

Clearly, submarine cable repair is a good business to be in. Cable repair ships are standing by in ports all over the world, on 24-hour call, waiting for a break to happen somewhere in their neighborhood. They are called *agreement ships*. Sometimes, when nothing else is going on, they will go out and pull up old abandoned cables. The stated reason for this is that the old cables present a hazard to other ships. However, if you do so much as raise an eyebrow at this explanation, any cable man will be happy to tell you the real reason: whenever a fisherman snags his net on anything—a rock, a wreck, or even a figment of his imagination—he will go out and sue whatever company happens to have a cable in that general vicinity. The cable companies are waiting eagerly for the day when a fisherman goes into court claiming to have snagged his nets on a cable, only to be informed that the cable was pulled up by an agreement ship years before.

IN WHICH THE HACKER TOURIST DELIGHTS IN CAIRO, THE MOTHER OF THE WORLD. ALEXANDRIA, THE FORMER HACKER HEADQUARTERS OF THE PLANET. THE LIGHTHOUSE, THE LIBRARIES, AND OTHER HAUNTS OF ANCIENT NERDS AND GEEKS. PROFOUND SIGNIFICANCE OF INTERSECTIONS. TRAVELS ON THE DESERT ROAD. LIBYA'S CONTACT WITH THE OUTSIDE WORLD RUDELY

SEVERED—THEN RESTORED! ENGINEER MUSALAMAND HIS PLANETARY INFORMA-TION NEXUS. THE VITALLY IMPORTANT CON-CEPT OF SLACK.

31° 12.841' N, 29° 53.169' E Site of the Pharos Lighthouse, Alexandria, Egypt

Having stood on the beach of Miura watching those miserable-but-plucky Japanese surfers, the hacker tourist had reached FLAG's easternmost extreme, and there was nothing to do except turn around and head west. Next stop: Egypt.

No visit to Egypt is complete without a stop in Cairo, but that city, the pinnacle of every normal tourist's traveling career, is strangely empty from a hacker tourist point of view. Its prime attraction, of course, is the pyramids. We visited them at five in the morning during a long and ultimately futile wait for the Egyptian military to give us permission to rendezvous with FLAG's cable-laying ship in the Gulf of Suez. To the hacker, the most interesting thing about the pyramids is their business plan, which is the simplest and most effective ever devised:

1. Put a rock on top of another rock.
2. Repeat (1) until gawkers arrive.
3. Separate them from their valuables by all conceivable means.

By contrast, normal tourist guidebooks have nothing good to say about Alexandria; it's as if the writers got so tired of marveling at Cairo and Upper Egypt that they had to vent their spleen somewhere. Though a town was here in ancient times, Alexandria per se was founded in 332 BC by Alexander the Great, which makes it a brand-new city by Egyptian standards. There is almost no really old stuff in Alexandria at all, but the mere memory of the landmarks that were here in its heyday suffice to make it much more important than Cairo from the weirdly distorted viewpoint of the hacker tourist. These landmarks are, or were, the lighthouse and the libraries.

The lighthouse was built on the nearby island of Pharos. Neither the building nor even the island exists any more. Pharos was eventually joined to the mainland by a causeway, which fattened out into a peninsula and became a minuscule bump on the scalp of Africa. The lighthouse was an immense structure, at some 120 meters the tallest building in the world for many centuries, and contained as many as 300 rooms. Somewhere in its upper stories a fire burned all night long, and its light was reflected out across the Mediterranean by some kind of rotating mirror or prism. This was a fine bit of ancient hacking in and of itself, but according to legend, the optics also had magnifying properties, so that observers peering through it during the daytime could see ships too distant to be perceived by the naked eye.

According to legend, this feature made Alexandria immune to naval assault as long as the lighthouse remained standing. According to another yarn, a Byzantine emperor spread a rumor that the treasure of Alexander the Great had been hidden within the lighthouse's foundation, and the unbelievably fatuous local caliph tore up the works looking for it, putting Pharos out of commission and leading to a military defeat by the Byzantine Empire.

Some combination or other of gullible caliphs, poor maintenance, and earthquakes eventually did fell the lighthouse. Evidently it toppled right into the Mediterranean. The bottom of the sea directly before its foundations is still littered with priceless artifacts, which are being catalogued and hauled out by French archaeologists using differential GPS to plot their findings. They work in the shadow of a nondescript fortress built on the site by a later sultan, Qait Bey, who pragmatically used a few chunks of lighthouse granite to beef up the walls—just another splinter under the fingernails of the historical preservation crowd.

You can go to the fortress of Qait Bey now and stare out over the ocean and get much the same view that the builders of the lighthouse enjoyed. They must have been able to see all kinds of weirdness coming over the horizon from Europe and western Asia. The Mediterranean may look small on a world map, but from Pharos its horizon seems just as infinite as the Pacific seen from Miura. Back then, knowing how much of the human world was around the Mediterranean, the horizon must have seemed that much more vast, threatening, and exciting to the Alexandrians.

Building the lighthouse with its magic lens was a way of enhancing the city's natural capability for looking to the north, which made it into a world capital for many centuries. It's when a society plunders its ability to look over the horizon and into the future in order to get short-term gain—sometimes illusory gain—that it begins a long slide nearly impossible to reverse.

The collapse of the lighthouse must have been astonishing, like watching the World Trade Center fall over. But it took only a few seconds, and if you were looking the other way when it happened, you might have missed it entirely—you'd see nothing but blue breakers rolling in from the Mediterranean, hiding a field of ruins, quickly forgotten.

31° 11.738' N, 29° 54.108' E Intersection of El Horreya and El Nabi Daniel, Alexandria, Egypt

Alexandria is most famous for having been the site of the ancient library. This was actually two or more different libraries. The first one dates back to the city's early Ptolemaic rulers, who were Macedonians, not Egyptians. It was modeled after the Lyceum of Aristotle, who, between other gigs, tutored Alexander the Great. Back in the days when people moved to information, instead of vice versa, this library attracted most of the most famous smart people in the world: the ultimate hacker, Archimedes; the father of geometry, Euclid; Eratosthenes, who was the first person to calculate the circumference of the earth, by looking at the way the sun shone down wells at Alexandria and Aswan. He also ran the library for a while and took the job seriously enough that when he started to go blind in his old age, he starved himself to death. In any event, this library was burned out by the Romans when they were adding Egypt to their empire. Or maybe it wasn't. It's inherently difficult to get reliable information about an event that consisted of the destruction of all recorded information.

The second library was called the Library of Cleopatra and was built around a couple of hundred thousand manuscripts that were given to her by Marc Antony in what was either a magnificent gesture of romantic love or a shrewd political maneuver. Marc Antony suffered from what we would today call "poor impulse control," so the former explanation is more likely. This library was wiped out by Christians in AD 391. Depending on which version of events you read, its life span may have overlapped with that of the first library for a few years, a few decades, or not at all.

Whether or not the two libraries ever existed at the same time, the fact remains that between about 300 BC and AD 400, Alexandria was by far the world capital of high-quality information. It must have had much in common with the MIT campus or Stanford in Palo Alto of more recent times: lots of hairy smart guys converging from all over the world to tinker with the lighthouse or to engage in pursuits that must have been totally incomprehensible to the locals, such as staring down wells at high noon and raving about the diameter of the earth.

The main reason that writers of tourist guidebooks are so cheesed off at Alexandria is that no vestige of the first library remains—not even a plaque stating "The Library of Alexandria was here." If you want to visit the site, you have to do a bit of straightforward detective work. Ancient Alexandria was laid out on a neat, regular grid pattern—just the kind of thing you would expect of a place populated by people like Euclid. The main east-west street was called the Canopic Way, and the main north-south street, running from the waterfront toward the Sahara Desert, was called the Street of the Soma.

The library is thought to have stood just south of their intersection.

Though no buildings of that era remain, the streets still do, and so does their intersection. Currently, the Canopic Way is called El Horreya Avenue, and the Soma is called El Nabi Daniel Street, though if you don't hurry, they may be called something else when you arrive.

We stayed at the Cecil Hotel, where Nabi Daniel hits the waterfront. The Cecil is one of those British imperial-era hotels fraught with romance and history, sort of like the entire J. Peterman catalog rolled into one building. British Intelligence was headquartered there during the war, and there the Battle of El Alamein was planned.

Living as they do, however, in a country choked with old stuff, the Egyptians have adopted a philosophy toward architecture that is best summed up by the phrase: "What have you done for me lately?" From this point of view, the Cecil is just another old building, and it's not even particularly old. As if to emphasize this, the side of the hotel where we stayed was covered with a rude scaffolding (sticks lashed together with hemp) aswarm with workers armed with sledgehammers, crowbars, chisels, and the like, who spent all day, every day, bellowing cheerfully at each other (demolition workers are the jolliest men in every country), bashing huge chunks of masonry off the top floor and simply dropping them—occasionally crushing an air conditioner on some guest's balcony. It was a useful reminder that Egyptians feel no great compulsion to tailor their cities to the specifications of guidebook writers.

This fact can be further driven home by walking south on Nabi Daniel and looking for the site of the Library of Alexandria. It is now occupied by office buildings probably not more than 100, nor less than 50, years old. Their openings are covered with roll-up steel doors, and their walls decorated with faded signs. One of them advertises courses in DOS, Lotus, dBase, COBOL, and others. Not far away is a movie theater showing *Forbidden Arsenal: In the Line of Duty 6*, starring Cynthia Khan.

The largest and nicest building in the area is used by an insurance company and surrounded by an iron fence. The narrow sidewalk out front is blocked by a few street vendors who have set up their wares in such a way as to force pedestrians out into the street. One of them is selling pictures of adorable kittens tangled up in yarn, and another is peddling used books. This is the closest thing to a library that remains here, so I spent a while examining his wares: a promising volume called *Bit by Bit* turned out to be an English primer. There were quite a few medical textbooks, as if a doctor had just passed away, and Agatha Christie and Mickey Mouse books presumably left behind by tourists. The closest thing I saw to a classic was a worn-out copy of *Oliver Twist*.

31° 10.916' N 29° 53.784' E Pompey's Pillar

The site of Cleopatra's library, precisely 1 mile away by my GPS, is viewed with cautious approval by guidebook writers because it is an actual ruin with a wall around it, a ticket booth, old stuff, and guides. It is right next to an active Muslim cemetery, so it is difficult to reach the place without excusing your way past crowds of women in voluminous black garments, wailing and sobbing heartrendingly, which all goes to make the Western tourist feel like even more of a penis than usual.

The site used to be the city's acropolis. It is a rounded hill of extremely modest altitude with a huge granite pillar on the top. To quote Shelley's "Ozymandias": "Nothing beside remains." A few sphinxes are scattered around the place, but they were obviously dragged in to give tourists something to look at. Several brutally impoverished gray concrete apartment buildings loom up on the other side of the wall, festooned with washing, crammed with children who entertain themselves by raining catcalls down upon the few tourists who straggle out this far. The granite pillar honors the Roman emperor Diocletian, who was a very bad emperor, a major Christian-killer, but who gave Alexandria a big tax break. The citizenry, apparently just as dimwitted as modern-day Americans, decided that he was a great guy and erected this pillar. Originally there was a statue of Diocletian himself on the top, riding a horse, which is why the Egyptians call it, in Arabic, *The man on horseback*. The statue is gone now, which makes this a completely mystifying name. Westerners call it *Pompey's Pillar* because that's the moniker the clueless Crusaders slapped on it; of course, it has absolutely nothing to do with Pompey.

The hacker tourist does not bother with the pillar but rather with what is underneath it: a network of artificial caves, carved into the sandstone, resembling nothing so much as a D & D player's first dungeon. Because it's a hill and this is Egypt, the caverns are nice and dry and (with a little baksheesh in the right hands) can be well lit too—electrical conduit has been run in and light fixtures bolted to the ceiling. The walls of these caves have niches that are just the right size and shape to contain piles of scrolls, so this is thought to be the site of the Library of Cleopatra. This complex was called the Sarapeum, or Temple of Sarapis, who was a conflation of Osiris and Apis admired by the locals and loathed by monotheists, which explains why the whole complex was sacked and burned by Christians in 391.

It is all rather discouraging, when you use your imagination (which you must do constantly in Alexandria) and think of the brilliance that was here for a while. As convenient as it is for information to come to us, libraries do have a valuable side effect: they force all of the smart people to come together in one place where they can interact with one another. When the information goes up in flames, those people go their separate ways. The synergy that joined them—that created the lighthouse, for example—dies. The world loses something.

So the second library is some holes in a wall, and the first is an intersection. Holes and intersections are both absences, empty places, disappointing to tourists of both the regular and the hacker variety. But one can argue that the intersection's continued presence is arguably more interesting than some old pile that has been walled off and embalmed by a historical society. How can an intersection remain in one place for 2,500 years? Simply, both the roads that run through it must remain open and active. The intersection will cease to exist if sand drifts across it because it's never used, or if someone puts up a building there. In Egypt, where yesterday's wonders of the world are today's building materials, nothing is more obvious than that people have been avidly putting up buildings everywhere they possibly can for 5,000 years, so it is remarkable that no such thing has happened here. It means that every time some opportunist has gone out and tried to dig up the street or to start putting up a wall, he has been flattened by traffic, arrested by cops, chased away by outraged donkey-cart drivers, or otherwise put out of action. The existence of this intersection is proof that a certain pattern of human activity has endured in this exact place for 2,500 years.

When the hacker tourist has tired of contemplating the profound significance of intersections (which, frankly, doesn't take very long) he must turn his attention to—you guessed it—cable routes. This turns out to be a much richer vein.

30° 58.319' N, 29° 49.531' E Alexandria Tollbooth, the Desert Road, Sahara Desert, Egypt

As we speed across the Saharan night, the topic of conversation turns to Hong Kong. Our Egyptian driver, relaxed and content after stopping at a roadside rest area for a hubbly-bubbly session (smoking sweetened tobacco in a Middle Eastern bong), smacks the steering wheel gleefully. "Ha, ha, ha!" he roars. "Miserable Hong Kong people!"

Alexandria and Cairo are joined by two separate, roughly parallel highways called the Desert Road and the Agricultural Road. The latter runs through cultivated parts of the Nile Delta. The Desert Road is a rather new, four-lane highway with a tollbooth at each end—tollbooths in the middle not being necessary, because if you get off in the middle you will die. It is lined for its entire length with billboards advertising tires, sunglasses, tires, tires, tires, bottled water, sunglasses, tires, and tires.

Perhaps because it is supported by tolls, the Desert Highway is a first-rate road all the way. This means not merely that the pavement is good but also that it has a system of ducts and manholes buried under its median strip, so that anyone wishing to run a cable from one end of the highway to the other—tollbooth to tollbooth—need only obtain a "permit" and ream out the ducts a little. Or at least that's what the Egyptians say. The Lan Tao Island crowd, who are quite discriminating when it comes to ducts and who share an abhorrence of all things Egyptian, claim that cheap PVC pipe was used and that the whole system is a tangled mess.

They would both agree, however, that beyond the tollbooths the duct situation is worse. The Alexandria Tollbooth is some 37 kilometers outside of the city center; you get there by driving along a free highway that has no ducts at all.

This problem is being remedied by FLAG, which has struck a deal with ARENTO (Arab Republic of Egypt National Telecommunications Organization—the PTT) that is roughly analogous to the one it made with the Communications Authority of Thailand. FLAG has no choice but to go overland across Egypt, just as in Thailand. The reasons for doing so here are entirely different, though.

By a freak of geography and global politics, Egypt possesses the same sort of choke point on Europe-to-Asia telecommunications as the Suez Canal gives it in the shipping industry. Anyone who wants to run a cable from Europe to East Asia has severely limited choices. You can go south around Africa, but it's much too far. You can go overland across all of Russia, as U S West has recently talked about doing, but if even a 170-kilometers terrestrial route across Thailand gets your customers fumbling for their smelling salts, what will they say about one all the way across Russia? You could attempt a shorter terrestrial route from the Levant to the Indian Ocean, but given the countries it would have to pass through (Lebanon and Iraq, to name two), it would have about as much chance of survival as a strand of gossamer stretched across a kick-boxing ring. And you can't lay a cable down the Suez Canal, partly because it would catch hell from anchors and dredgers, and partly because cable-laying ships move very slowly and would create an enormous traffic jam.

The only solution that is even remotely acceptable is to land the cable on Egypt's Mediterranean coast (which in practice means either Alexandria or Port Said) and then go overland to Suez, where the canal joins the Gulf of Suez, which in turn joins the Red Sea. The Red Sea is so shallow and so heavily trafficked, by the way, that all cables running through it must be plowed into the seafloor, which is a hassle, but obviously preferable to running a terrestrial route through the likes of Sudan and Somalia, which border it.

In keeping with its practice of running two parallel routes on terrestrial sections, FLAG is landing at both Alexandria and Port Said. From these cities the cables converge on Suez. Alexandria is far more important than Port Said as a cable nexus for the simple reason that it is at the westernmost extreme of the Nile Delta, so you can reach it from Europe without having to contend with the Nile. European cables running to Port Said, by contrast, must pass across the mouths of the Nile, where they are subjected to currents.

Engineer Mustafa Musalam, general manager of transmission for ARENTO's Alexandria office, is a stocky, affable, silver-haired gent. Egypt is one of those places where *Engineer* is used as a title, like *Doctor* or *Professor*, and Engineer Musalam bears the title well. In his personality and bearing he has at least as much in common with other highly competent engineers around the world as he does with other Egyptians. In defiance of ARENTO rules, he drives himself around in his own vehicle, a tiny, beat-up, but perfectly functional subcompact. An engineer of his stature is supposed to be chauffeured around in a company car. Most Egyptian service-industry professionals are masters at laying passive-aggressive head trips on their employers. Half the time, when you compensate them, they make it clear that you have embarrassed them, and yourself, by grossly overdoing it— you have just gotten it totally wrong, really pissed down your leg, and placed them in a terribly awkward situation. The other half of the time, you have insulted them by being miserly. You never get it right. But Engineer Musalam, a logical and practical-minded sort, cannot abide the idea of a driver spending his entire day, every day, sitting in a car waiting for the boss to go somewhere. So he eventually threw up his hands and unleashed his driver on the job market.

Charitably, Engineer Musalam takes the view that the completion of the Aswan High Dam tamed the Nile's current to the point where no one need worry about running cables to Port Said anymore. FLAG's surveyors obviously agree with him, because they chose Port Said as one of their landing points. On the other hand, FLAG's archenemy, SEA-ME-WE 3, will land only at Alexandria, because France Telecom's engineers refuse to lay cable across the Nile. SEA-ME-WE 3's redundant routes will run, instead, along the Desert Road and the Agricultural Road. Bandwidth buyers trying to choose between the two cables can presumably look forward to lurid sales presentations from FLAG marketers detailing the insane recklessness of SEA-ME-WE 3's approach, and vice versa.

At the dirt-and-duct level, the operation in Egypt is much like the one in Thailand. The work is being done by Consolidated Contractors, which is a fairly interesting multinational contracting firm that is based and funded in the Middle East but works all over the globe. Here it is laying six 100-mm ducts (10 inside Alexandria proper) as compared with only two in Thailand. These ducts are all PVC pipe, but FLAG's duct is made of a higher grade of PVC than the others— even than President Mubarak's duct.

That's right—in a nicely Pharaonic touch, one of the six ducts going into the ground here is the sole property of President Hosni Mubarak, or (presumably) whoever succeeds him as head of state. It is hard to envision why a head of state would want or need his own private tube full of air running underneath the Sahara. The obvious guess is that the duct might be used to create a secure communications system, independent of the civilian and military systems (the Egyptian military will own one of the six ducts, and ARENTO will

own three). This, in and of itself, says something about the relationship between the military and the government in Egypt. It is hardly
surprising when you consider that Mubarak's predecessor was mur-
dered by the military during a parade.

Inside the city, where ten rather than six ducts are being pre-
pared, they must occasionally sprout up out of the ground and run
along the undersides of bridges and flyovers. In these sections it is
easy to identify FLAG's duct because, unlike the others, it is galvanized steel instead of PVC. FLAG undoubtedly specified steel for its
far greater protective value, but in so doing posed a challenge for
Engineer Musalam, who knew that thieves would attack the system
wherever they could reach it—not to take the cable but to get their
hands on that tempting steel pipe. So, wherever the undersides of
these bridges and flyovers are within 2 or 3 meters of ground level,
Engineer Musalam has built in special measures to make it virtually
impossible for thieves to get their hands on FLAG's pipe.

For the most part, the duct installation is a simple cut-and-cover
operation, right down the median strip. But the median is crossed
frequently by nicely paved, heavily trafficked U-turn routes. To cut or
block one of these would be unthinkable, since no journey in Egypt is
complete without numerous U-turns. It is therefore necessary to bore
a horizontal tunnel under each one, run a 600-mm steel pipe down
the tunnel, and finally thread the ducts through it. The tunnels are
bored by laborers operating big manually powered augers. Under a
sign reading Civil Works: Fiberoptic Link around the Globe, the men
had left their street clothes carefully wrapped up in plastic bags, on
the shoulder of the road. They had kicked off their shoes and changed
into the traditional, loose, ankle-length garment. One by one, they
disappeared into a tunnel barely big enough to lie down in, carrying
empty baskets, then returned a few minutes later with baskets full of
dirt, looking like extras in some new Hollywood costume drama: *The
Ten Commandments Meets the Great Escape*.

We blundered across Engineer Musalam's path one afternoon.
This was sheer luck, but also kind of inevitable: other than ditch dig-

gers, the only people in the median strip of this highway are hacker tourists and ARENTO engineers. He was here because one of the crews working on FLAG had, while enlarging a manhole excavation, plunged the blade of their backhoe right through the main communications cable connecting Egypt to Libya—a 960-circuit coaxial line buried, sans conduit, in the same median. Libya had dropped off the net for a while until Mu'ammar Gadhafi's eastbound traffic could be shunted to a microwave relay chain and an ARENTO repair crew had been mobilized. The quality of such an operation is not measured by how frequently cables get broken (usually they are broken by other people) but by how quickly they get fixed afterward, and by this standard Engineer Musalam runs a tight ship. The mishap occurred on a Friday afternoon—the Muslim sabbath—the first day of a three-day weekend and a national holiday to boot—40 years to the day after the Suez Canal was handed over to Egypt. Nevertheless, the entire hierarchy was gathered around the manhole excavation, from ditch diggers hastily imported from another nearby site all the way up to Engineer Musalam.

The ditch diggers made the hole even larger, whittling out a place for one of the splicing technicians to sit. The technicians stood on the brink of the pit offering directions, and eventually they jumped into it and grabbed shovels; their toolboxes were lowered in after them on ropes, and their black dress trousers and crisp white shirts rapidly converged on the same color as the dust covered them. In the lee of an unburied concrete manhole nearby, a couple of men established a little refreshment center: one hubbly-bubbly and one portable stove, shooting flames like a miniature oil well fire, where they cranked out glass after glass of heavily sweetened tea. This struck me as more efficient than the American technique of sending a gofer down to the 7-Eleven for a brace of Super Big Gulps. Traffic swirled around the adjacent U-turn; motorists rolled their windows down and asked for directions, which were cheerfully given. Egyptian males are not afraid to hold hands with each other or to ask for directions, which does not mean that they should be confused with sensitive New Age males.

The mangled ends of the cable were cleanly hacksawed and stripped, and a 2-meter-long segment of the same type of cable was wrestled out of a car and brought into the pit. Two lengths of lead pipe were threaded onto it, later to serve as protective bandages for the splices, and then the splicing began, one conductor at a time. Engineer Musalam watched attentively while I badgered him with nerdy questions.He brought me up to speed on the latest submarine cable gossip. During the previous month, in mid-June, SEA-ME-WE 2 had been cut twice between Djibouti and India. Two cable ships, *Restorer* and *Enterprise,* had been sent to fix the breaks. But fire had broken out in the engine room of the *Enterprise* (maybe a problem with the dilithium crystals), putting it into repairs for four weeks. So *Restorer* had to fix both breaks. But because of bad weather, only one of the faults had been repaired as of July 26. In the meantime, all of SEA-ME-WE 2's traffic had been shunted to a satellite link reserved as a backup.

Satellite links have enough bandwidth to fill in for a second-generation optical cable like SEA-ME-WE 2 but not enough to replace a third-generation one like FLAG or SEA-ME-WE 3. The cable industry is therefore venturing into new and somewhat unexplored territory with the current generation of cables. It is out of the question to run such a system without having elaborate backup plans, and if satellites can't hack it anymore, the only possible backup is on another cable—almost by definition, a competing cable. So as intensely as rival companies may compete with each other for customers, they are probably cooperating at the same time by reserving capacity on each other's systems. This presumably accounts for the fact that they are eager to spread nasty information about each other but will never do so on the record.

I didn't know the exact route of SEA-ME-WE 3 and was intrigued to learn that it will be passing through the same building in Alexandria as SEA-ME-WE 1 and 2, which is also the same building that will be used by FLAG. In addition, there is a new submarine cable called Africa 1 that is going to completely encircle that continent, it being much easier to circumnavigate Africa with a cable-laying ship than to run ducts and cables across it (though I would like to see Alan Wall have a go at it). Africa 1 will also pass through Engineer Musalam's building in Alexandria, which will therefore serve as the cross-connect among essentially all the traffic of Africa, Europe, and Asia.

Though Engineer Musalam is not the type who would come out and say it, the fact is that in a couple of years he's going to be running what is arguably the most important information nexus on the planet.

As the sun dropped behind the western Sahara (I imagined Mu'ammar Gadhafi out there somewhere, picking up his telephone to hear a fast busy signal), Engineer Musalam drove me into Alexandria in his humble subcompact to see this planetary nexus.

It is an immense neoclassical pile constructed in 1933 by the British to house their PTT operations. Since then, it has changed very little except for the addition of a window air conditioner in Engineer Musalam's office. The building faces Alexandria's railway station across an asphalt square crowded with cars, trucks, donkey carts, and pedestrians.

I do not think any other hacker tourist will ever make it inside this building. If you do so much as raise a camera to your face in its vicinity, an angry man in a uniform will charge up to you and let you get a very good look at the bayonet fixed to the end of his automatic weapon. So let me try to convey what it is like:

The adjective *Blade-Runneresque* means much to those who have seen the movie. (For those who haven't, just keep reading.) I will, however, never again be able to watch *Blade Runner*, because all of the buildings that looked so cool, so exquisitely art-directed in the movie, will now, to me, look like feeble efforts to capture a few traces of ARENTO's Alexandria station at night.

The building is a titanic structure that goes completely dark at night and becomes a maze of black corridors that appear to stretch on into infinity. Some illumination, and a great deal of generalized din, sifts in from the nearby square through broken windows. It has received very limited maintenance in the last half-century but will probably stand as long as the pyramids. The urinals alone look like something out of Luxor. The building's cavernous stairwells consist of profoundly worn white marble steps winding around a central shaft that is occupied by an old-fashioned wrought-iron elevator with all of the guts exposed: rails, cables, counterweights, and so on. Litter and debris have accumulated at the bottom of these pits. At the top, nocturnal birds have found their way in through open or broken windows and now tear around in the blackness like Stealth fighters, hunting for insects and making eerie keening noises—not the twitter of songbirds but the alien screech of movie pterodactyls. Gaunt cats prowl soundlessly up and down the stairs. A big microwave relay tower has been planted on the roof, and the red aircraft warning lights hang in the sky like fat planets. They shed a vague illumination back into the building, casting faint cyan shadows. Looking into the building's courtyards you may see, for a moment, a human figure silhouetted in a doorway by blue fluorescent light. A chair sits next to a dust-fogged window that has been cracked open to let in cool night air. Down in the square, people are buying and selling, young men strolling hand in hand through a shambolic market scene. In the windows of apartment buildings across the street, women sit in their colorful but demure garments holding tumblers of sweet tea.

In the midst of all this, then, you walk through a door into a vast room, and there it is: the cable station, rack after rack after rack of gleaming Alcatel and Siemens equipment, black phone handsets for the order wires, labeled Palermo and Tripoli and Cairo. Taped to a pillar is an Arabic prayer and faded photograph of the faithful circling the Ka'aba. The equipment here is of a slightly older vintage than what we saw in Japan, but only because the cables are older; when FLAG and SEA-ME-WE 3 and Africa 1 come through, Engineer Musalam will have one of the building's numerous unused rooms scrubbed out and filled with state-of-the-art gear.

A few engineers pad through the place. The setup is instantly recognizable; you can see the same thing anywhere nerds are performing the kinds of technical hacks that keep modern governments alive. The Manhattan Project, Bletchley Park, the National Security Agency, and, I would guess, Saddam Hussein's weapons labs are all built on the same plan: a big space ringed by anxious, ignorant, heavily armed men, looking outward. Inside that perimeter, a surprisingly small number of hackers wander around through untidy offices making the world run.

If you turn your back on the equipment through which the world's bits are swirling, open one of the windows, wind up, and throw a stone pretty hard, you can just about bonk that used book peddler on the head. Because this place, soon to be the most important data nexus on the planet, happens to be constructed virtually on top of the ruins of the Great Library of Alexandria.

THE *LALLA ROOKH*

When William Thomson became Lord Kelvin and entered the second phase of his life—tooling around on his yacht, the *Lalla Rookh*—he appeared to lose interest in telegraphy and got sidetracked into topics that, on first reading, seem unrelated to his earlier interests— disappointingly mundane. One of these was depth sounding, and the other was the nautical compass.

At the time, depths were sounded by heaving a lead-weighted rope over the side of the ship and letting it pay out until it hit bottom. So far, so easy, but hauling thousands of meters of soggy rope, plus a lead weight, back onto the ship required the efforts of several sailors and took a long time. The U.S. Navy ameliorated the problem by rigging it so that the weight could be detached and simply discarded on the bottom, but this only replaced one problem with another one in that a separate weight had to be carried for each sounding. Either way, the job was a mess and could be done only rarely. This probably explains why ships were constantly running aground in those days, leading to a relentless, ongoing massacre of crew and passengers compared to which today's problem of bombs and airliners is like a Sunday stroll through Disney World.

In keeping with his general practice of using subtlety where moronic brute force had failed, Kelvin replaced the soggy rope with a piano wire, which in turn enabled him to replace the heavy weight with a much smaller one. This idea might seem obvious to us now, but it was apparently quite the brainstorm. The tension in the wire was so light that a single sailor could reel it in by turning a spoked wooden wheel.

The first time Kelvin tried this, the wheel began to groan after a while and finally imploded. Dental hygienists, or people who floss the way they do (using extravagantly long pieces of floss and wrapping the used part around a fingertip), will already know why. The first turn of floss exerts only light pressure on the finger, but the second turn doubles it, and so on, until, as you are coming to the end of the process, your fingertip has turned a gangrenous purple. In the same way, the tension on Kelvin's piano wire, though small enough to be managed by one man, became enormous after a few hundred turns. No reasonable wheel could endure such stress.

Chagrined and embarrassed, Kelvin invented a stress-relief mechanism. On one side of it the wire was tight, on the other side it was slack and could be taken up by the wheel without compressing the hub. Once this was out of the way, the challenge became how to translate the length of piano wire that had been paid out into an accurate depth reading. One could never assume that the wire ran straight down to the bottom. Usually the vessel was moving, so the lead weight would trail behind it. Furthermore, a line stretched between two points in this way forms a curve known to mathematicians as a catenary, and of course the curve is longer than a straight line between the same two points. Kelvin had to figure out what sorts of catenary curves his piano wire would assume under various conditions of vessel speed and ocean depth—an essentially tedious problem that seems well beneath the abilities of the father of thermodynamics.

In any case, he figured it out and patented everything. Once again he made a ton of money. At the same time, he revolutionized the field of bathymetry and probably saved a large number of lives by making it easier for mariners to take frequent depth soundings. At the same time, he invented a vastly improved form of ship's compass which was as big an improvement over the older models as his depth-sounding equipment was over the soggy rope. Attentive readers will not be surprised to learn that he patented this device and made a ton of money from it.

Kelvin had revolutionized the art of finding one's way on the ocean, both in the vertical (depth) dimension and in the horizontal (compass) dimensions. He had made several fortunes in the process and spent a great deal of his intellectual gifts on pursuits that, I thought at first, could hardly have been less relevant to his earlier work on undersea cables. But that was my problem, not his. I didn't figure out what he was up to until very close to the ragged end of my hacker tourism binge.

SLACK

The first time a cable-savvy person uses the word *slack* in your presence, you'll be tempted to assume he is using it in the loose, figurative way—as a layperson uses it. After the eightieth or ninetieth time, and after the cable guy has spent a while talking about the seemingly paradoxical notion of slack control and extolling the sophistication of his ship's slack control systems and his computer's slack numerical-simulation software, you begin to understand that slack plays as pivotal a role in a cable lay as, say, thrust does in a moon mission.

He who masters slack in all of its fiendish complexity stands

astride the cable world like a colossus; he who is clueless about slack
either snaps his cable in the middle of the ocean or piles it in a snarl
on the ocean floor—which is precisely what early 19th-century cable
layers spent most of their time doing.

The basic problem of slack is akin to a famous question underlying the mathematical field of fractals: How long is the coastline of
Great Britain? If I take a wall map of the isle and measure it with a
ruler and multiply by the map's scale, I'll get one figure. If I do the
same thing using a set of large-scale ordnance survey maps, I'll get
a much higher figure because those maps will show zigs and zags in
the coastline that are polished to straight lines on the wall map. But
if I went all the way around the coast with a tape measure, I'd pick
up even smaller variations and get an even larger number. If I did it
with calipers, the number would be larger still. This process can be
repeated more or less indefinitely, and so it is impossible to answer
the original question straightforwardly. The length of the coastline
of Great Britain must be defined in terms of fractal geometry.

A cross-section of the seafloor has the same property. The route
between the landing station at Songkhla, Thailand, and the one at Lan
Tao Island, Hong Kong, might have a certain length when measured
on a map, say 2,500 kilometers. But if you attach a 2,500-kilometer
cable to Songkhla and, wearing a diving suit, begin manually unroll-
ing it across the seafloor, you will run out of cable before you reach
the public beach at Tong Fuk. The reason is that the cable follows the
bumpy topography of the seafloor, which ends up being a longer distance than it would be if the seafloor were mirror-flat.

Over long (intercontinental) distances, the difference averages
out to about 1 percent, so you might need a 2,525-kilometer cable to
go from Songkhla to Lan Tao. The extra 1 percent is slack, in the sense
that if you grabbed the ends and pulled the cable infinitely tight (bar
tight, as they say in the business), it would theoretically straighten
out and you would have an extra 25 kilometers. This slack is ideally
molded into the contour of the seafloor as tightly as a shadow, running straight and true along the surveyed course. As little slack as

possible is employed, partly because cable costs a lot of money (for the FLAG cable, $16,000 to $28,000 per kilometer, depending on the amount of armoring) and partly because loose coils are just asking for trouble from trawlers and other hazards. In fact, there is so little slack (in the layperson's sense of the word) in a well-laid cable that it cannot be grappled and hauled to the surface without snapping it.

This raises two questions, one simple and one nauseatingly difficult and complex. First, how does one repair a cable if it's too tight to haul up?

The answer is that it must first be pulled slightly off the seafloor by a detrenching grapnel, which is a device, meant to be towed behind a ship, that rolls across the bottom of the ocean on two fat tractor tires. Centered between those tires is a stout, wicked-looking, C-shaped hook, curving forward at the bottom like a stinger. It carves its way through the muck and eventually gets under the cable and lifts it up and holds it steady just above the seafloor. At this point its tow rope is released and buoyed off.

The ship now deploys another towed device called a cutter, which, seen from above, is shaped like a manta ray. On the top and bottom surfaces it carries V-shaped blades. As the ship makes another pass over the detrenching grapnel, one of these blades catches the cable and severs it.

It is now possible to get hold of the cut ends, using other grapnels. A cable repair ship carries many different kinds of grapnels and other hardware, and keeping track of them and their names (like "long prong Sam") is sort of like taking a course in exotic marine zoology. One of the ends is hauled up on board ship, and a new length of cable is spliced onto it solely to provide excess slack. Only now can both ends of the cable be brought aboard the ship at the same time and the final splice made.

But now the cable has way too much slack. It can't just be dumped overboard, because it would form an untidy heap on the bottom, easily snagged. Worse, its precise location would not be known, which is suicide from a legal point of view. As long as a cable's position is pre-

cisely known and marked on charts, avoiding it is the responsibility
of every mariner who comes that way. If it's out of place, any snags are
the responsibility of the cable's owners.

So the loose loop of cable must be carefully lowered to the bottom
on the end of a rope and arranged into a sideways bight that lies
alongside the original route of the cable something like an oxbow
lake beside a river channel. The geometry of this bight is carefully
recorded with sidescan sonar so that the information can be forwarded to the people who update the world's nautical charts.

One problem: now you have a rope between your ship's winch
and the recently laid cable. It looks like an old-fashioned, hairy, organic jute rope, but it has a core of steel. It is a badass rope, extremely
strong and heavy and expensive. You could cut it off and drop it, but
this would waste money and leave a wild rope trailing across the seafloor, inviting more snags.

So at this point you deploy your submersible remotely operated
vehicle (ROV) on the end of an umbilical. It rolls across the seabed on
its tank tracks, finds the rope, and cuts it with its terrifying hydraulic
guillotine.

Sad to say, that was the answer to the easy question. The hard one
goes like this: You are the master of a cable ship just off Songkhla,
and you have taken on 2,525 kilometers of cable which you are about
to lay along the 2500-kilometer route between there and Tong Fuk
Beach on Lan Tao Island. You have the 1 percent of slack required.
But 1 percent is just an average figure for the whole route. In some
places the seafloor is rugged and may need 5 percent slack; in others
it is perfectly flat and the cable may be laid straight as a rod. Here's
the question: How do you ensure that the extra 25 kilometers ends up
where it's supposed to?

Remember that you are on a ship moving up and down on the
waves and that you will be stretching the cable out across a distance
of several kilometers between the ship and the contact point on

the ocean floor, sometimes through undersea currents. If you get it wrong, you'll get suspensions in the cable, which will eventually develop into faults, or you'll get loops, which will be snagged by trawlers. Worse yet, you might actually snap the cable. All of these, and many more entertaining things, happened during the colorful early years of the cable business.

The answer has to do with slack control. And most of what is known about slack control is known by Cable & Wireless Marine. AT&T presumably knows about slack control too, but Cable & Wireless Marine has twice as many ships and dominates the deep-sea cable-laying industry. The Japanese can lay cable in shallow water and can repair it anywhere. But the reality is that when you want to slam a few thousand kilometers of state-of-the-art optical fiber across a major ocean, you call Cable & Wireless Marine, based in England. That is pretty much what FLAG did several years ago.

IN WHICH THE HACKER TOURIST TREKS TO LAND'S END, THE HAUNT OF DRUIDS, PIRATES, AND TELEGRAPHERS. AN IDYLLIC HIKE TO THE TINY CORNISH TOWN OF PORTHCURNO. MORE FLAGON HOISTING AT THE CABLE STATION. LORD KELVIN'S HANDIWORK EXAMINED AND EXPLAINED. EARLY BITS. THE SURVEYORS OF THE OCEANS IN CHELMSFORD, AND HOW COMPUTERS PLAY AN ESSENTIAL PART IN THEIR WORK. ALEXANDER GRAHAM BELL, THE SECOND SUPREME NINJA HACKER MAGE LORD, AND HIS MISGUIDED ANALOG DETOUR. LEGACY OF KELVIN, BELL, AND FLAG TO THE WIRED WORLD.

50° 3.965' N, 5° 42.745' W Land's End, Cornwall, England

As anyone can see from a map of England, Cornwall is a good jumping-off place for cables across the Atlantic, whether they are laid westward to the Americas or southward to Spain or the Azores. A cable from this corner of the island needs to traverse neither the English Channel nor the Irish Sea, both of which are shallow and fraught with shipping. Cornwall also possesses the other necessary prerequisite of a cable landing site in that it is an ancient haunt of pirates and smugglers and is littered with ceremonial ruins left behind by shadowy occult figures. The cable station here is called Porthcurno.

Not knowing exactly where Porthcurno is (it is variously marked on maps, if marked at all), the hacker tourist can find it by starting at Land's End, which is unambiguously located (go to England; walk west until the land ends). He can then walk counterclockwise around the coastline. The old fractal question of "How long is the coastline of Great Britain" thus becomes more than a purely abstract exercise. The answer is that in Cornwall it is much longer than it looks, because the fractal dimension of the place is high—Cornwall is bumpy. All of the English people I talked to before getting here told me that the place was rugged and wild and beautiful, but I snidely assumed that they meant "by the standards of England." As it turns out, Cornwall is rugged and wild and beautiful even by the standards of, say, Northern California. In America we assume that any place where humans have lived for more than a generation has been pretty thoroughly screwed up, so it is startling to come to a place where 2,000-year-old ruins are all over the place and find that it is still virtually a wilderness.

From Land's End you can reach Porthcurno in two or three hours, depending on how much time you spend gawking at views, clambering up and down cliffs, exploring caves, and taking dips at small perfect beaches that can be found wedged into clefts in the rock.

Cables almost never land in industrial zones, first because such areas are heavily traveled and frequently dredged, second because of pure geography. Industry likes rivers, which bring currents, which are bad for cables. Cities like flat land. But flat land above the tide line implies a correspondingly gentle slope below the water, meaning that the cable will pass for a greater distance through the treacherous shallows. Three to thirty meters is the range of depth where most of the ocean dynamics are and where cable must be armored. But in wild places like Porthcurno or Lan Tao Island, rivers are few and small, and the land bursts almost vertically from the sea. The same geography, of course, favors pirates and smugglers.

On the other hand, what looks to a pirate like an accessible port of entry can be a remote refuge to a landlubber. Cornwall, like Wales, is one of the places where peculiar and unpopular Britishers have long gone to seek refuge—it was the last part of England to become English. And when Kublai Khan was storming China, the last Mongol emperor fled southward until he reached—you guessed it—Lan Tao Island, where he and his dynasty died.

But all becomes clear when you clamber over yet another headland and discover Porthcurno, a perfect beach of pale sand sloping gently out of clear turquoise water and giving way to a cozy valley that, a few miles inland, rises to the level of the inland plateau. To the hacker tourist, it comes as no surprise to learn that much of that valley has been owned by Cable & Wireless, or its predecessors, for more than a century. To anyone else, the only obvious hint that this place has anything to do with cables comes from the rusty yellow signs that stand above the beach proclaiming "Telephone Cable" as a feeble effort to dissuade mariners from using the bay for anchor practice.

It was here that the long-range submarine cable business, after any number of early-round knockdowns, finally dragged its bloody self up off the mat and really began to kick ass.

By the year 1870, Kelvin and others had finally worked the bugs out of the technology. A three-master anchored off this beach in that year and landed a cable that eventually ran to Lisbon, Gibraltar, Malta, Alexandria, Cairo, Suez, Aden (now part of Yemen), Bombay, over land to the east coast of India, then on to Penang, Malacca, Singapore, Batavia (later Jakarta), and finally to Darwin, Australia. It was Australia's first direct link to Great Britain and, hardly by coincidence, also connected every British outpost of importance in between. It was the spinal cord of the Empire.

The company that laid the first part of it was called the Falmouth, Gibraltar and Malta Telegraph Company, which is odd because the cable never went to Falmouth—a major port some 50 kilometers from Porthcurno. Enough anchors had hooked cables, even by that point, that "major port" and "submarine cable station" were seen to be incompatible, so the landing site was moved to Porthcurno.That was just the beginning: the company (later called the Eastern Cable Company, after all the segments between Porthcurno and Darwin merged) was every bit as conscious of the importance of redundancy as today's Internet architects—probably more so, given the unreliability of early cables. They ran another cable from Porthcurno to the Azores and then to Ascension Island, where it forked: one side headed to South America while the other went to Cape Town and then across the Indian Ocean. Subsequent transatlantic cables terminated at Porthcurno as well.

Many of the features that made Cornwall attractive to cable operators also made it a suitable place to conduct transatlantic radio experiments, and so in 1900 Guglielmo Marconi himself established a laboratory on Lizard Point, which is directly across the bay from Porthcurno, some 30 kilometers distant. Marconi had another station on the Isle of Wight, a few hundred kilometers to the east, and when he succeeded in sending messages between the two, he constructed a more powerful transmitter at the Lizard station and began trying to send messages to a receiver in Newfoundland. The competitive threat to the cable industry could hardly have been more obvious, and so the Eastern Telegraph Company raised a 60-meter mast above its Porthcurno site, hoisted an antenna, and began eavesdropping on Marconi's transmissions. A couple of decades later, after the Italian had worked the bugs out of the system, the government stepped in and arranged a merger between his company and the submarine cable companies to create a new, fully integrated communications monopoly called Cable & Wireless.

50° 2.602' N, 5° 39.054' W Museum of Submarine Telegraphy, Porthcurno, Cornwall

On a sunny summer day, Porthcurno Beach was crowded with holidaymakers. The vast majority of these were scantily clad and tended to face toward the sun and the sea. The fully clothed and heavily shod tourists with their backs to the water were the hacker tourists; they were headed for a tiny, windowless cement blockhouse, scarcely big enough to serve as a one-car garage, planted at the apex of the beach. There was a sign on the wall identifying it as the Museum of Submarine Telegraphy and stating that it is open only on Wednesday and Friday.

This was appalling news. We arrived on a Monday morning, and our maniacal schedule would not brook a two-day wait. Stunned, heartbroken, we walked around the thing a couple of times, which occupied about 30 seconds. The lifeguard watched us uneasily. We admired the brand-new manhole cover set into the ground in front of the hut, stamped with the year '96, which strongly suggested a connection with FLAG. We wandered up the valley for a couple of hundred meters until it opened up into a parking lot for beach-goers, surrounded by older white masonry buildings. These were well-maintained but did not seem to be used for much. We peered at a couple of these and speculated (wrongly, as it turned out) that they were the landing station for FLAG.

Tantalizing hints were everywhere: the inevitable plethora of manholes, networked to one another by long straight strips of new pavement set into the parking lot and the road. Nearby, a small junkheap containing several lengths of what to the casual visitor might look like old, dirty pipe but which on closer examination proved to be hunks of discarded coaxial cable. But all the buildings were locked and empty, and no one was around.

Our journey seemed to have culminated in failure. We then noticed that one of the white buildings had a sign on the door identifying it as The Cable Station—Free House. The sign was adorned with a painting of a Victorian shore landing in progress—a line of small boats supporting a heavy cable being payed out from a sailing ship anchored in Porthcurno Bay.

After coming all this way, it seemed criminal not to have a drink in this pub. By hacker tourist standards, a manhole cover counts as a major attraction, and so it was almost surreal to have stumbled across a place that had seemingly been conceived and built specifically for us. Indeed, we were the only customers in the place. We admired the photographs and paintings on the walls, which all had something or other to do with cables. We made friends with Sally the Dog, chatted with the proprietress, grabbed a pint, and went out into the beer garden to drown our sorrows.

Somewhat later, we unburdened ourselves to the proprietress, who looked a bit startled to learn of our strange mission, and said, "Oh, the fellows who run the museum are inside just now."

Faster than a bit speeding down an optical fiber we were back inside the pub where we discovered half a dozen distinguished gentlemen sitting around a table, finishing up their lunches. One of them, a tall, handsome, craggy sort, apologized for having ink on his fingers. We made some feeble effort to explain the concept of *Wired* magazine (never easy), and they jumped up from their seats, pulled key chains out of their pockets, and took us across the parking lot, through the gate, and into the museum proper. We made friends with Minnie the Cable Dog and got the tour. Our primary guides were Ron Werngren (the gent with ink on his fingers, which I will explain in a minute) and John Worrall, who is the cheerful, energetic, talkative sort who seems to be an obligatory feature of any cable-related site.

All of these men are retired Cable & Wireless employees. They sketched in for us the history of this strange compound of white buildings. Like any old-time cable station, it housed the equipment for receiving and transmitting messages as well as lodgings and support services for the telegraphers who manned it. But in addition it served as the campus of a school where Cable & Wireless foreign service staff were trained, complete with dormitories, faculty housing, gymnasium, and dining hall.

The whole campus has been shut down since 1970. In recent years, though, the gentlemen we met in the pub, with the assistance of a local historical trust, have been building and operating the Museum of Submarine Telegraphy here. These men are of a generation that trained on the campus shortly after World War II, and between them they have lived and worked in just as many exotic places as the latter-day cable guys we met on Lan Tao Island: Buenos Aires, Ascension Island, Cyprus, Jordan, the West Indies, Saudi Arabia, Bahrain, Trinidad, Dubai.

Fortunately, the tiny hut above the beach is not the museum. It's just the place where the cables are terminated. FLAG and other modern cables bypass it and terminate in a modern station up at the head of the valley, so all of the cables in this hut are old and out of service. They are labeled with the names of the cities where they terminate: Faial in the Azores, Brest in France, Bilbao in Spain, Gibraltar 1, Saint John's in Newfoundland, the Isles of Scilly, two cables to Carcavelos in Portugal, Vigo in Spain, Gibraltar 2 and 3. From this hut, the wires proceed up the valley a couple hundred meters to the cable station proper, which is encased in solid rock.

During World War II, the Porthcurno cable nexus was such a painfully obvious target for a Nazi attack that a detachment of Cornish miners were brought in to carve a big tunnel out of a rock hill that rises above the campus. This turned out to be so wet that it was necessary to then construct a house inside the tunnel, complete with pitched roof, gutters, and downspouts to carry away the eternal drizzle of groundwater. The strategically important parts of the cable station were moved inside. Porthcurno Bay and the Cable & Wireless campus were laced with additional defensive measures, like a fuel-filled pipe underneath the water to cremate incoming Huns.

Now the house in the tunnel is the home of the museum. It is sealed from the outside world by two blast doors, each of which consists of a foot-thick box welded together from inch-thick steel plate. The inner door has a gasket to keep out poison gas. Inside, the building is clean and almost cozy, and except for the lack of windows, one is not conscious of being underground.

Practically the first thing we saw upon entering was a fully functional Kelvin mirror galvanometer—the exquisitely sensitive detector that sent Wildman Whitehouse into ignominy, made the first transatlantic cable useful, and earned William Thomson his first major fortune. Most of its delicate innards are concealed within a metal case. The beam of light that reflects off its tiny twisting mirror shines against a long horizontal screen of paper, marked and numbered like a yardstick, extending about 10 inches on either side of a central zero point. The light forms a spot on this screen about the size and shape of a dime cut in half. It is so sensitive that merely touching the machine's case—grounding it—causes the spot of light to swing wildly to one end of the scale.

At Porthcurno this device was used for more than one purpose. One of the most important activities at a cable station is pinpointing the locations of faults, which is done by measuring the resistance in the cable. Since the resistance per unit of length is a known quantity, a precise measurement of resistance gives the distance to the fault. Measuring resistance was done by use of a device called a Wheatstone bridge. The museum has a beautiful one, built in a walnut box with big brass knobs for dialing in resistances. Use of the Wheatstone bridge relies on achieving a null current with the highest attainable level of precision, and for this purpose, no instrument on earth was better suited than the Kelvin mirror galvanometer. Locating a mid-ocean fault in a cable therefore was reduced to a problem of twiddling the dials on the Wheatstone bridge until the galvanometer's spot of light was centered on the zero mark.

The reason for the ink on Ron Werngren's fingers became evident when we moved to another room and beheld a genuine Kelvin siphon recorder, which he was in the process of debugging. This machine represented the first step in the removal of humans from the global communications loop that has culminated in the machine room at cable landing stations like Ninomiya.

After Kelvin's mirror galvanometer became standard equipment throughout the wired world, every message coming down the cables had to pass, briefly, through the minds of human operators such as the ones who were schooled at the Porthcurno campus. These were highly trained young men in slicked hair and starched collars, working in teams of two or three: one to watch the moving spot of light and divine the letters, a second to write them down, and, if the message were being relayed down another cable, a third to key it in again.

It was clear from the very beginning that this was an error-prone process, and when the young men in the starched collars began getting into fistfights, it also became clear that it was a job full of stress. The stress derived from the fact that if the man watching the spot of light let his attention wander for one moment, information would be forever lost. What was needed was some mechanical way to make a record of the signals coming down the cable. But because of the weakness of these signals, this was no easy job.

Lord Kelvin, never one to rest on his laurels, solved the problem with the siphon recorder. For all its historical importance, and for all the money it made Kelvin, it is a flaky-looking piece of business. There is a reel of paper tape which is drawn steadily through the machine by a motor. Mounted above it is a small reservoir containing perhaps a tablespoon of ink. What looks like a gossamer strand emerges from the ink and bends around through some delicate metal fittings so that its other end caresses the surface of the moving tape. This strand is actually an extremely thin glass tube that siphons the ink from the reservoir onto the paper. The idea is that the current in the cable, by passing through an electromechanical device, will cause this tube to move slightly to one side or the other, just like the spot of light in the mirror galvanometer. But the current in the old cables was so feeble that even the infinitesimal contact point between the glass tube and the tape still induced too much friction, so Kelvin invented a remarkable kludge: he built a vibrator into the system that causes the glass tube to thrum like a guitar string so that its point of contact on the paper is always in slight motion.

Dynamic friction (between moving objects) is always less than static friction (between objects that are at rest with respect to each other). The vibration in the glass siphon tube reduced the friction against the paper tape to the point where even the weak currents in a submarine cable could move it back and forth. Movement to one side of the tape represented a dot, to the other side a dash. We prevailed upon Werngren to tap out the message Get Wired. The result is on the cover of this magazine, and if you know Morse code you can pick the letters out easily.

The question naturally arises: How does one go about manufacturing a hollow glass tube thinner than a hair? More to the point, how did they do it 100 years ago? After all, as Worrall pointed out, they needed to be able to repair these machines when they were posted out on Ascension Island. The answer is straightforward and technically sweet: you take a much thicker glass tube, heat it over a Bunsen burner until it glows and softens, and then pull sharply on both ends. It forms a long, thin tendril, like a string of melted cheese stretching away from a piece of pizza. Amazingly, it does not close up into a solid glass fiber, but remains a tube no matter how thin it gets.

Exactly the same trick is used to create the glass fibers that run down the center of FLAG and other modern submarine cables: an ingot of very pure glass is heated until it glows, and then it is stretched. The only difference is that these are solid fibers rather than tubes, and, of course, it's all done using machines that assure a consistent result.

Moving down the room, we saw a couple of large tabletops devoted to a complete, functioning reproduction of a submarine cable system as it might have looked in the 1930s. The only difference is that the thousands of miles of intervening cable are replaced with short jumper wires so that transmitter, repeaters, and receiver are contained within a single room.

All the equipment is built the way they don't build things anymore: polished wooden cabinets with glass tops protecting gleaming brass machinery that whirrs and rattles and spins. Relays clack and things jiggle up and down. At one end of the table is an autotransmitter that reads characters off a paper tape, translates them into Morse code or cable code, and sends its output, in the form of a stream of electrical pulses, to a regenerator/retransmitter unit. In this case the unit is only a few feet away, but in practice it would have been on the other end of a long submarine cable, say in the Azores. This regenerator/retransmitter unit sends its output to a twin siphon-tube recorder which draws both the incoming signal (say, from London) and the outgoing signal as regenerated by this machine on the same paper tape at the same time. The two lines should be identical. If the machine is not functioning correctly, it will be obvious from a glance at the tape.

The regenerated signal goes down the table (or down another submarine cable) to a machine that records the message as a pattern of holes punched in tape. It also goes to a direct printer that hammers out the words of the message in capital letters on another moving strip of paper. The final step is a gummer that spreads stickum on the back of the tape so that it may be stuck onto a telegraph form. (They tried to use pregummed tape, but in the tropics it only coated the machinery with glue.)

Each piece of equipment on this tabletop is built around a motor that turns over at the same precise frequency. None of it would work—no device could communicate with any other device—unless all of those motors were spinning in lockstep with one another. The transmitter, regenerator/retransmitter, and printer all had to be in sync even though they were thousands of miles apart.

This feat is achieved by means of a collection of extremely precise analog machinery. The heart of the system is another polished box that contains a vibrating reed, electromagnetically driven, thrumming along at 30 cycles per second, generating the clock pulses that keep all the other machines turning over at the right pace. The reed is as precise as such a thing can be, but over time it is bound to drift and get out of sync with the other vibrating reeds in the other stations.

In order to control this tendency, a pair of identical pendulum clocks hang next to each other on the wall above. These clocks feed steady, one-second timing pulses into the box housing the reed. The reed, in turn, is driving a motor that is geared so that it should turn over at one revolution per second, generating a pulse with each revolution. If the frequency of the reed's vibration begins to drift, the motor's speed will drift along with it, and the pulse will come a bit too early or a bit too late. But these pulses are being compared with the steady one-second pulses generated by the double pendulum clock, and any difference between them is detected by a feedback system that can slightly speed up or slow down the vibration of the reed in order to correct the error. The result is a clock so steady that once one of them is set up in, say, London, and another is set up in, say, Cape Town, the machinery in those two cities will remain synched with each other indefinitely.

This is precisely the same function that is performed by the quartz clock chip at the heart of any modern computing device. The job performed by the regenerator/retransmitter is also perfectly recognizable to any modern digitally minded hacker tourist: it is an analog-to-digital converter. The analog voltages come down the cable into the device, the circuitry in the box decides whether the signal is a dot or a dash (or if you prefer, a 1 or a 0), and then an electromagnet physically moves one way or the other, depending on whether it's a dot or a dash. At that moment, the device is strictly digital. The electromagnet, by moving, then closes a switch that generates a new pulse of analog voltage that moves on down the cable. The hacker tourist, who has spent much of his life messing around with invisible, ineffable bits, can hardly fail to be fascinated when staring into the guts of a machine built in 1927, steadily hammering out bits through an electromechanical process that can be seen and even touched.

As I started to realize, and as John Worrall and many other cable-industry professionals subsequently told me, there have been new technologies but no new ideas since the turn of the century. Alas for Internet chauvinists who sneer at older, "analog" technology, this rule applies to the transmission of digital bits down wires, across long distances. We've been doing it ever since Morse sent "What hath God wrought!" from Washington to Baltimore.

(Latitude & longitude unknown) Cable & Wireless Marine, Chelmsford, England

[Note: I left my GPS receiver on a train in Bristol and had to do without it for a couple of weeks until Mr. Gallagher, station supervisor at Preston, Lancashire, miraculously found it and sent it back to me. Chelmsford is a half-hour train ride northeast of London.]

When last we saw our hypothetical cable-ship captain, sitting off of Songkhla with 2,525 kilometers of very expensive cable, we had put him in a difficult spot by asking the question of how he could ensure that his 25 kilometers of slack ended up in exactly the right place. Essentially the same question was raised a few years ago when FLAG approached Cable & Wireless Marine and said, in effect: "We are going to buy 28,000 kilometers of fancy cable from AT&T and KDD, and we would like to have it go from England to Spain to Italy to Egypt to Dubai to India to Thailand to Hong Kong to China to Korea to Japan. We would like to pay for as little slack as possible, because the cable is expensive. What little slack we do buy needs to go in exactly the right place, please. What should we do next?"

So it was that Captain Stuart Evans's telephone rang. At the time (September 1992), he was working for a company called Worldwide

Ocean Surveying, but by the time we met him, that company had been bought out by Cable & Wireless Marine, of which he is now general manager—survey. Evans is a thoroughly pleasant middle-aged fellow, a former merchant marine captain, who seemed just a bit taken aback that anyone would care about the minute details of what he and his staff do for a living. A large part of being a hacker tourist is convincing people that you are really interested in the nitty-gritty and not just looking for a quick, painless sound bite or two; once this is accomplished, they always warm to the task, and Captain Evans was no exception.Evans's mission was to help FLAG select the most economical and secure route. The initial stages of the process are straightforward: choose the landing sites and then search existing data concerning the routes joining those sites. This is referred to as a desk search, with mild but unmistakable condescension. Evans and his staff came up with a proposed route, did the desk search, and sent it to FLAG for approval. When FLAG signed off on this, it was time to go out and perform the real survey. This process ran from January to September 1994.

Each country uses the same landing sites over and over again for each new cable, so you might think that the routes from, say, Porthcurno to Spain would be well known by now. In fact, every new cable passes over some virgin territory, so a survey is always necessary. Furthermore, the territory does not remain static. There are always new wrecks, mobile sand waves, changes in anchorage patterns, and other late-breaking news.

To lay a cable competently you must have a detailed survey of a corridor surrounding the intended route. In shallow water, you have relatively precise control over where the cable ends up, but the bottom can be very irregular, and the cable is likely to be buried into the seabed. So you want a narrow (1 kilometer wide) corridor with high resolution. In deeper water, you have less lateral control over the descending cable, but at the same time the phenomena you're looking at are bigger, so you want a survey corridor whose width is 2 to 3 times the ocean depth but with a coarser resolution. A resolution of 0.5 percent of the depth might be considered a minimum standard, though the FLAG survey has it down to 0.25 percent in most places. So, for example, in water 5,000 meters deep, which would be a somewhat typical value away from the continental shelf, the survey corridor would be 10 to 15 kilometers in width, and a good vertical resolution would be 12 meters.

The survey process is almost entirely digital. The data is collected by a survey ship carrying a sonar rig that fires 81 beams spreading down and out from the hull in a fan pattern. At a depth of 5,000 meters, the result, approximately speaking, is to divide the 10-kilometer-wide corridor into grid squares 120 meters wide and 175 meters long and get the depth of each one to a precision of some 12 meters.

The raw data goes to an onboard SPARC station that performs data assessment in real time as a sort of quality assurance check, then streams the numbers onto DAT cassettes. The survey team is keeping an eye on the results, watching for any formations through which cable cannot be run. These are found more frequently in the Indian than in the Atlantic Ocean, mostly because the Atlantic has been charted more thoroughly.

Steep slopes are out. A cable that traverses a steep slope will always want to slide down it sideways, secretly rendering every nautical chart in the world obsolete while imposing unknown stresses on the cable. This and other constraints may throw an impassable barrier across the proposed route of the cable. When this happens, the survey ship has to backtrack, move sideways, and survey other corridors parallel and adjacent to the first one, gradually building a map of a broader area, until a way around the obstruction is found. The proposed route is redrafted, and the survey ship proceeds.

The result is a shitload of DAT tapes and a good deal of other data as well. For example, in water less than 1,200 meters deep, they also use sidescan sonar to generate analog pictures of the bottom—these look something like black-and-white photographs taken with a point light source, with the exception that shadows are white instead of black. It is possible to scan the same area from several different directions and then digitally combine the images to make something that looks just like a photo. This may provide crucial information that would never show up on the survey—for example, a dense pattern of anchor scars indicates that this is not a good place to lay a cable. The survey ship can also drop a flowmeter that will provide information about currents in the ocean.

The result of all this, in the case of the FLAG survey, was about a billion data points for the bathymetric survey alone, plus a mass of sidescan sonar plots and other documentation. The tapes and the plots filled a room about 5 meters square all the way to the ceiling. The quantity of data involved was so vast that to manage it on paper, while it might have been theoretically possible given unlimited resources, was practically impossible given that FLAG is run by mortals and actually has to make money. FLAG is truly an undertaking of the digital age in that it simply couldn't have been accomplished without the use of computers to manage the data. Evans's mission was to present FLAG with a final survey report. If he had done it the old-fashioned way, the report would have occupied some 52 linear feet of shelf space, plus several hefty cabinets full of charts, and the inefficiency of dealing with so much paper would have made it nearly impossible for FLAG's decision makers to grasp everything.

Instead, Evans bought FLAG a PC and a plotter. During the summer of 1994, while the survey data was still being gathered, he had some developers write browsing software. Keeping in mind that FLAG's investors were mostly high-finance types with little technical or nautical background, they gave the browser a familiar, easy-to-use graphical user interface. The billion data points and the sidescan sonar imagery were boiled down into a form that would fit onto 5 CD-ROMs, and in that form the final report was presented to FLAG at the end of 1994. When FLAG's decision makers wanted to check out a particular part of the route, they could zoom in on it by clicking on a map, picking a small square of ocean, and blowing it up to reveal several different kinds of plots: a topographic map of the seafloor, information abstracted from the sidescan sonar images, a depth profile along the route, and another profile showing the consistency of the bottom—whether muck, gravel, sand, or hard rock. All of these could be plotted out on meterwide sheets of paper that provided a much higher-resolution view than is afforded by the computer screen.

This represents a noteworthy virtuous circle—a self-amplifying trend. The development of graphical user interfaces has led to rapid growth in personal computer use over the last decade, and the coupling of that technology with the Internet has caused explosive growth in the use of the World Wide Web, generating enormous demand for bandwidth. That (in combination, of course, with other demands) creates a demand for submarine cables much longer and more ambitious than ever before, which gets investors excited—but the resulting project is so complex that the only way they can wrap their minds around it and make intelligent decisions is by using a computer with a graphical user interface.

HACKING WIRES

As you may have figured out by this point, submarine cables are an incredible pain in the ass to build, install, and operate. Hooking stuff up to the ends of them is easy by comparison. So it has always been the case that cables get laid first and then people begin trying to think of new ways to use them. Once a cable is in place, it tends to be treated not as a technological artifact but almost as if it were some naturally occurring mineral formation that might be exploited in any number of different ways.

This was true from the beginning. The telegraphy equipment of 1857 didn't work when it was hooked up to the first transatlantic cable. Kelvin had to invent the mirror galvanometer, and later the siphon recorder, to make use of it. Needless to say, there were many other Victorian hackers trying to patent inventions that would enable more money to be extracted from cables. One of these was a Scottish-Canadian-American elocutionist named Alexander Graham Bell, who worked out of a laboratory in Boston.

Bell was one of a few researchers pursuing a hack based on the phenomenon of resonance. If you open the lid of a grand piano, step on the sustain pedal, and sing a note into it, such as a middle C, the strings for the piano's C keys will vibrate sympathetically, while the D strings will remain still. If you sing a D, the D strings vibrate and the C strings don't. Each string resonates only at the frequency to which it has been tuned and is deaf to other frequencies.

If you were to hum out a Morse code pattern of dots and dashes, all at middle C, a deaf observer watching the strings would notice a corresponding pattern of vibrations. If, at the same time, a second person was standing next to you humming an entirely different sequence of dots and dashes, but all on the musical tone of D, then a second deaf observer, watching the D strings, would be able to read that message, and so on for all the other tones on the scale. There would be no interference between the messages; each would come through as clearly as if it were the only message being sent. But anyone who wasn't deaf would hear a cacophony of noise as all the message senders sang in different rhythms, on different notes. If you took this to an extreme, built a special piano with strings tuned as close to each other as possible, and trained the message senders to hum Morse code as fast as possible, the sound would merge into an insane roar of white noise.

Electrical oscillations in a wire follow the same rules as acoustical ones in the air, so a wire can carry exactly the same kind of cacophony, with the same results. Instead of using piano strings, Bell and others were using a set of metal reeds like the ones in a harmonica, each tuned to vibrate at a different frequency. They electrified the reeds in such a way that they generated not only acoustical vibrations but corresponding electrical ones. They sought to combine the electrical vibrations of all these reeds into one complicated waveform and feed it into one end of a cable. At the far end of the cable, they would feed the signal into an identical set of reeds. Each reed would vibrate in sympathy only with its counterpart on the other end of the wire, and by recording the pattern of vibrations exhibited by that reed, one could extract a Morse code message independent of the other messages being transmitted on the other reeds. For the price of one wire, you could send many simultaneous coded messages and have them all sort themselves out on the other end.

To make a long story short, it didn't work. But it did raise an interesting question. If you could take vibrations at one frequency and combine them with vibrations at another frequency, and another, and another, to make a complicated waveform, and if that waveform could be transmitted to the other end of a submarine cable intact, then there was no reason in principle why the complex waveform known as the human voice couldn't be transmitted in the same way. The only difference would be that the waves in this case were merely literal representations of sound waves, rather than Morse code sequences transmitted at different frequencies. It was, in other words, an analog hack on a digital technology.

We have all been raised to think of the telephone as a vast improvement on the telegraph, as the steamship was to the sailing ship or the electric lightbulb to the candle, but from a hacker tourist's point of view, it begins to seem like a lamentable wrong turn. Until Bell, all telegraphy was digital. The multiplexing system he worked on was purely digital in concept even if it did make use of some analog properties of matter (as indeed all digital equipment does). But when his multiplexing scheme went sour, he suddenly went analog on us.

Fortunately, the story has a happy ending, though it took a century to come about. Because analog telephony did not require expertise in Morse code, anyone could take advantage of it. It became enormously popular and generated staggering quantities of revenue that underwrote the creation of a fantastically immense communications web reaching into every nook and cranny of every developed country.

Then modems came along and turned the tables. Modems are a digital hack on an analog technology, of course; they take the digits from your computer and convert them into a complicated analog waveform that can be transmitted down existing wires. The roar of white noise that you hear when you listen in on a modem transmission is exactly what Bell was originally aiming for with his reeds. Modems, and everything that has ensued from them, like the World Wide Web, are just the latest example of a pattern that was established by Kelvin 140 years ago, namely, hacking existing wires by inventing new stuff to put on the ends of them.

It is natural, then, to ask what effect FLAG is going to have on the latest and greatest cable hack: the Internet. Or perhaps it's better to ask whether the Internet affected FLAG. The explosion of the Web happened after FLAG was planned. Taketo Furuhata, president and CEO of IDC, which runs the Miura station, says: "I don't know whether Nynex management foresaw the burst of demand related to the Internet a few years ago—I don't think so. Nobody—not even AT&T people—foresaw this. But the demand for Internet transmission is so huge that FLAG will certainly become a very important pipe to transmit such requirements."

John Mercogliano, vice president—Europe, Nynex Network Systems (Bermuda) Ltd., says that during the early 1990s when FLAG was getting organized, Nynex executives felt in their guts that something big was going to happen involving broadband multimedia transmission over cables. They had a media lab that was giving demos of medical imaging and other such applications. "We knew the Internet was coming—we just didn't know it was going to be called the Internet," he says.

FLAG may, in fact, be the last big cable system that was planned in the days when people didn't know about the Internet. Those days were a lot calmer in the global telecom industry. Everything was controlled by monopolies, and cable construction was based on sober, scientific forecasts, analogous, in some ways, to the actuarial tables on which insurance companies predicate their policies.

When you talk on the phone, your words are converted into bits that are sent down a wire. When you surf the Web, your computer sends out bits that ask for yet more bits to be sent back. When you go to the store and buy a Japanese VCR or an article of clothing with a Made in Thailand label, you're touching off a cascade of information flows that eventually leads to transpacific faxes, phone calls, and money transfers.

If you get a fast busy signal when you dial your phone, or if your Web browser stalls, or if the electronics store is always low on inventory because the distribution system is balled up somewhere, then it means that someone, somewhere, is suffering pain. Eventually this pain gets taken out on a fairly small number of meek, mild-mannered statisticians—telecom traffic forecasters—who are supposed to see these problems coming.

Like many other telephony-related technologies, traffic forecasting was developed to a fine art a long time ago and rarely screwed up. Usually the telcos knew when the capacity of their systems was going to be stretched past acceptable limits. Then they went shopping for bandwidth. Cables got built.

That is all past history. "The telecoms aren't forecasting now," Mercogliano says. "They're reacting."

This is a big problem for a few different reasons. One is that cables take a few years to build, and, once built, last for a quarter of a century. It's not a nimble industry in that way. A PTT thinking about investing in a club cable is making a 25-year commitment to a piece of equipment that will almost certainly be obsolete long before it reaches the end of its working life. Not only are they risking lots of money, but they are putting it into an exceptionally long-term investment. Long-term investments are great if you have reliable long-term forecasts, but when your entire forecasting system gets blown out of the water by something like the Internet, the situation gets awfully complicated.

The Internet poses another problem for telcos by being asymmetrical. Imagine you are running an international telecom company in Japan. Everything you've ever done, since TPC–1 came into Ninomiya in '64, has been predicated on circuits. Circuits are the basic unit you buy and sell—they are to you what cars are to a Cadillac dealership. A circuit, by definition, is symmetrical. It consists of an equal amount of bandwidth in each direction—since most phone conversations, on average, entail both parties talking about the same amount. A circuit between Japan and the United States is something that enables data to be sent from Japan to the U.S., and from the U.S. to Japan, at the same rate—the same bandwidth. In order to get your hands on a circuit, you cut a deal with a company in the States. This deal is called a correspondent agreement.

One day, you see an ad in a magazine for a newfangled thing called a modem. You hook one end up to a computer and the other end to a phone line, and it enables the computer to grab a circuit and exchange data with some other computer with a modem. So far, so good. As a cable-savvy type, you know that people have been hacking cables in this fashion since Kelvin. As long as the thing works on the basis of circuits, you don't care—any more than a car salesman would care if someone bought Cadillacs, tore out the seats, and used them to haul gravel.

A few years later, you hear about some modem-related nonsense called the World Wide Web. And a year after that, everyone seems to be talking about it. About the same time, all of your traffic forecasts go down the toilet. Nothing's working the way it used to. Everything is screwed up.

Why? Because the Web is asymmetrical. All of your Japanese Web customers are using it to access sites in the States, because that's where all the sites are located. When one of them clicks on a button on an American Web page, a request is sent over the cable to the US. The request is infinitesimal, just a few bytes. The site in the States promptly responds by trying to send back a high-resolution, 24-bit color image of Cindy Crawford, or an MPEG film of a space shuttle mission. Millions of bytes. Your pipe gets jammed solid with incoming packets.

You're a businessperson. You want to make your customers happy. You want them to get their millions of bytes from the States in some reasonable amount of time. The only way to make this happen is to purchase more circuits on the cables linking Japan to the States. But if you do this, only half of each circuit is going to be used—the incoming half. The outgoing half will carry a miserable trickle of packets. Its bandwidth will be wasted. The correspondent agreement relationship, which has been the basis of the international telecom business ever since the first cables were laid, doesn't work anymore.

This, in combination with the havoc increasingly being wrought by callback services, is weird, bad, hairy news for the telecom monopolies. Mercogliano believes that the solution lies in some sort of bandwidth arbitrage scheme, but talking about that to an old-time telecrat is like describing derivative investments to an old codger who keeps his money under his mattress. "The club system is breaking down," Mercogliano says.

Somewhere between 50° 54.20062' N, 1° 26.87229 W AND 50° 54.20675' N, 1° 26.95470 W Cable ship *Monarch*, Southampton, England

John Mercogliano, if this is conceivable, logs even more frequent-flier miles, to even more parts of the planet, than the cable layers we met on Lan Tao Island. He lives in London, his office is in Amsterdam, his territory is Europe, he works for a company headquartered in Bermuda that has many ties to the New York metropolitan area and that does business everywhere from Porthcurno to Miura. He is trim, young-looking, and vigorous, but even so the schedule occasionally takes its toll on him, and he feels the need to just get away from his job for a few days and think about something—anything—other than submarine cables. The last time this feeling came over him, he made inquiries with a tourist bureau in Ireland that referred him to a quiet, out-of-the-way place on the coast: a stately home that had been converted to a seaside inn, an ideal place for him to go to get his mind off his work. Mercogliano flew to Ireland and made his way overland to the place, checked into his room, and began ambling through the building. The first thing he saw was a display case containing samples of various types of 19th-century submarine cables. It turned out that the former owner of this mansion had been the captain of the *Great Eastern*, the first of the great deep-sea cable-laying ships.

The *Great Eastern* got that job because it was by a long chalk the largest ship on the planet at the time—so large that its utter uselessness had made it a laughingstock, the *Spruce Goose* of its day. The second generation of long-range submarine cables, designed to Lord Kelvin's specifications after the debacle of 1857, were thick and heavy. Splicing segments together in mid-ocean had turned out to be problematical, so there were good reasons for wanting to make the cable in one huge piece and simply laying the whole thing in one go.

It is easier to splice cables now and getting easier all the time. Coaxial cables of the last few decades took some 36 to 48 hours to splice, partly because it was necessary to mold a jacket around them. Modern cables can be spliced in more like 12 hours, depending on the number of fibers they contain. So modern cable ships needn't be quite as great as the *Great Eastern*.

Other than the tank that contains the cable, which is literally nothing more than a big round hole in the middle of the ship, a cable ship is different from other ships in two ways. One, it comes with a complement of bow and stern thrusters coupled to exquisitely sensitive navigation gear on the bridge, which give it unsurpassed precision-maneuvering and station-keeping powers. In the case of *Monarch*, a smaller cable repair ship that we visited in Southampton,

England, there are at least two differential GPS receivers, one for the bow and one for the stern—hence the two readings given at the head of this section. Each one of them reads out to five decimal places, which implies a resolution of about 1 centimeter.

Second, a cable ship has two winches on board. But this does not do justice to them, as they are so enormous, so powerful, and yet so nimble that it would almost be more accurate to say that a cable ship *is* two floating winches. Nearly everything that a cable ship does reduces, eventually, to winching. Laying a cable is a matter of paying cable out of a winch, and repairing it, as already described, involves a much more complicated series of winch-related activities.

As Kelvin figured out the hard way, whenever you are reeling in a long line, you must first relieve all tension on it or else your reel will be crushed. The same problem is posed in reverse by the cable-laying process, where thousands of meters of cable, weighing many tons, may be stretched tight between the ship and the contact point on the seafloor, but the rest of the cable stored on board the ship must be coiled loosely in the tanks with no tension on them at all. In both cases, the cable must be perfectly slack on the ship end and very tight on the watery end of the winching machinery. Not surprisingly, then, the same machinery is used for both outgoing and incoming winch work.

At one end of the ship is a huge iron drum some 3 meters in diameter with a few turns of cable around it. As you can verify by wrapping a few turns of rope around a pipe and tugging, this is a very simple way to relieve tension on a line. It is not, however, very precise, and here, precise control is very important. That is provided by something called a linear engine, which consists of several pairs of tires mounted with a narrow gap between them (for you baseball fans, it is much like a pitching machine). The cable is threaded through this gap so that it is gripped on both sides by the tires. *Monarch*'s linear engine contains 16 pairs of tires which, taken together, can provide up to 10 tons of holdback force. Augmented by the drums, which can

be driven by power from the ship's main engines, the ultimate capacity of *Monarch*'s cable engines is 30 tons.

The art of laying a submarine cable is the art of using all the special features of such a ship: the linear engines, the maneuvering
thrusters, and the differential GPS equipment, to put the cable exactly where it is supposed to go. Though the survey team has examined a corridor many thousands of meters wide, the target corridor
for the cable lay is 200 meters wide, and the masters of these ships
take pride in not straying more than 10 meters from the charted
route. This must be accomplished through the judicious manipulation of only a few variables: the ship's position and speed (which are
controlled by the engines, thrusters, and rudder) and the cable's tension and rate of payout (which are controlled by the cable engine).

One cannot merely pay the cable out at the same speed as the ship
moves forward. If the bottom is sloping down and away from the ship
as the ship proceeds, it is necessary to pay the cable out faster. If the
bottom is sloping up toward the ship, the cable must come out more
slowly. Such calculations are greatly complicated by the fact that the
cable is stretched out far behind the ship—the distance between the
ship and the cable's contact point on the bottom of the ocean can be
more than 30 kilometers, and the maximum depth at which (for example) KDD cable can be laid is 8,000 meters. Insofar as the shape of
the bottom affects what the ship ought to be doing, it's not the shape
of the bottom directly below the ship that is relevant, but the shape of
the bottom wherever the contact point happens to be located, which
is by no means a straightforward calculation. Of course, the ship is
heaving up and down on the ocean and probably being shoved around
by wind and currents while all this is happening, and there is also
the possibility of ocean currents that may move the cable to and fro
during its descent.

It is not, in other words, a seat-of-the-pants kind of deal; the
skipper can't just sit up on the bridge, eyeballing a chart, and twiddling a few controls according to his intuition. In practice, the only

way to ensure that the cable ends up where it is supposed to is to calculate the whole thing ahead of time. Just as aeronautical engineers
create numerical simulations of hypothetical airplanes to test their
coefficient of drag, so do the slack control wizards of Cable & Wireless
Marine use numerical simulation techniques to model the catenary
curve adopted by the cable as it stretches between ship and contact
point. In combination with their detailed data on the shape of the
ocean floor, this enables them to figure out, in advance, exactly what
the ship should do when. All of it is boiled down into a set of instructions that is turned over to the master of the cable ship: at such and
such a point, increase speed to x knots and reduce cable tension to y
tons and change payout speed to z meters per second, and so on and
so forth, all the way from Porthcurno to Miura.

"It sounds like it would make a good videogame," I said to Captain
Stuart Evans after he had laid all of this out for me. I was envision-
ing something called SimCable. "It would make a good videogame,"
he agreed, "but it also makes a great job, because it's a combination
of art and science and technique—and it's not an art you learn overnight. It's definitely a black art."

Cable & Wireless's Marine Survey department has nailed the
slack control problem. That, in combination with the company's fleet
of cable-laying ships and its human capital, makes it dominant in the
submarine cable-laying world.

By "human capital" I mean their ability to dispatch weather-
beaten operatives such as the Lan Tao Island crowd to difficult places
like Suez and have them know their asses from their elbows. As we
discovered on our little jaunt to Egypt, where we tried to rendezvous
with a cable ship in the Gulf of Suez and were turned back by the
Egyptian military, one doesn't just waltz into places like that on short
notice and get stuff to happen.

In each country between England and Japan, there are hoops that
must be jumped through, cultural differences that must be understood, palms that must be greased, unwritten rules that must be re-

spected. The only way to learn that stuff is to devote a career to it. Cable & Wireless has an institutional memory stretching all the way back to 1870, when it laid the first cable from Porthcurno to Australia, and the British maritime industry as a whole possesses a vast fund of practical experience that is the legacy of the Empire.

One can argue that, in the end, the British Empire did Britain surprisingly little good. Other European countries that had pathetic or nonexistent empires, such as Italy, have recently surpassed England in standard of living and other measures of economic well-being. Scholars of economic history have worked up numbers suggesting that Britain spent more on maintaining its empire than it gained from exploiting it. Whether or not this is the case, it is quite obvious from looking at the cable-laying industry that the Victorian practice of sending British people all over the planet is now paying them back handsomely.

The current position of AT&T versus Cable & Wireless reflects the shape of America versus the shape of the British Empire. America is a big, contiguous mass, easy to defend, immensely wealthy, and basically insular. No one comes close to it in developing new technologies, and AT&T has always been one of America's technological leaders. By contrast, the British Empire was spread out all over the place, and though it controlled a few big areas (such as India and Australia), it was basically an archipelago of outposts, let us say a network, completely dependent on shipping and communications to stay alive. Its dominance was always more economic than military—even at the height of the Victorian era, its army was smaller than the Prussian police force. It could coerce the natives, but only so far—in the end, it had to co-opt them, give them some incentive to play along. Even though the Empire has been dissolving itself for half a century, British people and British institutions still know how to get things done everywhere.

It is not difficult to work out how all of this has informed the development of the submarine cable industry. AT&T makes really, really good cables; it has the pure technology nailed, though if it doesn't stay on its toes, it'll be flattened by the Japanese. Cable & Wireless doesn't even try to make cables, but it installs them better than anyone else.

THE LEGACY

Kelvin founded the cable industry by understanding the science, and developing the technology, that made it work. His legacy is the ongoing domination of the cable-laying industry by the British, and his monument is concealed beneath the waves: the ever growing web of submarine cables joining continents together.

Bell founded the telephone industry. His legacy was the Bell System, and his monument was strung up on poles for all to see: the network of telephone wires that eventually found its way into virtually every building in the developed world. Bell founded New England Telephone Company, which eventually was absorbed into the Bell System. It never completely lost its identity, though, and it never forgot its connection to Alexander Graham Bell—it even moved Bell's laboratory into its corporate headquarters in Boston.

After the breakup of the Bell System in the early 1980s, New England Telephone and its sibling Baby Bell, New York Telephone, joined together to form a new company called Nynex, whose loyal soldiers are eager to make it clear that they see themselves as the true heirs of Bell's legacy.

Now, Nynex and Cable & Wireless, the brainchildren of Bell and Kelvin, the two supreme ninja hacker mage lords of global telecommunications, have formed an alliance to challenge AT&T and all the other old monopolies.

We know how the first two acts of the story are going to go: In late 1997, with the completion of FLAG, Luke ("Nynex") Skywalker, backed up on his Oedipal quest by the heavy shipping iron of Han ("Cable & Wireless") Solo, will drop a bomb down the Death Star's ventilation shaft. In 1999, with the completion of SEA-ME-WE 3, the Empire will Strike Back. There is talk of a FLAG 2, which might represent some kind of a *Return of the Jedi* scenario.

But once the first FLAG has been built, everyone's going to get into the act—it's going to lead to a general rebellion. "FLAG will change the way things are done. They are setting a benchmark," says Dave Handley, the cable layer. And Mercogliano makes a persuasive case that national telecom monopolies will be so preoccupied, over the next decade, with building the "last mile" and getting their acts together in a competitive environment that they'll have no choice but to leave cable laying to the entrepreneurs.

That's the simple view of what FLAG represents. It is important to remember, though, that companies like Cable & Wireless and Nynex are not really heroic antimonopolists. A victory for FLAG doesn't lead to a pat ending like in *Star Wars*—it does not get us into an idealized free market. "One thing to bear in mind is that Cable & Wireless *is* a club and they are rigorously anticompetitive wherever they have the opportunity," said Doug Barnes, the cypherpunk. "Nynex and the other Baby Bells are self-righteously trying to crack open other companies' monopolies while simultaneously trying to hold onto their domestic ones. The FLAG folks are merely clubs with a smidgin more vision, enough business sense to properly reward talent, and a profound desire to make a great pile of money."

There has been a lot of fuss in the last few years concerning the 50th anniversary of the invention of the computer. Debates have raged over who invented the computer: Atanasoff or Mauchly or Turing? The only thing that has been demonstrated is that, depending on how you define *computer*, any one of the above, and several others besides, can be said to have invented it.

Oddly enough, this debate comes at a time when stand-alone computers are seeming less and less significant and the Internet more so. Whether or not you agree that "the network is the computer," a phrase Scott McNealy of Sun Microsystems recently coined, you can't dispute that moving information around seems to have much broader appeal than processing it. Many more people are interested in email and the Web than were interested in databases and spreadsheets.

Yet little attention has been paid to the historical antecedents of the Internet—perhaps partly because these cable technologies are much older and less accessible and partly because many Net people want so badly to believe that the Net is fundamentally new and unique. Analog is seen as old and bad, and so many people assume that the communications systems of old were strictly analog and have just now been upgraded to digital.

This overlooks much history and totally misconstrues the technology. The first cables carried telegraphy, which is as purely digital as anything that goes on inside your computer. The cables were designed that way because the hackers of a century and a half ago understood perfectly well why digital was better. A single bit of code passing down a wire from Porthcurno to the Azores was apt to be in sorry shape by the time it arrived, but precisely because it was a bit, it could easily be abstracted from the noise, then recognized, regenerated, and transmitted anew.

The world has actually been wired together by digital communications systems for a century and a half. Nothing that has happened during that time compares in its impact to the first exchange of messages between Queen Victoria and President Buchanan in 1858. That was so impressive that a mob of celebrants poured into the streets of New York and set fire to City Hall.

It's tempting to observe that, so far, no one has gotten sufficiently excited over a hot new Web page to go out and burn down a major building. But this is a little too glib. True, that mob in the streets of New York in 1858 was celebrating the ability to send messages quickly across the Atlantic. But, if the network is the computer, then in retrospect, those torch-bearing New Yorkers could be seen as celebrating the joining of the small and primitive computer that was the North American telegraph system to the small and primitive computer that was the European system, to form The Computer, with a capital C.

At that time, the most important components of these Computers—the CPUs, as it were—were tense young men in starched collars. Whenever one of them stepped out to relieve himself, The Computer went down. As good as they were at their jobs, they could process bits only so fast, so The Computer was very slow. But The Computer has done nothing since then but get faster, become more automated, and expand. By 1870, it stretched all the way to Australia. The advent of analog telephony plunged The Computer into a long dormant phase during which it grew immensely but lost many of its computerlike characteristics.

But now The Computer is fully digital once again, fully automatic, and faster than hell. Most of it is in the United States, because the United States is large, free, and made of dirt. Largeness eliminates troublesome borders. Freeness means that anyone is allowed to patch new circuits onto The Computer. Dirt makes it possible for anyone with a backhoe to get in on the game. The Computer is striving mightily to grow beyond the borders of the United States, into a world that promises even vaster economies of scale—but most of that world isn't made of dirt, and most of it isn't free. The lack of freedom stems both from bad laws, which are grudgingly giving way to deregulation, and from monopolies willing to do all manner of unsavory things in order to protect their turf.

Even though FLAG's bandwidth isn't that great by 1996 Internet standards, and even though some of the companies involved in it are, in other arenas, guilty of monopolistic behavior, FLAG really is going to help blow open bandwidth and weaken the telecom monopolies.

In many ways it hearkens back to the wild early days of the cable business. The first transatlantic cables, after all, were constructed by private investors who, like FLAG's investors, just went out and built cable because it seemed like a good idea. After FLAG, building new high-bandwidth, third-generation fiber-optic cable is going to seem like a good idea to a lot of other investors. And unlike the ones who built FLAG, they will have the benefit of knowing about the Internet, and perhaps of understanding, at some level, that they are not merely stringing fancy telephone lines but laying down new traces on the circuit board of The Computer. That understanding may lead them to create vast amounts of bandwidth that would blow the minds of the entrenched telecrats and to adopt business models designed around packet-switching instead of the circuits that the telecrats are stuck on.

If the network is The Computer, then its motherboard is the crust of Planet Earth. This may be the single biggest drag on the growth of The Computer, because Mother Earth was not designed to be a motherboard. There is too much water and not enough dirt. Water favors a few companies that know how to lay cable and have the ships to do it. Those companies are about to make a whole lot of money.

Eventually, though, new ships will be built. The art of slack control will become common knowledge—after all, it comes down to a numerical simulation problem, which should not be a big chore for the ever-expanding Computer. The floors of the oceans will be surveyed and sidescanned down to every last sand ripple and anchor scar. The physical challenges, in other words, will only get easier.

The one challenge that will then stand in the way of The Computer will be the cultural barriers that have always hindered cooperation between different peoples. As the globe-trotting cable layers in Papa Doc's demonstrate, there will always be a niche for people who have gone out and traveled the world and learned a thing or two about its ways.

Hackers with ambitions of getting involved in the future expansion of The Computer could do a lot worse than to power down their PCs, buy GPS receivers, place calls to their favorite travel agents, and devote some time to the pursuit of hacker tourism.

The motherboard awaits.

THE SALON INTERVIEW
(2004)

The author of "Cryptonomicon" and the "Baroque Cycle" talks about the brighter side of Puritanism, the feud between Newton and Leibniz, and the literary world's grudge against science fiction.

INTERVIEW BY LAURA MILLER

Rumor had it that Neal Stephenson would follow "Crypto-nomicon," his bestselling 1999 novel combining present-day high-tech entrepreneurs and World War II–era derring-do, with a similar tale of fugitive data and high adventure set sometime in the near future. Last year, with the publication of the first of the three-volume "Baroque Cycle," "Quicksilver," Stephenson revealed that he'd turned the dial on his time machine in the other direction. "Quicksilver," written by hand with a fountain pen in an alcove lined with a huge map of early 18th-century London, immersed the author and his legions of devoted readers in one of the most intellectually exciting and politically momentous periods of history. It was the age of such scientific geniuses as Isaac Newton, Gottfried Wilhelm von Leibniz and the undersung polymath Robert Hooke, and also the time when our modern economic systems began to take form.

Unusual subjects for fiction, perhaps, but Stephenson makes the "Baroque Cycle" a weirdly effective mix of high-octane tutorial and ripping yarn. To balance such cerebral characters as Newton and Daniel Waterhouse (Puritan ancestor of the Waterhouses, crack mathematicians and programmers, in "Cryptonomicon"), he introduces Jack Shaftoe, aka the King of the Vagabonds and his sometime-paramour turned countess and financial whiz, Eliza. Shaftoe, like his descendant Bobby in "Cryptonomicon," skips from one outlandish but irresistibly entertaining exploit to the next, barely escaping with his skin intact: war, thieves, prison, pirates—you name it. As for Eliza, well, she's the kind of girl who encrypts top-secret military information in her cross-stitch embroidery and surreptitiously handles the investments of half the court of Louis XIV. The second volume in the "Cycle," "The Confusion," published on April 19, continues the saga, with an even more lavish serving of the feats of Jack and Eliza.

Stephenson found time for an interview during the course of a road trip, in a borrowed 40-foot R.V., across the high desert of Washington State from Spokane to his home in Seattle. It was a long conversation.

What inspired the "Baroque Cycle"?

It was an unexpected byproduct of "Cryptonomicon." One of the things I wanted to talk about in that book was the history of computing and its relationship to society. I was talking to Stephen Horst, a philosophy professor at Wesleyan, and he mentioned that Newton for the last 30 years of his life did very little in the way of science as we normally think of it. His job was to run the Royal Mint at the Tower of London. I'd been thinking a lot about gold and money, which were themes in "Cryptonomicon."

At the same time, I read a book by George Dyson called "Darwin Among the Machines," in which he talks about the deep history of computing and about Leibniz and the work he did on computers. It wasn't just some silly adding machine or slide rule. Leibniz actually thought about symbolic logic and why it was powerful and how it could be put to use. He went from that to building a machine that could carry out logical operations on bits. He knew about binary arithmetic. I found that quite startling. Up till then I hadn't been that well informed about the history of logic and computing. I hadn't been aware that anyone was thinking about those things so far in the past. I thought it all started with [Alan] Turing. So, I had computers in the 17th century. There's this story of money and gold in the same era, and to top it all off Newton and Leibniz had this bitter rivalry. I decided right away that I was going to have to write a book about that.

Pretty soon I was thinking this was an exceptionally apt time in which to set a novel. There were so many wild and improbable things going on then that made for good material. The siege of Vienna where the Turks penetrated into Europe is a thing that's almost inconceivable to us today. That was the deepest into Europe that they got. That's a pretty dramatic little happening. Things like the Barbary pirates and 800 other different flavors of pirates, Spanish treasure galleons, the wars of Louis XIV, the scientific revolution, the plague, the Great Fire of London. All that falls into the period of time when Newton and Leibniz were alive.

The rivalries between the various scientists you write about are so bitter, it's surprising even to someone who already knows that science isn't this Olympian, rational activity totally removed from human pettiness.

Science was new and they didn't know how to do it yet. Science was and is a somewhat contentious thing. Someone's got a theory and they promulgate that theory and then something else comes along and alters, improves on or even flatly contradicts it. Now that we've got 350 years of perspective on this, scientists understand that this is how it's done and there's a mechanism in place for how to do it. It's refereed journals and it's become institutionalized. They didn't have that perspective on it. They couldn't stand back and say, Well, my theory may get contradicted here and there, but this guy who's contradicting it will get contradicted in turn. They didn't have that expectation. They didn't have journals. The first two journals were the *Journale de Savants*, which was about 1665, and the *Proceedings of the Royal Society*, which was right about the same time. Leibniz had to found his own journal in order to publish his own work. They were kind of banging around in the dark trying to figure out how to do this.

Hooke, for example, when he figured out how arches work, published it as an anagram. He condensed the idea into this pithy statement: "The ideal form of an arch is the form of a chain hanging, flipped upside down." Then he scrambled the letters to make an anagram and published it. That way, he wasn't giving away the secret, but if somebody came along a few years later and claimed that they'd invented it, he could just unscramble what he'd published. He was establishing precedence.

Hooke squabbled with [Christiaan] Huygens over a bunch of clock-related inventions. This kind of thing was just rife. It came to a head in a grotesque way in the priority dispute over [who invented] the calculus. That was so embarrassing to the whole institution of science and people were so nauseated by it that it taught everyone a lesson. After that, no one would dream of doing what Newton did, which was to invent something really important and then sit on it for 30 years.

I'm still baffled as to why he'd do that.

It was a combination of things. Again, the institutions of science didn't exist. Even if he'd wanted to publish it there were no journals at the time. The prevailing ethos that he would have been brought up in was alchemy, which was called the "esoteric brotherhood." They were completely of a mind that you didn't publish your results, at least not in a way that was intelligible to anyone. So if you read the alchemical recipes of Paracelsus or Robert Boyle or any of those people who practiced this, they're all couched in metaphor. You have to know what stands for what to understand the recipe. They even thought that some of the Greek myths were disguised alchemy recipes, like the myth of Cadmus, who sowed the teeth that grew into soldiers, which they thought was a set of instructions to make some kind of compound. It wouldn't have occurred to Newton anyway to make any new material public. He didn't care at all for fame or getting attention.

But you'd think they'd care about the advancement of their field.

They didn't have the sense of progress, I think, though that's debatable. I talked to one historian of math and science who thinks they very much did. Another thing about the calculus is that it was very controversial because it involves adding up infinitesimal quantities to make something, which is an iffy proposition. Newton was very thin-skinned and would become very withdrawn and bitter when people made even routine criticisms of his work. He didn't want to put it out and then have to spend all his time defending it. Later in the 19th century the mathematical profession finally said, Look, as currently written, this is nonsense, so we've got to tear it down and go back to the beginning. They had to go back and build some serious mathematical underpinnings beneath the calculus. They could see that it worked, but the way in which it had been proved was no longer acceptable. Newton may have suspected that, intuited that, and so was afraid to bring it out.

It's odd that so few historical novelists set their books in the late 17th century, when you think about it. The changes in the air were so huge.

That was one of my reactions, too, when I started getting into this. You see a lot about the late 18th century, the time of the Revolution, you see a lot about the Civil War and the Victorian era. There have been some books about this era published recently—"An Instance of the Fingerpost," "A Conspiracy of Paper," about the fall of the South Sea company in 1721. But it's strangely underrepresented.

Maybe that's because most novelists tend to be interested in literary history. The age of Johnson is exciting, and the age of Dickens, but not so much this time, in terms of great writers.

Well, in this period you've got Milton. He's coming out with "Paradise Lost" at the same time as the plague, the fire, the founding of the Royal Society. You've got [John] Bunyan, "Pilgrim's Progress," although that's a hard book for people to take these days. That's not anyone's favorite book.

Also, for a modern readership, the religious disputes of that time are pretty complicated and hard to follow. And people took them so seriously, which is difficult to relate to if you're secular-minded.

I think you're on to something in saying that one off-putting thing to people about this period is the religious aspect of it, and also the politics, which are also pretty closely entwined. Milton and Bunyan are intensely religious people and every word they write comes straight from their religion. This was pre-Enlightenment. There were a few people running around with the secular ideas that we accept as being the norm today, but most of these people were religious and really meant it. Newton was that way; Leibniz was that way. They argued about religion, but they did so from the standpoint of people who really took it seriously. I found that an interesting thing to tackle as a writer because these people were so different from the people who are likely to read this book.

You're remarkably sympathetic to the Puritans, too, which is unusual these days.

I have a perverse weakness for past generations that are universally reviled today. The Victorians have a real bad name, and the word "Puritan" is never used except in a highly pejorative way, despite the fact that there are very strong Victorian and Puritan threads in our society today, and despite the fact that the Victorians and Puritans built the countries that we live in. The other one, by the way, is the '50s. Someday I'll have to write a '50s novel.

The reason why people are so vituperative about those generations is not because they know anything about the history, but because they're really talking about splits within our culture today that they're worried about. In the same spirit that I wrote a Victorian novel earlier in my career, I figured it might be a kick to see what to do with some Puritans. Not hip, jaded, cool Puritans, but honest-to-god, fire-breathing Puritans. Drake [Waterhouse, Daniel's father] is an arch-Puritan, but by no means exaggerated. There were a million guys like this running around England in those days. He became the patriarch of this family of people who have to respond to his larger-than-life status and extreme commitment to religion.

What do you admire about the Puritans?

They were tremendously effective people. They completely took over the country and they created an army pretty much from scratch that kicked everyone's ass. This is not always a good thing. They were guilty of some very bad behavior in Ireland, for example. But any way you slice it they were very effective. Cromwell was a tremendous military leader. A lot of that effectiveness was rooted in the fact that they had money, in part because persecuted religious minorities, if they're not persecuted out of existence, often manage to achieve disproportionate wealth. It happened with Jews, Armenians, Huguenots. Earlier in this project, I could have rattled off five more. They have to form private trading networks and lend each other money. They're unusually education conscious. Puritans—and when we say Puritans, we're talking about a whole grab bag of religious groups—tended to prize literacy and education. I'm sure they had a higher literacy rate than the general English population. Literacy and education make people more effective.

Another answer is that they very early on adopted a set of views on social topics that everyone now takes for granted as being basic tenets of Western civilization. They were heavily for free enterprise. They didn't want the state interfering in private property. Now our whole system is built on that. We tend to forget that someone had to come up with that idea and fight for it. And those people did. The separation of church and state—in the absence of that separation, Puritans and other religious minorities couldn't exist. You had to belong to your parish church. Things like registering births, deaths and marriages, which are state functions to us now, were handled solely by the parish churches. If you didn't belong, you didn't exist legally. You had no choice, you had to tithe. It's often said that Cromwell admitted the Jews to England. He disestablished the church and made it possible for churches other than the established one to legally exist. That's what enabled Jews to come back and start living there. Opposition to slavery got its start among different Puritan sects. To be fair, there were Catholic theologians who objected to it, too, but in the English-speaking world it started out as a fringe belief among Quakers and some other groups and spread from there to become a tenet of Methodism and Episcopalianism and basically all churches.

Another thing that some people might find surprising is how religious the scientists are—though they called themselves natural philosophers back then. We tend to think of science and religion as being fundamentally opposed.

A lot of secular, modern people claim to be disillusioned whenever they learn that any smart person is religious. That's applicable to Newton as it is to any other religious smart person.

And then there was alchemy, which was a major preoccupation for Newton.

Alchemy is a whole different bag because it seems wacky, nuts to us. That's kind of how it's presented in the early part of the "Baroque Cycle." In everything that you've read so far, you're seeing alchemy through Daniel's eyes, and he hates it. He can't believe that Newton is buying into it at all and feels that fooling around with it has caused Newton to associate with the wrong crowd. At the beginning Newton is every bit as much of the correct young Puritan as Daniel is.

These men were discovering properties like gravity and the movement of the planets, but they also believed there was a whole spiritual realm as well.

They certainly believed in sin, temptation, the devil and witches as being real things. They were trying to integrate the new scientific way of thinking into that without destroying the old beliefs that are important to them. At the time, I think alchemy didn't have the occult connotation that it might have now. It was an alternate way of thinking about matter, and it was comparatively modern. A lot of smart people believed in it, and a lot of them were perfectly devout Christians, Jews or Muslims. Since then it's gotten associated with occult practices and one of the chores I've got in this book is to try to keep those two things apart.

Daniel thinks that it's fraudulent. It's old, it's wrong, it's being swept away by the new science, which he sees in Robert Hooke, for example. If you read the text of "Micrographia" [Hooke's famous book of illustrations of objects observed through various lenses], Hooke goes through and demolishes a bunch of alchemical ideas and talks about light and heat and oxygen—he doesn't use the word "oxygen," but that's what he's talking about—in ways that are modern. Daniel thinks, why doesn't Newton get with the program and abandon this old system? It's clear that a lot of the people practicing it are frauds and second-raters, when there are people like Hooke inventing a whole new chemistry that actually makes sense. Later on, the vision of this is going to become a little more nuanced.

How did Newton and Leibniz reconcile their scientific studies with their religion?

Newton and Leibniz and other people at the same time are struggling to come up with a system of understanding the world that lets them have their cake and eat it too. There are some holes in the system that Newton presents in "Principia Mathematica" that he's aware of and wants to plug, and you can make a case that the reason he spent so much time on alchemy is that he saw it as a way to finish this grand project. It wasn't like this nutty, eccentric, oddball thing. It was a carefully thought-out part of his grand strategy for his life's work. He was going to publish a book on alchemy called "Praxis" that was going to be as great as or greater than "Principia Mathematica" and supply the missing bits.

At the same time Leibniz is toiling away on a totally different system that's meant to achieve the same goal. It's really the clash between those two systems that's the story, not who invented the calculus first. What Newton and Leibniz were arguing about was broad metaphysical topics of absolute space and time: Do we have free will, and if so, what does that mean? What's a miracle?

Why do you think people find the religious leanings of great scientists so disappointing? Why should they be mutually exclusive?

It's reductionism. You have to be able to reduce everything to interactions among particles. You can't have anything other than that.

There are also the attacks on science made by some religious groups.

The fundamentalist churches nowadays do a much better job of promulgating their views and are much more vocal and outspoken, and if you're a secular person who doesn't have much interaction with organized religion, then the only time you ever see a Christian, it's someone saying that evolution is a lie and the world is only 6,000 years old. It's very easy to miss the fact that the Catholic Church and all the mainline Protestant denominations long ago accepted evolution and have no problem with it at all. I frequently run into militantly secular types who think that all Christians, for example, deny the theory of evolution. That accounts for a certain amount of the militancy of secular types in public discourse. They just can't believe people believe this stuff. It seems patently idiotic to them.

Do you think that reductionist view of science is insufficient?

Steve Horst is working on a book right now called "Mind in the World of Nature," where he talks about our standard method of doing science that Galileo got started—which is, you break a system down into its parts, you understand the parts, and then you build back up from that to figure out how to explain observable parts. That's a description of how all science has been done for a long time. He's making the argument that a lot of science doesn't necessarily fit that mold: biological science, psychology. There are plenty of cases you can point to, even in mathematics, where being able to break things down into its smallest components doesn't really get you anywhere. It doesn't give you an explanation that's really worth anything. If you look at cellular automata, for example: Sure, each automaton can be explained as a unit, but that's not what's interesting. What's interesting is the really complicated emergent behaviors that you can get out of a whole bunch of these things acting at once. There's really no grid to cross that gap.

Yet we're often led to believe that these things are better understood than they are. Biologists complain that it doesn't make much sense to talk about having "decoded" the genome when how the coding in genes is used to make proteins is still something of a mystery.

My friend Alvy Ray Smith would say that [the making of proteins from genes] is computation. I would avoid the term "mystery." The materialist types just go nuts—that's their word still. To call somebody a mysterian is their way of flicking somebody off the board. At some level there may be no mystery. You may be able to understand everything if you take the time and trouble to figure out how it all works. But it doesn't give you anything useful, and in the meantime there's lots of perfectly good science you can do by observing the top-level behaviors. People who do cell biology are doing perfectly good science—you can't claim that they're not doing science.

How much is the "Baroque Cycle" linked to "Cryptonomicon"?

People can decide for themselves how much of a piece they are. I stuck certain little details in "Cryptonomicon" that will make no sense whatsoever unless you've read "Baroque Cycle," but they're so small that you could read through them and not really notice them.

Do you ever worry that the sheer bulk of information you're putting across in the "Baroque Cycle" might overwhelm your readers?

You're seeing it in the context of a story that's hopefully exciting. That makes it more fun to read. I believe that to encounter that kind of material in a story draws people in and gives them a real sense of immediacy, that it was really happening. You want to create a complete picture—the smells, the look of it, how it worked economically, where the money went. You want to get all that in there.

The birth of modern banking stuff seems like the most daunting thing to turn into entertainment. What interested you about this?

The fact that it was invented. At some point it doesn't exist and then suddenly it's there. They had a market that was basically one stock, which was Dutch East India stock and various derivatives of that. But it still had all the features of the modern stock market. A lot of that stuff got transplanted to London around the time of the Glorious Revolution. The Dutch came over and established links between Amsterdam and London. That's where it really flourished. One thing that London added to the mix that really made it go was a modern banking system. We see them coming up with the idea of it in "Quicksilver," and we see it coming together in "The Confusion," and then we see it operating with various complications in the last volume, "The System of the World." A lot of the people who had a hand in it were the same Royal Society types who were cutting up dogs and pursuing all these other science endeavors.

Speaking of the dogs, some of those descriptions are pretty hard to take.

This is what these guys did. They did it a lot. They went through a lot of dogs in that way.

With something like that, there's only so many different ways for a writer to address it. You can erase it, pretend it didn't happen, and avoid talking about it just because it's unpleasant and you don't want these characters to seem like evil people. But that's not an honest way to go about it. You can turn it into a piece of propaganda to show they were irredeemably vile people, but they weren't. If you're an animal rights advocate, you'll disagree with that and say they were. But to write a book that feels like propaganda for that point of view . . . no one would read it. It wouldn't make a good story. So the one thing you're left with is to address the ambiguity of these people and the ambiguity of what they did.

Again, some people won't see any ambiguity. But if you look for it in these Royal Society accounts, it's clear that at a certain point some of these guys started to feel pretty disgusted by what they were doing and they find excuses to avoid doing it anymore. I just decided to present it pretty much as it's described in the historical accounts and leave it to the reader to think about what it means. They had peculiar ideas about pain and what kind of organisms felt pain and which didn't. Of course, they were really just rationalizations. It was believed that black people didn't feel as much pain, also.

The other half of the equation was that they were all feeling pain all the time. Even the most fortunate ones had lice and you name it. They had it. The incidence of bladder stones, something that nobody gets anymore, was incredibly high.

I'd never heard of those.

People get kidney stones still, but they don't seem to get bladder stones anymore. I asked a couple of people why, and you get a vague answer like "changes in diet" or what have you. I think they rarely drank water. They were just drinking alcoholic beverages all the time. Nobody in the world drank water, except maybe Indians and people who lived in really pristine places. That's kind of my pet theory: Every culture can be kind of defined by what they drink in order to avoid dying of diarrhea. In China it's tea. In Africa it's milk or animal blood. In Europe it was wine and beer.

Do you see yourself as part of any particular literary tradition?

I absolutely look to—consciously, knowingly look back on—those 19th-century serialized, potboiler novelists as people who are on to something. They got something right. There was something about living in that environment that made these guys incredibly productive. Dickens was the same deal. I do not have the sheer guts that it would take to serialize something. Before you've written the last chapter, the first chapter has already been published, so you can't go back and change anything to make it all work out. I just do not have the sheer chutzpah to start publishing stuff before it's all done. Mine is a pretty risk-averse strategy.

What do you think makes those writers different from "serious" writers today?

I don't think they spent a lot of time agonizing about their art. I think that they found gainful employment producing stuff that was meant to be entertaining, that readers of the Strand magazine would enjoy reading. A lot of it was forgettable, but guess what, a lot of what those kinds of people wrote is now thought of as literature. I've published books that probably aren't literature, but to me it just feels easier and more natural to sit down and produce the material and let the chips fall where they may.

Let's talk about writing. Do you have some plan for what you're trying to do with your books? They're such an unusual combination of what we call right-brain and left-brain material.

For me it begins and ends with story. I'm not a great self-analyzer. I don't think a lot about process. Usually it starts with "Hey, wouldn't it

be a great yarn if . . . ?" Because if you don't have that, you've got nothing. What I'm doing here is writing novels, and novels—never mind
what anyone else might tell you—novels are pop entertainment, and
they have to tell a story and they have to engage the emotions. There
are a few basic tricks they use to do that. One is to tell a good yarn and
the other is to make you feel empathy for the characters involved in
the doings of that yarn, but you've got to have that yarn. That's what
I seize on first. That's what gives me confidence that I've got a pony I
can ride. Characters tend to come out of that, and ideas—I don't know
where they come from. The yarn that got me going on "Quicksilver"
was Newton pursuing and prosecuting an archvillain in London at
the same time as the dispute with Leibniz is at its peak.

**Do you see yourself as moving away from the speculative fiction you
wrote early on? "Cryptonomicon" was set entirely in the present
and past. The "Baroque Cycle" is an entirely historical novel.**

But "Cryptonomicon" was nominated for a Hugo Award. I was
very happy about that. This gets into a whole conversation about the
sociology of writers and the literary world. There's a long-standing
tendency of so-called literary writers and critics to say mean things
about science fiction. A lot of science fiction writers don't care, but
the ones who do care feel wounded by that and get defensive. That
leads to a common thing that happens when a science fiction writer
has achieved some success and gets a readership outside the pure science fiction world. A lot of science fiction people become nervous that
this writer perceives himself as trapped in some kind of notional science fiction ghetto and is trying to break out of it.

Some people in the science fiction world are ever alert to anyone
who's showing signs of that. I don't begrudge them that. I understand
where they're coming from. So I always make it clear that I consider
myself a science fiction writer. Even the "Baroque Cycle" fits under
the broader vision of what science fiction is about.

And what's that?

Fiction that's not considered good unless it has interesting ideas in it. You can write a minimalist short story that's set in a trailer park or a Connecticut suburb that might be considered a literary master-piece or well-regarded by literary types, but science fiction people wouldn't find it very interesting unless it had somewhere in it a cool idea that would make them say, "That's interesting. I never thought of that before." If it's got that, then science fiction people will embrace it and bring it into the big-tent view of science fiction. That's really the role that science fiction has come to play in literature right now. In arty lit, it's become uncool to try to come to grips with ideas per se.

I don't know if that's really true. Don DeLillo, for example, writes about ideas, and he's widely revered by literary writers.

He's less idea oriented now than in the past. If you look at "The Names" or "Great Jones Street," at the core of both of those novels is a conceit that is very science fiction, in a way. I didn't see that as much in "Underworld." You could look on him as a guy who used to write some pretty good science fiction. You could probably find readers and critics who'd say he used to write this iffy stuff with all these geeky ideas, but now he's matured. This is one of these "perception is real-ity" deals. If you look at science fiction, it's a self-defining community and they know what they like. They've got their own frame of refer-ence for looking at books. If you read the fine print in the reviews in the back of *Locus* magazine, there's a real intellectual movement rep-resented by the discourse going on in those reviews. It's consciously apart from the mainstream literary world.

One side effect of books getting so little coverage is that different areas of literary activity or excitement often don't seem to know that each other exists. And the literary establishment often isn't

aware of what most people are reading. What's most visible in the press isn't necessarily what's reaching the majority of the readers.

There's an interesting phenomenon where . . . I first noticed this when I was in a bar with a fantasy novelist having a few drinks. We got to the point in the evening when we had the "How big is yours?" conversation. We compared sales figures for "Snow Crash" with this other fellow's latest and I think he'd sold more than I had and he was dumbfounded and so was I. It turns out that there's a whole lot of writers like that, who sell impressive numbers of books. Compared to some of those people I don't sell that many copies. I do fine, but the fact is for some reason I get attention that's out of proportion to actual sales. What was new to me is that there were people like that, mastodons, who I'd never even heard of.

People see you as having become a crossover writer. Are you deliberately trying to bridge that gap with your more recent work, to reach readers who ordinarily wouldn't consider science fiction?

But I got a big review in the New York Times for "Zodiac"! I think I got one for "The Big U," actually, but I'd have to go back and check. I've heard from people, "Oh, I don't like science fiction but someone talked me into reading this book." There was some of that happening, certainly. But this is not what I ever think about. I try to follow my nose and write what I want to write and do it in a way that's presentable and engaging for people. Everything beyond that is a marketing decision. I don't think of myself that way and people don't think of themselves that way.

Do you worry about losing your old audience?

The "Baroque Cycle" is about science, right? And it's got ideas in it. So to me it'll appeal to people who read science fiction. There's always been a lot of historical stuff in science fiction. Kim Stanley Robinson just published "The Years of Rice and Salt"—which is a kind of historical novel. It's been going on for a long time. Even when I was a kid, reading science fiction stories and books, every so often I'd run across one that happened to be set in the historical past. That was considered to be within the normal bounds of what these people write about.

There was a review of "Cryptonomicon" with a line in it that struck me as interesting. The guy said, "This is a book for geeks and the history buffs that they turn into." I'm turning into one. I'm in this history book club, which is not all geeks but it's definitely got some serious geeks in it. It's been going for four or five years maybe. We're all consistently dumbfounded by how interesting history is when you read it yourself compared to how dull it was when they made you study it in school. We can't figure out why there's that gap. I think they try to cover too broad a sweep at once so you never get down to the individual people and their stories. It's all generalities.

You come from a scientific family, don't you?

Both my grandfathers had Ph.D.'s in the sciences. My dad's dad was a physicist and my mom's dad was a biochemist. My dad is an electrical engineering professor. I have uncles who are scientists. More than anything, growing up in a university town got me interested in it. First we lived in Champaign-Urbana and then Ames, Iowa. Ames is the home of a university with a strong orientation toward science, technology, engineering. The community where I grew up, half the parents of the kids I hung out with were Ph.D. science types.

Were you interested in science as a kid?

I was always one of these little science geek guys who would do little experiments and build things. If you call blowing things up experiments, there were a lot of chemistry experiments. We played with model rockets. It was a freedom to mess around with things. Ames was the site of the Manhattan Project facility where they would take uranium ore that they'd truck down from Canada and extract uranium metal from it and then send the uranium on to Oak Ridge to be enriched. There were all kinds of facilities there for dealing with rare earths and radioactive elements. They also had a big agricultural engineering school. We did a thing in my Cub Scout troop where one of the dads got a bunch of corn seeds that were all from the same plant, divided them up into little bags, carried them across campus to another dad of one of the other scouts who worked with radioactive stuff, and he carried it down to the hot room in the basement and exposed these seeds to radiation, some hot isotope that they had down there. These were handed out to use at the next meeting and we were each supposed to take these home and plant them and at the end of the month a prize was given out to the healthiest plant and another to the weirdest mutation. We got some really weird-looking plants out of that. I've never had a green thumb, so mine died, but I don't think it had anything to do with radiation.

I'm surprised you wound up as a novelist.

I started out as a physics major. I should have stuck with it. At some point I got interested in geography. There were fun people in that department to hang around with, and they had easier access to computers there, particularly to computer graphics terminals. I came within a couple credits of getting a double major, physics and geography. I could have gotten a physics degree, but I was ready to leave school, so I left.

How did you wind up writing your first novel?

I think my plan was to drive to the West Coast. I had this old pickup truck that I was going to do it in and I got as far as Iowa before I got it into my head that I should overhaul the engine of this pickup truck. It was burning oil. I was having to stop every 150 miles and put in a quart of oil. Now that's not so bad. It would have made a lot more sense to buy a couple of cases of oil, but I have always had this fatal weakness for getting involved in the physical nitty-gritty of stuff. It seemed like a cool idea that I'd take apart this engine and fix it up with my own two hands. I launched into that and I was doing it in an unheated garage in Iowa in January. I was 21. It was bitterly cold and the engine was all dirty. If you know what you're doing, you steam-clean the engine first, and I didn't do that. I did a bunch of things wrong. It turned into a lengthy, grinding, unpleasant process. But I got it done, got the engine to work right, but I'd lost my momentum to go out West and do something there. My sole assets at that point were the value of the gasoline in the tank of this vehicle, in my parents' garage.

So I decided to write my second novel. I'd written one in Boston, kind of a starter novel. Kind of a fantasy novel, I guess you could say. "The Big U" is No. 3. The second novel was an epic fantasy.

Were you inspired by Tolkien?

I was very consciously trying to do something that was not like Tolkien. This is a novel with a lot of geography in it. It was set on a planet that had a peculiar geography. It was geography-driven, geographical fiction.

Was that the point that you started to get serious about writing?

I felt like I was starting to get a little bit of traction as a writer. I wasn't publishing anything, but I was starting to get the hang of it, and I knew what to do better next time. I got a day job in an office and started working on this third book, which became "The Big U." The bottom line is that eventually it sold. It needed a lot of work because of the way I'd written it. There's a theory or a paradigm of how to write that I'd imbibed without knowing that I'd imbibed it. Somewhere out there is the platonic ideal of the thing you're trying to write and your rough draft is just a shadow of it. You toil through one draft after another trying to make it better. I sort of did that with "The Big U" and then I very consciously tried to do it with the thing I wrote after that, which never got published.

What happened to that book?

I had been reading all these accounts by other writers about how they produced their magnum opus and they all followed something I'll call the distillation narrative. Which was: "I sat down and wrote a manuscript that was a foot thick and it had some good stuff in it, but it was too long. So I rolled up my sleeves and went to work and edited. Toiled. I cut and scraped. I hacked. I shortened and rearranged and got it down to six inches, but it still wasn't good enough. So I went back and yada yada yada. And eventually I wound up with this trim little manuscript that had all the good parts in it."

That was a reassuring theory of how to write because it didn't require you to sit down every day and turn out good material. Instead it required you to sit down for eight hours a day and produce a huge volume of material and hope that there was something good in it. Then you'd go back later and cut out all the crap. Whatever works, but it failed for me, and it failed kind of expensively in the sense that I spent two or three years on that and produced a miserable, incoherent pile and sort of ruined a decent enough idea. I ended up feeling very anxious when I got to the end of the process and came to terms with the fact that this was not a publishable book. Then I panicked and wrote another book very quickly that got almost immediately accepted for publication and that was "Zodiac."

How did you change your writing process after that?

I did figure out that I tended to write good stuff first thing in the morning. So I had all this free time in the rest of the day that I had to occupy with something other than writing. Because if I sat and wrote, I'd just bury the good stuff I'd written in crap and have to excavate it later. I did some construction work with a friend of mine. Basically the work habit I developed out of all that was of setting things up so I could write in the morning and then stop and exercise my penchant for getting into the nitty-gritty details of physical things. Not because that was productive in any way but because it kept me from screwing up whatever I happened to be writing. I tried to pattern things that way ever since. That's worked fairly well.

One of things you like to do on the side is dabble in programming. Do you see similarities between writing code and writing fiction?

I think there are common threads between writing and programming. That's a really easy statement for people to misunderstand and twist around so I'm a little leery of making it. All I'm saying is that the thing you're making—the novel or the computer program—has got a very complicated and finely wrought hierarchical structure to it. The structure has to work right or the whole thing fails. But the only way you can work on it is by hitting one character at a time. You're building this thing one character at a time while having to maintain the whole structure in your head. That description applies equally well to programming and novel writing even though they're very different activities.

I agree that comparing the two could raise hackles in some quarters. People like to believe that one activity is entirely aesthetic and emotional and the other is entirely rational.

That's a misconception. I justify say that by referring to the work of Antonio Damasio, who's a friend of mine. He's written a few books about the brain, and the one that's most relevant to this discussion is "Descartes' Error." The error he's complaining about is the idea that reason and emotion are different things. He tells a story about a patient who suffered a very specific localized kind of brain damage that was blocking a certain kind of interaction between how he thought and how he felt. In certain situations, this guy was better than other people at certain things. When driving on ice he didn't panic and he knew all the rules, how to turn the steering wheel and keep his car under control, and he was able to drive when other people were skidding off the road. But if you asked him to schedule an appointment and gave him two dates to choose between, this guy could sit there for an hour, dithering over this simple choice. Every possible contingency or scenario that could play out would flash up in his head, and he didn't know how to choose between them.

Damasio is arguing that one of the innate faculties of our brain is that we can envision a wide range of possible scenarios and then sort through them very quickly not by logic but through a kind of process of the emotions. Emotions associated with a particular scenario cause us to prune off whole sets of options. He claims that chess masters work that way. Part of the time it's this very logical, rational thing, but part of the time it's "This gives me the willies. I'm not going there." Damasio quotes in this book scientists like Einstein who quite explicitly say that their process of sifting through ideas and deciding where to go with their research has a very strong emotional component to it. I don't buy the idea of a split between a rational and an emotional mind. I suspect that idea is a lot more common among nonscientists. I think there's a whole complex of factors behind scientists being pegged as emotionally remote or out of touch with their feelings.

I was amazed to discover that you wrote these three 1,000-page books by hand, but some writers do say that writing by hand puts them in better touch with that kind of intuition.

I do it all on paper. I started that with the "Baroque Cycle." "Cryptonomicon" is the last book I wrote typing it into a computer. I use a fountain pen. The entire thing is in longhand.

Is that your method from now on?

I think so. It's hard to say, because I tend to invent a whole different system for writing each book. This may turn out to be something
just for these books.

**Considering the period you're writing about, maybe you should
have tried writing it with a quill.**

I thought about it. But that seemed a little over the top. What I figured out a long time ago is that, while I don't get blocked that much,
when I got really blocked and couldn't get going on something, what
always worked was to get away from the computer and sit down somewhere with a piece of paper and a pen and just start writing. So I
thought, if this works so well to get the juices flowing, is there any
reason why I shouldn't try to write more that way? This was around the
same time I was discarding the whole notion that one had to produce
tons of material every day. The fact that it's slower is not a problem
because I wasn't worried anymore about producing a lot fast. I like
the fact that it never crashes, you can't lose your work. Occasionally
after I've typed it and I'm editing it onscreen, I may add a paragraph at
the keyboard but that's probably not more than a few pages out of the
entire "Cycle." Basically, every word was written with a fountain pen.

**It's incredible how much you've produced in the past few years
while only writing in the morning. What do you do with the rest of
the day?**

Ever since about '85 or '86 I've indulged my penchant for getting
into physical stuff. A lot of the time I'd do projects, whatever interested me. I'd build a model rocket or work on an electronic circuit or
write a little computer program or work on the house or the car. There
was a long series of things like that I would do.

Then I started skewing towards things that were really impractical, because if I got into practical things, I'd get into trouble. I'd work on a computer program and then I'd think, "Hey, there's a business opportunity here." And then I'd get distracted. Or I'd start a house remodeling project, wiring some outlets or something like that, and something would happen and I'd run afoul of the inspector and get into some kind of situation-comedy tangle that would make it hard for me to work in the morning. I ended up doing a lot of rocket building, large model rockets. That turned into me being on the advisory board of this space company in Seattle, Blue Origin.

Is it a research outfit, or do they actually make things?

It's intended to be very much a making-things kind of operation, but right now it's in a hiring and getting-ready stage.

Correct me if I'm wrong, but doesn't building rockets cost a fortune?

It does cost a fortune, but that's not my department. I'm a member of the advisory board with machine shop privileges. I go in there and try to make myself useful in an advisory capacity inasmuch as a science fiction writer can. Time will tell. Here I have to get really vague because it's not my company and I don't have an ownership stake in it, and so we're no longer talking about my intellectual property, as it were. I tend to rapidly become bored with the more abstract parts of it. I want to go off and lift heavy objects and operate a plate grinder.

BLIND SECULARISM
(1993)

Fear none of those things which thou shalt suffer: behold, the devil shall cast some of you into prison, that ye may be tried; and ye shall have tribulation 10 days: be thou faithful unto death, and I will give thee a crown of life.

—REVELATION 2:10

In 870, the Danes assaulted a community of nuns at Colding-ham, Scotland, and were flabbergasted to discover that, following the example of one Ebbe (later St. Ebbe the Younger), they had gashed their lips and noses with razors, rendering themselves so gruesome as to put to flight any lustful thoughts.

The nonplused invaders ended up burning the place down, and its inhabitants with it, and thus joined a long series of practical-minded sorts who have failed to understand the faithful. The roster of baffled infidels includes many Romans, at Masada and when they were martyring early Christians, and missionary-killing aborigines the world over. Now we can add the Bureau of Alcohol, Tobacco and Firearms, the Federal Bureau of Investigation and much of the news media.

The day after the Branch Davidians immolated themselves, I happened to drive past Boeing Field in Seattle. The spot where the E-4B airborne nuclear command post used to appear, surrounded by fences, lights and guards, is now occupied by shiny new 737's and 757's waiting to be delivered to customers around the world. The prospect of nuclear war has faded with astonishing suddenness. Even the ozone hole is shrinking, another apocalypse to scratch off the list. Yet the Branch Davidians got just the apocalypse they were looking for.

Our cultures used to be almost hereditary, but now we choose them from a menu as various as the food court of a suburban shopping mall. Ambition, curiosity, talent, sexuality or religion can draw us to new cities and cultures, where we become foreigners to our parents. Synthetic cultures are nimbler than old ones, often imprudently so. They have scattered so widely that they can no longer hear each other and now some have gone so far afield that they have passed through the apocalypse while the rest of us are watching it on TV.

The smorgasbord of new cultures is probably a good thing, and for every person it makes crazy, there are probably a hundred it keeps sane. But new cultures lead to new forms of culture shock, and new ways for us to misunderstand each other.

No three cultures could be more mutually incomprehensible than the trinity at Waco: Branch Davidians, G-men and the media. This is not because they came from different places; on the contrary, it is easy to imagine members of all three groups growing up in the same small town in the Middle West, starting out as schoolmates and winding up on opposite sides of barricades shouting gibberish at one another.

Waves of police, each more heavily armed and psychologically refined than the last, were dispatched to Waco, but came no closer to understanding the cultists than did local cops. Still, they came closer than the news media. Before the flames had even died out, journalists were complaining about the lack of on-the-scene fire engines—as if the trigger-happy cultists, dodging the battering rams and tear gas to slosh lantern fuel across the floors of their own home, amounted to just another predictable public health hazard, like cryptosporidium in Milwaukee.

> ... and God shall will wipe away all tears from their eyes.
>
> —REVELATION 7:17

Tear gas hurts, even if you have a gas mask, and the Branch Davidians withstood it with the same fortitude as the razor-wielding nuns of Coldingham. Looking out their windows at the weird tanks sent to assault them, the cultists could not have failed to notice their resemblance to the hellish tormentors prophesied in their favorite book of the Bible: "and they had breastplates, as it were breastplates of iron [Revelation 9: 9–10] . . . and out of their mouths issued fire and smoke and brimstone [Revelation 9:18]."

The F.B.I. was surprised by the fire because it apparently did not take David Koresh's religion at face value. Now many commentators find fault with the Government, and in so doing misunderstand Branch Davidians even more miserably than the F.B.I. (The agency's bombardment of the compound with amplified rock and Tibetan chants shows that it understood synthetic-culture shock at least well enough to use it as a weapon.) The pundits (and Congressional inquisitors) who find fault with the F.B.I.'s approach and who suggest that anyone other than the cultists themselves is to blame for the deaths are just as out of it as the Danes in 870.

In weighing the morality of the Branch Davidians, it is not necessary to go any deeper than the fact that they were abusers, (allegedly) molesters and (finally) murderers of their own children. But has our society really secularized to the point where we are so bewildered by people with sincere religious faith? The F.B.I. can perhaps be forgiven for not having seen it in the Branch Davidians' words—but how can the critics fail to recognize it in their deeds?

In my adopted city, the sun is out for once, illuminating the flowery payoff of a long, rainy spring. No apocalypses seem imminent and the citizens, few of whom were actually born here, are pursuing the customs of their chosen cultures. Around here, this means a lot of young people in bright clothes, healthier than you or me, riding bikes, drinking espresso, and typing away on their PowerBooks—activities that would doubtless meet the approval of the journalists who patronize the Branch Davidians by scolding the F.B.I. The scene is as shiny and inviting as the spring snow on the glaciated slopes of the Cascades, which conceals jagged crevasses hundreds of feet deep. Still it is a better place to live and to raise children than older societies that held up people like St. Ebbe the Younger as role models.

For many, the heavy eschatological issues that lie just below the surface of religion are simply too icky and troublesome to think about. But in a society where multiculturalism has become a new creed, it would not hurt for some of us to spend some time trying to see things from the standpoint of a sincerely religious person, just as we would for a differently abled sexual minority.

Though I have recently started going back to church, I am as full of doubts and skepticism as many full-blown atheists. Even so it doesn't take much of a stretch to understand that the Branch Davidians didn't think death was such a bad thing. One does not have to believe David Koresh was the Messiah to understand that he wasn't kidding. Next time the organs of secular society find themselves pointing their cameras and gun barrels into a compound full of Scripture-toting survivalists, a perusal of the lives of saints or the story of Masada might be illuminating.

TIME MAGAZINE ARTICLE
ABOUT *ANATHEM*
(2012)

—An army of Western citizen-soldiers marches into Mesopo-
tamia. Their mission: to replace a cruel dictator with a friendly
leader. The dictator's conscript army scatters like chaff before the
heavier armor and superb discipline of the Westerners. But the new
leader turns out to be a slippery con man. A quick victory turns into
a long stay. Soldiers and commanders fall victim to sneak attacks.
The folks at home are dismayingly quick to forget about their faraway
army. Their journey home turns into an ordeal, the soldiers harried
by an elusive foe skilled at asymmetrical warfare. They finally come
home to a country they hardly recognize, whose people are uneasy
with hardened combat veterans in their midst, and whose political
leadership is worried about how they will upset the balance of power.

That's Anabasis, written 2500 years ago by Xenophon.

—The greatest military power in the world sends its army into a populous Middle Eastern country. The stated purpose: to overthrow its capricious, torture-prone dictator and return the land to its former state of peace and prosperity. The ulterior motive: to seize control of its resources, which will pay for the invasion once the people are given the modern Western-style government they yearn for. Sharp resistance from the dictator's elite troops soon crumbles before the invaders' overwhelming firepower and mobility. The dictator flees into hiding in the desert, where he long evades his pursuers. The invaders march into his capital and are astounded by the wealth and luxury of his palaces. But they don't get the welcome they were expecting. Religious leaders exhort the common people to fight them. Faceless jihadists abduct stragglers and decapitate them or hold them for ransom. The foreigners build fortified zones in the major cities. The expected swag never materializes. Food and provisions must be imported from home at great cost. No expense is spared to bring the long-suffering troops the comforts of home. This lavish operation, however, is soon riddled with corruption. Faced with other demands on military resources, Napoleon Bonaparte decides to leave Egypt in August 1799.

—On August 1st, 2007, the I-35W bridge in Minneapolis collapses during rush hour . . .

"Hey, wait a sec!" you might be saying, "I thought this was another diatribe about the war in Iraq . . . how does a rusty bridge figure into it?"

The answer: I'm interested in a larger topic: the attention span of our society. Bear with me.

Literate people used to spend a lot of time reading books, but during the Internet years those have begun to seem more and more like a distinct minority: a large and relatively well-off minority, to be sure, but one that simply doesn't register in the electronic media, as vampires are invisible in mirrors. They are out there somewhere, the book-readers in their millions, and they are talking to each other.

Books, though, and the thoughts that go through the heads of their readers, are too long and complex to work on the screen—be it a talk show, a PowerPoint presentation, or a web page. Bookish people sense this. They don't object to it. They don't favor electronic media anyway. So why should they make a fuss if those media Photoshop them out of the national scene? They know how to find each other and to have the long conversations that nourish their bookish souls.

A few years ago I began thinking that the bookish people of the world were becoming a little bit like medieval monks, living austere but intellectually complex lives in voluntary seclusion from a gaudy and action-packed secular world. I've written a novel, *Anathem*, based on that premise.

It's paradoxical, I suppose, to write a long book about how no one reads long books any more: an ambiguity I'll have a hard time explaining on talk shows.

If bookishness were just a niche pastime, like stamp collecting or waveboarding, none of this would really matter. But it's more than that. It is the collective memory and the accumulated wisdom of our species.

The rough-and-ready intellectual consensus of the mid–Twentieth Century is being pushed out by a New Superstition whose victims can find testimony on the Internet for anything they choose to believe. The only cure for it is reading books, and lots of them. When all things bookish are edited out of public discourse, strange things happen, or seem to. When our societal attention span becomes shorter than the lifetime of a steel bridge over a river, what appears to be a solid strip of highway can suddenly fall out from under us. Like a portent from the medieval world.

EVERYTHING AND MORE
FOREWORD
(2003)

When I was a boy growing up in Ames, Iowa, I belonged to a Boy Scout troop whose adult supervision—consisting almost entirely of professors from the Iowa State University of Science and Technology—devised the following project for us to pursue when not occupied with dodgeball and clove hitches. One of the scouts' dads—an eminent professor of agricultural engineering—obtained, from a lab in his department, a sack of genetically identical corn kernels, carried them across campus, and handed them off to one of the other scouts' dads: a physicist employed by the Ames Laboratory. This was an offshoot of the Manhattan Project. The uranium enriched at Oak Ridge, and used in the first atomic bombs, had been refined from its ore by a process developed at Ames. Dad #2, who had been present at the startup of the world's first atomic pile in a racquetball court at the University of Chicago, carried the seeds into a hot room buried a couple of stories beneath one of the Ames Lab's buildings and handed it off to a mechanical arm that carried it behind a thick wall of yellowish lead-laced glass and set it down in the vicinity of something that was radioactive. After a certain amount of time had passed, he retrieved the irradiated seeds and brought them to the next meeting of our Scout troop and distributed them to the boys. I distinctly remember looking at the kernels in the palm of my hand and noting that they had been washed with paint or ink of two or three different colors, and, though the color code was not explained to us (not, at least, before the expiration of my attention span), I caught the spoor of the Scientific Method, and guessed that different batches had been exposed to greater or lesser amounts of radiation. In any case, we were directed to take these seeds home and plant them and water them. In a few weeks' time, we would bring the results to a meeting where two prizes would be handed out: one for the tallest, healthiest corn plant, the other for the weirdest mutation. And indeed we ended up with both: proud stalks that would do any Iowa farmer proud, and plants, in many cases quite beautiful, that were scarcely recognizable as belonging to the relevant taxonomic phylum. If anyone had asked us "do you imagine that other scout troops in other towns are doing anything remotely like this" we would, after some higher-brain activity, have guessed no. No one asked, however, and so our lower brains assimilated the whole scenario as normal, like playing catch and making s'mores.

I draw the reader's attention, in other words, to the phenomenon of the Midwestern American College Town, which, in a completely self-aware tip of the stylistic hat to David Foster Wallace, I will denominate the MACT. For the final autobiographical note that I will make in this Foreword is to say that in 1960, when I was six months old, my parents and I moved to the archetypal, if somewhat larger-than-normal, MACT of Champaign-Urbana, Illinois, so that my father could get to work on his Ph.D. Two years later, when David

Foster Wallace was six months old, his family moved to the same town on the same errand (his dad is a philosopher, mine an electrical engineer). He and I lived in the same MACT only until 1966, when my family moved to the smaller, but no less quintessential, MACT of Ames. I never met him, unless we happened to share a slide or a swingset in some Champaign-Urbana park. Each of us went to Massachusetts for higher education and then landed for a while in a different MACT: Iowa City in my case, Bloomington-Normal, Illinois, for DFW.

The irradiated-corn anecdote might have already said everything there's to say about the culture of the MACT, but, since DFW and I seem to have been MACT products all the way, there are a few particulars that might be worth drawing out in a more discursive manner. So here goes.

PEOPLE WHO OFTEN FLY BETWEEN THE EAST AND WEST COASTS OF THE UNITED States will be familiar with the region, stretching roughly from the Ohio to the Platte, that, except in anomalous non-flat areas, is spanned by a Cartesian grid of roads. They may not be aware that the spacing between roads is exactly one mile. Unless they have a serious interest in 19th-Century Midwestern cartography, they can't possibly be expected to know that when those grids were laid out, a schoolhouse was platted at every other road intersection. In this way it was assured that no child in the Midwest would ever live more than $\sqrt{2}$ miles from a place where he or she could be educated. Secondary schools were presumably sited according to some less rigid scheme, and universities were generally doled out two to a state. According to a convention that obtains pretty consistently across all states west of Ohio, a given state, call it X, is allotted a "University of X" and an "X State University." "University of X" has been a University, as opposed to a College, from its inception, and generally houses all of the prestigious Arts-and-Sciences departments, the law school, and the medical school. "X State University" frequently started out as "X State College" and only acquired the more august "University" designation within the second half of the Twentieth Century. It is, more often than not, a land-grant institution, practical-minded, skewed toward agricultural, veterinary, and engineering departments while showing a decent respect for the liberal arts.

Normal Schools—the third tier—were post-secondary institutions whose purpose was to train the teachers who would staff those every-other-mile schoolrooms on the Cartesian road grid. The same inflationary pressure that turned X State College into X State University eventually caused these to get promoted to "University of [geographical modifier] X" or "[geographical modifier] X University," which is how we got the University of Northern Iowa, Eastern Illinois University, and many others.

The result is a network of public universities, typically situated in small cities (population, say, between twenty and two hundred thousand) and scattered about the upper Midwest at intervals of approximately one tank of gas. Precisely because of their proximity (spang in the middle of their catchment areas); their unprepossessing rank in the academic hierarchy; their practical, down-to-earth emphases; and their athletic teams, which entertain the surrounding areas, which are too sparsely populated to support professional squads, these institutions have escaped the censure/taint of elitism or ivory towerism that, deservedly or not, tends to get slapped onto private, coastal universities by those elements of society who, when depicted cinematically, are generally shown brandishing torches and pitchforks. This may have changed during the 21st Century because of the politicization of science, but none of that existed in the MACT of the mid- to late-20th Century, when most people's attitudes toward science were shaped more by antibiotics, the polio vaccine, and moon rockets than current this-can't-be-happening controversies over evolution and global warming.

According to numerical metrics of selectivity, academic prestige, etc.—and believe me, these are exactly the kinds of yardsticks by which these people rule everything—these schools tend to be somewhere behind the prestigious and older private schools of the coasts (not because the people are any dumber but because it is part of their mission to pull in the whole spectrum of academic talent whereas coastal institutions are lodged in well-defined strata). That combined with the habitually dour and self-deprecating, not to say passive-aggressive, character of residents of the upper Midwest, has left them with chips on their shoulders and an embarrassing tendency to denote themselves as "The Harvard of the Midwest" or what-have you. Seen in a longer perspective and without the overlay of coast-vs.-Midwest politics, however, the achievements of the state universities are more remarkable, and certainly more unusual, in that one would not necessarily expect newish, publicly funded institutions to be able to make such respectable showings in competition with far older, privately funded schools that have nothing to do except pile up their endowments century after century and educate the cleverest, best-prepared scions of powerful families.

I describe, here, a situation that existed during the second half of the Twentieth Century. It might be different now. But in those days, graduate students and faculty members U-Hauled from MACT to MACT somewhat in the manner of Arabs oasis-hopping across otherwise inhospitable terrain, and all of the MACTs, *mutatis mutandis*, were the same. Only the school colors and mascots really differed.

Geographical isolation is key to MACT culture. If you have an academic position in, say, greater Boston, you are spending your working days in a culture similar to that of the MACT, but when you go back to your house in Saugus or your apartment in Allston-Brighton, you're in a place where, even if you're not making more money than the people around you, you do enjoy an at least theoretically exalted status by virtue of your advanced degree and your prestigious job. Some people will treat you with a degree of deference. Even those who don't remind you of what an odd duck you are in the larger scheme. Whereas if you are in a MACT you are accorded no sense of specialness whatsoever.

And, remember, these are the professors themselves I'm talking about. The professors' *kids*, growing up in a community where all of the other kids had Ph.D. parents, never acquired in the first place, and so did not have to lose, their sense of belonging to a special, or even an unusual, class.

There are certain other peculiarities of the MACT that might find their place in a longer treatment of the topic, such as the way that garbage collectors' sons and farmers' daughters ended up being treated the same as everyone else, as long as they were smart, and the way that grad students from what were in those days seen as extremely exotic and remote places (Thailand, Afghanistan, Nigeria) were surprised, not always happily, to see their children fully and unquestioningly integrated into small-town Midwestern society, going to keggers and t.p.-ing their friends' houses as if their ancestors had come over on the *Mayflower*.

The premise of this Foreword, which will be nailed to the mast very shortly, is that in *Everything and More*, David Foster Wallace is speaking in a language and employing a style of inquiry that might strike people who have not breathed the air of Ames, Bloomington-Normal, and Champaign-Urbana as unusual enough to demand some sort of an explanation. And that, lacking such background, many of DFW's critics fall into a common pattern of error, which consists of attempting to explain his style and approach by imputing certain stances or motives to him, then becoming nonplussed, huffy, or downright offended by same. It's a mistake that befuddles MACT natives who see this book as simply what it is: one of the other smart kids trying to explain some cool stuff.

THE REGRETTABLE FACT THAT (BARRING POSSIBLE RANDOM PLAYGROUND EN-counters) I never actually met Mr. Wallace is not necessarily a disqualification from writing a Foreword. For that, all that is strictly required is some familiarity with the work being introduced. But since anyone can read *Everything and More*, that hardly makes for a unique, or even an unusual, qualification, and so my strategy here will be to predicate certain things of DFW and his work, based solely on our common MACT provenance, that are wild guesses, but that I'm pretty sure are right. This could be developed at heinous length, but since what you are reading is merely a foreword to the actual book ("booklet"—DFW) I am going to lay my core thesis directly on the line and put it to you that this is all about a quintessentially MACTish denial, or at least shrugging-off, of an attitude toward knowledge that in the Greek tradition is conveyed in the story of Prometheus and, in the Judeo-Christian, in that of Eve.

Here, in a conjectural version of this Foreword that was more dignified and old-school, those two myths would be recounted and glossed. Matters being what they are, I will encourage anyone unfamiliar with them to consult Google before proceeding. These are meant to be scary, cautionary tales to keep Bronze Age peons from asking difficult questions of their betters. To say that they have outlived their usefulness is wrong, since they were never useful to begin with. At some level, though, we've all imbibed them and they can be invoked in rhetoric to elicit certain predictable responses. By and large, these enure to the benefit of those who have acquired lots of knowledge. You might not think so, for the Promethean myth is ostensibly a knock on academics. Not so ostensibly, though, it gives scientists a reason to put on priestly airs and, by hinting at the perhaps not-so-priestly stances of their counterparts in other countries, haul down defense grants. And it gives non-scientists an implicit pitchfork to brandish in the scientists' faces. Accordingly, a kind of deal has been struck in which both scientists and non-scientists have ended up accepting the Promethean myth as being a passable model of reality. Call this the Promethean consensus. The Promethean consensus is something that no one would ever admit to believing in, if you pinned them down and tried to get them to engage in that level of introspection, but is universally hammered home by every movie and TV show about science and a good many books as well, and obviously underlies the public postures that scientists are expected to adopt.

Once you've bought into it, the only two stances you can really take toward the Promethean consensus are to respect its rules or to wilfully break them. You are either a priest or a bad boy. Priest because, if you are one of the keepers of the academic flame and are willing to allow that some of your knowledge is dangerous, you can get a lot of mileage out of intoning the right solemn and portentous sound bites. Bad boy because the downside of the Promethean myth has largely gone away. No one is getting expelled from the Garden of Eden or being chained to a rock to have his liver torn by vultures any more. It's true that modern-day scientists have to take their share of flak, but, with the exception of people who run girls' schools in Afghanistan, or the occasional biomed researcher who's run afoul of animal-rights activists, they no longer have to dodge pitchforks. And so if you're one of the people who actually has access to Promethean-grade knowledge, there's no longer much personal risk, and so, to the extent that the knowledge is perceived as dangerous, it can just feel kind of cool, in a naughty way, like you're a teenager who just figured out where Dad hides the keys to his gun cabinet.

Neither of these seemed to be going on with the irradiated corn seeds. Clearly, giving that kind of stuff to kids is non-priestly behavior. But when they were handed out at the scout meeting, or when we were exposed to sacred knowledge in countless other ways in the MACT, it was never done with an attitude of "we're getting away with something—aren't we being naughty" but rather "here's some interesting and perhaps useful knowledge that any well-brought-up young person will want to have."

So the Promethean consensus is not much in evidence in the MACT. After I went Coastal, I committed a string of social gaffes in which I failed to address or introduce some Ph.D.-endowed person with the correct title. We simply never did this where I grew up because it would have given us the faintly comical affect of characters in *The Crucible* addressing one another as "Goodman this" and "Goodwife that" (in our town there was one man, not employed in academia, who had a Ph.D., and who insisted on being addressed by his title. The view taken of him by everyone else might most politely be described as bemused).

In the preceding paragraph I am using a somewhat tawdry rhetorical shortcut by making fun of people who are pompous about academic titles, and readers from academic, but non-MACT, environments are probably getting hot under the collar and feeling as though they've been ill used by a thoroughly odious hit-and-run straw-man argument, so let me make clear right away that it's way more complicated than I'm making it sound, and that professors at Harvard and Cambridge and Bologna and Berkeley address one another by their first names all the time.

But I am, however crudely, trying to direct the reader's attention to the fact that, even among academics who ride bicycles to work and wear T-shirts and blue jeans and eschew use of formal titles, there are certain strictures and rules and bright lines and hierarchies that Must Be Respected and that people who violate them can find themselves the object of crazily vehement retribution. And here I feel I am on firmer rhetorical ground since anyone who has spent time on any rung of that ladder will probably have at least one face-burning anecdote about how he or she ran afoul of these strictures and got crucified in a faculty meeting or a letter to the editor or rampant email thread. I put it to you that, improbable as it might seem, MACT natives can grow up not being keenly aware of those rules, somewhat as the Eloi never twigged to the fact that they were Morlock chow. As I have tried to demonstrate with the irradiated-corn anecdote, the MACT breeds an anti-Promethean nonchalance that really rubs some people the wrong way. Every paragraph of *Everything and More* is imbued with it.

IT IS AN EXPECTATION, AND A REASONABLE ENOUGH ONE, THAT ANYONE who ventures to write about mathematics must make some kind of positive advance or else shut up. Exceptions are made for occasional review articles, which summarize other results without presenting new material per se, but even a review needs to be written to sufficiently exacting standards that a serious, let us say Ph.D.-level, student of the field in question can take every statement in the thing at face value and never be exposed to the risk that some part of it, in retrospect, might be found to have been glossed over, rearranged, or out-and-out screwed up. So if one is playing by the rules of academic publishing, writing an intellectually serious book about math that engages in some rearrangement and glossing over, as DFW explicitly does in *Everything and More*, is not looked on favorably.

Another practice that seems to make tenured academics practically hop up and down in rage is the crossing of boundaries between sub-sub-disciplines (or, in the case of history, geographical regions or chronological epochs) to write articles that pull together a number of threads and point out common themes among them. The exact reasons for this taboo are probably best left to anthropologists or psychologists, but I infer that this sort of thing is viewed as a privilege gained only with age and emeritus-level distinction and that to write any such material before the age of 60 gets one designated as a whippersnapper, which, in the academic world, is the setup for retributive measures of a severity normally seen only in Greek myths.

So the rules of the academic publishing road are both strict and cruelly enforced. This imposes some narrow and hard limits on what smart people can get away with writing about, which are sufficiently restrictive that some effort goes into finding loopholes. The biggest of these appears to be science fiction. SF novelists arrogate to themselves and, by convention, are readily afforded, a kind of court jester's immunity. And indeed there have been any number of hard science professors who have donned the motley, taken up the pen, and written more or less successful works of hard science fiction as a way of dodging those two terrible strictures against popularization/simplification, and synoptic pulling-together-of-diverse-strands.

It is also permissible for serious academics to write books that are explicitly targeted at general readers, though again this tends to be viewed as whippersnapperish behavior if indulged in too early in one's career.

To this point, then, we have two categories of books-about-real-science-for-non-specialist-readers: the hard SF novel and the popularizing book written by an actual scientist. There is a third category, in which a writer, well-educated, but without formal credentials in the field in question, immerses himself in the subject matter and then does his level best to explain it. There is a tendency, which is by no means a bad thing, for such books to become somewhat self-referential and autobiographical as the author tells the tale of his own self-education. While the premise, explained this way, sounds dodgy, these books can be really good, since the writer knows what it's like to not understand the material, and can tell the story of learning it as a narrative.

A fourth category, seemingly quite different from #3 but in some ways similar, is the History of Science book, which generally takes the form of a narrative about the efforts of one or more scientists to figure something out. Here the questing author of the Type 3 book is replaced, as protagonist, by the actual scientist who figured it all out in the first place.

Again, this Foreword might be a more respectable—certainly it would be longer—document if it now listed specific examples of each of the above-mentioned four types of books and engaged in some actual literary criticism. But anyone who is bothering to read an introduction by an SF novelist to a book about infinity by DFW probably has examples of all four types on her bookshelf and so this will be left, as the saying goes, as an exercise for the reader. Just to be clear, though, I will list some examples:

Type 1: Any fiction by Gregory Benford

Type 2: *A Brief History of Time* by Stephen Hawking

Type 3: *1491* by Charles Mann

Type 4: *Einstein in Berlin* by Tom Levenson

What is clearly true about all of these types of books is that they are safe to write, in the sense that critically-minded readers from the academic world will fairly quickly say to themselves, "ah, this is one of those" and then, if they wish to criticize them, will do so according to the rules of that type.

Everything and More occupies a hard-to-pin-down space in the Venn diagram that has been taking shape in preceding paragraphs (and before going into detail on that, I'll just supply the premonitory information that books without a clear coordinate on the Venn diagram tend to make people crazy, since this makes it unclear which set of interpretive and critical ground rules is to be applied).

To begin with, DFW was arguably a science fiction writer (*Infinite Jest*), although he probably would not have classified himself as such. Of course *Everything and More* is not SF, or even F, at all, *pace* some of its detractors, but the mere fact of DFW's having been an SF kind of guy muddies the taxonomic waters before we have even gotten started. Novelists—who almost by definition hold motley and informal credentials, when they are credentialed at all—make for an uneasy fit with the academic world, where credentials are everything. And writers who produce books on technical subjects aimed at non-technical readers are doomed to get cranky reviews from both sides: anything short of a fully peer-reviewed monograph is simply wrong and subject to censure from people whose job it is to get it right, and any material that requires unusual effort to read undercuts the work's claim to be accessible to a general audience. So in writing a book such as *Everything and More*, DFW reminds us of the soldier who earns a medal by calling in an artillery strike on his own position; with the possible elaboration that in this case he's out in the middle of no-man's land calling in strikes from both directions.

DFW's degree was in modal logic, which, if you haven't seen it, is indistinguishable, by almost all laymen, from pure math, though even more punishingly abstract than mathematics could ever be. Though he did not pursue that career to a Ph.D. and an academic post, the fact that he was able to study such a recondite field at all clearly marks him out as having had what it took to be a hard science/math/ logic professional, and, therefore, in the eyes of hard-math critics, as fair game. We must therefore ask whether *Everything and More* is to be taken as a serious technical book by an actual scientist, or a popularization. Its editors clearly asked for the latter and eventually took delivery of something closer to the former. Which is not to say that DFW makes actual technical advances in mathematics—he doesn't, and doesn't try or claim to—but that he immersed himself in the material in a way that the editors of this series could not reasonably have asked or expected any writer to do, and pitched many parts of the text at a higher technical level than is generally considered a good move in books whose mission it is to popularize science. Which, if all DFW cared about was getting a uniformly rapturous critical reception, might not have been the best tactical approach. But he doesn't appear to have been this kind of guy at all.

In immune-system lingo, the equation-laden sections of *Everything and More* cause it to express certain antigens that arouse the retributive ardor of hard-science and math reviewers. The analogy being apposite here because the immune system, when aroused, can elicit a range of reactions from a mild sense that something isn't right, to irritation, to hives, to full-on T-cell counterattack and organ rejection.

Finally, *Everything and More*, in many sections, alternates between being a Type 3 and a Type 4 (see above taxonomic breakdown) in that, part of the time, we are getting autobiographical material about how DFW learned mathematics, mostly under one Dr. Goris, and part of the time it becomes a History of Science book in which we learn about the lives and careers of Dedekind, Weierstrass, Cantor, et al.

Having as it were set all of those pieces out on the board, the weakest possible claim that I can now assert is that I really like this book and that, as I was reading it, it never even occurred to me to be troubled, confused, annoyed, or nonplussed by any of the features alluded to: the fact that it was written by a fiction writer, the excursions into highly technical discourse, the caveats—clearly and repeatedly stated by DFW—that the technical bits simplified and glossed over material in a way that wouldn't be satisfactory to mathematicians, and the use of both autobiographical, and just plain biographical, material. My advice, therefore, dear reader, is that you simply read it, and that if you happen to be a math major you then peruse some of the trenchant criticisms of the book that have appeared in the mathematical literature, and improve your understanding of the pure-math content by studying peer-reviewed documents on the same topics, and, in general, make sure that this is not the last thing you read on the topic before your orals.

Having supplied that exhortation I will add one piece of advice about how to read this book, which is to relax and pay no attention—beyond, of course, reading and enjoying it—to one feature of this book that has engendered an absurd volume of critical boggling, namely, DFW's habit of employing informal pop/slang expressions in close juxtaposition with high-end vocabulary and while talking about fancy stuff. This is nothing except good writing. The vernacular is often the most expressive wing of the language. DFW could write high-powered prose better than just about anyone but he well knew the value of mixing it with informal day-to-day English, and, though he was especially good at it, it's worth keeping in mind that he was hardly the first great English writer to do so. For every Milton who kept it all on an elevated plane there was a Shakespeare who knew how to sock us in the chops with some well-timed plain talk (among reviewers with humanities degrees, it also seems compulsory to make some remark—or, just as well, to go on at some length—on "post-modernism," a topic of zero interest to most actual readers).

I infer that some whose academic reputations have been put into play by the assignment to write a review of this book have felt provoked or confused by DFW's disinclination or outright refusal to don the mortarboard—the lofty academic style of expression—that's expected of people who want to thrive within that system, but that can be swapped out, by novelists, in favor of the court jester's cap 'n' bells. A dead giveaway being the habit of following a quote from DFW's prose by "(*sic*)." As long as you are not the sort of person who is in the habit of using "(*sic*)" after quoting others' work in your own written communications, you should be okay with the style in which *Everything and More* has been written.

THE FOREGOING HAS BEEN ALL NEGATIVE, NOT IN THE POP-PSYCH SENSE OF adopting a dispiriting tone, but in the purely technical sense that it has been about negating a number of predicates (DFW didn't buy into the Promethean consensus, *Everything and More* doesn't fit into such-and-such bubble on the Venn diagram, certain criticisms of the book aren't that interesting or useful to most readers). I would like to end with something positive (both in the pop-psych and the technical senses). DFW's writing reflects an attitude that is lovely: a touching, and for the most part well-founded, belief that you can explain anything with words if you work hard enough and show your readers sufficient respect. While it has probably existed in other times and places, it is a Midwestern American College Town attitude all the way.

As an explanation for milder allergic reactions—and, having proselytized DFW's writing to many friends over the years, I've seen a few—some readers posit (often vaguely and fretfully) that there is some archness or smart-assery in DFW's literary style. This, to me anyway, is an unsupportable conclusion, given the obvious love that DFW brings to what he's writing about, and his explicitly stated opposition to irony-as-lifestyle in his essay *E Unibus Pluram*. Why do people see it when it's not there? It's something to do with the fact that his conspicuous verbal talent and wordplay create a nagging sense among some readers that there's a joke here that they're not getting or that they are somehow being made fools of by an agile knave. Which DFW was not.

To me *Everything and More* reads, rather, as a discourse from a green, gridded prairie heaven, where irony-free people who've been educated to a turn in those prairie schoolhouses and great-but-unpretentious universities sit around their dinner tables buttering sweet corn, drinking iced tea, and patiently trying to explain even the most recondite mysteries of the universe, out of a conviction that the world must be amenable to human understanding, and that if you can understand something, you can explain it in words: fancy words if that helps, plain words if possible. But in any case you can reach out to other minds through that medium of words and make a connection. Handing out irradiated corn kernels to a troop of Boy Scouts, and writing books that explain difficult matters in disarmingly informal language, are the same act, a way of saying *here is something cool that I want to share with you for no reason other than making the spark jump between minds*. If that is how you have been raised, then to explain anything to anyone is a pleasure. To explain difficult things is a challenge. And to explain the infamously difficult ideas that were spawned in chiliastic profusion during the late Nineteenth and early Twentieth Centuries (Infinities, Relativity, Quantum Mechanics, Hilbert's problems, Gödel's Proof) is Mount Everest.

So in reading *Everything and More*, cleverness or verbal pyrotechnics or archness are not the emotional tone that comes through to me, but a kind of open-soulness and desire to connect that were touching before, and heartbreaking after, David Foster Wallace succumbed, at the age of 46, to a cruel and incurable disease. Because of this we will not have the opportunity to enjoy and profit from many other explanations that it was in his power to supply on diverse topics, lofty and mundane, and so we must content ourselves with what he did leave behind—an impossibility given the pleasure and the insight he gave us in *Everything and More*, and his obvious ability to have provided much more, had fortune treated him with as much consideration as he did his readers.

THE GREAT SIMOLEON CAPER

(1995)

Hard to imagine a less attractive life-style for a young man just out of college than going back to Bismarck to live with his parents—unless it's living with his brother in the suburbs of Chicago, which, naturally, is what I did. Mom at least bakes a mean cherry pie. Joe, on the other hand, got me into a permanent emotional headlock and found some way, every day, to give me psychic noogies. For example, there was the day he gave me the job of figuring out how many jelly beans it would take to fill up Soldier Field.

Let us stipulate that it's all my fault; Joe would want me to be clear on that point. Just as he was always good with people, I was always good with numbers. As Joe tells me at least once a week, I should have studied engineering. Drifted between majors instead, ended up with a major in math and a minor in art—just about the worst thing you can put on a job app.

Joe, on the other hand, went into the ad game. When the Internet and optical fiber and HDTV and digital cash all came together and turned into what we now call the Metaverse, most of the big ad agencies got hammered—because in the Metaverse, you can actually whip out a gun and blow the Energizer Bunny's head off, and a lot of people did. Joe borrowed 10,000 bucks from Mom and Dad and started this clever young ad agency. If you've spent any time crawling the Metaverse, you've seen his work—and it's seen you, and talked to you, and followed you around.

Mom and Dad stayed in their same little house in Bismarck, North Dakota. None of their neighbors guessed that if they cashed in their stock in Joe's agency, they'd be worth about $20 million. I nagged them to diversify their portfolio—you know, buy a bushel basket of Krugerrands and bury them in the backyard, or maybe put a few million into a mutual fund. But Mom and Dad felt this would be a no-confidence vote in Joe. "It'd be," Dad said, "like showing up for your kid's piano recital with a Walkman."

Joe comes home one January evening with a magnum of champagne. After giving me the obligatory hazing about whether I'm old enough to drink, he pours me a glass. He's already banished his two sons to the Home Theater. They have cranked up the set-top box they got for Christmas. Patch this baby into your HDTV, and you can cruise the Metaverse, wander the Web and choose from among several user-friendly operating systems, each one rife with automatic help systems, customer-service hot lines and intelligent agents. The theater's subwoofer causes our silverware to buzz around like sheet-metal hockey players, and amplified explosions knock swirling nebulas of tiny bubbles loose from the insides of our champagne glasses. Those low frequencies must penetrate the young brain somehow, coming in under kids' media-hip radar and injecting the edfotainucational muchomedia bitstream direct into their cerebral cortices.

"Hauled down a mother of an account today," Joe explains. "We hype cars. We hype computers. We hype athletic shoes. But as of three hours ago, we are hyping a currency."

"What?" says his wife, Anne.

"Y'know, like dollars or yen. Except this is a new currency."

"From which country?" I ask. This is like offering lox to a dog: I've given Joe the chance to enlighten his feckless bro. He hammers back half a flute of Dom Perignon and shifts into full-on Pitch Mode.

"Forget about countries," he says. "We're talking Simoleons—the smart, hip new currency of the Metaverse."

"Is this like E-money?" Anne asks.

"We've been doing E-money for e-ons, ever since automated-teller machines," Joe says, with just the right edge of scorn.

"Nowadays we can use it to go shopping in the Metaverse. But it's still in U.S. dollars. Smart people are looking for something better."

That was for me. I graduated college with a thousand bucks in savings. With inflation at 10% and rising, that buys a lot fewer Leinenkugels than it did a year ago.

"The government's never going to get its act together on the budget," Joe says. "It can't. Inflation will just get worse. People will put their money elsewhere."

"Inflation would have to get pretty damn high before I'd put my money into some artificial currency," I say.

"Hell, they're all artificial," Joe says. "If you think about it, we've been doing this forever. We put our money in stocks, bonds, shares of mutual funds. Those things represent real assets—factories, ships, bananas, software, gold, whatever. Simoleons is just a new name for those assets. You carry around a smart card and spend it just like cash. Or else you go shopping in the Metaverse and spend the money online, and the goods show up on your doorstep the next morning."

I say, "Who's going to fall for that?"

"Everyone," he says. "For our big promo, we're going to give Simoleons away to some average Joes at the Super Bowl. We'll check in with them one, three, six months later, and people will see that this is a safe and stable place to put their money."

"It doesn't inspire much confidence," I say, "to hand the stuff out like Monopoly money."

He's ready for this one. "It's not a handout. It's a sweepstakes."
And that's when he asks me to calculate how many jelly beans will fill
Soldier Field.

Two hours later, I'm down at the local galaxy-class grocery store,
in Bulk: a Manhattan of towering Lucite bins filled with steel-cut
rolled oats, off-brand Froot Loops, sun-dried tomatoes, prefabri-
cated s'mores, macadamias, French roasts and pignolias, all dispensed into your bag or bucket with a jerk at the handy Plexiglas
guillotine. Not a human being in sight, just robot restocking machines trundling back and forth on a grid of overhead catwalks and
surveillance cameras hidden in smoked-glass hemispheres. I stroll
through the gleaming Lucite wonderland holding a perfect 6-in. cube
improvised from duct tape and cardboard. I stagger through a glit-
ter gulch of Gummi fauna, Boston baked beans, gobstoppers, Good &
Plenty, Tart'n Tiny. Then, bingo: bulk jelly beans, premium grade. I
put my cube under the spout and fill it.

Who guesses closest and earliest on the jelly beans wins the Simoleons. They've hired a Big Six accounting firm to make sure everything's done right. And since they can't actually fill the stadium with
candy, I'm to come up with the Correct Answer and supply it to them
and, just as important, to keep it secret.

I get home and count the beans: 3,101. Multiply by 8 to get the
number in a cubic foot: 24,808. Now I just need the number of cubic
feet in Soldier Field. My nephews are sprawled like pithed frogs
before the HDTV, teaching themselves physics by lobbing antimatter
bombs onto an offending civilization from high orbit. I prance over
the black zigzags of the control cables and commandeer a unit.

Up on the screen, a cartoon elf or sprite or something pokes its
head out from behind a window, then draws it back. No, I'm not a paranoid schizophrenic—this is the much-hyped intelligent agent who
comes with the box. I ignore it, make my escape from Gameland and
blunder into a lurid district of the Metaverse where thousands of in-
fomercials run day and night, each in its own window. I watch an ad
for Chinese folk medicines made from rare-animal parts, genetically

engineered and grown in vats. Grizzly-bear gallbladders are shown growing like bunches of grapes in an amber fluid.

The animated sprite comes all the way out, and leans up against the edge of the infomercial window. "Hey!" it says, in a goofy, exuberant voice, "I'm Raster! Just speak my name—that's Raster—if you need any help."

I don't like Raster's looks. It's likely he was wandering the streets of Toontown and waving a sign saying WILL ANNOY GROWNUPS FOR FOOD until he was hired by the cable company. He begins flying around the screen, leaving a trail of glowing fairy dust that fades much too slowly for my taste.

"Give me the damn encyclopedia!" I shout. Hearing the dread word, my nephews erupt from the rug and flee.

So I look up Soldier Field. My old Analytic Geometry textbook, still flecked with insulation from the attic, has been sitting on my thigh like a lump of ice. By combining some formulas from it with the encyclopedia's stats . . .

"Hey! Raster!"

Raster is so glad to be wanted that he does figure eights around the screen. "Calculator!" I shout.

"No need, boss! Simply tell me your desired calculation, and I will do it in my head!"

So I have a most tedious conversation with Raster, in which I estimate the number of cubic feet in Soldier Field, rounded to the nearest foot. I ask Raster to multiply that by 24,808 and he shoots back: 537,824,167,717.

A nongeek wouldn't have thought twice. But I say, "Raster, you have Spam for brains. It should be an exact multiple of eight!" Evidently my brother's new box came with one of those defective chips that makes errors when the numbers get really big.

Raster slaps himself upside the head; loose screws and transistors tumble out of his ears. "Darn! Guess I'll have to have a talk with my programmer!" And then he freezes up for a minute.

My sister-in-law Anne darts into the room, hunched in a don't-mind-me posture, and looks around. She's terrified that I may have a date in here. "Who're you talking to?"

"This goofy I.A. that came with your box," I say. "Don't ever use it to do your taxes, by the way."

She cocks her head. "You know, just yesterday I asked it for help with a Schedule B, and it gave me a recipe for shellfish bisque."

"Good evening, sir. Good evening, ma'am. What were those numbers again?" Raster asks. Same voice, but different inflections—more human. I call out the numbers one more time and he comes back with 537,824,167,720.

"That sounds better," I mutter.

Anne is nonplussed. "Now its voice recognition seems to be working fine."

"I don't think so. I think my little math problem got forwarded to a real human being. When the conversation gets over the head of the built-in software, it calls for help, and a human steps in and takes over. He's watching us through the built-in videocam," I explain, pointing at the fish- eye lens built into the front panel of the set-top box, "and listening through the built-in mike."

Anne's getting that glazed look in her eyes; I grope for an analog analogy. "Remember *The Exorcist*? Well, Raster has just been possessed, like the chick in the flick. Except it's not just Beelzebub. It's a customer-service rep."

I've just walked blind into a trap that is yawningly obvious to Anne. "Maybe that's a job you should apply for!" she exclaims. The other jaw of the trap closes faster than my teeth chomping down on my tongue: "I can take your application online right now!" says Raster.

My sister-in-law is the embodiment of sugary triumph until the next evening, when I have a good news/bad news conversation with her. Good: I'm now a Metaverse customer-service rep. Bad: I don't have a cubicle in some Edge City office complex. I telecommute from home—from her home, from her sofa. I sit there all day long, munching through my dwindling stash of tax-deductible jelly beans, wearing an operator's headset, gripping the control unit, using it like a puppeteer's rig to control other people's Rasters on other people's screens, all over the U.S. I can see them—the wide-angle view from their set-top boxes is piped to a window on my screen. But they can't see me—just Raster, my avatar, my body in the Metaverse.

Ghastly in the mottled, flattening light of the Tube, people ask me inane questions about arithmetic. If they're asking for help with recipes, airplane schedules, child-rearing or home improvement, they've already been turfed to someone else. My expertise is pure math only.

Which is pretty sleepy until the next week, when my brother's agency announces the big Simoleons Sweepstakes. They've hired a knot-kneed fullback as their spokesman. Within minutes, requests for help from contestants start flooding in. Every Bears fan in Greater Chicago is trying to calculate the volume of Soldier Field. They're all doing it wrong; and even the ones who are doing it right are probably using the faulty chip in their set-top box. I'm in deep conflict-of-interest territory here, wanting to reach out with Raster's stubby, white-gloved, three-fingered hand and slap some sense into these people.

But I'm sworn to secrecy. Joe has hired me to do the calculations for the Metrodome, Three Rivers Stadium, RFK Stadium and every other N.F.L. venue. There's going to be a Simoleons winner in every city.

We are allowed to take 15-minute breaks every four hours. So I crank up the Home Theater, just to blow the carbon out of its cylinders, and zip down the main street of the Metaverse to a club that specializes in my kind of tunes. I'm still "wearing" my Raster uniform, but I don't care—I'm just one of thousands of Rasters running up and down the street on their breaks.

My club has a narrow entrance on a narrow alley off a narrow side street, far from the virtual malls and 3-D video-game amusement parks that serve as the cash cows for the Metaverse's E-money economy. Inside, there's a few Rasters on break, but it's mostly people "wearing" more creative avatars. In the Metaverse, there's no part of your virtual body you can't pierce, brand or tattoo in an effort to look weirder than the next guy.

The live band onstage—jacked in from a studio in Prague—isn't very good, so I duck into the back room where there are virtual racks full of tapes you can sample, listening to a few seconds from each song. If you like it, you can download the whole album, with optional interactive liner notes, videos and sheet music.

I'm pawing through one of these racks when I sense another avatar, something big and shaggy, sidling up next to me. It mumbles something; I ignore it. A magisterial throat-clearing noise rumbles in the subwoofer, crackles in the surround speakers, punches through cleanly on the center channel above the screen. I turn and look: it's a heavy-set creature wearing a T-shirt emblazoned with a logo HACKERS 1111. It has very long scythe-like claws, which it uses to grip a hot-pink cylinder. It's much better drawn than Raster; almost Disney-quality.

The sloth speaks: "537,824,167,720."

"Hey!" I shout. "Who the hell are you?" It lifts the pink cylinder to its lips and drinks. It's a can of Jolt. "Where'd you get that number?" I demand. "It's supposed to be a secret."

"The key is under the doormat," the sloth says, then turns around and walks out of the club.

My 15-minute break is over, so I have to ponder the meaning of this through the rest of my shift. Then, I drag myself up out of the couch, open the front door and peel up the doormat.

Sure enough, someone has stuck an envelope under there. Inside is a sheet of paper with a number on it, written in hexadecimal notation, which is what computer people use: 0A56 7781 6BE2 2004 89FF 9001 C782—and so on for about five lines.

The sloth had told me that "the key is under the doormat," and I'm willing to bet many Simoleons that this number is an encryption key that will enable me to send and receive coded messages.

So I spend 10 minutes punching it into the set-top box. Raster shows up and starts to bother me: "Can I help you with anything?"

By the time I've punched in the 256th digit, I've become a little testy with Raster and said some rude things to him. I'm not proud of it. Then I hear something that's music to my ears: "I'm sorry, I didn't understand you," Raster chirps. "Please check your cable connections—I'm getting some noise on the line."

A second figure materializes on the screen, like a digital genie: it's the sloth again. "Who the hell are you?" I ask.

The sloth takes another slug of Jolt, stifles a belch and says, "I am Codex, the Crypto-Anarchist Sloth."

"Your equipment requires maintenance," Raster says. "Please contact the cable company."

"Your equipment is fine," Codex says. "I'm encrypting your back channel. To the cable company, it looks like noise. As you figured out, that number is your personal encryption key. No government or corporation on earth can eavesdrop on us now."

"Gosh, thanks," I say.

"You're welcome," Codex replies. "Now, let's get down to biz. We have something you want. You have something we want."

"How did you know the answer to the Soldier Field jelly-bean question?"

"We've got all 27," ' Codex says. And he rattles off the secret numbers for Candlestick Park, the Kingdome, the Meadowlands . . .

"Unless you've broken into the accounting firm's vault," I say, "there's only one way you could have those numbers. You've been eavesdropping on my little chats with Raster. You've tapped the line coming out of this set-top box, haven't you?"

"Oh, that's typical. I suppose you think we're a bunch of socially inept, acne-ridden, high-IQ teenage hackers who play sophomoric pranks on the Establishment."

"The thought had crossed my mind," I say. But the fact that the cartoon sloth can give me such a realistic withering look, as he is doing now, suggests a much higher level of technical sophistication. Raster only has six facial expressions and none of them is very good.

"Your brother runs an ad agency, no?"

"Correct."

"He recently signed up Simoleons Corp.?"

"Correct."

"As soon as he did, the government put your house under full-time surveillance."

Suddenly the glass eyeball in the front of the set-top box is looking very big and beady to me. "They tapped our infotainment cable?"

"Didn't have to. The cable people are happy to do all the dirty work—after all, they're beholden to the government for their monopoly. So all those calculations you did using Raster were piped straight to the cable company and from there to the government. We've got a mole in the government who cc'd us everything through an anonymous remailer in Jyvaskyla, Finland."

"Why should the government care?"

"They care big-time," Codex says. "They're going to destroy Simoleons. And they're going to step all over your family in the process."

"Why?"

"Because if they don't destroy E-money," Codex says, "E-money will destroy them."

The next afternoon I show up at my brother's office, in a groovily refurbished ex-power plant on the near West Side. He finishes rolling some calls and then waves me into his office, a cavernous space with a giant steam turbine as a conversation piece. I think it's supposed to be an irony thing.

"Aren't you supposed to be cruising the I-way for stalled motorists?" he says.

"Spare me the fraternal heckling," I say. "We crypto-anarchists don't have time for such things."

"Crypto-anarchists?"

"The word panarchist is also frequently used."

"Cute," he says, rolling the word around in his head. He's already working up a mental ad campaign for it.

"You're looking flushed and satisfied this afternoon," I say. "Must have been those two imperial pints of Hog City Porter you had with your baby-back ribs at Divane's Lakeview Grill."

Suddenly he sits up straight and gets an edgy look about him, as if a practical joke is in progress, and he's determined not to play the fool.

"So how'd you know what I had for lunch?"

"Same way I know you've been cheating on your taxes."

"What!?"

"Last year you put a new tax-deductible sofa in your home office. But that sofa is a hide-a-bed model, which is a no-no."

"Hackers," he says. "Your buddies hacked into my records, didn't they?"

"You win the Stratolounger."

"I thought they had safeguards on these things now."

"The files are harder to break into. But every time information gets sent across the wires—like, when Anne uses Raster to do the taxes—it can be captured and decrypted. Because, my brother, you bought the default data-security agreement with your box, and the default agreement sucks."

"So what are you getting at?"

"For that," I say, "we'll have to go someplace that isn't under surveillance."

"Surveillance!? What the . . ." he begins. But then I nod at the TV in the corner of his office, with its beady glass eye staring out at us from the set-top box.

We end up walking along the lakeshore, which, in Chicago in January, is madness. But we hail from North Dakota, and we have all the cold-weather gear it takes to do this. I tell him about Raster and the cable company.

"Oh, Jesus!" he says. "You mean those numbers aren't secret?"

"Not even close. They've been put in the hands of 27 stooges hired by the government. The stooges have already FedEx'd their entry forms with the correct numbers. So, as of now, all of your Simoleons—$27 million worth—are going straight into the hands of the stooges on Super Bowl Sunday. And they will turn out to be your worst public-relations nightmare. They will cash in their Simoleons for comic books and baseball cards and claim it's safer. They will intentionally go bankrupt and blame it on you. They will show up in twos and threes on tawdry talk shows to report mysterious disappearances of their Simoleons during Metaverse transactions. They will, in short, destroy the image—and the business—of your client. The result: victory for the government, which hates and fears private currencies. And bankruptcy for you, and for Mom and Dad."

"How do you figure?"

"Your agency is responsible for screwing up this sweepstakes. Soon as the debacle hits, your stock plummets. Mom and Dad lose millions in paper profits they've never had a chance to enjoy. Then your big shareholders will sue your ass, my brother, and you will lose. You gambled the value of the company on the faulty data-security built into your set-top box, and you as a corporate officer are personally responsible for the losses."

At this point, big brother Joe feels the need to slam himself down on a park bench, which must feel roughly like sitting on a block of dry ice. But he doesn't care. He's beyond physical pain. I sort of expected to feel triumphant at this point, but I don't.

So I let him off the hook. "I just came from your accounting firm," I say. "I told them I had discovered an error in my calculations—that my set-top box had a faulty chip. I supplied them with 27 new numbers, which I worked out by hand, with pencil and paper, in a conference room in their offices, far from the prying eye of the cable company. I personally sealed them in an envelope and placed them in their vault."

"So the sweepstakes will come off as planned," he exhales. "Thank God!"

"Yeah—and while you're at it, thank me and the panarchists," I shoot back. "I also called Mom and Dad, and told them that they should sell their stock—just in case the government finds some new way to sabotage your contest."

"That's probably wise," he says sourly, "but they're going to get hammered on taxes. They'll lose 40% of their net worth to the government, just like that."

"No, they won't," I say. "They aren't paying any taxes."

"Say what?" He lifts his chin off his mittens for the first time in a while, reinvigorated by the chance to tell me how wrong I am. "Their cash basis is only $10,000—you think the IRS won't notice $20 million in capital gains?"

"We didn't invite the IRS," I tell him. "It's none of the IRS's damn business."

"They have ways to make it their business."

"Not any more. Mom and Dad aren't selling their stock for dollars, Joe."

"Simoleons? It's the same deal with Simoleons—everything gets reported to the government."

"Forget Simoleons. Think CryptoCredits."

"CryptoCredits? What the hell is a CryptoCredit?" He stands up and starts pacing back and forth. Now he's convinced I've traded the family cow for a handful of magic beans.

"It's what Simoleons ought to be: E-money that is totally private from the eyes of government."

"How do you know? Isn't any code crackable?"

"Any kind of E-money consists of numbers moving around on wires," I say. "If you know how to keep your numbers secret, your currency is safe. If you don't, it's not. Keeping numbers secret is a problem of cryptography—a branch of mathematics. Well, Joe, the crypto-anarchists showed me their math. And it's good math. It's

better than the math the government uses. Better than Simoleons'
math too. No one can mess with CryptoCredits."

He heaves a big sigh. "O.K., O.K.—you want me to say it? I'll say
it. You were right. I was wrong. You studied the right thing in college
after all."

"I'm not worthless scum?"

"Not worthless scum. So. What do these crypto-anarchists want,
anyway?"

For some reason I can't lie to my parents, but Joe's easy. "Nothing," I say. "They just wanted to do us a favor, as a way of gaining some
goodwill with us."

"And furthering the righteous cause of World Panarchy?"

"Something like that."

Which brings us to Super Bowl Sunday. We are sitting in a skybox
high up in the Superdome, complete with wet bar, kitchen, waiters
and big TV screens to watch the instant replays of what we've just seen
with our own naked, pitiful, nondigital eyes.

The corporate officers of Simoleons are there. I start sounding them out on their cryptographic protocols, and it becomes clear
that these people can't calculate their gas mileage without consult-
ing Raster, much less navigate the subtle and dangerous currents of
cutting-edge cryptography.

A Superdome security man comes in, looking uneasy. "Some, uh,
gentlemen are here," he says. "They have tickets that appear to be au-
thentic."

It's three guys. The first one is a 300 pounder with hair down to
his waist and a beard down to his navel. He must be a Bears fan because he has painted his face and bare torso blue and orange. The
second one isn't quite as introverted as the first, and the third isn't
quite the button-down conformist the other two are. Mr. Big is carrying an old milk crate. What's inside must be heavy, because it looks
like it's about to pull his arms out of their sockets.

"Mr. and Mrs. De Groot?" he says, as he staggers into the room.

Heads turn towards my mom and dad, who, alarmed by the appearance of these three, have declined to identify themselves. The guy makes for them and slams the crate down in front of my dad. "I'm the guy you've known as Codex," he says. "Thanks for naming us as your broker."

If Joe wasn't a rowing-machine abuser, he'd be blowing aneurysms in both hemispheres about now. "Your broker is a half-naked blue-and-orange crypto-anarchist?"

Dad devotes 30 seconds or so to lighting his pipe. Down on the field, the two-minute warning sounds. Dad puffs out a cloud of smoke and says, "He seemed like an honest sloth."

"Just in case," Mom says, "we sold half the stock through our broker in Bismarck. He says we'll have to pay taxes on that."

"We transferred the other half offshore, to Mr. Codex here," Dad says, "and he converted it into the local currency—tax free."

"Offshore? Where? The Bahamas?" Joe asks.

"The First Distributed Republic," says the big panarchist. "It's a virtual nation-state. I'm the Minister of Data Security. Our official currency is CryptoCredits."

"What the hell good is that?" Joe says.

"That was my concern too," Dad says, "so, just as an experiment, I used my CryptoCredits to buy something a little more tangible."

Dad reaches into the milk crate and heaves out a rectangular object made of yellow metal. Mom hauls out another one. She and Dad begin lining them up on the counter, like King and Queen Midas unloading a carton of Twinkies.

It takes Joe a few seconds to realize what's happening. He picks up one of the gold bars and gapes at it. The Simoleons execs crowd around and inspect the booty.

"Now you see why the government wants to stamp us out," the big guy says. "We can do what they do—cheaper and better."

For the first time, light dawns on the face of the Simoleons CEO. "Wait a sec," he says, and puts his hands to his temples. "You can rig it so that people who use E-money don't have to pay taxes to any government? Ever?"

"You got it," the big panarchist says. The horn sounds announcing the end of the first half.

"I have to go down and give away some Simoleons," the CEO says, "but after that, you and I need to have a talk."

The CEO goes down in the elevator with my brother, carrying a box of 27 smart cards, each of which is loaded up with secret numbers that makes it worth a million Simoleons. I go over and look out the skybox window: 27 Americans are congregated down on the 50-yard line, waiting for their mathematical manna to descend from heaven. They are just the demographic cross section that my brother was hoping for. You'd never guess they were all secretly citizens of the First Distributed Republic.

The crypto-anarchists grab some Jolt from the wet bar and troop out, so now it's just me, Mom and Dad in the skybox. Dad points at the field with the stem of his pipe. "Those 27 folks down there," he says. "They didn't get any help from you, did they?"

I've lied about this successfully to Joe. But I know it won't work with Mom and Dad. "Let's put it this way," I say, "not all panarchists are long-haired, Jolt-slurping maniacs. Some of them look like you—exactly like you, as a matter of fact."

Dad nods; I've got him on that one.

"Codex and his people saved the contest, and our family, from disaster. But there was a quid pro quo."

"Usually is," Dad says.

"But it's good for everyone. What Joe wants—and what his client wants—is for the promotion to go well, so that a year from now, everyone who's watching this broadcast today will have a high opinion of the safety and stability of Simoleons. Right?"

"Right."

"If you give the Simoleons away at random, you're rolling the dice. But if you give them to people who are secretly panarchists—who have a vested interest in showing that E-money works—it's a much safer bet."

"Does the First Distributed Republic have a flag?" Mom asks, out of left field. I tell her these guys don't look like sewing enthusiasts. So, even before the second half starts, she's sketched out a flag on the back of her program. "It'll be very colorful," she says. "Like a jar of jelly beans."

LOCKED IN
(2011)

The phenomena of path dependence and lock-in can be illus-
trated with many examples, but one of the most vivid is the gear we
use to launch things into space. Rockets are a very old invention. The
Chinese have had them for something like a thousand years. Francis
Scott Key wrote about them during the War of 1812 and we sing about
them at every football game. As late as the 1930s, however, they remained small, experimental, and failure-prone.

There is no way, of course, to guess how rockets might have developed, or failed to, were it not for the fact that, during the 1940s,
the world's most technically sophisticated nation came under the absolute control of a crazy dictator who decreed that vast physical and
intellectual resources should be hurled into the project of creating
rockets of hitherto unimagined size.

These rockets, which were known as V-2s, were worse than useless from a military standpoint, in the sense that the same resources would have produced a much greater effect had they been devoted instead to the production of U-boats or Messerschmitts. Accordingly, the victorious nations showed only modest interest in their development following the war. It is reasonable to suppose that little more would have been done with them, had it not been for another event, happening at the same time, even more bizarre and incredible than the seizure of absolute control over a modern nation-state by a genocidal madman. I refer, of course, to the sudden and completely unexpected development of nuclear weapons, undertaken over the course of a very few years by a top-secret crash program atop a mesa in New Mexico.

Atomic bombs turned out to be expensive, dirty, controversial, and of limited military use (it was difficult to find targets sufficiently large to be worth using them on). So they might have fizzled out, were it not for the fact that there just happened to be another victorious nation, controlled by a dictator, every bit as evil as the V-2 maker, but not so crazy, who insisted that his nation, the USSR, had to have atomic bombs too. Moreover, the conditions existing in the USSR then were such as to enable the development of that bomb in near-perfect secrecy. The United States could only guess at what the Soviets were doing; and given the stakes, they naturally tended to make the scariest guesses possible. The military logic of nuclear warfare forced them to develop the hydrogen bomb.

Rockets and H-bombs are made for each other. The rockets of the 1950s and 1960s were so expensive, and yet so inaccurate, that their only effective military use was lobbing bombs of inconceivably vast destructive power in the general direction of large urban areas.

Conversely, because those bombs were so destructive (making it tricky to drop them out of a manned aircraft without killing the crew) and the consequences of a first strike so dire, ICBMs—which could be launched from hardened, dispersed silos, as contrasted with bombers, which must take off from concentrated, vulnerable air bases— were the best way to deliver them.

Vast, nation-bankrupting expenditures were now directed to the development of such rockets. In *Dark Sun*, Richard Rhodes estimates the cost of the nuclear weapons and missile programs at $4 trillion in the United States and the USSR *each*.

Since the countries were on opposite sides of the planet, the rockets had to be large enough to throw their payload halfway around the world: only a small step short of putting payloads into orbit.

The unthinkable destructiveness of nuclear warfare now led the two superpowers to compete by proxy in other arenas, notably the exploration of space. Astronauts became heroic figures. Killing them accidentally became a no-no. A "failure is not an option, price is no object" mentality became prevalent.

To recap, the existence of rockets big enough to hurl significant payloads into orbit was contingent on the following radically improbable series of events:

1. World's most technically advanced nation under absolute control of superweapon-obsessed madman

2. Astonishing advent of atomic bombs at exactly the same time

3. A second great power dominated by secretive, superweapon-obsessed dictator

4. Nuclear/strategic calculus militating in favor of ICBMs as delivery system

5. Geographic situation of adversaries necessitating that ICBMs must have near-orbital capability

6. Manned space exploration as propaganda competition, unmoored from realistic cost/benefit discipline.

The above circumstances provide a remarkable example of path dependency. Had these contingencies not obtained, rockets with orbital capability would not have been developed so soon, and when modern societies became interested in launching things into space they might have looked for completely different ways of doing so.

Before dismissing the above story as it as an aberration, consider that the modern petroleum industry is a direct outgrowth of the practice of going out in wooden, wind-driven ships to hunt sperm whales with hand-hurled spears and then boiling their heads to make lamp fuel.

We move now to the phenomenon of lock-in.

Space travel has not proved nearly as useful to the human race as boys of my generation were once led to believe, but it does have one application—unmanned satellites—that is extremely lucrative to the civilian economy and of the highest imaginable importance to the military and intelligence worlds.

It is illuminating here, though utterly conjectural, to imagine a dialog, set in the offices of a large telecommunications firm during the 1960s, between a business development executive and an engineer.

BIZ DEV GUY: WE COULD MAKE A PREPOSTEROUS AMOUNT OF MONEY FROM communications satellites.

Engineer: It will be expensive to build those, but even so, nothing compared to the cost of building the machines needed to launch them into orbit.

Biz dev guy: Funny you should mention that. It so happens that our government has already put $4 trillion into building the rockets and supporting technology we need. There's only one catch.

Engineer: Okay, I'll bite. What is the catch?

Biz dev guy: Your communications satellite has to be the size, shape, and weight of a hydrogen bomb.

AS SATELLITES BECAME IMPORTANT, THE EARLY H-BOMB-HURLING ROCKETS were modified to the point where they became unrecognizable. A quick scan of the Wikipedia entry for the Titan rocket family tells the story in pictures: this machine started out in the late 1950s as an ICBM but, as the military and economic importance of launching

satellites became obvious, underwent a lengthy series of modifica-
tions, evolving beyond recognition. Similar stories can be told about
the Atlas and Thor-Delta families and some of their Soviet counterparts. Since H-bomb-hurlers, even heavily upgraded ones, were not
big enough to launch large manned space vehicles such as Apollo,
entirely new rocket families such as the Saturn were developed. So
it would be erroneous to suggest that more recent satellite design-
ers have been limited by the H-bomb form factor in the way that they
might have been at the dawn of the Space Age.

That is not, however, the most important way that rockets generate lock-in. In order to understand this it's necessary to know a few
things about (1) the physical environment of rocket launches, (2) the
economics of the industry, and (3) the way it is regulated; or, to be
more precise, the way it interacts with government.

1. The designer of a rocket payload, such as a communications satellite, has much more to worry about than merely limiting the payload to a given size, shape, and weight. The payload must be designed
to survive the launch and the transition through various atmospheric
regimes into outer space. As we all know from watching astronauts
on movies and TV, there will be acceleration forces, relatively modest
at the beginning, but building to much higher values as fuel is
burned and the rocket becomes lighter relative to its thrust. At some
moments, during stage separation, the acceleration may even reverse
direction for a few moments as one set of engines stops supplying
thrust and atmospheric resistance slows the vehicle down. Rockets
produce intense vibration over a wide range of frequencies; at the
upper end of that range we would identify this as noise (noise loud
enough to cause physical destruction of delicate objects), at the lower
range, violent shaking. Explosive bolts send violent shocks through
the vehicle's structure. During the passage through the ionosphere,
the air itself becomes conductive and can short out electrical gear.
Enclosed spaces must be vented so that pressure doesn't build up in
them as the vehicle passes into vacuum. Once the satellite has reached

orbit, sharp and intense variations in temperature as it passes in and out of the earth's shadow can cause problems if not anticipated in the engineering design. Some of these hazards are common to all things that go into space, but many are unique to rockets.

2. If satellites and launches were cheap, a more easygoing attitude toward their design and construction might prevail. But in general they are, pound for pound, among the most expensive objects ever made *even before* millions of dollars are spent launching them into orbit. Relatively mass-produced satellites, such as those in the Iridium and Orbcomm constellations, cost on the order of $10,000/lb. The communications birds in geostationary orbit—the ones used for satellite television, e.g.—are two to five times as expensive, and ambitious scientific/defense payloads are often $100,000 per pound. Comsats can only be packed so close together in orbit, which means that there is a limited number of available slots—this makes their owners want to pack as much capability as possible into each bird, helping jack up the cost. Once they are up in orbit, comsats generate huge amounts of cash for their owners, which means that any delays in launching them are terribly expensive. Rockets of the old school aren't perfect—they have their share of failures—but they have enough of a track record that it's possible to buy launch insurance. The importance of this fact cannot be overestimated. Every space entrepeneur who dreams of constructing a better mousetrap sooner or later crunches into the sickening realization that, even if the new invention achieved perfect technical success, it would fail as a business proposition simply because the customers wouldn't be able to purchase launch insurance.

3. Rockets—at least, the kinds that are destined for orbit, which is what we are talking about here—don't go straight up into the air. They mostly go horizontally, since their purpose is to generate horizontal velocities so high that centrifugal force counteracts gravity. The initial launch is vertical because the thing needs to get off the pad and out of the dense lower atmosphere, but shortly afterwards it bends its

trajectory sharply downrange and begins to accelerate nearly horizontally. Consequently, all rockets destined for orbit will pass over
large swathes of the earth's surface during the ten minutes or so that
their engines are burning. This produces regulatory and legal complications that go deep into the realm of the absurd. Existing rockets,
and the launch pads around which they have been designed, have been
grandfathered in. Space entrepeneurs must either find a way to negotiate the legal minefield from scratch or else pay high fees to use the
existing facilities. While some of these regulatory complications can
be reduced by going outside of the developed world, this introduces
a whole new set of complications since space technology is regulated
as armaments, and this imposes strict limits on the ways in which
American rocket scientists can collaborate with foreigners. Moreover, the rocket industry's status as a colossal government-funded
program with seemingly eternal lifespan has led to a situation in
which its myriad contractors and suppliers are distributed over the
largest possible number of Congressional districts; anyone who has
witnessed Congress in action can well imagine the consequences of
giving it control over a difficult scientific and technological program.

Dr. Jordin Kare, a physicist and space launch expert to whom I
am indebted for some of the details mentioned above, visualizes the
result as a triangular feedback loop joining big expensive launch systems; complex, expensive, long-life satellites; and few launch opportunities. To this could be added any number of cultural factors (the
engineers populating the aerospace industry are heavily invested in
the current way of doing things); the insurance and regulatory factors mentioned above; market inelasticity (cutting launch cost in half
wouldn't make much of a difference); and even accounting practices
(how do you amortize the non-recoverable expenses of an innovative
program over a sufficiently large number of future launches?).

To employ a commonly used metaphor, our current proficiency in
rocket-building is the result of a hill-climbing approach; we started
at one place on the technological landscape—which must be consid-

ered a random pick, given that it was chosen for dubious reasons by a maniac—and climbed the hill from there, looking for small steps that could be taken to increase the size and efficiency of the device. Sixty years and a couple of trillion dollars later, we have reached a place that is infinitesimally close to the top of that hill. Rockets are as close to perfect as they're ever going to get. For a few more billion dollars we might be able to achieve a microscopic improvement in efficiency or reliability, but to make any game-changing improvements is not merely expensive; it's a physical impossibility.

There is no shortage of proposals for radically innovative space launch schemes that, if they worked, would get us across the valley to other hilltops considerably higher than the one we are standing on now—high enough to bring the cost and risk of space launch down to the point where fundamentally new things could begin happening in outer space. But we are not making any serious effort as a society to cross those valleys. It is not clear why. A temptingly simple explanation is that we are decadent and tired. But none of the bright young up-and-coming economies seem to be interested in anything besides aping what the U.S. and the USSR did years ago. We may, in other words, need to look beyond strictly U.S.-centric explanations for such failures of imagination and initiative. It might simply be that there is something in the nature of modern global capitalism that is holding us back. Which might be a good thing, if it's an alternative to the crazy schemes of vicious dictators. Admittedly, there are many who feel a deep antipathy for expenditure of money and brainpower on space travel when, as they never tire of reminding us, there are so many problems to be solved on earth. So if space launch were the only area in which this phenomenon were observable, it would be of concern only to space enthusiasts. But the endless BP oil spill of 2010 highlighted any number of ways in which the phenomena of path dependency and lock-in have trapped our energy industry on a hilltop from which we can gaze longingly across not-so-deep valleys to much higher and sunnier peaks in the not-so-great distance.

Those are places we need to go if we are not to end up as the Ottomon Empire of the 21st Century, and yet in spite of all of the lip service that is paid to innovation in such areas, it frequently seems as though we are trapped in a collective stasis. As described above, regulation is only one culprit; at least equal blame may be placed on engineering and management culture, insurance, Congress, and even accounting practices. But those who do concern themselves with the formal regulation of "technology" might wish to worry less about possible negative effects of innovation and more about the damage being done to our environment and our prosperity by the mid–Twentieth Century technologies that no sane and responsible person would propose today, but in which we remain trapped by mysterious and ineffable forces.

INNOVATION STARVATION
(2011)

My lifespan encompasses the era when the United States of
America was capable of launching human beings into space. Some of
my earliest memories are of sitting on a braided rug before a hulk-
ing black-and-white television, watching the early Gemini missions.
This summer, at the age of 51—not even old—I watched on a flat-panel
screen as the last Space Shuttle lifted off the pad. I have followed
the dwindling of the space program with sadness, even bitterness.
Where's my donut-shaped space station? Where's my ticket to Mars?
Until recently, though, I have kept my feelings to myself. Space exploration has always had its detractors. To complain about its demise
is to expose oneself to attack from those who have no sympathy that
an affluent, middle-aged white American has not lived to see his boy-
hood fantasies fulfilled.

Still, I worry that our inability to match the achievements of the
1960s space program might be symptomatic of a general failure of

our society to get big things done. My parents and grandparents wit-nessed the creation of the airplane, the automobile, nuclear energy, and the computer, to name only a few. Scientists and engineers who came of age during the first half of the 20th century could look for-ward to building things that would solve age-old problems, transform the landscape, build the economy, and provide jobs for the burgeon-ing middle class that was the basis for our stable democracy.

The Deepwater Horizon oil spill of 2010 crystallized my feeling that we have lost our ability to get important things done. The OPEC oil shock was in 1973—almost 40 years ago. It was obvious then that it was crazy for the United States to let itself be held economic hostage to the kinds of countries where oil was being produced. It led to Jimmy Carter's proposal for the development of an enormous synthetic fuels industry on American soil. Whatever one might think of the merits of the Carter presidency or of this particular proposal, it was, at least, a serious effort to come to grips with the problem.

Little has been heard in that vein since. We've been talking about wind farms, tidal power, and solar power for decades. Some progress has been made in those areas, but energy is still all about oil. In my city, Seattle, a 35-year-old plan to run a light rail line across Lake Washington is now being blocked by a citizen initiative. Thwarted or endlessly delayed in its efforts to build things, the city plods ahead with a project to paint bicycle lanes on the pavement of thoroughfares.

In early 2011, I participated in a conference called Future Tense, where I lamented the decline of the manned space program, then pivoted to energy, indicating that the real issue isn't about rockets. It's our far broader inability as a society to execute on the big stuff. I had, through some kind of blind luck, struck a nerve. The audience at Future Tense was more confident than I that science fiction (SF) had relevance—even utility—in addressing the problem. I heard two theories as to why:

1. The Inspiration Theory. SF inspires people to choose science and engineering as careers. This much is undoubtedly true, and somewhat obvious.

2. The Hieroglyph Theory. Good SF supplies a plausible, fully thought-out picture of an alternate reality in which some sort of compelling innovation has taken place. A good SF universe has a coherence and internal logic that makes sense to scientists and engineers. Examples include Isaac Asimov's robots, Robert Heinlein's rocket ships, and William Gibson's cyberspace. As Jim Karkanias of Microsoft Research puts it, such icons serve as hieroglyphs—simple, recognizable symbols on whose significance everyone agrees.

Researchers and engineers have found themselves concentrating on more and more narrowly focused topics as science and technology have become more complex. A large technology company or lab may employ hundreds or thousands of persons, each of whom can only address a thin slice of the overall problem. Communication among them can become a mare's nest of email threads and PowerPoints. The fondness that many such people have for SF reflects, in part, the usefulness of an over-arching narrative that supplies them and their colleagues with a shared vision. Coordinating their efforts through a command-and-control management system is a little like trying to run a modern economy out of a Politburo; letting them work toward an agreed-on goal is something more like a free and largely self-coordinated market of ideas.

SF HAS CHANGED OVER THE SPAN OF TIME I AM TALKING ABOUT—FROM THE 1950s (the era of the development of nuclear power, jet airplanes, the space race, the computer) to now. Speaking broadly, the techno-optimism of the Golden Age of SF has given way to fiction written in a generally darker, more skeptical and ambiguous tone. I myself have tended to write a lot about hackers—trickster archetypes who exploit the arcane capabilities of complex systems devised by faceless others.

Believing we have all the technology we'll ever need, we seek to draw attention to its destructive side effects. This seems foolish, though, now that we find ourselves saddled with technologies like Japan's ramshackle 1960's-vintage reactors at Fukushima. The imperative to develop new technologies and implement them on a heroic scale no longer seems like the childish preoccupation of a few nerds with slide rules. It's the only way for the human race to escape from its current predicaments. Too bad we've forgotten how to do it.

"You're the ones who've been slacking off!" proclaimed Michael Crow, the President of Arizona State University (and one of the other speakers at Future Tense), when I spoke with him recently. He was referring, of course, to SF writers. The scientists and engineers, he seemed to be saying, are ready, and looking for things to do. Time for the SF writers to start pulling their weight and supplying big visions that make sense. Hence the Hieroglyph project, an effort to produce an anthology of new SF that will be in some ways a conscious throwback to the practical techno-optimism of the Golden Age.

CHINA IS FREQUENTLY CITED AS A COUNTRY THAT IS NOW EXECUTING ON BIG Stuff, and there's no doubt that they are constructing dams, high-speed rail systems, and rockets at an extraordinary clip. But those are not fundamentally innovative. Their space program, like all other countries' (including our own), is just parroting work that was done 50 years ago by the Soviets and the Americans. A truly innovative program would involve taking risks (and accepting failures) to pioneer some of the alternative space launch technologies that have been advanced by researchers all over the world during the decades dominated by rockets.

Imagine a factory mass-producing small vehicles, about as big and about as complicated as refrigerators, which roll off the end of the assembly line, are loaded with space-bound cargo, and topped off with non-polluting liquid hydrogen fuel, then exposed to the intense concentrated heat of an array of ground-based lasers or microwave antennas. Heated to temperatures beyond what can be achieved by a chemical reaction, the hydrogen erupts from a nozzle on the base of the device and sends it rocketing into the air. Tracked through its flight by the lasers or the microwaves, the vehicle soars into orbit carrying a larger payload for its size than a chemical rocket could ever manage, but the complexity, expense, and jobs remain grounded. For decades, this has been the vision of such researchers as physicists Jordin Kare and Kevin Parkin. A similar idea, using a pulsed ground-based laser to blast propellant from the backside of a space vehicle, was being talked about by Arthur Kantrowitz, Freeman Dyson, and other eminent physicists in the early 1960s.

If that sounds too complicated, then consider the 2003 proposal of Geoff Landis and Vincent Denis to construct a 20-kilometer-high tower using simple steel trusses. Conventional rockets launched from its top would be able to carry twice as much payload as comparable ones launched from ground level. There is even abundant research, dating all the way back to Konstantin Tsiolkovsky, the father of astronautics beginning in the late 19th century, to show that a simple tether—a long rope, tumbling end-over-end while orbiting the earth—could be used to scoop payloads out of the upper atmosphere and haul them up into orbit without the need for engines of any kind. Energy would be pumped into the system using an electrodynamic process with no moving parts.

All promising ideas, and just the sort of thing that used to get an earlier generation of scientists and engineers fired up about actually building something.

But to get an idea of just how far away our current mindset is from being able to attempt innovation on such a scale, consider the fate of the space shuttle's external tanks, or ETs. Dwarfing the vehicle itself, the ET was the largest and most prominent feature of the space shuttle as it stood on the pad. It remained attached to the shuttle—or perhaps it makes as much sense to say that the shuttle remained attached to it—long after the two strap-on boosters had fallen away. The ET and the shuttle remained connected all the way out of the atmosphere and into space. Only after the system had attained orbital velocity was the tank jettisoned and allowed to fall into the atmosphere, where it was destroyed on re-entry. At a modest marginal cost, the ETs could have been kept in orbit indefinitely. The mass of the ET at separation, including residual propellants, was about twice that of the largest possible Shuttle payload, so not destroying them would have roughly tripled the total mass launched into orbit by the Shuttle. ETs could have been connected to build constructs that would have humbled today's International Space Station. The residual oxygen and hydrogen sloshing around in them could have been combined to generate electricity and produce tons of water, a commodity that is vastly expensive and desirable in space. But in spite of hard work and passionate advocacy by space experts who wished to see the tanks put to use, NASA—for reasons both technical and political—sent every single one of them to fiery destruction in the atmosphere. Viewed as a parable, it has much to tell us about the difficulties of innovating in other spheres.

INNOVATION CAN'T HAPPEN WITHOUT ACCEPTING THE RISK THAT IT MIGHT fail. The vast and radical innovations of the mid-20th century took place in a world that, in retrospect, looks insanely dangerous and un-stable. Possible outcomes that the modern mind identifies as serious risks might not have been taken seriously—supposing they were no-ticed at all—by people habituated to the Depression, the World Wars, and the Cold War, in times when seat belts, antibiotics, and many vaccines did not exist. Competition between the Western democ-racies and the communist powers obliged the former to push their scientists and engineers to the limits of what they could imagine, and supplied a sort of safety net in the event that their initial efforts did not pay off. A grizzled NASA veteran once told me that the Apollo moon landings were communism's greatest achievement.

In his recent book *Adapt: Why Success Always Starts with Failure*, Tim Harford outlines Charles Darwin's discovery of a vast array of distinct species in the Galapagos Islands—a state of affairs that contrasts with the picture seen on large continents, where evolutionary experiments tend to get pulled back towards a sort of ecological consensus by interbreeding. "Galapagan isolation" vs. the "nervous corporate hierarchy" is the contrast staked out by Harford in assessing the ability of an organization to innovate.

Most people who work in corporations or academia have witnessed something like the following: A number of engineers are sitting together in a room, bouncing ideas off each other. Out of the discussion emerges a new concept that seems promising. Then some laptop-wielding person in the corner, having performed a quick Google search, announces that this "new" idea is, in fact, an old one—or at least vaguely similar—and has already been tried. Either it failed, or it succeeded. If it failed, then no manager who wants to keep his or her job will approve spending money trying to revive it. If it succeeded, then it's patented and entry to the market is presumed to be unattainable, since the first people who thought of it will have "first-mover advantage" and will have created "barriers to entry." The number of seemingly promising ideas that have been crushed in this way must number in the millions.

What if that person in the corner hadn't been able to do a Google search? It might have required weeks of library research to uncover evidence that the idea wasn't entirely new—and after a long and toilsome slog through many books, tracking down many references, some relevant, some not. When the precedent was finally unearthed, it might not have seemed like such a direct precedent after all. There might be reasons why it would be worth taking a second crack at the idea, perhaps hybridizing it with other innovations from other fields. Hence the virtues of Galapagan isolation.

The counterpart to Galapagan isolation is the struggle for survival on a large continent, where firmly established ecosystems tend to blur and swamp new adaptations. Jaron Lanier, a computer scientist, composer, visual artist, and author of the recent book *You Are Not a Gadget: A Manifesto*, has some insights about the unintended consequences of the Internet—the informational equivalent of a large continent—on our ability to take risks. In the pre-Net era, managers were forced to make decisions based on what they knew to be limited information. Today, by contrast, data flows to managers in real time from countless sources that could not even be imagined a couple of generations ago, and powerful computers process, organize, and display the data in ways that are as far beyond the hand-drawn graph-paper plots of my youth as modern video games are to tic-tac-toe. In a world where decision-makers are so close to being omniscient, it's easy to see risk as a quaint artifact of a primitive and dangerous past.

The illusion of eliminating uncertainty from corporate decision-making is not merely a question of management style or personal preference. In the legal environment that has developed around publicly traded corporations, managers are strongly discouraged from shouldering any risks that they know about—or, in the opinion of some future jury, *should have known* about—even if they have a hunch that the gamble might pay off in the long run. There is no such thing as "long run" in industries driven by the next quarterly report. The possibility of some innovation making money is just that—a mere possibility that will not have time to materialize before the subpoenas from minority shareholder lawsuits begin to roll in.

Today's belief in ineluctable certainty is the true innovation-killer of our age. In this environment, the best an audacious manager can do is to develop small improvements to existing systems, climbing the hill, as it were, toward a local maximum, trimming fat, occasionally eking out the occasional tiny innovation—like city planners painting bicycle lanes on the streets as a gesture toward solving our energy problems. Any strategy that involves crossing a valley—accepting short-term losses to reach a higher hill in the distance—will soon be brought to a halt by the demands of a system that celebrates short-term gains, tolerates stagnation, but condemns anything else as failure. In short, a world where big stuff can never get done.

WHY I AM A BAD CORRESPONDENT (1998)

Writers who do not make themselves totally available to everyone, all the time, are frequently tagged with the "recluse" label. While I do not consider myself a recluse, I have found it necessary to place some limits on my direct interactions with individual readers. These limits most often come into play when people send me letters or e-mail, and also when I am invited to speak publicly. This document is a sort of form letter explaining why I am the way I am.

When I read a novel that I really like, I feel as if I am in direct, personal communication with the author. I feel as if the author and I are on the same wavelength mentally, that we have a lot in common with each other, and that we could have an interesting conversation, or even a friendship, if the circumstances permitted it. When the novel comes to an end, I feel a certain letdown, a loss of contact. It is natural to want to recapture that feeling by reading other works by the same author, or by corresponding with him/her directly.

All of this seems perfectly reasonable—I should know, since I have had these feelings myself! But it turns out to be a bad idea. To begin with, a novel has roughly the same relationship to a conversation with the author, as a movie does to the actors in it. A movie represents many person-years of work distilled into two hours, and so everything sounds and looks perfect. But if you have ever met a movie actor in person, you know that they are not quite as dazzling and witty (or as tall) as the figures they play in movies. This seems obvious but it always comes as a bit of a letdown anyway.

Likewise, a novel represents years of hard work distilled into a few hundred pages, with all (or at least most) of the bad ideas cut out and thrown away, and the good ideas polished and refined as much as possible. Interacting with an author in person is nothing like reading his novels. Just about everyone who gets an opportunity to meet with an author in person ends up feeling mildly let down, and in some cases, grievously disappointed.

Authors are participants in a kind of colloquy that joins together all literate persons, and so it seems only reasonable that they should from time to time stop writing fiction for a few hours or days, and attend public events, such as conventions, signings, panels, seminars, etc., where they should exchange ideas with other authors and with other members of society. Therefore, authors such as myself frequently receive invitations to do exactly that.

Letters or e-mail from readers, and invitations to speak in public, might seem like very different things. In fact they are points on a common continuum; they have more in common than is obvious at first. The e-mail message from the reader, and the invitation to speak at a conference, are both requests (in most cases, polite and absolutely reasonable requests) for the author to interact directly with readers.

Normally, my only interaction with readers is to go to a FedEx drop box every couple of years and throw in the manuscript of a completed novel. It seems reasonable enough to ask for a little bit more than that! After all, the time commitment is very small: a few minutes tapping out an e-mail message, or a day trip to a conference to speak.

For some authors, this works, but in my case, it doesn't. There is little to nothing that I can offer readers above and beyond what appears in my published writings. It follows that I should devote all my efforts to writing more material for publication, rather than spending a few minutes here, a day there, answering e-mails or going to conferences.

Writing novels is hard, and requires vast, unbroken slabs of time. Four quiet hours is a resource that I can put to good use. Two slabs of time, each two hours long, might add up to the same four hours, but are not nearly as productive as an unbroken four. If I know that I am going to be interrupted, I can't concentrate, and if I suspect that I might be interrupted, I can't do anything at all. Likewise, several consecutive days with four-hour time-slabs in them give me a stretch of time in which I can write a decent book chapter, but the same number of hours spread out across a few weeks, with interruptions in between them, are nearly useless.

The productivity equation is a non-linear one, in other words. This accounts for why I am a bad correspondent and why I very rarely accept speaking engagements. If I organize my life in such a way that I get lots of long, consecutive, uninterrupted time-chunks, I can write novels. But as those chunks get separated and fragmented, my productivity as a novelist drops spectacularly. What replaces it? Instead of a novel that will be around for a long time, and that will, with luck, be read by many people, there is a bunch of e-mail messages that I have sent out to individual persons, and a few speeches given at various conferences.

That is not such a terrible outcome, but neither is it an especially good outcome. The quality of my e-mails and public speaking is, in my view, nowhere near that of my novels. So for me it comes down to the following choice: I can distribute material of bad-to-mediocre quality to a small number of people, or I can distribute material of higher quality to more people. But I can't do both; the first one obliterates the second.

Another factor in this choice is that writing fiction every day seems to be an essential component in my sustaining good mental health. If I get blocked from writing fiction, I rapidly become depressed, and extremely unpleasant to be around. As long as I keep writing it, though, I am fit to be around other people. So all of the incentives point in the direction of devoting all available hours to fiction writing.

I am not proud of the fact that some of my e-mail goes unanswered as a result. It is never my intention to be rude or to give well-meaning readers the cold shoulder. If I were a commercial best-seller, I would have enough money to hire a staff to look after my correspondence. As it is, my books are bought by enough people to provide me with a sort of middle-class lifestyle, but not enough to hire employees, and so I am faced with a stark choice between being a bad correspondent and being a good novelist. I am trying to be a good novelist, and hoping that people will forgive me for being a bad correspondent.

PERMISSIONS

A version of "Slashdot Interview" previously appeared on Slashdot.org.

A version of "Metaphysics in the Royal Society 1715–2010" previously appeared in *Seeing Further: The Story of Science & the Royal Society* edited by Bill Bryson. Published by HarperCollins in 2010.

A version of "It's All Geek to Me," "Turn On, Tune In, Veg Out," and "Blind Secularism" previously appeared in *The New York Times*.

A version of "Spew," "In the Kingdom of Mao Bell (selected excerpts)," and "Mother Earth, Mother Board" previously appeared in *Wired* magazine and on Wired.com.

A version of "The Salon Interview" previously appeared on Salon.com. Grateful acknowledgment is given to Laura Miller for allowing Harper-Collins Publishers to include the introduction and interview questions in "The Salon Interview."

A version of *"Everything and More* Foreword" previously appeared as the foreword in *Everything and More: A Compact History of Infinity* by David Foster